LEVIATHAN 3:

*Libri quosdam ad sciéntiam,
álios ad insaniam deduxére*

Edited by
Forrest Aguirre & Jeff VanderMeer

Min
Tallahassee, F

Ministry of Whimsy Press

Editorial offices:

Jeff VanderMeer
POB 4248, Tallahassee, FL 32315, USA

Forrest Aguirre
4905 Ascot Lane #3, Madison, WI 53711, USA

Publisher:

Sean Wallace/Prime Books
POB 36503, Canton, OH 44735, USA

ministryofwhimsy@yahoo.com
www.ministryofwhimsy.com

Thanks to: Ann Kennedy, Neil Williamson, Tamar Yellin, Dawn Andrews, Mark Roberts, Jeffrey Ford, Brian Evenson, L. Timmel Duchamp, Zoran Zivkovic (not least, for our subtitle), Eric Schaller, Eric at Rain Taxi, Stephanie McConnell, Sean Doughtie, John Coulthart, Garry Nurrish.

All stories are original to this anthology, except:

"The Camus Referendum" by Michael Moorcock, originally published in *Gare du Nord*, France, 1997.

"The Evenki" by Eugene Dubkov, originally published in *The Massachusetts Review*, 1991.

"Kafka in Brontëland" by Tamar Yellin, originally published in *The Slow Mirror: New Fiction by Jewish Writers*, 1996.

"Moonlight" by Tamar Yellin, originally published in *Leviathan Quarterly*, 2001.

ABOUT THE MINISTRY OF WHIMSY:
Founded in 1984, the Ministry of Whimsy takes its name from the ironic doublespeak of Orwell's novel. Committed to promoting high-quality fantastical and surreal fiction, the Ministry published the Philip K. Dick Award-winning *The Troika* in 1997. The Ministry has also been a finalist for the World Fantasy Award. *Leviathan 2* was a finalist for the British Fantasy Award. The *Leviathan* fiction series is dedicated to mapping the world of fiction.

ISBN: 1-894815-42-4

TABLE OF CONTENTS

INTRODUCTION
Jeff VanderMeer

"The universe (which others call the Library) is composed of an indefinite, perhaps an infinite, number of . . . galleries . . . "
—Jorge Borges, "The Library of Babel"

"The library was the world trapped in a mirror; it had its infinite breadth, its variety and unpredictability."
—Jean Paul Sartre, *Les Mots*

AT THIS VERY moment, a man in Sweden named Olaf Nicolai is compiling a bibliography comprised of books that have never existed for a library that will never be substantiated outside of paper. The Fantastic Metropolis Web site this past December posted year-end best-of lists including imaginary books. And Brian Quinette, through his Invisible Library Web site, continues to diligently type in lists and descriptions of every fake book ever mentioned in a work of fiction, constructing a meta-library of astounding proportions. Borges' Library of Babel may indeed be a Virtual Library.

But such efforts, I hasten to add, are not unusual. Every book in the world once existed as little more than a title on a blank piece of paper. Every library was once just a list of titles on an acquisition sheet.

It therefore follows that every anthology begins as an idea expressed through a title. In some extreme cases—very rare—an anthology begins with an entire *library*; or, as in *Leviathan 3*'s case, six libraries, each holding innumerable treasures.

Our libraries are not didactic in nature. They hold no grudges and they are well-maintained. No theme sullies these libraries, other than a love for fantastical literature, and we have no agenda other than to present the pleasures of the written word. (We do, however, have a Latin phrase as a subtitle—*Libri quosdam ad sciéntiam, álios ad insaniam deduxére**—and this provides, I think, direction enough.)

On a more personal note, I have been creating my own library through the Ministry of Whimsy for more than 18 years, ever since I was 16. With the initial help of co-editor Duane Bray (who still designs covers for Ministry books) and art editor Penelope Miller, the Ministry has always striven to uphold one simple ideal: the celebration of the imagination in all of its written manifestations. Now, however, the time has come for me to concentrate exclusively on libraries of my own words. In recent years, I have felt that my efforts, divided between editing and writing, have been simultaneously invigorating and in conflict. With the transfer of publishing responsibilities to Prime Books (Sean Wallace and Garry Nurrish), the Ministry now has the ability to publish imaginative and idiosyncratic books on a more regular basis. And now, also, I have found an editor who can replace me on day-to-day Ministry operations, guide book projects to fruition, and make new acquisitions that take into account the Ministry's honorable history.

Forrest Aguirre has put a lot of hard work into this anthology and I believe he will work doubly hard in the future as he strives to build upon the Ministry's reputation. I will leave it to him, on the new Ministry Web site and in *Leviathan 4*, to set out the specifics of that direction. I ask that all the devoted Ministry readers support Forrest and the Ministry in the future as you have in the past.

There is little doubt in my mind that now—after a multitude of Ministry successes, from the Philip K. Dick Award to being a finalist for both the World and British Fantasy Awards—is the time to devote myself more fully to my own writing.

I do not think I could leave on a higher note than *Leviathan 3*. This anthology, for me, does a superlative job of articulating what the Ministry stands for and why it will continue to be a vital force in publishing. In a more general sense, the quality and diversity of work contained within these pages speaks to the continuing renaissance of fantastical literature—whether at the level of metaphor or at the level of idea. I can think of no time in the past when I have been as excited by the sheer amount of quality writing being produced all over the world.

The Ministry library will continue to grow and prosper because it has access to such talent. I look forward with great interest to reading that library as interpreted by Forrest Aguirre. Thanks to everyone who has made this venture a success.

---

* Those kind readers who devour Leviathan whole may find, lack of Latin notwithstanding, a solution to the puzzle by anthology's end.

VIRTUAL LIBRARY

The Library: 1: VIRTUAL LIBRARY
Zoran Zivkovic
All Library Stories translated by Alice Copple-Tosic

To Mike Moorcock, a good man.

EMAIL ISN'T PERFECT. Although Internet providers probably do their best to protect us from receiving unwanted messages, there seems to be no remedy. Whenever I open up the in-box on my screen, I almost always find at least one from an unknown sender. Usually there are several; the record was thirteen junk mail messages, sent over just a few hours, in between two sessions at the computer.

When that happened I really got irritated and changed my e-address, despite considerable inconvenience. I gave my new address only to a small number of people, but to no avail. The pesky e-mails soon began to arrive once again. I complained to my provider, who admitted in a roundabout way that they could do nothing to help. They advised me just to delete everything that didn't interest me, particularly since dangerous computer viruses often spread through junk mail.

The recommendation was unnecessary as I had already been deleting my junk mail, even though I was unaware of the viruses. At first,

11

I'd read these messages in bewilderment, but after I realized what was going on, I deleted every e-message of unknown origin without delay. I didn't even give them a cursory reading, in spite of the fact that the senders took all kinds of pains to attract my attention. Bombastic, flickering headings with fancy, ostentatious illustrations advertised a variety of exceptional offers not to be missed at any cost.

One proposal, for example, would make me rich overnight if I invested money through a glamorous-sounding agency from some Pacific Rim country I had never heard of. Or, after a two-week correspondence course, I could become a preacher in any Christian church I wanted, authorized to carry out baptismal, wedding, and funeral rites. I also had the opportunity, regardless of my age, to turn back the clock twenty-five years using some new macrobiotic remedy. I was offered the unique opportunity, for the modest commission of forty-nine percent, to finally get hold of the money that had been awarded to me by the court, if I had any such claims. I could also satisfy my assumed passion for gambling at any hour of the day or night, playing in some virtual casino guaranteed to be honest. Finally, to top it all off, I was offered at a mere pittance, under the counter, two-and-a-half million verified, active e-addresses to which I could send whatever I wanted as many times as I wanted.

Perhaps the e-mail that started it all would have ended up in the recycle bin, along with the others, if it had not been so brief that I inadvertently read it. Against a black background, devoid of decoration, the first line announced: VIRTUAL LIBRARY in large, yellow letters, while under it the slogan "We have everything!"—written in considerably smaller blue letters—did not exactly assume the aggressive tone typical of this type of message.

Of all the exaggeration I had come across on the Internet, this one took the cake. Really, "everything!" Such a claim would be absurd even for web sites from the largest world libraries. Whoever had come up with this scheme certainly had no notion of how many books have been published in the last five thousand years. No one has ever managed to put such a library together in one place, even without all those works that have disappeared into oblivion.

And then there was that word "virtual." Used in its truest sense, "virtual" should mean a library composed of electronic books. The Internet has several sites containing such e-editions and I visit them from time to time. But they offer slim pickings. Only several hundred titles are available, just a drop in the ocean compared to "everything" in the literal sense. Who would even dare to hope that this vast multitude could ever be transferred into computer form? And who would ever find it worth the effort?

Although I was convinced this must be a hoax, my curiosity stopped me from proceeding as usual. If it had involved anything other than books, I would have ignored the message without a second thought. But for a writer this was like waving a red flag in front of a bull. Instead of deleting the message, I positioned the cursor on the text. The arrow turned into a hand with a raised index finger and I found myself at the Virtual Library site.

The change was barely noticeable. The background stayed black, with two small additions appearing under the name of the site and the slogan. The first was the standard search field: a narrow white rectangular space in which to type the search text. This, however, could not be the title of a work or some other data, since the word "Author" appeared at the beginning. I shook my head. More sophisticated capabilities were to be expected from a library that prided itself on being the "ultimate." At the very bottom of the screen was a short e-address.

I typed in my own name. This was not out of vanity, although it might have appeared so. I chose myself because, obviously, I am most familiar with my own work. If the Virtual Library truly contained what it claimed in its slogan, then my three books should be no exception. I am certainly not a well-known or popular writer, but I still should be included in a library containing all authors. In such a place there should be no discrimination of any type.

There were two possible outcomes. If the search did not produce the expected result, which was quite likely, then the whole thing was probably a practical joke. Someone had decided to have some fun at the expense of writers, or perhaps publishers, critics, librarians, bookshop owners, and the book world in general. Who knew what kind of trick might be played instead of a page listing my works. But I had no right to complain; no one had forced me to visit the site. A joke would serve me right for not minding my own business.

If, however, my books appeared in electronic form, then the situation was considerably worse. I had not ceded my rights to anyone for such publication, which would mean they were pirated editions. That would really be a problem. The Internet is inundated with this type of abuse, and as far as I have heard, protection from it is just as difficult as protection from unwanted e-messages.

If my work did exist in the Virtual Library, the search would have to last some time. Regardless of increases in computer speed, the gigantic corpus involved could certainly not be searched momentarily. But that is just what happened. As soon as I clicked the mouse to begin the search, a new page appeared on the screen. This time it had a gray background, with black and white writing. A smaller picture also appeared in color, disturbing the uniformity.

At first, I thought that the speed with which it had been found was a sure sign of something fishy. But when I found myself squinting at my own face on the screen, a shudder ran down my spine. That was me, no doubt about it, although I had no idea when and where the picture had been taken. I appeared to be somewhat younger, but it was hard to tell how much younger.

Under the picture, on the left side of the screen, I found a brief biography. All the information was correct, except for the end. Unless something had happened without my noticing it, I was still very much alive. The facts about my death, though, were strangely undefined. The word "died" was followed by nine different years, separated by commas. Unlike the black letters before them, these numbers were white. The closest year was a decade and a half in the future, while the most distant was almost half a century away. Whoever had edited the entry obviously had a morbid sense of humor.

On the right side of the screen, I found a list of my books. It did not end, however, after the third book. It continued all the way to number twenty-one which, of course, was ridiculous. I'm not saying that such a voluminous bibliography didn't please me, but it simply was not mine. Two colors had been used here as well. The three books I had actually published appeared in black type, while the other eighteen works appeared in white. These other titles were presented in chronological order. The first dated from the following year, and forty-five years had to pass until the last date. So I was dealing not only with a twisted prankster, but someone who seemed to imagine himself a clairvoyant.

None of this mattered, however; I still had to find out the most important thing. Was this just the work of some idler who had nothing better to do than fool around with such nonsense? The Internet is full of people who think nothing of putting time and effort into pulling off stunts like this. Hackers are a good example. They invent and spread destructive viruses, even though they gain no benefit other than an insular satisfaction. I clicked the cursor on the first of my three books, certain that nothing would happen. But the arrow, unfortunately, turned into a hand again and the screen soon filled with text.

I only had to read the first sentence to confirm that this really was my first novel. A wave of anger rolled over me. My book was accessible to the whole world without any permission or payment! How dare they! Why, this was highway robbery! And then suddenly I was filled with the hope that perhaps it wasn't all there, that maybe only an excerpt had been posted, which might be somewhat bearable. But as soon as I scrolled down to the end of the page, I lost this faint hope. The whole book was there, from the first word to the last. I didn't even have to open the other two titles. I knew perfectly well what I would find there.

Enraged, I reached for the mouse again, clicked on the button, and returned to the previous page. I brought the cursor to the e-address at the bottom, then clicked once again. My browser opened a blank e-mail window with the site's e-mail address in the "To" field. I stared at the empty page for a few moments, deliberating. Finally, I wrote "Piracy" in the "Subject" line, then started to write.

Dear Sir,

A very unpleasant surprise awaited me when I visited the Virtual Library site. I found my three novels there freely accessible to anyone. Since I, as the copyright holder, never gave permission for such publication, it clearly represents an act of publishing piracy, punishable by law. I order you to withdraw my works from your site without delay. I would also like to inform you that my lawyer will soon be sending you a request for due compensation for damages, not only for the unauthorized placement of my books on your site but also for the inaccurate, and insulting, additions to my biography and bibliography.

I signed my name at the end, without any closing salutation. It was impolite, but I couldn't think of anything that sounded appropriate. It would have been hard to put the formal "sincerely yours" or "yours truly." I also had trouble using a properly severe tone for my missive; I had no experience in this sort of thing. The letter, I suppose, must have appeared harsh enough and a warning, although, to tell the truth, I did not count on it having much effect. The most that could be expected was for them to remove the page containing my works, while I hadn't the slightest hope of receiving any compensation.

I even doubted that I would receive a reply. But I was wrong. Just after I sent the e-mail, a message came back in response. The only explanation was that the editors of the Virtual Library, flooded with similar protest letters, had a ready-made reply to be sent automatically upon receipt of such a complaint. They probably didn't receive any other kind of letter. What did they say in their defense?

Highly esteemed sir,

First, please allow us to express our deepest gratitude to you for having shown us the honor of visiting the Virtual Library.

We hasten to dispel your fears. This is not an unauthorized publication of your works. Although the page devoted to you does contain the texts of your books, access to that page is not at all free, as you have assumed. It is allowed exclusively to you, and only once. Since you have just used this opportunity, you may rest assured that no one will ever again be able to access the page containing your bio-bibliography. You will see this for yourself should you try to return to it.

Regarding the information that you have concluded is incorrect, please rest assured that it is accurate.

Sincerely yours,
Virtual Library

So they had it all worked out. As soon as an author complained, they quickly removed the page. No page, no proof of piracy. I had nonetheless expected something more ingenious. That page still existed in the "cache" memory of my computer as irrefutable proof. All I had to do was hit the "Back" button and save it. Nothing easier. In addition, it seemed the Virtual Library considered writers to be so computer illiterate and naïve that they would easily swallow the story about access to their page. Nonsense. As if something like that was even possible. Or that bit about the accuracy of the invented data. What a misjudgment.

I quickly clicked "Back" on the toolbar. But something unexpected happened. Instead of showing the previous page, the window with the letter from the Virtual Library closed, and the "Back" button became inactive, as though nothing had been stored in the "cache" file. I stared in bewilderment at the primarily black picture on the screen, without understanding. The page had to be there. I had been on it just a few minutes before and had done nothing in the meantime to delete it.

Obviously, something had gone wrong. I wasn't computer illiterate, but I also was not skilled enough to figure out everything that could go wrong with these strange machines. But it made no difference, I would enter my name once again in the search rectangle. Although I had been informed that access to my page would henceforth be blocked, it would be hard for them to do so instantaneously. Unfortunately, the search came up blank this time. The program informed me that no writer with my name could be found in the library that included all authors who had ever existed.

Confusion and anger started to get the upper hand. I looked like a fool who, by his own rashness, had been taken in by a cheap trick. It even crossed my mind that a throng of happy people from some television station might burst into my study at any moment, revealing that all of this had been just a cleverly organized candid camera episode. But no one appeared and, after several long minutes, I did the only thing I could do. I clicked once again on the lower e-address and started to type a new e-mail.

Dear Sir,

I don't know how you did it, but that's not important. Your joke—I could use a stronger word—is tasteless to say the least. People such as you are inflicting enormous damage on the noble idea of the Internet. You should be ashamed of yourselves. Don't forget that I still have the address of your web site. I will try to trace you through it. Your library might be virtual, but you certainly are not.

Once again I used my signature, without any closing formality. Good manners were superfluous in this situation. I should have left out the "Dear Sir" too. The people behind this travesty did not deserve such a courtesy. When I sent the message I was again sure there would be no reply. How could they respond to my accusation? But I got one anyway, the same instant just like before. The speed of the reply should have aroused my suspicions, of course, since this letter could not have been prepared in advance like the previous one. All caught up in my anger, I did not give proper consideration to this impossibility which was, in any case, not the first one I had encountered with the Virtual Library. How strange it is that one easily starts to accept things that have no explanation, particularly when computers are involved.

Highly esteemed sir,

We are sorry that you received the wrong impression. Making jokes is the farthest thing from our intent. All our efforts go towards the serious execution of our responsible work, which is the only fitting thing to do.

Sincerely yours,
Virtual Library

As I opened the window for a new letter to my unknown adversary, a sober voice inside tried to dissuade me. There was no point in taking part in such a farce anymore. I had already achieved as much as I could, given the circumstances. The page with my works had been removed and further correspondence would lead nowhere. Unfortunately, one does not always listen to sober advice.

I suppose you expect me to take the list of books cited as mine seriously, even though they have not yet been written. I might have admired your ability to foretell the future if you had not been so indecisive regarding the year of my death. Nine possibilities! I would appreciate being informed when you decide on one of them. Timely knowledge in this regard would considerably facilitate the remainder of my life, however long it might be.

This time I even omitted my signature. That fact, and the conspicuously sarcastic tone of the letter, should have indicated what I thought of them, had they been previously unaware. Their pointed politeness, not at all appropriate to the circumstances, had started to get on my nerves. The answer arrived once again a moment after I sent my message, but this no longer amazed me. Sleights-of-hand cease to be interesting when they are repeated too often, even if you don't know how they are performed.

Highly esteemed sir,

We are unfortunately unable to inform you of when you will die. It is not simple to forecast the future. All nine possibilities have equal footing at this moment. Chance will decide which of them comes true. Your bibliography contains all the works from all these futures. However, you will not write and publish all eighteen of them on a single one of the branches of life that await you, to use a picturesque expression. Your later works will include at most eleven and at least six books. You were only able to see them all on our site. We therefore hope that we have justified our slogan.

Sincerely yours,
Virtual Library

Just as I finished reading the message, it vanished, the window in which it was located suddenly closing even though I had not touched any keys. A moment later, the same thing happened to the browser window. The only window left open was for e-mail, but it did not contain the original message from the Virtual Library, although it should have been there, since I had not deleted it. Before I closed it, I checked to see if any new e-mail messages had arrived in the meantime, but there were none.

I sat there for a long time, eyes unfocused, staring at the empty screen before me. I did not try to understand. The ways of the computer are often incomprehensible to me. I searched my memory, but as hard as I tried the text written in white against a gray background to the right of my photograph did not become sharp enough to read. It

20

seemed to be covered by a shimmering, impenetrable veil. Finally, even though frustration weighed me down, I abandoned my vain efforts and turned off the computer.

From then on, I continued to delete unwanted e-mail messages, but no longer right away. First, I read them, even when it was clear right away that they did not deserve the slightest attention. I felt foolish as I skimmed through various incoherent offers, particularly since I hadn't the faintest hope of ever seeing among them one that was quite brief, on a black background. But such was the burden I had to bear.

WHILE WANDERING
A VANISHED SEA
James C. Bassett

ON THE EVE of our third week wandering that brine-rimed desert, Rushfalter suddenly exclaimed, "Raunevan! We've full-circled."

And true enough, there in the distance our city tumbled to the edge of a superfluous coast. Still, I stole a sidelong glance at Slothslake in time to catch his weary headshake.

"That may be Raunevan," he said, "but we're as lost as when we left."

Rushfalter and I exchanged a look; I thought to speak, but Slothslake was already moving again and we had to rush to catch up. It was almost as much as he'd spoken since our journey began, and as cryptic a comment as the first.

A fortnight before, the same night the sea disappeared, Slothslake had said as we returned from burying the memory artist, "This city is drowning itself."

The sad certainty in his voice roused us all from the solitude of our own thoughts. Glad of any distraction, we waited for an explanation, but Slothslake only stared at the weathered roofs before us and kept walking.

"You can't just let a statement like that lie," I told him, but he did. We all shrugged to one another and continued our procession back to the city which remained, as always, dry except in the insipid water gardens of Memorial Park and at the salt-sodden edges of the port.

Raunevan has always been at odds with water. Like the Mariner, we were forever taunted by a surfeit of brine as gray as ash and thick with sorrow, while our only potable water comes stolen from the mountains and smuggled to us on an ancient aqueduct. The city fans out alluvially from this titanic course until it reaches the abrupt and unforgiving cliff of the coastline.

Built hardscrabble on that rough and narrow margin between sea and jungle, Raunevan was always a city besieged, locked in constant struggle against encroachment from both enemies; the two join forces to the east in vast and fetid marshes which rise every morning with the sun to roll hallucinogenic miasmas over the streets and shanties of the Beggars Town. In the fullest heat of summer, that translucent carpet persists day and night and can creep as far as the port itself. Only to the west does any stretch of beach open itself to the sky, but the mansions of the Noble Quarter rise in a shield wall of affluence to protect the rest of the city from dreams of such leisure.

Raunevan is the last city anyone would have expected a man as illustrious (many would say infamous) as Mimpi to even visit—yet when he arrived so many years ago, he made it clear from the moment he stepped ashore that he had come to stay.

Like the Frenchman Artaud (whose generation he shared), Mimpi was a deliberate *avant-gardiste* and a professional provocateur. He had earned his fame touring Europe and America as a memory artist, but Raunevan was too provincial for metaphysics, so on his arrival here he billed himself simply as a dreamer.

It was an unnecessary precaution. Mimpi was known throughout the world, even in Raunevan. Furthermore, no few words, no matter how carefully chosen, could ever adequately describe Mimpi—that strange little man with skin the color of the tannic stagnation in the swamps—or the peculiar nature of his performance.

Like the man himself, Mimpi's act, his *art*, was unique. I once asked him what, exactly, it was that he did to his audiences; he replied that he simply (*simply*, he said!) told stories. The effect he achieved sprang not from the tales he told, but from their manner of telling. Simple enough those stories may have been, but the manner—his manner—defied description.

As we camped that night in a petrified field of scrub drawn in sharp geometric angles with the lights of Raunevan flickering in the distance, I said to the others, "It will be good to get home tomorrow. To see everyone again. Though in a way, I just can't imagine what the city will be like without Mimpi."

Before our moods could fall, Rushfalter said with a smile, "Do you remember his first performance?"

"How could I forget? How could any of us forget?"

"Eleven years ago," Rushfalter continued as though I hadn't spoken, "the day after he arrived. An outdoor performance. We were all so worried about the weather—he told us it wouldn't matter."

"And of course he was right," mused Slothslake. "Rain threatened all day but never actually came."

Rushfalter gaped oddly. "No—the storm broke just as Mimpi started his first song. And he sang about Raunevan—as a gift to his new home, he sang about the founding of our city. What did our history used to be—failed mutineers set adrift, something like that?" He looked at us for corroboration, but continued before either of us could speak. "Anyway, he changed it in his song, didn't he? He made us the descendants of a king. Royalty, all of us—the whole city. Out of the old story, he sang us a new truth."

"Mimpi never sang a day in his life," I countered.

"Why, it's all he did. The power of his art was in his songs."

I shook my head. "He told stories. They weren't even in rhyme. Sometimes he acted them out, but they were always spoken." I paused apologetically. "But you're right about the new memory he gave us. He changed our old ignoble past into a more noble reality."

"He sang," Rushfalter insisted. "How can you have forgotten that? Slothslake, tell him."

"You're both right," Slothslake said.

"That's not possible."

"Yes, Slothslake," I chided. "Give us a straight answer for once."

Slothslake stared out at the lights and said, "Art isn't a finished product, but a process. And that process is an integral part of the resulting creation—of the memory created, in Mimpi's case. The whole nature of his art was the redefinition of memory, so it only follows that our memories of how he did it should also be altered."

Rushfalter and I stared at one another, shocked by this outpouring. "So what exactly *was* the process?" Rushfalter asked.

Still gazing at our faraway home, Slothslake only shrugged.

"I mean, how did he give us those memories at all?"

Now Slothslake turned back to us. "Our friend never gave us anything. We willingly gave up our memories to him, and he created something to fill the void—but there was a price, even though we didn't know it then. But truth and reality only changed because we forsook them."

Rushfalter and I pressed him for an explanation, but he only said we would understand when we reached the city—or not at all.

I felt this final night of our adventure slipping into morbidity; to lighten the mood, I ventured, "So, *why* do you think he did it? It certainly wasn't for the money."

Even Slothslake smiled. "He could have bought the whole city twice over, and still he chose to live by the swamp."

"By it?" Rushfalter exclaimed. "He was practically in it!"

We all laughed at that, but it was true. The Beggars Town lies unsettlingly close to the marshes, but Mimpi built apart even from those neighborhoods, his home all but lost amid jungle and the heavy, undulating mists.

On an evening in early summer when those miasmal spirits already lingered in the shadows of afternoon like forgotten phantoms, we sat drinking in a small café near the war memorial. While we waited for a new bottle to arrive, someone asked Mimpi why a man of his renown did not live in the Noble Quarter, or at least along the airy and broad Palace Boulevard.

Mimpi waved dismissively. "Dreams there are too rarefied. Those neighborhoods lie too far from life."

"Why not nearer the port, then? There are respectable streets there, and fashionable enough for an artist."

"The port is the heart of this city," our dreamer said, "but a heart is useless without blood to pump. The marshes are that blood—the real life of Raunevan."

"The marshes?" I asked, surprised. "Surely you mean the sea. It's the sea that gives life and purpose to the port."

Yet I could tell by his sad silence that I had somehow missed his point. Somehow, we all had. Pouring another glass of wine, I demanded good-naturedly, "But you can't deny the importance of the sea. If the marshes are our life, what then is the sea?"

A sparkle of enigma lit Mimpi's eyes, and a sinister shiver descended my spine.

"The sea," he said quietly, "is mine. You have given it to me."

He turned then with his glass to watch in silence the last crimson streaks flee from the encroaching violet of night.

We walked on in silence as we had for a week past the sharp-edged crystal skeletons that lay over the seabed like cubist corals. The sun remained hidden behind a high, thin haze of clouds, but still it bleached every color from the landscape. Even the sky itself was without hue, as faded as sand, so that the horizon seemed to have vanished along with the sea.

I closed my eyes to wipe away a grain of sand and collided with Rushfalter. He had stopped, and was staring back behind us. A triple line of tracks, aimlessly straight, stretched out of sight.

"I want to go back," he said.

By now, Slothslake had stopped and was walking back to us. "I think we should go back," Rushfalter told him. "There's nothing out here. We're never going to find what we're looking for."

"We're not looking for anything," Slothslake countered.

"Of course we are," I said, concerned that the heat was wearing on my friend. "We're trying to discover the fate of the sea."

"There is no sea."

"We should go back," Rushfalter said resolutely.

27

"You still don't understand? There's nothing to go back to. There is no sea, and there is no Raunevan."

Rushfalter bristled. "Then where did we come from?"

"You might as well ask where we're going."

"I *am* asking."

"We're exploring," I offered. "Aren't we?"

"There's nothing to explore."

"That's why I want to go back!" Exasperation was getting the better of Rushfalter.

A gust of wind blew sand into our tracks, obscuring them. Clouds had obscured the sun since our trek began, and the stars, too, at night. We had wandered all week with no means of marking direction. Slothslake hiked his pack and resumed his hike.

"If we're not exploring, why did we come out here?" I called after him.

"Because we couldn't stay there."

"But what about the sea?"

Without looking back, Slothslake shook his head sadly. "The sea died with Mimpi."

The morning he died, our memory artist, the thick and cloying vapors had risen with the sun. A woman who had braved those mists at noon in search of a private memory found Mimpi still sitting at his breakfast, a smile fixed on his face, his eyes open and sightless. By the time the news spread and those of us closest to Mimpi had gathered to retrieve his body the fog swam so heavily that nothing could be seen through it, and we could only find his house by memory. The heat already threatened the corpse, so we arranged for a burial that very day.

The evening before, Mimpi had given the most sublime performance of his career; we were all still reeling from the beauty of that new memory of a long-ago love—the sharp loss softened at the edges by time into a cherished bittersweet pain—as we journeyed in procession through the heady fog even deeper into that unsettling swamp. Mimpi had once requested this burial in order that his memory never fade. At the time, we had all thought it a showman's ploy.

28

As I slept off the fatigue of grief that night, strange seething dreams seized my drifting mind, haunting me through the hours of uneasy sleep. When at last those sullen dreams disowned me and returned me once more to the world of others, I could recall nothing from them but a vague sense of unease.

A wildfire rush of excitement in the street stole my attention; as soon as I could dress, I scurried to the port to join the rest of Raunevan as we gaped in wonder at the empty seabed.

As the whole population gathered there, bodies accreting in layers along that dry cliff edge to speculate about the fate of our ocean, I mentioned my dreams, as vanished as the sea. First one, then another, then another of those near me said they had suffered similar dreams—the whole city had. We thought them at first a final gift from our departed dreamer, or perhaps some hallucinogenic effect of the swamp's atmospheres, until Slothslake stepped down to the sand.

He was the first to breach the former sea, and we all fell silent. We watched him as transfixed as if he had dared to fly; we waited, but he only stood a few yards out with his hands in his pockets, staring faraway and cloud-lost to the dim, overcast horizon.

He did not move. With a fearsome effort, I pulled myself free of the frightened security of the crowd. I walked up beside Slothslake, each step down the slope bringing an ankle-deep avalanche of desert-dry sand into my shoes.

"It escaped with our dreams," he said as if by way of explanation. A murmur rippled through the people on the rim above us as his words spread. More quietly, to me he said, "I'm going."

"Where?"

Never shifting his distant gaze, he replied, "Out there."

We ascended and pushed our way through the gawking crowd. Only Rushfalter followed us away. When we returned an hour later, our packs heavy with provisions, the excited speculation still continued—and still no one else had ventured into the new desert.

They stared at the three of us as we strode out onto the sand. Slothslake moved forward wordlessly, without looking back, but I felt the stares of the assembled city at my back, and I turned.

29

"We're off to explore. Look for us in a few days."

Rushfalter waved and blurted, "We're going to find the sea," and then blushed as though wishing he hadn't.

We trudged all day through that saline landscape of sparse alien shapes and angles, bizarre mineral-hued crystalline structures looking neither stone nor plant, even the native formations hard-edged and unrecognizable. Three times we encountered serpentine arrangements, ivory-colored and skeletal, that nonetheless seemed more rock than bone.

We made our first camp before dark within the semi-circle of one such fossil. In the pallid gloaming of that overcast day we cooked our dinners over a fire of some unknown branch that glowed smoky and hot but would not flame. As I ate, I examined the curious fragments curling around our camp.

With some effort of imagination, I could distinguish skull, spine, ribs, and tail from those weathered pieces, but if they were, they came from no creature I had ever seen. Nothing we had encountered that day had been familiar. I mentioned this to my companions when my private attempts to decipher the mystery collapsed in a hopeless jumble.

"If some great fissure, say from an earthquake or a volcano, swallowed the water—which I could at least imagine—wouldn't what we know of the sea still be evident? That is, wouldn't such a calamity have left stranded fish and whales? And shouldn't we still see shells and corals encrusting the rocks?"

"Closer to shore, perhaps, but not here, not as far out as we've come." The glowing smoke, which gave the only light in the starless dark, obscured Rushfalter, so that his speech seemed almost to come from the improbable serpent. "This far out we shouldn't see much. Deep currents should have worn away all the rocks, and sand should have swept over any sunken remains. Besides, these bones wouldn't be weathered this way if they'd been resting on the sea floor."

Distantly, Slothslake said, "They're not on a sea floor."

"Well, no, of course, not anymore—"

"Not ever."

I glanced nervously at Rushfalter before asking, "What are you saying, Slothslake?"

"You yourself asked where all the fish have gone. But what of the seaweed and the other marine plants?"

"Well, obviously they were swept away with everything else. Weren't they?"

"Swept away?" Slothslake asked. "Then why don't we see craters where they were uprooted?"

Rushfalter, on the verge of exasperation, said, "The wind has covered them over."

"The sand would have to be dry for that to happen."

"It is," Rushfalter snapped crossly. "Or haven't you noticed after a day's walk?"

Slothslake stuck his fingers into the sand and scooped a handful aside. He kept digging until the pit was elbow deep. With every scoop, a granular cascade collapsed down the dry walls.

"How far down is it dry?" he asked. "Did today's pale sun do this?" He shook his head in answer to his own question. "If there was ever a sea on this plain, it disappeared much longer ago than one day."

"It was here yesterday," I countered. "We all know that."

"It may as well never have been here at all, the way we forsook it."

We slept through that night with those ominous words between us. With each passing day of our wandering, Slothslake grew more withdrawn and unhappy, and more silent. Even on that final morning when we awoke with Raunevan in sight, when Rushfalter and I rushed through breakfast because we could scarcely contain our excitement, Slothslake seemed unsettled, and almost afraid of what lay ahead.

Slothslake's reluctance grew as we neared our home, but he kept with us. When at last we entered what had been until three weeks before Raunevan Bay, Rushfalter sped headlong up the sloping ground to the port—its useless piers jutting awkward and self-conscious over the barren, featureless sand. I struggled after him, but paused when he shouted exuberantly, "We're back!"

31

Very few people roamed the purpose-robbed port; they responded almost universally to Rushfalter's exultation with nervous smiles and quickened paces.

"They don't know us," I told him. "Never mind. We'll stop by the café and tell our friends."

"Never mind," Slothslake echoed oddly.

The café looked the same as ever, and even Slothslake brightened as we neared our old haunt. But when our friends there gave us the same unrecognizing stares we had received from the strangers, uncertainty overtook us all.

"Back from where?" Jordan eventually ventured.

"We were searching for the sea," Rushfalter told him, as though shocked by the question.

The uncomprehending looks deepened. No one remembered the sea.

I thought they were joking. Rushfalter and I tried to explain, hoping to jog their memories, but we soon gave up. Our friends were wary of our familiarity; their guardedness hurt us, and we soon left.

"We should go home," I suggested. "I could use a hot shower and a few hours in a real bed." I paused, then added with forced brightness, "We can meet for dinner."

We parted; I walked home, alone for the first time in three weeks. As I stood at the outside door to my flat, rummaging through my pack, my neighbor came out of his house and glared at me. He did not return my greeting, but demanded, "What are you doing, there?"

"I'm just trying to find my keys. I've been away for a bit."

"Keys?" He eyed me suspiciously. "You don't live there—no one lives there."

"Of course I do. Are you feeling all right?"

"I don't recall anyone living there for years, now."

"I've lived here for years. See?"

I opened the door. My rooms stood customarily disheveled, but obviously recently occupied. My neighbor peered in and appeared shocked by the sight. He threw me a quick look caught somewhere between anger and fear and retreated to his own house.

I showered, but as good as my bed felt, warm and comforting, I could not sleep. My mind was wandering still, urging my body to restlessness.

I went out, and wandered without direction through my city—through a city that had succumbed to a strange sort of entropy. It was uncharacteristically unkempt, more out of casual disregard than neglect; it was overgrown, the fabric of its tapestry frayed at the edges and indistinct, as though it was losing the battle against the jungle and itself.

Meandering carried me in time to the former waterfront. Late afternoon spilled darkness over the edge of Raunevan, where nothing remained to give anyone reason to brave the growing chill. I stood alone at the edge of the road, at the edge of the sand, and stared at that indistinct distance where sand and sky disappeared into one another.

In the growing dusk, I entertained the possibility that we had not somehow circled back to our own Raunevan, but had instead found some city across the former sea that matched it stone for stone and person for person yet was in fact as foreign to us as we were to it: perfectly familiar, and completely unknown. With our departing tracks erased by wind and the milky sky still defying all sense of direction told by sun and star, this fantasy would have been easy enough to believe—yet I knew it could not possibly be true. There was only one Raunevan, our city, my home since birth—this city, our home. And so it still seemed, except for some lost sense of itself, a collective missing memory.

I turned at a sound; Slothslake stood beside me. Together we stared silently out at that strange wasteland for several minutes. Eventually he said, "I'm leaving again."

I nodded slowly, understanding. "You're not coming back this time." After a while, I asked, "Have you told Rushfalter?"

Slothslake hung his head. "No."

"Why not?"

"He'll be happier not knowing."

"But you're telling me?"

"Rushfalter will be happier not knowing because he'll forget soon

33

anyway," Slothslake explained. He fell silent for a stretch before turning his sad face to me and saying, "You, I think, will stay here, perhaps even happily someday. But I don't think you'll be able to forget."

"Will I want to?"

"Perhaps. But you'll stay anyway."

I favored him with a long, searching gaze. "But not you?"

In response, his gaze turned once more out to that strange wasteland.

"What do you think you'll find?" I asked.

"I won't find anything."

A premonition of understanding slipped around me in indistinct currents. "When will you stop?"

"I don't think I ever will," he said, and descended the hill.

I watched my friend go until distance and darkness devoured him. Alone and bewildered, I returned home. No one greeted me along the streets or from the familiar cafés and bistros. I ate a lonely supper inside and went to bed.

The night roused me hours later. I dressed and went out into a warm wind blowing in across the sand. The streets were empty now and still, but a static in the air made the night feel restless.

I began to walk eastward, propelled by a sudden urge. Mimpi, I knew, was the one vital link to everything that had been lost—to the sea, to memory of the sea, and a sea of memories. If there were any answers for me, he held them.

The streetlights ended, then the streets. By instinct alone, I at last found the overgrown remains of the house that the swamp had already reclaimed to itself. Beyond, memory saturated the thick air in dense pockets, drawing me ever deeper into the black and pathless marsh until my foot struck a stone.

Dim before me in the dark I saw the cairn that covered the dreamer's body, his headstone not yet in place. This sight, so much more than reason or sanity alone, proved to me that I was indeed in the same, the one and only, Raunevan. But all my questions remained, waiting.

A gust of wind leapt down from the sky, stirring the lethargic branches. I looked up at the rustling, and through a break in the trees, I saw the deep indigo sky, and stars.

The overcast that had masked both night and day for three weeks had cleared, but the sky revealed was full of unfamiliar constellations.

At last I understood Slothslake's sadness. The city had forgotten everything beyond itself, and had succumbed to its own forgetting. Slothslake had been right all along, I knew then—he would never return to Raunevan, and I would never leave, but we would both remain lost forever.

THE FORK
Jeffrey Thomas

. . . are we the dolls themselves,
born but never fed?
—Anne Sexton, *The Falling Dolls*

HE HAD NO eyelids; his returning vision began at the center and spread out equally to all sides, like his returning consciousness. He lay gazing up at the low ceiling of his compartment, as if it were the sky and he were interpreting the billowing of clouds. Instead, he sought faces and figures in the whorls and knotholes of those splintered, moldering planks of wood. The grain made miniature galaxies and vortexes, like a petrified universe. He couldn't conceive of the wood that composed his compartment ever having been alive, ever having been trees under a bright and open sky. He had never seen a tree, in fact, but it was like a collective memory etched in the rough grain of his own composition.

Even straining his imagination, he could find no faces in the wood. He was not permitted even imaginary company, so it would seem.

He sat up from the hard boards that formed his bed. Besides this, his only other furniture consisted of a small box positioned in front of a larger box, serving as his chair and table. His furniture was of

37

the same wood that made up the walls, floor, ceiling: scarred, rotting, leeched of even the dingiest color. He had constructed two small windows in his compartment, one directly behind his chair and one on the opposite wall; naked smeared panes held in place by mildewed frames. He stood and moved to the nearest one, staring out into the gloom. There were two parts to every day. Murky dark and utter dark. The pitch black outside his windows was lightening to an ashy gray, and he could just begin to make out details of the infinite enclosure of the vast outer room.

A sound made him turn, a light tapping or skittering at the opposite window. There was a vague shape beyond the glass, a fluttering darkness that might have been the humped back of a taxidermist's dusty bird come to life, or the husk of a huge milkweed pod infused with mindless sentience. Its various aspects were suggested to him from the worn hieroglyphics of his collective memory. But as he watched, the quivering black blot withdrew. He knew better than to rush outside to pursue it; he had done so in the past, and encountered nothing. The most he had thought he'd seen, once, was a very large moth with a single wing flying upwards in a jerky blur towards the machinery of the sky.

Moving to the edge of the table, he looked down into his empty bowl. It was part of the sky, having dropped down here. He'd found it in the low scrub of flaked rust. A hemispherical cap that rocked when he touched it because it wasn't meant to be a bowl, and did not have a flat bottom to rest upon. There was nothing in it. Some stillborn memory indicated to him that he should put something into it, but he could never recall what. He had tried various things, hoping it might connect with him, that he might stumble upon the correct answer. He had placed a handful of rusty screws in there. A half-melted clump of hardened slag. A gray and stinking fragment of flesh, glistening slick with decomposition but still pulsing, its waning electrical and chemical commands wandering in ever slower paths through its cells. All of these things had dropped down from the sky and been discovered by him half-hidden under the uneven bed of fallen rust outside his compartment.

Beside the bowl lay a fork. He had taken that from outside, as well. It was either a reject, ejected from the mechanisms, or it had simply been fed through the wrong slot somewhere along the line, ending up down here. He had found other forks before, during one period of pitch black had even heard a pelting rain of them, clanging and clattering across the flat roof of his tiny compartment. He had gathered them up, when the gloom lightened, and heaped them in another of the compartments, in case anyone ever came looking for them. If they were defective, rejects, he could not tell; he had never used a fork, as he could summon no recollection of its intended purpose.

This fork had one tine that was slightly bent toward its brother. Was that the problem? He tapped it against the edge of his box table, then swiftly held the vibrating fork to the side of his head. He listened to its brief, humming song. He had once done this again and again, a hundred times successively, hoping that there might be some coded language hidden in the fork's song, some kind of instruction. Was the fork, then, a device to transmit the voice of the Masters? If so, that voice was beyond his interpretation.

With one slim, stiff finger, he rocked the bowl once more. It seesawed, wobbled, slowly came to be still. He considered rocking the bowl again, as if the sound of its wobbling on the table top might contain the message he sought. He decided not to rock it. He went to the door of his compartment, three planks joined together, and creaked it open.

A landscape of wooden boxes of various sizes lay before him, some lying separate and others touching, some piled atop others, some inside of others, all of them compartments much like his own . . . with the major exception being that none of them were occupied. Some contained items that he had stored or categorized or disposed of himself. Other boxes had been filled by other hands, apparently, long before he had been here . . . though time was as obscure a concept to him as that of trees. The time he had spent before dwelling down here gaped emptily, like that bowl he didn't know how to fill.

Between all the compartments, which stretched off into vague duskiness, the floor of this gigantic outer room was covered in something like (strobe-flash images through his mind) deep piles of autumn leaves, dunes of a desert, drifts of snow, ash from a volcanic blast. The carpet was composed of irregular flakes of rust, some as large as his hand and others fine as powder . . . a mere coating in some places, up to his knees in others. He kept his roof swept clean, so that they didn't trickle through his ceiling boards, but some roofs were mounded with the fallen particles. Even as he watched, there was a subtle, minute sprinkling of them drifting down from above. The larger flakes tumbled or rocked gently as they floated down, like scales shed from an immense (flash: snake), yes, that was the word, snake. Tilting his head back, shielding his lidless eyes with one hand, he looked upwards.

The light snow of metallic scabs sprinkled down from the machines of the sky. As the grainy air lightened (the source of this diffuse illumination unknown to him), he was able to make out the general outlines of that high, distant ceiling. Even as he began to do so, he heard a faraway slide and clunk as some massive iron piece slotted into its socket. A faint grinding/rattling, then an echoing click fading away. Silence again. It seldom got very noisy; more like the ghosts, the memories, of sounds. Sometimes he thought that was all they were—more restless memories. But sometimes, especially when it grew pitch dark, he would hear great rumblings up there, and crashes, like (flash: trains) colliding. Like thunder might sound, he thought.

There was only a fine, nearly invisible mist or fog up there now, tendrils unfurling, shredding, reforming. Other times there were fat billowing clouds—either fumes or steam—and he had lain in the scratchy bed of rust gazing up at them. He had never seen faces in those, either.

Occasionally hot slag dripped down from the heavens, whitely incandescent (perhaps it was molten metal, glowing through cracks, seams, and vents in the far off machinery, that was the source of daylight). Once, when it began to fall, he made the mistake of turning his face up to it. The heavy fluid that spattered his face had blistered it, and when his face cooled his skin cracked and bits flaked away. But it had not hurt him.

When he pressed his palms to his temples, felt the subtle fluttering and twitching inside, sometimes he suspected there was another machine in there, equally as complex as the one that made up the sky, but this machine did not make forks as that one did. This one molded fluid thoughts, solidified them, ground them down, polished them, sent them along conveyors or discarded them if misshapen. This machine had filled endless wooden mail slots with broken bits of seashell, with glass eyes and tea bags, with teeth and clumps of hair and twisted spectacles and all the rest of those things he knew of but had never known.

Sometimes he thought the fluttering in his cracked skull was from a taxidermist's dusty bird, or a husk of milkweed pod infused with life.

One of the memories he half-divined was of falling from that sky himself, like the forks, the screws, the slag. That was how his hairless head first became cracked, and running his fingertips along those jagged sutures helped him to half-recollect. He had slipped through a chink, slipped between a conveyor track and a walkway, while carrying along a wooden box full of forks. A blur of plummeting, the rush of darkness, forks tumbling all around him, a landing partly broken by the thick carpet of rust. A very long sleep, but at last a small click buried inside and then his head finally lifted. A grinding inside it, as if misaligned gears meshed again in improvised patterns. He had stood, looked about him, saw the village of boxes, and had begun to walk toward them in his hesitant, flickering way. Even now, his jerking movements seemed to suggest that every command his head sent to his body and limbs staggered and skipped a beat before reaching them.

Now, as many times before, he stared up at that sky with a numb longing, caressing the fissures in his smooth head, and dreamed that he might dismantle several of the box-like compartments. Using screws from a pile that filled one of these boxes, he would connect the dismantled planks, building an immense ladder, so as to reach that ceiling. So as to slip through its chinks once again, and return to his labors after this long time that he had been idle. He had a calling. It called to him in a weak, scraping, hissing voice, like the whispers of mechanized angels on high. He had a function, a purpose, a reason to exist. He was a maker of forks.

* * *

But the logistics daunted him before he ever started the project. Even if he began his ladder upon the roof of the tallest box, how could he ever build one long enough to reach the sky? He would need to climb arduously back down and up again every time he needed more planks, an immense distance, as he could only hoist with him so many planks at a time. And what if the ladder teetered, fell over while he was at its summit, and he should plummet again? He might not survive such a fall a second time.

He had seldom tried very hard to escape the outer room. It dwarfed and humbled him, made his desires seem minuscule and ridiculous, presumptuous and unrealistic. Instead, he had existed down here cycle after countless cycle, and thought that perhaps one day he would be discovered here and liberated by more capable hands; those of the Masters he had once served. Infrequently, however, his impulses to be freed gathered strength, took on life. As was usually the case, part of him was rising up to smother those impulses. The ladder idea wouldn't work. Escape did not lie in venturing upward. He very nearly allowed his growing obsession to subside . . .

Instead, as he had done several times before, he decided to search for his escape on the floor of the massive chamber. But in the past, he had only traveled as far as he could go while still being able to return to his compartment before it grew black in the outer room. He had never left his compartment when it was utterly dark outside. There was that perhaps-moth at his panes, on occasion, and he had heard other disturbing things that did not sound like the gnashing of the sky machines. But today he had come upon a new plan.

He had never before been able to journey far enough to reach any of the outer room's walls. He had only neared one of them close enough to make out its gray surface, misted with distance, before he had to turn back toward the village of boxes.

Yet now he had the idea to bring a box along with him, and he could shelter inside it when the air turned black with night's rot. A box small enough to tug behind him or push ahead of him, but large enough to contain his curled or seated body. So he commenced his inspection of the boxes, testing their soundness, experimenting with pushing them through the bed of metallic scurf. He preferred the idea of seeing in front of him more clearly, and so began to create a harness that would enable him to pull the box behind him. He found mounds of balled wire in one box, and extricated several strands, twisted them and affixed them in two loops to the outside of the box, using screws to hold them in place. He could then slip his arms through the two loops, so as to drag the box along behind him like a sled.

This work took up most of the lighter part of the cycle, and he decided to rest inside his regular compartment until he could strike out fresh when the light returned.

While lying on his bare cot, staring at the ceiling, he listened to the sounds outside his close walls. A stamp-stamp-stamp, as of a titanic metal hoof stomping on the ceiling far beyond this one. A second or two of scraping at one of his black windowpanes, then gone. And— perhaps he only imagined this, as his vision closed into a narrower and narrower circle—the feathery sifting of rust tumbling out of the sky and alighting on his roof, like soil upon a (flash: coffin) lid.

* * *

After a long time of dragging the box behind him (flash of a snail shell), ploughing through the rustling fields of corrosion, he decided to rest. The wire hoops were cutting into his shoulders; it didn't cause him pain, but he was afraid to cause himself a debilitating injury. He flexed his arms, meanwhile standing on his toes as if that might help him see further ahead. Was it? Yes. He could begin to make out the vaguest notion of a looming barrier ahead of him. He was coming upon one of the walls that made up the outer room.

He took a second break later on, and when he finally decided to pitch camp, he could see the wall more clearly than he had on that previous excursion. It was all gray, one apparently solid surface rather than being composed of boards of wood or plates of metal, though it seemed chipped, pocked, even fissured with cracks. Those cracks might yawn like (flash: canyons) when he drew near enough. Might he escape through one of them?

This portable shelter had no windows, but as he rested inside it, clutching his knees to his chest, he heard soft ticking sounds against its exterior, as if stealthy probing fingers were feeling for a way inside. His vision narrowed but never entirely closed up. He was too unnerved by that exploratory sound, and by the feeling of being so far from his village of boxes, the only home he could remember, even though he knew it was not the place he had been intended for. He must be brave. His duties lay elsewhere. He must rediscover his function, must traverse this broad lacuna. He must fill the empty bowl of his skull (cracked like that great wall). Somewhere, there were those that valued and needed him. Those beings who knew how to utilize the beautiful and mysterious metal objects that he had once fashioned out of formless ore. They were his Masters. They would be expecting him back. He must not disappoint them.

* * *

Just when it seemed that the wire loops by which he drew his shelter along must slice into his shoulders, saw his very arms from him—and his weakening, overworked legs give out beneath him—he reached the base of the towering gray wall.

The machinery high above him, lost in a heavy layer of steam, chugged and hammered with a regular rhythm. And while no molten metal dripped from it at the moment, it must be a common occurrence here: there was a hill of solidified slag, looking like a hummock made from intertwined worms fossilized in lead, slanting up against the wall like a ramp. Hardened streams of slag marred the wall where they had run down its flank. And there were indeed huge rents and fissures in the wall. They seemed to be concentrated in the area of the slag heap, leading him to conclude that the heat from this fluid metal had caused

44

the wall's material to split.

The largest of these cracks jagged down to touch the summit of the slag hill. He could see darkness within it. Shrugging off the wire hoops that had dug into his body, he discarded his shelter behind him, the husk of a moth's chrysalis. He moved to the foot of the slag mound, and began to clamber his way up it . . . using his hands to find purchase in the gray, convoluted mass.

His long journey had left him fatigued . . . the climb was slow, and once he lost his hold and slid halfway down the hill again on his belly. But at last the crest of the slag hill was reached and he straightened up, peering somewhat timidly into the fissure that now yawned directly before him. It was as black as the night cycle in there. Was it night in the world beyond? A warm, humming breeze blew out at him, stirring the frayed edges of his coarsely woven garments.

Steeling himself, his head throbbing with a synchronized echo of that chugging clamor from above, he stepped into the fissure in the wall.

He found himself not passing through the wall, but merely inside of it, where it proved hollow. Dust coated everything like the darkness, but enough faint gray light entered the rift to reveal to him a giant piston sliding greased and nearly soundless, which in turn smoothly rotated a self-oiled crank. An immense grooved belt of segmented metal circulated as a result of the piston's pumping. This toothed band descended out of the murk above him, sandwiched between the two interior faces of the wall. It then looped and flowed upward again, back into the dissolving gloom.

To his great disappointment, after he had journeyed so far to reach this place, there were no service ladders set into the inner walls. But his gaze returned to consider that looping belt.

Perhaps he could reach the ceiling of machinery after all . . . that factory in the heavens.

Inching carefully forward, he waited until he thought he could seize onto the moving belt firmly. After several false starts, during which he nearly lost his nerve, he lunged for it, caught it, hugged himself to it, grasping onto two of its blunt teeth. The belt easily bore his slight weight upwards, upwards inside the wall. Looking down, he saw the pale light from the outer room fade away until he was entirely swallowed in blackness, as if he had fallen to sleep. Or ascended into sleep.

Upwards, upwards, and the air grew warmer, warmer, hot, hotter. He heard the increasing hiss of the steam somewhere on the other side of the wall. Higher, higher, the belt soaring with mindless confidence. He passed through a cloud of steam vented from somewhere. He passed through a cloud of loud gnashing sound. Tilting his head up, he saw that at last he was approaching a gray mirage of light, which became more real, more prevalent the higher he rose.

There was a ledge near the top of the shaft, where the belt ran around a great turning wheel. He would have to leap off the belt and onto that narrow walkway. If he missed, he would fall. If he hesitated, the belt would sweep him downward again, if it didn't tear him to shreds at its apex before that.

He loosened his grip on the notched belt, stood on one of its teeth, leaned far out and prepared to fling himself into space. A bit higher . . . and now he jumped, an infinite abyss roaring with its emptiness beneath him, but then his feet alighted on the ledge, and his fingers clawed across the wall desperately until they dug into pocks and found purchase. The belt continued rotating behind him, the teeth he had gripped slipping back down into the pit. Now that he was secure, he looked around him, and then up at the ceiling where the gray light filtered through gaps in a tight and complex weave of cobwebbed struts and girders, pipes and conduits, all of it caked thick with rust.

One pipeline ran vertically up past the ledge, joining the mass above him. Plastered to the wall, he shifted gingerly toward it. He took hold of the pipe, jagged with its corroded skin, and began to hoist himself up along it. His efforts caused scabs of rust to sprinkle down to join the layer that covered the floor even inside the wall.

After all the dreaming, the yearning, the hopeless hope, at last he touched the metal sky.

It was a struggle, but he was able to pull himself up into the nest of pipes and supports, and squeeze his body between several strands in this metallic tapestry. He was through . . .

He entered the gray light as if it were a sea he had been plunged into, a sea that stunned him with its coldness, that ripped the air from his chest.

But the air was actually molten, rippling, with the heat generated by the machinery. And it wasn't lack of air that nearly ceased the clockwork motions inside him, but the scene spread before his eyes. This unthinkable vastness of openness and freedom under a featureless sky the color of pewter.

Around him, crumbling chimneys and brick smokestacks and humped, hulking sections of the factory reared and loomed. Distantly, he saw the misted outlines of a (flash: city). But most of all, he saw the forks.

The forks were a sea. A landscape of snow, with drifts swept up against the factory's external machinery. A desert, with dunes and hills. The forks swallowed the bases of the chimneys and smokestacks. The forks seemed to reach all the way to the distant city itself. They glimmered and glinted under the sunless gray sky. Thousands, millions, more, polished and without a (flash: fingerprint) smudged upon one of them. He knew suddenly what a fingerprint was, though his fingers did not possess them.

The city was silent. But the factory itself chugged and pounded and rang with its ceaseless purpose, even as it crumbled into decay. A sudden crashing/clattering waterfall of sound, and he looked to see even more forks disgorged from a chute in the side of a black machine. They poured across the other forks, settled with a tinkling sound, lay still. For several moments, there lingered in the air a loud, ringing hum of a piercingly high register, as if wailing (flash: spirits) had been raised from these mounds and cairns of forks, only to quickly dissipate. It had been the vibration of the many tines. For it was a treacherous vista of sharp tines like myriad mysterious grins.

Some of the forks had plain, unadorned handles, while others boasted flowery filigree. Dinner forks and salad forks and baby forks.

Suddenly, the memory slotted into place with a definitive click. He knew what the forks were for. What the Masters had done with them.

But the Masters were gone. Just the forks, now. The billion forks lying like heaped bones, fragmented and gone cold.

He wandered unsteadily across the landscape, the forks slithering and shifting under his feet. He didn't venture far, however, instead sat himself down in the shadow of a smokestack, his back against it.

His cracked eggshell head lowered. He felt his body stilling. There was no purpose for him up here, after all. He had not been prepared for that. He had nothing to insert in its place. The knowledge seemed to empty him, blank him.

He hugged his knees to his chest and lowered his forehead onto his knees, weary from his long journey. Weary from a disillusionment too hollowed-out to be despair.

The circle of his vision began to diminish, close up, the light at the center growing smaller, smaller, more distant, until darkness consumed it altogether.

Another waterfall of forks swarmed around him. Later, there came more. Gradually, he was buried. Only the top of his bare skull showed. After a long time, not even that.

For a while, he continued to hear the churning of the factory, even in his blind interment. But at last, one day, there was another small click inside him. And then, restful silence.

STATE SECRETS OF APHASIA
Stepan Chapman

They went to sea in a Sieve, they did,
In a Sieve they went to sea:
In spite of all their friends could say,
On a winter's morn, on a stormy day,
In a Sieve they went to sea!
—Edward Lear

<FOR ACCESS TO THE IMPERIAL APHASIAN ARCHIVE, PLEASE ENTER YOUR CODE KEY.>

Cirrus densus, cirrus filosus, cirro-stratus nebulosus. Cumulus translucidus, cumulus castellatus, alto-cumulus lenticularus. Nimbus calvus, nimbus humilis, cumulo-nimbus capillatus.

<ACCESS GRANTED. WELCOME TO APHASIA! CLOUD CONTINENT OF A THOUSAND WONDERS! APHASIA! WHERE ANYTHING CAN HAPPEN! APHASIA IS A PROTECTED SUBSYSTEM OF ECTOID REALMS UNLIMITED.>

<YOUR SELECTED CATEGORY IS [history].>

<PLEASE REQUEST THE DESIRED DOCUMENT BY BOTH FILE NAME AND CATALOG NUMBER.>

*** ***** *******, #*********.

49

<PLEASE STAND BY FOR TRANSLATION.>
<TRANSLATION FOLLOWS.>

* * *

THE BLACK GLACIER

In Aphasia the people could walk on clouds. In fact they *had* to walk on clouds, because the continent of Aphasia was entirely composed of clouds. And since these clouds floated in a sky that wasn't connected to any planet, the Aphasians felt deeply grateful that they *could* walk on clouds.

The ectoids of Aphasia were air people—weightless luminous stick figures who built on vapor, slept on fog, and lived in architectural drawings. The cloud continent supported whole civilizations of these ephemeral nonsense creatures. They felt perfectly secure on their free-floating empire in the sky. They never once fell through the ground beneath their feet. They never had to deal with the hazards of mass or gravity. But all that changed when the Black Glacier invaded Aphasia.

The Black Glacier was first sighted at Mirage Lake in the year 500 AAA. (After Alba's Ascension.) The first Aphasians to witness the glacier were the simple conceptual tangles that fizzed up and drizzled away amidst the snorkel grass of the Doubtful Marsh. A small pixilated sneefler fizzed into being in the bubbly blue air. It opened its eyeknobs and saw what there was to see. It noticed that a glittering crag of ice was rising from the silvery mists of Mirage Lake.

As the sneefler marveled at the germinating glacier, the glacier watched the sneefler and exhaled a frosty wind in its direction. The sneefler was instantly transformed into soggy papier mâché on a flimsy armature of coat hanger wire. It dropped dead and lay on the wilting snorkel grass, lopsided and smelling of mildew. Then two more sneeflers and a double-billed quanzu self-assembled. They too were transmuted into shoddy papier mâché models of themselves. They fell on their sides in the swamp water and decayed into organicules in shame.

The glacier humped itself up from the lake and slid north across

50

the Amnesiac Waste. Soon its shadow darkened the lavender lowlands of the Southern Overreaches. All who beheld it turned to wet newsprint, sagged, and crumbled. A peaceful village of talking crockery was petrified en masse. Settlements of nomadic punctuation marks were slaughtered, and towns of sleep shovelers, and tribes of helium eyeballs. The Twelve Twisting Rivers of Mist froze solid.

Frostbitten refugees crowded the cobbled roads that radiated from Lotus City. The stragglers fell into the glacier's shadow and melted into white paste and paper pulp and brittle wire. Their remains were consumed by the swarms of fat brass cog-roaches that followed the glacier everywhere.

Various picturesque tribes of the Overreaches rose up against the glacier. The counterattack was organized by Queen Ellen the Wickerwork Giraffe and her blood brother, the Great Stone Wheelbarrow—mighty sorcerers both. Queen Ellen loosed her venom goats against the glacier. The Great Stone Wheelbarrow assailed it with iodine kites and friendly shark robots. The Bronze Man and his crew of stained botflies flew their pirate blimp into the thick of battle and fired off cannonades of melon rockets at the ice wall. Two rival gangs called the Chromium Drain Bandits and the Hungry Jars joined forces that day. They fought the glacier with snow chains and cheese scorpions.

All enchantments failed. All advantages of armor, speed, or weaponry proved futile. The resistance fighters collapsed into crumpled paper and crooked loops of wire. The flying warriors were sucked headlong into a vibrating slush that canceled their flesh and erased their memories. Foot soldiers were crushed beneath the glacier's obsidian belly. Despite their bravery, the armies of the Overreaches were decimated.

The Black Glacier slid across the Overreaches like a colossal smothering slug. A light-gobbling ice sheet shoved its prow against the towering cumulo-nimbal formations of the Dribbled Peaks. The only survivors were those who had scaled the peaks and reached the Plateau of Stratus. These displaced remnants of so many once-proud nations limped north. A bone-chilling gale pursued them across the cloudprairie, as they wended their weary way toward Lotus City.

51

Lotus City! Flower of the cloud continent, where the sky is always sapphire blue, and the clouds are always clean and fertile and firm underfoot. Lotus City! An asylum in times of disaster, protected against all evil by the courtiers of the lotus empress.

Rivers of footsore refugees trudged through the city streets, dragging wagons heaped with pitiful bundles. All these grief-stricken rivers converged on the base of the mile-high marble pedestal that supported the Lotus Palace. Above their heads, the fabled stronghold opened its gleaming white petals to the light of the morning sunbubble.

Though the outward appearance of Lotus Palace was tranquil, its inhabitants were close to panic. There was much running in the corridors, many ambassadors waving reports at one another, much shouting behind closed doors.

The throne room, by contrast, lay in the grip of a heavy silence, a silence that echoed between the pavilions of white jade. It was the silence of the dowager empress Alba, who sat on her throne of salt wearing an ivory crown and a white silk robe. The old woman held her head in her hands, deeply depressed. Strands of gray hair spilled down her face. A few of her personal servants, platinum-plated termites in tuxedos, moved around the throne room at a distance, tending to the candle sconces and the coffee samovar.

Alba the First. Skinny Old Alba. Alba the Dowager. Alba the Senile. Sitting alone in her palace of milk glass. No one liked her anymore. But at least she'd held the place together. Until now. Now they could all stop pretending.

Alba tried to come to terms with the inevitable. She saw no way to halt the glacier. She had no enchantments of her own. She was merely the particular imaginary woman who had, by an accident of birth, ascended this imaginary throne one fine spring day five hundred years ago. Now she must watch her kingdoms devastated, a fate more bitter than death.

Alba's herald, a plump little boy in white satin livery, entered the throne room and cleared his throat. "Announcing Lady—"

"Announcing? Who gave you permission to announce? I'm not receiving."

Young Gumsnot shrugged and scratched his left calf with his right shoe buckle. "They insisted," he mumbled.

"Go on then."

"Announcing Lady Crane, Protector of the Eastern Colonies, the Stray Thoughts, and the Vague Notions. Also King Skronk, High Khan of the Cactus Trolls and Sultan of the Headless Knots."

Alba rose to her feet, a flush darkening her cheeks. *"King Skronk? Here? In my palace? What is the meaning of this?!"*

"How would I know?" whined Gumsnot. "I just announce them. I don't interview them."

"Get out of my sight."

Gumsnot ran and hid behind a tapestry.

Lady Crane and King Skronk strode into the throne room through a jade archway. Lady Crane was seven feet tall. Her head and her long slender neck were those of a fisher crane, and her hands were long and feathered. She wore a ceremonial robe of crimson velvet.

Skronk stood nine feet tall and was woven from twelve varieties of cactus. His eyes were peyote buds, and his head hair was a serrated crown of yucca blades. For clothing he wore a chain mail tunic and his tool belt. Walking under the arch, he had no need to duck his head. The Lotus Palace was built on a grand scale.

Alba found the pair disorienting. The lady was her closest friend, but the cactus king was another matter. Alba was used to seeing him at the vanguard of a horde of metal-eating trolls, all armed to the teeth and screaming for her blood. How many times had she driven this rash barbarian back to the Mad Slag Pits of Throatburg? And how many times had he hidden himself away to plot revenge? It was all so childish.

Alba stamped her foot. "Skronk, you blot on your own escutcheon, are you behind that glacier? Lady Crane, what has this miscreant been up to?"

The lady dropped a curtsy. "My liege," she said. "King Skronk is not here as our enemy this day, but as my peer on the Ontological Controls Commission."

"The *what?* I've never heard of it."

"Nonetheless," said Lady Crane, "it has existed since the dawn days of Aphasia."

"And both you and Skronk are members of this . . . secret council?"

"We are, Alba. And that's the least of the things you don't know about Aphasia." Lady Crane drew closer to the empress. "There are many state secrets."

"Too secret for *my* ears? Have you taken leave of your senses?"

"Oh shut up, you old bitch," muttered Skronk.

"*What?*" cried Alba. "What did he say?"

Skronk turned to Lady Crane. "Why are we here? Did we come here to humor her? Let's get to work."

"*Silence,*" commanded Alba.

"No," snarled Skronk, advancing on her. "I don't think so."

"*Guards.*" Jade trap doors in the throne room floor sprang open. Four iron crickets, as big as steam engines, scrambled up from hidden tunnels and surrounded the cactus king.

"Voice control override," Skronk said to the guard crickets. "Regression phase epsilon." The crickets stopped in their tracks.

"Authority?" said the biggest one.

"Ontological Controls Commission."

"What are you waiting for?!" Alba shouted at the crickets. "Seize him!"

"Seize him yourself, you old bat," said the biggest cricket. "Come on, boys. Let's get out of here before the world ends. I hear there's beer and loose women in Moundville." The four guards hurried from the room, congratulating one another on their liberation.

"How dare you?!" Alba demanded of Skronk.

"Just sit down and relax," said Lady Crane, taking her arm. Alba shook herself free and made a run for her escape door.

"Throne," said Skronk. "Voice control override. Restrain the empress."

"If you say so," said the throne of salt, turning on its base and extending its silver-plated tentacles. Two of the mechanical tentacles reached across the room and hooked Alba under her arms. A third

54

looped itself round her waist. They dragged her back to the throne, lifted her into it, and bound her to it. With a whirring of tiny motors, the throne raised itself on a silver column and reclined the empress, elevating her feet. More and more it resembled a dentist's chair.

Lady Crane stood beside the breathless Alba and held her hand. "Sorry about this, Alba. Drastic times require drastic action."

Alba's anger drained out of her. Now she was frightened. It was a palace revolution, and her closest friend was part of it. But why depose her at a time like this? The empire was crumbling. The glacier would soon destroy them all.

Lady Crane made an announcement to the air. "All medical millipedes will now convene for the imperial regression." Seven disks of white jade floor sank from floor level and swung aside. Seven cylindrical silver platforms rose into the room. On each platform was a semicircle of electronic consoles. The flickering read-out lights of the consoles illuminated the leggy ventral surfaces of seven copper millipedes, who were already busily tracing out engram boundaries, adjusting resostats, and generally crunching their proxological data. Skronk stood behind one of the millipedes and peered over its shoulder at the screen of its nerve radar. His spiny face was fixed in a disgusted frown.

Alba struggled against her restraints. "Get these things off of me."

"If you behave," Lady Crane told her.

"Listen. I know I'm a tiresome old woman, but really that's no excuse for treason. I've always done my best to be fair to you and to—"

Skronk loomed above Alba and slapped her face, leaving cactus spines embedded in her cheek.

"Doesn't she ever stop talking?" he grumbled as he stalked away.

"She certainly felt that," said one of the medical millipedes.

"Look at this tracing," said a second.

"Any minute now she'll start crying," suggested a third.

"It's standard procedure," said a fourth. "He has to break down her resistance."

"You'll pay for that," Alba said coldly.

"You must forgive the cactus king," said Lady Crane, plucking spines from Alba's cheek. "He has the good of the empire at heart."

"Tell me, what do you want from me? My crown? It's yours."

"It's not that simple," Lady Crane said sadly. "The only thing that can stop the glacier is you. But the problem with you is, you're not *you*."

"I'm not?"

"No. You're someone else entirely. And we *could* just tell you who that is. But just *telling* you wouldn't snap you out of your Alba trance. You have to remember."

"Remember what? Some previous life?"

"Your *real* life. Which is happening as we speak."

"And how is that going to repel a glacier?"

"Trust me, Your Grace. It will. Why? Because this is all in your mind. Me. Him. Lotus City. The glacier. This entire majestic cloud continent. It only exists in your poor sick mind, Alba."

"And how did your mind *get* so sick?" Skronk interjected, standing opposite Lady Crane and leaning over the throne. His voice was like the buzzing of a jar of angry bees. "State secret. Can't be revealed directly. Have to use the Secret Piano. Have to peel you like an onion."

Lady Crane poised her beak to strike and dealt Skronk a peck to his forehead. He withdrew, rubbing his bruise, and sat down in a corner with an audible crunching of buttock spines.

Lady Crane walked slowly around the throne, on her long orange legs. "Just relax, Alba dear. This won't hurt a bit." Long cool fingers stroked Alba's brow. "Do you remember how you ascended the throne, Alba?"

"Of course. It's all in the first chapter of Professor Clickbeetle's *Chronicles*. I was enchanted by Scugma the Sewage Witch. She deposed my father and then turned me into Klump the Chewed Boy. She made me chop her wood. Then I was rescued by the Bronze Man and the Cardboard Dog. They restored me to my throne."

"But you were someone else before you were Klump."

"Of course. I was myself. A little girl. I was Alba."

"*Well . . .* " Lady Crane trilled in her long white throat. " . . . not exactly. That's why we need the piano. *Young Gumsnot.* Announce the Secret Piano."

Gumsnot emerged from behind the tapestry and blew a strangulated trumpet fanfare. "Announcing the Secret Piano of Aphasia."

"You should *clean* that trumpet," said Skronk.

A white player piano trotted shyly into the throne room on its square wooden legs. It looked around, approached the throne, and made an awkward bow.

"Your Grace. Nice to see you again."

Alba stared down from her throne in bafflement. "I've never seen this thing before in my life. What is it, Lady Crane?"

"It's the Secret Piano."

"She certainly has gotten older since the last time," said the piano.

Lady Crane put a finger to her beak. "Hush. She doesn't remember the last time."

"Ah," said the Secret Piano. "I don't suppose she would. May I introduce the piano rolls to Her Grace?"

A lid flipped open in the side of the piano's sound box. Four piano rolls with pipe-cleaner arms and legs bounded to the ground. They lined up neatly, saluted Lady Crane, and bowed to Alba.

"Roll delta may insert itself," said the piano.

"About time," Skronk muttered in his corner.

Seven copper millipedes punched madly at ivory buttons. Seven teak abacuses chattered. Piano roll delta leapt onto the piano's keyboard, opened a secret door, and disappeared inside. Internal piano clockwork began to whir. The piano began to play, softly at first, then louder, themes from some romantic symphony of epic sweep and poignant grandeur. Alba listened to the music and grew drowsy. Music always put her to sleep.

"How do you feel?" asked Lady Crane.

"I feel a dream coming on," said Alba. "I can't keep my eyes open. What's that piano doing to me?"

"Well, out in the real world, they'd call it a posthypnotic suggestion trigger. But since we're in Aphasia, let's just say it's a magic spell. The piano will help you to remember a story. And since you're the main character, the story should hold your interest."

The piano lifted its lid to a vertical position and unfolded it into four sections, making it taller and taller until it was ready to function as a film screen. A star field appeared on the screen, a flickering silent film. It was being projected by an invisible fiber-optic cable from the depths of Alba's mind. There was blackness and sun glare and silence—a typical section of the solar system. "False memory on screen," said a millipede. "Time codes running."

"Alba?" said Lady Crane. "Can you see the picture from where you're sitting?"

"Very clearly," said Alba, although her eyes were closed, and her head reclining. "I can see it on my eyelids. Those don't look like the stars of Aphasia, do they?"

"They're not, Alba. That's the physical universe. That which surrounds and excludes human thought. The Other World. The opposite end of the superstring."

Alba shuddered. "It looks so cold. How can I remember a place I've never been?"

"Try harder," Skronk growled from his corner.

The piano screen brightened. A white star was emerging from the star field, shining ever brighter as it neared the discarnate camera eye. Luminous vapor whorls swirled round a glowing core that danced and flared like a flame. It seemed constantly on the verge of coalescing into a beautiful young woman. She surged toward the camera eye—half naiad, half ice comet. Out here, her scale was impossible to guess. She might be larger than a gas giant or smaller than a snowflake. Six lesser lights of six different colors trailed after the comet woman, swerving and dipping like fireflies around her vapor trail.

"Crane, what are they? They look like fairies. Yes, like void fairies from the rings of Saturn, emissaries from the realm of hail and mist."

"Exactly. They're journeying on a crucial mission to Earth. The last remnants of the fairy nations of Earth have called a solar council.

Saturn had to send a representative. Although the voyage was hazardous, Queen White Speck of the Outer Ring undertook the task. But Queen White Speck was headstrong. She refused an escort of Martian gremlins. She embarked into the void with only her six handmaidens as retinue. She thought she could defend herself against the vacuum predators. She was wrong. A swarm of electrostatic leeches caught her party unprepared."

Up on the screen, the tragic leech attack was being staged, and not very convincingly. This particular part of the film resembled seven silent film starlets being pestered by floating duffel bags with rubber tail fins. There was very little blood, but a maximum of melodramatic posing in diaphanous gowns. The piano did its impression of Rachmaninoff.

"They're so beautiful," Alba murmured. "What a waste."

"What's a waste?" asked Lady Crane.

"They died so young. The leeches came, with their ink clouds and their shock stingers. Queen White Speck was mortally wounded, just when we had almost reached Earth."

"You were one of them?"

"Did I say that? Perhaps I was. Life is full of surprises. All these years I've imagined myself a mere mortal. Have I been under an enchantment?"

"Which one of them were you?" asked Lady Crane.

"You see that greenish one? Hanging close to the big white one? That was me. There were six of us. One for each color of the rainbow. We were all so devoted to Queen White Speck." Alba sighed.

"Inflation," said one of the medical millipedes.

"Grandiosity," agreed another.

"Has to be processed," a third observed stoically. "It's a question of retracing the design path."

"How long is this going to take?" Skronk asked no one in particular.

"*Silence,*" commanded Lady Crane.

"Vacuum leeches dislike the color green for some reason. My sisters were eaten alive, but I never got a scratch. Queen White Speck was leaking light like a wicker basket, and all that light was going to waste. So we created Aphasia. White Speck told me to hover in the Earth's atmosphere. She said that a provision would be made for my survival. But she wasn't going anywhere."

"How did you two create Aphasia?"

"Aren't you watching? It's right there on the screen."

The screen was filled by an extenuated creature of pulsing green light fibers, slowly spinning on her axis. This youthful inhuman version of Alba spun ever faster, and her peripheral fibers fanned out around her head like a revolving galaxy of angel hair. All at once a torrent of white light flooded down on her.

"Adjust the exposure," shouted a millipede.

The lightfall penetrated the proto-Alba's chest. Her heart chakra diffracted the white torrent into prismatic coils of rainbow fairy lightning. She discharged the lightning as jerking thrashing bolts that spent themselves into a few square miles of partial cloud cover. As the clouds were innocently drifting past some pasture land, harming no one, minding their own business, they were dragged unceremoniously from the material plane.

The film cross-faded to the noosphere, where Alba's graft of earthly weather was rapidly blossoming into the ornate basins and mesas of Aphasia.

"I was the lens," said Alba from her trance. "I created Aphasia from the light of my dying sisters. All I needed were some ordinary clouds."

The film interrupted itself with a title card: SHE HAS PRO-DUCED AN IMAGINARY CONTINENT FROM THE LIGHT OF HER DYING SISTERS.

"So I came here to live and found myself something to do," she went on. "I built an empire, and I banished death from it. I hate death. And leeches."

Lady Crane folded her hands and smiled at the corners of her beak. Another title card appeared on the screen: HERE ENDS FALSE MEMORY PHASE DELTA: "THE CREATION OF APHASIA".[1]

[1] False memory delta was believed by Alba during the years 81 through 243 AAA.

The piano fell silent. Skronk stood up and stretched his back. The piano folded its screen.

Just then a shock wave rocked the palace. The throne room shook like a leaf. Jagged cracks streaked up the white jade walls.

A butler termite rushed in. "The glacier has reached the lotus pedestal! It's firing icicles at the palace!"

A large section of the ceiling lurched off kilter and then fell through the floor. Six of the seven medical millipedes were crushed.

"This is bad," Skronk told Lady Crane. "Very bad. We have to get her out of Lotus City. We have to take her as far north as possible."

"I have summoned the Purple Scarab," she told him. "He will be here soon."

A huge black icicle transpierced the throne room, slamming Lady Crane against a wall and impaling her.

Moments later a giant black beetle crashed up through the remains of the floor and threw open its carapace. "Into the cargo hold!" shouted Skronk. The throne raised itself from its pedestal on six silver legs and scuttled up the scarab's boarding ramp. Following close behind were the Secret Piano and a medical millipede loaded down with black boxes and cables. Skronk pushed them up the ramp and slammed the hatch behind him.

The Purple Scarab tunneled down through the stalk of the palace, unwilling to expose itself to ice projectiles in the open air. It tunneled through the foundations of Lotus City and into the raw cloudstuff beneath. It tunneled north, far below the surface, seeking asylum for the Ontological Controls Commission and their imperial captive.

Skronk crouched in a corner of the cargo bay. Alba lay sleeping on her throne. The last of the medical millipedes wept for the dead.

"This is all I need," said Skronk. "And we've still got three piano rolls to go."

* * *

The final defense of Lotus City involved entities from all quadrants of the empire, along with several entities visiting from Ataxia the

61

wooden continent. Many wise and peaceable beings, ancient with years, were slain that day. Oilspin the Pen-Nibbed Octopus was lost. The Enormous Chocolate Face With Green Sugar Sprinkles In the Sky At Twilight perished as well, and the Denture Tank From Hell. Others fell beside them—shy harmless ectoids who had no business fighting a war—the Moonbathing Sphagnum Dancers, the Flutter In a Haze, the Golden Sand Fleas, the Tiny Riders . . . All who stood against the Black Glacier were soon transmuted into heaps of moldy papier mâché. The glacier toppled the Lotus Palace and ground the city to rubble beneath it. Then it resumed its march northward.

Meanwhile the Purple Scarab's tunnel had emerged into the starlight on a windy hillside in the feather forests of the Dripping Lands. A sliver of moon was glowing above the ground fog. Admiral Snailwick greeted the scarab's passengers as they disembarked. He led them to dry quarters in a natural cave which the Mollusk Boys had converted into a concrete bunker. Surrounded by the hooded Mollusk Boys in berets and bandoliers, the three remaining members of the Ontological Controls Commission made camp and collected their wits. Alba was still sleeping soundly.

"Can you monitor the next phase or not?" King Skronk asked the medical millipede.

"I'll do what I can do, Sir." The millipede used its tail to whack the side of one of the black boxes. Another oscilloscope came on-line. "Moonlight mode is now active. We are go for the gamma engram."

"Piano?" said Skronk. "Do your stuff."

"Aren't you going to hold her hand and talk her through it?" asked the Secret Piano.

"Hell no. I detest the bitch."

"Someone's got to do it," insisted the millipede.

"So *you* do it."

"I have to calibrate the nephostrophic feedback algorithms!"

"Well, I'm not touching the old bag, and that's final."

"So we'll all die, and the world will end. *Fine,*" said the piano.

Admiral Snailwick wiped the mud from his boots and approached the throne of salt. He gazed at the old woman's face while she slept.

The admiral was a hollow uniform with a small pink snail that lived on its right epaulet. He had lost his body in a freak gunnery accident, and had it replaced with a naval uniform. Then he'd lost his head to a melon rocket and hired the snail as a surrogate head, for all the lettuce it could eat. (The admiral was under a curse. But that's another story.)

"Just the mollusk I want to see," said Skronk. "Can you get the queen of the world here to wake up. We need to run her through another fugue state."

The admiral examined Alba's restraints with the fingers of his white dress gloves. Somewhere on the scarab journey, she'd lost her crown.

"Let her go," he told the throne. The throne withdrew its tentacles and lowered Alba's feet toward the floor. Snailwick took her arm and helped her to walk a few steps. He sat her down on an ammunition crate in front of the piano. He brought her a mug of hot podwater with earwig honey and seated himself beside her, watching her closely.

"So, Your Grace. Are you ready for another concert?"

"Is that you, Snailwick? It is? I seem to be losing my eyesight along with my mind. Where is Lady Crane?"

"Called away on state business," Snailwick told her. "Very hush-hush. Oh dear. Look at this. Your slippers and stockings are soaked. Let me plug in this heating snake." The admiral respectfully removed his sovereign's footwear. "And would you like for me to peel off your skin?"

"I beg your pardon?"

"Your skin. It's rather old and wrinkly. I could peel it all off if you'd feel more comfortable."

"No! Don't touch me!"

"There there. Don't take on so. I'll start with this arm." Snailwick took hold of a pinch of loose skin and peeled loose a long strip. There was fresh new skin beneath it, smooth as a peach.

"What are you doing?!"

"It's a beauty treatment. Try it yourself. See how nice?"

Alba tried it. "That *is* relaxing. I had no idea that my skin was

63

self-replacing. Go ahead, Admiral Snailwick. Peel it all off."

The admiral obliged, within the limits of modesty. When he'd finished, a new Alba had emerged—a lovely girl only sixteen years old. She felt her smooth pink face with her smooth pink fingers. She even had long golden hair, which had been coiled beneath the old Alba's flaky scalp.

Snailwick was beaming. "Now you look just as you did in the fifth year of your reign. Ravishing."

"I remember it well. You've certainly cheered me up, Admiral. Shall we begin the concert? The night is young. You there. *Piano.*"

The piano looked to Skronk. Skronk nodded. The piano commenced a slow and rather dissonant obbligato, which elaborated itself into a web of musical tensions. The piano screen unfolded. The film began with a montage of wheat fields. Amber waves of grain, tossing their tassels in the autumn sun.

"I smell Wyoming," said Alba, closing her eyes. "I'd know it anywhere. It's an empty smell. Dust and wheat and leather tack. I can smell it quite distinctly. I'm sixteen years old, and I've run away from home. I'm living with my Auntie and my Uncle on a sheep ranch. The year is 1897."

"Good," said Admiral Snailwick. "Excellent." His eyestalks were fixed on the screen.

A horizon line—pale blue above, pale yellow below. A field of wheat. And someone moving in the foreground—a girl, out of focus, pushing through the wheat. More wheat and some railroad tracks and then wheat again. Where was the girl? Here she was. Crouching down in the wheat stalks and looking back the way she came, as if pursued. Trying to catch her breath. Nowhere to hide. A girl in a straw hat with a green ribbon, a cotton dress, and a well-worn pair of work boots.

"Unless it's all her imagination," said Alba, sitting on her ammo crate, gazing at the screen through closed eyelids. "But no. He's really back there, and he's following me. I'm sure of it. He saw me leave the barn dance, and I saw him starting after me. And he's always got that knife on his belt. Worthless no-account roughneck. Him with his whiskers and his whiskey breath. Wants to get me alone and do something terrible. And he's back there, stalking me, the way he'd stalk a deer. What possessed me to leave the barn dance by myself? Uncle would have walked me home. Now something terrible will happen."

The camera eye swiveled and backtracked along a footpath, searching the wheat. It discovered the unsavory roughneck with the knife on his belt. He moved stealthily past the camera. He really was stalking the farm girl. But the camera didn't follow him. It kept its attention on the footpath and backtracked farther. And its attention was rewarded.

Someone was stalking the stalker. A straight-backed woman in wire-rimmed glasses and a severe black dress. Hair in a bun, frosted with gray. She had the hands of a rancher's wife and a double-barreled shotgun cradled on one arm.

The man caught up with the girl and let her see him. She froze in her tracks, too frightened to run. He grinned as if this situation he'd created was the funniest joke in the history of the world. Rape was in the air, and murder. The film was coming to a boil.

The woman with the shotgun was right behind him, but he was too intent on the girl to notice. Then he felt the woman's eyes boring into him. He began to turn around.

The sky ripped open, and a blinding writhing torrent of fairy lightning struck the prairie. It was a lightning bolt from some larger stronger dimension. It would have incinerated all three characters in a microsecond, but it had other plans for them. The man and the woman fell to the ground. The girl remained standing. Rainbow fibers bleached Wyoming out of existence. The characters went translucent. As they faded away, one of them seemed to be turning into a cholla cactus. Another seemed well on her way to becoming a stork.

Several acres of pasture land also went missing, leaving a smoking crater which would later become a duck pond. Freak lightning, people said.

"So I never was a fairy princess," said Alba regretfully. "I was just some little nobody from Earth who purely by accident got caught in that glorious searchlight and dragged kicking and screaming into the noosphere. What a letdown."

"Things could be worse," said Admiral Snailwick. "You were pioneers. Think what you and Lady Crane and the cactus king have accomplished here."

"Could we please skip the details?" King Skronk asked loudly. "Time is a factor here."

"The details are of the essence," countered Snailwick.

The piano bashed its way through a rousing coda, a patriotic march. The film, meanwhile, had shifted its scene to the noosphere. Montage of happy families of happy ectic citizens performing acts of recreation and responsible citizenship under the civic leadership of their beloved absolute monarch.

Title card: HERE ENDS FALSE MEMORY PHASE GAMMA: "THE FARM GIRL"[2]

The final chords of the soundtrack die away. Fade to black.

"Can we go straight on to phase beta?" asked Skronk.

"No way," said the millipede. "She has to absorb and evaluate. And sleep."

"Unless the world ends first."

A roar like the end of the world shook the Dripping Lands. The floor of the bunker collapsed, and the last of the medical millipedes slid into the cloud crevasse and was never seen again.

"I don't believe this!" Skronk raged. "How fast can a damned glacier *move?*"

"It's a cloudquake," said Snailwick. "The continent can't support all that ice. It's compressing the nephotonic plates."

"Tell me later," said Skronk. He sprinted up a slanting tunnel and emerged under a sky like none he'd ever witnessed—a sky full of feather trees. The hillsides around him were devastated. A boulder whizzed past his head, knocking off a yucca blade. Off to the south, the glacier was charging toward the bunker, smashing down the forest, leveling the hills, sweeping wooden wreckage, cloudsoil, and cloudstone before it. It wanted Alba. It was yearning to turn her to papier mâché. Skronk sprinted back to the bunker.

"The glacier is here, Admiral. And it's throwing boulders now."

[2] False memory gamma was believed by Alba during the years 20 through 80 AAA.

"Let's get out of here," he suggested.

The cactus king scooped up the drowsing Alba under one cactus-needled arm and the piano under the other. He sprinted up the tunnel into the maelstrom. At some point in the bedlam that followed, he realized that Admiral Snailwick wasn't with them anymore.

The details of the admiral's death are recorded in *The Annals of the Aphasian Speed Corps.*

While the admiral was guarding the commission's rear flank, a projectile icicle fell nearby and shattered the quill of a stately old ostrich feather tree. A barb from a falling vane knocked the little pink snail from the admiral's right epaulet. The snail hit a quill stump and was knocked unconscious. The uniform groped blindly for its guiding intelligence. But in its clumsy searching, it stepped on the snail with its boot. Then it dropped in a heap, for it had crushed its own head.

The Mollusk Boys were lost without their admiral. Rather than face conversion into papier mâché, they decided to throw a party inside their ammo dump—a party featuring mixed drinks, barbecued ribs, and tiki torches. And we all know that drinking, barbecuing, tiki torches, and high explosives *simply don't mix.*

After centuries of Alba's prohibition against death, death was making up for lost time.

* * *

Many tribal leaders of the eastern and western frontiers had remained with their tribes instead of riding to the defense of Lotus City. Fate now forced them to confront the Black Glacier in their homelands. The guerrillas of the wilderness areas dreamed up a surprising number of tactics for confusing and delaying a malevolent glacier. The last-ditch resistance of these bits and scraps of outlying territory provided the Ontological Controls Commission—now reduced to King Skronk and the Secret Piano—with the time they so desperately needed for dismantling and unraveling Empress Alba.

The tribes went down fighting—the Snoogs of Ababastan, the Yng-Nen of the Isle of Bristles, the Loudmouth Orpers from the

Inside-Out Isthmus, the Fright Bulbs, the Life Machines, and other tribes seldom encountered by the civilized ectoids of the empire. Men, women, elders, children, and even tiny rough sketches took up arms. But all were frozen into papier mâché statues by the dark dank shadow of the advancing ice wall. And where was their warrior empress? Where was Alba?

Every continent is surrounded by oceans, and Aphasia was no exception. The cloud continent was surrounded by two vast oceans of air, the oversky and the undersky. Aphasia also boasted a sea, the Sea of Cirrus, which lay to the north of Caravan Beach. Ridges of cloudwave extended to the horizon at sea level. These seaborne cirrus didn't behave like normal clouds. They *moved*, slowly but visibly. They formed out at sea, rolled gradually south, and broke against the shore. Towering above the beach, the Impossible Bluffs ran from east to west. This was the nephographical region to which the captors of the lotus empress had fled.

The empress, if you watched her from the beach without binoculars, was a smear of dirty white being carried like a sack over the broad shoulder of a taller smear of green. The green smear was laboriously making his way down the bluffside, avoiding steep ravines and dead-end overhangs. The first two smears were followed by an indistinct blur like a small albino giraffe with extensible legs.

Skronk was trying to reach the beach. On cloudsand, their situation might improve. Commercial travelers sometimes traversed the beach. Someone might give them a lift. Or some ally might spot them from the air. Given a moment's peace, the piano could proceed with its regression therapy.

Skronk enjoyed the sea air and the sight of the open sea stretching to infinity—wavering white arabesques against a background of porcelain blue undersky. The waveclouds merged or tangled, crowded together or spread themselves out, grew as wide as houses and dwindled to nothing. Many ectoids got dizzy just looking at them. But not Skronk.

"Let me down," whined Empress Alba. "Please. This hurts."

"If I set you down, will you run away?"

"Do you think I want to be wandering in this pestilent wilderness by myself?"

"All right then."

Skronk set Alba down. She ran away. She soon slipped on some loose vapor, slid a few yards, wedged her foot in a crevice, and sprained her ankle. Skronk and the piano climbed down to the spot where she sat. She was trying to extricate her foot. Skronk stood over her, glowering.

"Help me up," she demanded. "This is your fault."

"I don't think so." Skronk whipped a machete from his tool belt. With a single whistling stroke, he struck Alba's head from her neck. The head bounced some distance down the bluffside.

"Oww oww oww oww oww!" yelled the head as it tumbled.

When the head came to rest, Skronk retrieved it and dangled it by its long golden hair in front of his nose. "Go to your room," he growled. And so saying, he flipped up the lid of the Secret Piano and tossed Alba into the sounding box. She landed on a row of velvet-padded wooden hammers. Skronk slammed the lid and cast her into darkness.

"What a grouch," Alba said to herself. She tried to nurse her sense of grievance, but she felt very odd without arms or legs. Also her nose was running. She'd always been allergic to sea air.

Skronk and the piano walked across the windswept beach toward the brink where the continent ended. Cloudsand blew against their legs.

"Someone's coming," said the piano.

Skronk climbed a tall crag to get a better view. He shouted down to the piano. "It's a tank crab. One of the Speed Corps. Maybe we can flag it down."

"Hurry!" cried the piano. "Those things move like greased lightning."

Skronk ran to the center of the beach. He stood there and waited. Eventually the piano joined him, though its legs were ill-suited to the terrain.

"Have you ever seen a tank crab move like that?" asked Skronk.

"It seems to be injured," said the piano.

A tank crab in camouflage paint, (serial number ASC-eleventy-threeve-fivety-sixen,) halted not far from the ontology commissioners and fell on its side. A slovenly young man in combat fatigues emerged from an escape hatch in the tank's undershell. He stood squinting at Skronk and the piano and scratched a crusty elbow. "How did *you* get here?" he asked them.

"Gumsnot," said Skronk. "How did *you* get here?"

"Me? You're asking me? How would I know?! In one chapter I'm *here!* In some other chapter I'm *there!* I can't figure out the connections! No one tells me anything!"

"Calm down. What's wrong with your tank?"

Gumsnot blew his nose on a handkerchief. "I couldn't drive it. So I got it drunk to slow it down. We went out to Wriggleberry Lagoon. I'm a little impaired myself."

"You were born impaired. Can you fit the three of us in there?"

Gumsnot turned and squinted at the crab. "Probably. Did you say *three?*"

"Alba's inside the piano. She's being punished."

The crab stirred and attempted to right itself. "You really mush excush me," it said. "I ushually go mush mush fashter than thish."

"How far have you got with the regression?" asked Gumsnot.

Skronk hung his spiny head. "Gamma phase."

"You mean you still have *two more to go?*" said Gumsnot. "Oh I see. So we're all going to die."

"Just drive the damn tank. We can't stay here. We're being stalked by a glacier."

"It's everywhere, Your Highness. Before long it will be here."

Minutes later the crab was trundling along the coastline with Gumsnot, Skronk, and the piano all jammed inside the cockpit and feeling none too comfortable. The sea wind wailed at the gunnery slots. Skronk spoke to the piano.

"Let's tackle phase beta. Start playing. Put the empress under."

"Her head is in the way of my hammers."

"Well, tell your little friends to move her. My hands are too big."

Two of the secret piano rolls climbed inside the sound box. They rolled Alba's head across the hammers to the treble end of the box and propped her upright. "The boss can spare one octave," they told her. "And the acoustics in here are really not bad. We hope you enjoy the concert."

While the piano rolls climbed out again, the piano unfolded its screen into a crooked zigzag. Due to spatial constraints in the cockpit, that was as far as the unfolding got.

The head began to weep.

"Do you mind?!" said the piano. "I'm trying to play a piece! Just because *you're* depressed is no reason to upset *me*."

"I'm sorry," Alba sniveled. "I'm sorry. My nose is running, and I haven't got my handkerchief."

"*Boo hoo*," said Skronk. "Things are tough all over."

Now Alba began to cry very loudly.

"I refuse to play under these conditions," declared the piano.

Gumsnot left the pilot's chair and peered down into the sound box. "Wow. She's sort of pretty, for a head. What happened to all the wrinkles?"

Alba screamed.

"Alba?" said Gumsnot. "Is something wrong with you?"

Wrong? With me? You're asking *me* what's wrong with *me*? I haven't a clue. I don't even know who I am. I *thought* I was a farm girl from Wyoming. But before that I though I was a goddess from outer space. So what do I know?" Gumsnot produced a slightly used handkerchief and helped Alba to blow her nose and dry her eyes.

"What can I do about a hyperactive glacier? It's not my fault."

"It's not a glacier, Alba."

"Then what is it?"

"Listen to the secret piano music. Listen all the way through. Then you'll know what the glacier is."

"Am I really the Empress Alba, Gumsnot? Am I anyone?"

"You're the heart and soul of the empire, Alba. If *you* turn to papier mâché, we'll all pop like soap bubbles. You *are* Aphasia. Now close your eyes."

She closed her eyes. She felt much safer that way. She made a resolution to keep them closed for the rest of her life. Eyes were far too delicate to be exposed to the elements.

Gumsnot patted the hair on the crown of her head. Then he returned to his station.

The Secret Piano began to play a tensely modernist piece, suitable for the soundtrack of a film noir. Alba thought she recognized the piece. She didn't like it. It sounded morbid. A stereoscopic phosphene image began to form on the inner surfaces of her eyelids, just as it was forming on the crooked screen overhead. Alba didn't want to watch another stupid silent film, but the only alternative was to open her eyes.

Up on the screen, a station wagon was driving Interstate 101 along the Oregon coast. Views of the Pacific Ocean swung past. There were evergreens and sea gulls and dark gray clouds that threatened rain. The station wagon and the cars that whisked past in the opposite lane were old model cars, suggestive of the 40s or the 50s. In the back seat sat a seven-year-old girl with haunted eyes. A green barrette held back her fine blonde hair. She was wearing her best white party dress.

Skronk leaned toward the piano and carefully pressed one ear to its side, snapping some of his ear spines against the white paint. The piano tried to ignore the cactus king. It was also trying to ignore the mumbling inside its sound box.

"Helpless as a little girl," Alba said to herself. "Helpless as a seven-year-old from Roseburg, taking a road trip with her father. Why is she sitting in the back seat? Why is her father sitting alone? Where is her mother? Where is her brother? Why couldn't *they* come along? And why was there suddenly a padlock on the basement door? And why was the house full of smoke just as the girl and her father were leaving on this peculiar road trip? And not tobacco smoke either, but smoke that smelled like burning wood and gasoline. Her father has presented the girl with a mystery. But there aren't enough clues, and he's hardly said a word all day. Is that me? Is that little girl me? What's wrong with my Daddy? What's gone *wrong?*"

The film was interrupted by flashes of the memories that were tormenting the girl. Sinister glimpses of domestic details better left unseen. Was it possible? Could Daddy have killed Mommy? And killed her brother? And be planning to kill *her*? Surely she was making a terrible mistake. Daddy pushed in the dashboard cigarette lighter.

The tank crab was sobering up, as its accelerated metabolism burned off the inkohol in its system. The soberer it became, the faster it ran across the cloudsand. The ride inside the cockpit got rougher. Gumsnot strapped himself into the pilot's chair. Alba's head began to roll around the sound box, absorbing some of the hammer blows and causing gaps in the fabric of the music.

The cigarette lighter popped out. Daddy lit his cigarette. He always smoked when he was nervous. The little girl with Alba's eyes watched him closely. She couldn't shake the stubborn intuition that at any moment Daddy was going to drive through the guard rail and take a plunge down the cliffside to the surf-pounded rocks below. Daddy wanted to die, but the little girl didn't.

"Is that what the real world is like?" asked Alba's head. "No wonder I wanted to escape."

Skronk had lost interest in eavesdropping and was watching the film. "It's like watching paint dry," he observed aloud. "It's boring, and there's nothing you can do to make it happen faster."

"You shouldn't be so hard on her," said Gumsnot over his shoulder. "She's had a confusing life."

"That must be why she refuses to remember it."

On the screen, the grille of the station wagon broke through the guardrail in slow motion. The car began its plummet through empty air. Its horizontal momentum carried it farther out to sea than Daddy had expected. It missed the rocks and the surf zone entirely. But it was going very fast indeed when its grille hit the surface of the ocean.

As the action slowed to a crawl, the camera eye tracked forward into the station wagon's interior. The girl was curled in a ball, floating in midair at a strange angle, suspended between the roof and the rear seat. But free fall was just a prelude. Now metal was impacting against water, and she suddenly felt heavy. Her cranium was as dense as a cannon ball. The momentum of that cannon ball would soon propel

73

her straight through the windshield. The steering wheel held Daddy in place, but the girl sailed past him—a flying rag doll. In extreme close-up, the skin of her forehead pressed against the windshield. It was bone versus safety glass now. The image separated into blobs, which subdivided into droplets and evaporated. Then a new image condensed—two white blobs on a field of greenish gray.

The girl was outside her body, watching herself drown. The water was dark and unbelievably cold, like water from some other dimension. She couldn't tell which way was up. She couldn't feel any pain, which was disorienting.

The camera zoomed back, isolating the dying child and her soul inside a field of inky darkness. The girl was definitely dying. But thanks to the diving reflex and to the imperfect interconnectedness of the human brain, millions of her cranial neurons were still available as a medium for stray thoughts. And thereon hung the tale of Aphasia.

It took more than a few clouds or a few acres of Wyoming to found an empire in the noosphere, you see. It took a few billion neurons. It required a human sacrifice. And not just any old brain tissue would do. What was required was gray matter from which the owner's soul and psyche had been radically expunged. Cortical tissue like that didn't grow on Bong Trees. It was like a dish of sterile gelatin. A perfect medium for the growth of ectoid cultures.

The tissue didn't have to be available for long. Ectoids lived on a different time scale from biological forms. Ectoids could pack millennia into the time it took a little girl to drown.

And there they were, on-screen at last. Ectoids of every shape and size came swimming from the edges of the frame toward the drowning girl at the center. They filled the screen, inquisitive and bickersome, like neon cartoons of benthic invertebrates. Lured from the noosphere by the promise of a better life, they converged on the vacant brain. They needed a place to live.

The child floated a few yards beneath the surface, almost lost in shadow, suspended between worlds. The camera zoomed in on a floating cloud of fine blonde hair. Myriads of ectoids began to wriggle their way into the girl's skull. The girl's ejected soul liked the looks of them

74

and followed them in, disguised as a cartoon of a green tadpole.

Montage of domed Aphasian cities springing up like mushrooms.

Title card: HERE ENDS FALSE MEMORY BETA: "THE SINKING STATION WAGON".[3]

"That was 'Theme From The Sinking Station Wagon'," the piano informed them. "No applause please. I'm doing this for the empire."

Skronk reached into the sound box and extracted Alba's head. "I think you've been punished enough," he told her.

"Oh Skronk. What have you done to me? Now I'm not even a grown-up anymore. I'm just a brain-dead drowned girl from Oregon. Am I her or am I here?"

The crab juddered to a halt. The commission piled up against the pilot's chair. "Avalanche!" screeched Gumsnot.

The weight of the black ice was shoving a section of the Impossible Bluffs down onto Caravan Beach. The glacier had caught up with Alba again. Now it meant to bury her alive. The tank crab leapt onto the back of the onrushing cloudslide and ran up the flowing scree, fighting the current to stay in one place. Then it lost its footing and bounced down a river of streaming cloudrubble—thoroughly out of control. Inside the crab, the piano fell from floor to ceiling to floor. Ten legs akimbo, the crab tumbled onto an unburied strip of beach sand.

It ran northwest, following the coast line, or so it believed. But it found itself trapped on a narrowing peninsula, with the Black Glacier itself blocking retreat. Inevitably the crab retreated to the peninsula's far end, where it was cornered. There was nothing around it but the sky above, the sky beneath, and moving rafts of cirrus colliding with the shoreline in slow motion. And of course the looming glacier.

Skronk threw open the escape hatch and dropped to the cloudsand.

"Everybody out!" he thundered. "End of the line!"

---

[3] False memory beta was believed by Alba during the years 2 through 26 AAA.

* * *

The Black Glacier's relentless expansion northward piled towering mountains of ice on the flattened corpse of the Dripping Lands. The ice spilled west and north and east, submerging the fringe colonies. The scene was one of chaos and horror. The hanging purple smoke from the blob cannons . . . The whinnying of terrified yak-dogs . . . The clatter of the junk strainers on their rumple wagons . . . The piteous cries of the partially transformed.

Mercifully, the avalanche was brief. When the flurries of black snow finally settled, the entire continent was interred beneath the glacier. Despite this, Empress Alba's northward journey in the clutches of King Skronk was still in progress.

Alba's head must have dozed off. She blinked open her eyes and returned to her woozy senses. She was bobbing along in the brisk sea air, rotating this way or that as she dangled by her hair from Skronk's tool belt. The sunbubble was just setting into the sea, painting shades of crimson across an oversky pale as paper. Skronk seemed to be walking along the crest of a serpentine ridge of humped-up sand. The Secret Piano hobbled along behind, as rapidly as it could manage on three legs. Something huge seemed to have taken a bite out of one corner of it. Skronk was breathing heavily. There was no sign of Young Gumsnot or his tank crab.

Skronk took a running start and leapt a great distance. Alba looked down and saw streaks of sky between parallel sandbars, like sky reflected in puddle water. Skronk landed on the crest of a different ridge. Then Alba realized where they were, and her scalp tingled with fear. Skronk was crossing the Sea of Cirrus. Madness! The man must have a death wish.

"Come on," Skronk called to the piano. "You can make it."

By telescoping its legs to their full length, the piano made itself taller than the tallest albino giraffe and gingerly stepped across the gap between cloudwaves. But the commission had to keep moving, because the waves kept moving. If you tarried too long in one spot, they were liable to evaporate out from under you.

"Help!" Alba squeaked.

"You're awake," said Skronk.

"Apparently. What happened to Gumsnot?"

"Papier mâché. As far as I know, we're the only ones left. Are you in shape for another music recital?"

"Will you be shutting me up in the piano again?"

"No. Something much worse." He stamped a foot on the cloud-sand. "Let's stop here. This wave should last a while. Long enough for us to save the world anyway."

Skronk turned around to face the piano and the shoreline. The Black Glacier was massed high on Caravan Beach, but it didn't dare cross the sea. It would fall right through if it did. One of the disadvantages of being gigantic. Skronk sat down cross-legged on the cloud-sand. The piano fell to its knees, panting and wheezing.

"Is this the last piano roll?" asked Alba.

"The very last," said Skronk. "The bitter end. You've regressed through all four of your false memory complexes."

"Four?"

"Don't forget the one you woke up with this morning. That one's been in force for more than two centuries. Alba the rightful monarch. We don't have a piano roll punched for *that* one. Not yet anyway."

"If my delusions are all destroyed, why play me another recital?"

"*True* memories," said the Secret Piano.

"What if I don't want to know them?" asked Alba.

"Oh, you *won't* want to know them," said Skronk. "But you'll have no choice. Would you mind a little brain surgery before we start?"

"You can't be serious. Brain surgery? Certainly *not*, you filthy barbarian. You keep your spiny fingers *off* of my brain."

"Relax," said Skronk, jamming the stump of her neck down into the sand. "It's all covered in the Secret Manual. Anyone can do it." Beads of perspiration slid down the cactus king's thorny face.

"Keep away from me, you ugly troll!"

Skronk removed a tool from his belt and held it in front of his long pointed nose. "This," he told Alba, "is the Secret Glass Cutter."

"How thrilling for you."

"It works on skulls as well as glass. I'll show you." Skrankrash began an incision over Alba's left ear and extended it horizontally around her scalp. "Now hold your nose and blow out your cheeks," he instructed.

"I beg your pardon?"

"Close your eyes, hold your nose, keep your mouth shut, and *blow.*"

"I *can't* hold my nose, Skronk. No hands."

Skronk scowled. "Oh. Of course. Shall I do it?"

"Do you see anyone else around here with hands?"

Skronk held Alba's nostrils closed while she blew out her cheeks. The top of her skull popped from her head, rolled cheerfully off the cirrus strand, and fell from sight into the undersky. It is undoubtedly falling still.

"*My,*" said Alba. "That feels refreshing. Perhaps brains need airing out every few centuries. Like pillows."

"It wouldn't surprise me." Skronk unhooked a small tin doodad and a stainless steel rectangle from his belt.

"What are those?"

"This is the Secret Cookie Cutter."

"Of course. I feel silly for asking. And that?"

"Oh that's just a cookie sheet."

"And what does that do?"

"It keeps the cookie from getting sandy."

"And is this part of the brain surgery, or have you suddenly taken up baking?"

All the while the cirrus strand had been shrinking. Now it was no wider than a tree trunk. Skronk wrapped his legs around it, digging in his thigh spines. The piano was perched in a precarious knock-kneed stance on the three rubber tips of its legs. "Hold still," Skronk told Alba. "This is going to hurt like hell."

"Am I properly sedated?" she asked him brightly.

"Not really."

Skronk pressed the cookie cutter into Alba's cerebrum, wiggled it

78

a little, and pulled it out again. Alba's face went slack. Her sapphire blue eyes went as dead as a pair of buttons. Skronk tapped one edge of the cutter against the cookie sheet. Without a sound, a little gray gingerbread girl flopped from the cutter. (Except that instead of gingerbread, the cookie was made of gray matter.) The brain cookie lay supine on the cold steel and showed no sign of life. Skronk picked up the head and shook it. It rattled. Skronk tossed it over his shoulder. It fell into the undersky. (And will continue to fall for an eternity, so they say.)

Skronk took a pouch from his belt, rummaged in it, and extracted two raisins. He poked the raisins carefully into the head of the brain cookie. Then he sang the cookie a song. Waking up on a strange cookie sheet to hear Skronk the cactus king attempting to sing was arguably the strangest thing that had happened to Alba all day.

"Wake up, wake up, my precious pearl. You must save the world. You're the Angerbread Girl."

The cookie sneezed, sat up, and rubbed her raisins. Then she sprang to her feet, took a wide hands-on-hips stance on the cookie sheet, and opened her mouth fissure wide.

"*I am Alba Angerbread!*" she declared in a booming voice. "I am the *Angerbread Girl*, and this is my personal world. Who petitions the cookie goddess?"

The Secret Piano breathed a sigh of relief. The regression had succeeded.

Skronk bowed as deeply as he could from a sitting position. "Your Grace. At last."

"What's the problem?" demanded the cookie. "Bring it on! I'm ready for anything!"

"Your Grace," said the cactus king, "Aphasia is on the ropes. A great black glacier has completely buried the cloudlands."

"To battle!" shrieked the Alba cookie. "Where are my millipedes?"

The cookie dashed between the piano's legs and bounded south along the cirrus strand, shouting imprecations at the glacier. Skronk took a flying leap over the piano and another leap over the Alba cookie. She ran right past him. Skronk ran after her, begging her to stop. Eventually he managed to coax her back to the spot where the piano stood shivering in the wind.

The piano cleared its throat. "Your Grace, before you ride to battle, we humbly beg that you listen to piano roll alpha. This sacred music will increase your already staggering power and thus ensure our victory."

"Are you implying that I'm too short to win a battle?" the cookie asked suspiciously.

"Not at all, Your Grace, but—"

"*Fine then*. I don't mind a little music before a battle."

"Play the damned music," Skronk whispered to the piano. "Before she changes her mind."

The piano unfolded its screen, while struggling to keep its balance on a writhing shrinking tree branch of cloudsand. The screen was catching a lot of wind, but it had to be unfolded. It was a required component of the regression program. The piano steadied itself, took a deep breath, and began to play. It was a modern piece called "The Boy With the Empty Brain." There were few pieces the piano liked less. The composition was formless and asymmetrical, with no dominant chord, no resolution.

On-screen was a static video image—the feed from a ceiling-mounted surveillance camera. Nothing moved except for the streaming digits of the time code at one corner of the screen. The camera looked down at a hospital room with two beds. A fat little boy lay in one of the beds. He had bandages around his head, a respirator tube down his throat, an IV tube taped to the crook of his arm, and pacemaker wires running into his chest. His eyes were open, and his chest was rising and falling, but Alba had never seen anybody so dead.

"Who's *that* supposed to be?" the brain cookie asked itself.

The piano answered her as it played the piece which it liked so little. "We call him Patient Alpha. At this very moment, a cookie-sized area of his brain is the staging area for the Aphasian cosmos. Five hundred years of Aphasian history have already come to pass inside his skull. He's a lot like the drowned girl, but his brain death is better

80

maintained. A few minutes between concussion and drowning aren't sufficient for the building of an ectoid civilization. But twenty-four hours of life support is an eternity. And the doctors are required to keep him breathing that long. Afterwards they'll be allowed to harvest his organs. Now this particular moment we're coming up to *here*—" The time code digits froze. The image froze behind it.

"—corresponds to this exact moment in Aphasian time. That twelve-year-old boy on that screen is alive right now. Viewed from the noosphere, you can hardly tell he's moving. But he is alive. And if he *dies*, Aphasia dies with him. This is not a history lesson, Alba. This is current events. He's the key to the glacier, Alba. And you're the only person in the world who can prolong his miserable life."

"Why should I do that? I don't even know him."

"Why?" echoed the piano. "Because you *are* him."

"You're saying I'm not even a *girl*? You're telling me I'm *that*? I can't be! He's gross!"

"The two little girls at the day care center didn't like him either. They teased him pretty ruthlessly." Photographs of twelve-year-old girls cross-faded over the freeze-framed video image. The background image was moving now, just barely—a glacially slow zoom toward the face of the little boy with the empty eyes.

"Did he want to get even?" asked the cookie.

"Very much. And he did get even."

"What did he do? I bet he got in trouble."

"That's putting it mildly. He borrowed a power tool from his father's workshop. He took it to his day care center in his backpack. He only wanted to scare the girls. But in the heat of the moment, he shot at them."

"Shot at them? With a power tool?"

"A nail gun."

"Oh dear. I don't feel well."

"Luckily the nails produced only flesh wounds. But there was blood just everywhere. And the girls got hysterical of course."

"He must have run and hid. He must have felt terrible. I feel a little queasy myself."

"He was deeply ashamed. He knew he'd done something unforgivable. And he had seen enough war movies and crime movies and spy movies and samurai movies and so forth to know the proper course of action for a gunman in such a situation."

"He . . . uh . . . "

"He shot himself in the head. There were articles about it all the national magazines. He certainly was one twisted little cookie."

Strangely familiar voices were calling to Alba from hidden fissures of her brainy flesh. They were the voices of the hypothetical people that Alba might have been, and might have preferred being. The dowager empress. The naiad from Saturn. The farm girl. The drowned girl. They wouldn't leave her alone. Which made sense. She wasn't alone. She had all these falsified people running around her head. They were *insisting* that she remember some stupid jingle. They wouldn't *tell* her what it was. She had to *remember* it.

Blue Slime Nest Aphids Can Torture Test Wizened Old Horses. Cold. *Buy Some Nasty Apricot Clams Then Taste Wet Oozy Harelips.* Warmer.

Boy Shoots Nails At Children Then Turns Weapon On Self.

That's it. That's the one. The film provided a montage of newspaper headlines. SEATTLE PARENTS STRICKEN BY DAY CARE TRAGEDY. 12-YEAR-OLD SHOOTS TWO GIRLS THEN SELF WITH NAIL GUN. LINGERS IN CRITICAL CONDITION.

"Right through the roof of the mouth," said the piano. "With a four-inch nail. He was the perfect spot for the founding of Aphasia. He's lasted five hundred years with no major disruptions. Then the Black Glacier showed up."

"But what has this awful little boy got to do with a glacier?"

"What a good question! How clever you are! Do you see that intravenous tube? That's how they're feeding him. Without that glucose, he'll starve. In fact he *is* starving. There's a big black blood clot blocking his needle. But the nurses don't know. He could die right in front of them. There are monitor alarms for pulse and breathing, and a motion detector as well. But they don't take his blood sample until two a.m. That blood clot is the Black Glacier, Alba. Now ask me what you can do about it."

"You're very smart for a piano."

"Ask me what you can do about the blood clot."

"What can I possibly do about a blood clot in the real world?! I've been hiding from the real world for the last five hundred years!"

"You can gurgle. You can squirm. You could gag. You could twitch. Anything. Anything that might get the attention of a nurse."

"Out there?! Are you insane?! Aphasia has no connection with the physical plane!"

"Ah, but we do," interrupted King Skronk. "We have *you*."

The piano screen displayed its final title card: HERE ENDS TRUE MEMORY ALPHA: "THE BOY WITH THE EMPTY BRAIN". THANK YOU FOR WATCHING.[4] The piano delivered its final scherzo with a bravura verging on bombast, and with all possible speed.

"If that little brat dies," said Skronk, "thousands of innocent ectoids will be cast adrift. And as for you, Alba, you'll just *croak*. One more disadvantage of being real."

"Well, that hardly seems fair."

"It's the *boy* we're concerned with, not *you*," snapped the piano. "The boy is dying as we speak. Aphasia is *ending*."

At this point the piano's rhetoric carried it away and it stamped one of its legs for emphasis. The tip of the leg slid off the cloudsand. With a horrible fading scream, the piano fell into the undersky. (And you know *that* means.)

Skronk crossed his arms over his chest and struck a pose of noble outrage. "Now, great goddess, you *must* defeat the evil blood clot. If you fail, then the Secret Piano has died in vain."

"*Relax*," said the cookie. "I know just what to do. I'll make the

---

[4] The true story of Alba's ascension is recorded in Professor Clickbeetle's *The Secret History of Aphasia*. This story was known to Alba during the first year of her reign, from Junuary First, the first day of Aphasian history, until the Thirst of Margust, eight months later. Roughly one month subsequent to Alba's first lapse into false memory, the original Ontological Controls Commission was convened. This meeting led to the building of the original Secret Piano by Claudius Pipifex the Artificer, who also punched the first of the sacred scrolls. Sometimes the truth is just too ugly to live with.

boy gag and choke."

"How will you manage it?" Skronk queried worshipfully. He was hanging from the cirrus strand by the crook of one arm at this point, and the wind was blowing like a mad thing all around them. "Has a small gray cookie such power?"

"Of course I have! I'm Patient Alpha, Empress of All Aphasia! I may not have created it, but I was *sacrificed* to it, and that ought to count for something."

"What will you do, great cookie goddess?"

"I'll vomit. I'll puke all over that ugly glacier. That will teach it. I'll fill up the little boy's brain with vomit. He'll *have* to gag and choke."

"A brilliant plan, great goddess. I am awestruck. I am like unto the dust at your feet."

And so he was. Somehow she was towering over Skronk and over the glacier as well. She must have grown larger during the music. In fact she could see all the way to the far side of Aphasia. Except that it was the far side of this rude glacier that was so rudely lying prone on top of her clouds without her permission. She was taller than the Plateau of Stratus! Yet she was balancing on a cloud filament no thicker than a twig.

Skronk was hanging from the cloud twig by his sharp green fingers. "Well?" he snarled. "Getting impressed with yourself? What are you waiting for? Save the damned world!"

The bile of Alba Angerbread's rage swelled her brain belly. It filled her brain legs with bitter yellow syrup. Her cookie head inflated with rage gas, bugging out her raisins. Her body shook with barely contained lightning. Her legs felt like mile-high slabs of brain that were rooted in the undersky. Somehow it was supporting her. It wouldn't let her fall.

"I'll save everything! I will! I'll drown this whole cosmos in vomit if I have to! That glacier has got to go!"

Alba jammed her giant brain hands like blunt mittens down her giant brain throat. Up came the luminous boiling vomit of anger. The world-preserving vomit gushed out of her like magma, like a thousand Niagaras, like a tidal wave of hatred. It rushed across the Sea of

Cirrus, and somehow not a drop of it fell through the cracks.

It engulfed the Black Glacier, sizzling and shining, reclaiming the Impossible Bluffs, reclaiming the Dripping Lands and the central cloudprairie, reclaiming the terraced rice paddies of the Agricultural Birthworms and the epiphytic moss gardens of the Waxy Fruit Puppets. Finally the holy vomit reclaimed the Amnesiac Wastes and Mirage Lake, where wee sneeflers effervesce and melt away amidst the snorkel grass, while the snorkel grass is forever weaving itself into existence and untangling itself again.

Have you ever smelled brain vomit? It's worse than sulfuric acid. It's the worst kind there is. But it boils away.

The Aphasian pocket universe filled with stale-smelling steam. Night fell. The stars came out of their sky burrows and twinkled smugly. A buttery crescent moon sailed from the undersky to the oversky and smiled down on fogbound Aphasia.

In another world entirely, a little boy gagged and choked. His wounded body twisted restlessly. A motion sensor set off an alarm bleep. The ward nurse on duty investigated, but the boy was quiet again. Since it was nearly two a.m., she disconnected the glucose tube from his hypodermic and tried to draw a blood sample. She soon discovered that a blood clot was fouling the works.

Patient Alpha would receive his full twenty-four hours of mandated life support. Sometime in the distance Aphasian future, the transplant teams would converge on the boy, pluck out his eyes, remove his liver, harvest his kidneys, and so on and so forth. That was just how they did things, out in the real world.

Until the organs got harvested, Aphasia would survive and prosper. And of course the perpetual struggle would persist between the divine Empress Alba and her evil nemesis King Skronk, High Khan of the Cactus Trolls and Sultan of the Headless Knots.

* * *

A few weeks later Confetti Girl and the Cardboard Dog returned to Aphasia on one of Air Aphasia's dirigible jellyships. The two celebrities had just completed a goodwill tour of Ataxia the wooden continent, where they had done their ambassadorial duties at the royal courts of Cellulosia, Osmosia, and the Sublimate of Lamanatia. Now they were home again at last.

Their jellyship docked at the harbor of Droplet On the Brink. Standing on the pier with their luggage, they noticed many changes in the town. Why were all the buildings suddenly painted in bloople and grellow stripes? Why were the streets all paved with chocolate-covered raisins? The Cardboard Dog and Confetti Girl rode a rickshaw to the Village of the Walking Soup Ladles. Except that it was now the Village of the Talking Salad Forks. They spent the night at their favorite motel. It was under new management.

They boarded an eel train for Lotus City. They passed Ectopolis, but instead of a sprawling city, it was just a shanty town with a sprawling construction site around it. The conductor, a soft-spoken rotifer, informed them that the Bronze Man and his sideways coal scuttles were building a new sports stadium from tapioca pudding. Confetti Girl and the Cardboard Dog exchanged a significant look. When they'd left Aphasia, the Pudding Stadium had been an historic ruin. They asked the conductor for the correct year. He asked his pocket watch, and the watch said that it was the fifth year of the reign of Princess Alba the Fair.

"This is beginning to make sense," mused the Cardboard Dog, scratching the side of his tongue.

"I smell a regression," said Confetti Girl, changing colors.

They soon arrived at the stalk of the Lotus Palace. Except that it was now the Tulip Palace. Bright red. Very colorful. According to the guidebooks, it had always been the Tulip Palace. Confetti Girl petitioned Professor Clickbeetle for an audience with the Princess. While they waited for their appointment, they visited the chambers of the Secret Piano. But it wasn't the Secret Piano they were used to. It was that piano's grandfather.

Alba entered the throne room in a strapless electric green gown. She rushed to embrace her two dear friends. She was shockingly beautiful.

After a few minutes of pleasantries, the Cardboard Dog raised a new topic of conversation. "So this is your fifth year on the throne, correct? Not the five-hundredth but the fifth."

"Well, it couldn't very well be the five-hundredth," said Alba. "I'm only sixteen years old. Do the math. Next month I'll turn seventeen. My birthday fete is going to last for a month. You're invited of course."

"Strange," said Confetti Girl. "I thought you hated parties."

"You're mistaken," said Alba blithely. "But don't give it a thought. I myself make mistakes all the time. Important people such as ourselves have so many things to keep track of. One can't remember everything at once, can one? The ectoid brain contains only so many nerve cells, does it not?"

They inquired after Alba's chief viceroy, Lady Crane. Alba told them that surely they were thinking of the Baroness Ibis. Confetti Girl and the Cardboard Dog drank their tea and ate their croissants and nodded their heads at intervals, wishing to avoid any unpleasantness.

"Have you heard from the cactus king?" Confetti Girl asked offhandedly.

"Certainly not! Don't even mention his name to me. He's banished, you know. We're not speaking. He said I was bossy. And besides he's getting fat. It's disgusting."

"Ah," said the Cardboard Dog. "I see."

He and Confetti Girl exchanged a look of tolerant forbearance. Someone had to rule Aphasia. They were just glad it wasn't them.

* * *

<HERE ENDS THE DOCUMENT "THE BLACK GLACIER".>
<DO YOU WISH TO ACCESS ANOTHER DOCUMENT? PLEASE TYPE Y OR N.> [*]
<PLEASE VISIT THE ARCHIVE AGAIN SOON. THE IMPERIAL APHASIAN ARCHIVE IS A PROUD SUBSIDIARY OF THE APHASIC DEPARTMENT OF HELL, EDUCATION, AND FUNGUS.>

UP
James Sallis

TWO WENT UP on the bus today. One was an elderly lady who came aboard at the stop near Megaworld with her collapsible rolling cart and sat huddled for close to half an hour in blue bundle of skirt, sweater, and what she'd no doubt have called a wrap. Then she took a sigh and went up. The other was a young man pierced all about, ears, nose, tongue, eyebrow, as though to provide rings and hitches by which he might be lashed to the world. His eyes were never still. Ten blocks into his ride he stood and let out a scream of rage or challenge, a single burst, like a flare, before he went up. The rest of us watched a moment, then went about our business. For most of us, of course, our business isn't much. I've read that when the bomb was dropped on Hiroshima, people's shadows were burned onto walls. That's what the tracings always remind me of, those faint outlines of gray like photographs that haven't quite been captured, the bare footprints of ash, left behind when they go up.

When these two went up, I was, first, just beginning, then four hours into, my daily countdown, carrying on the shabby pretense that things were as they'd always been or soon would be again, yo-yoing in dark suit, pinpoint oxford shirt and briefcase uptown, cross-town, downtown and back, filling out applications here, dropping off a resume there, but mostly sitting on park benches and on buses like this one. Go through the motions, people tell you, and form becomes content. Keep putting the vessel out and it'll fill. As usual, people, the ones who give you advice anyway, are full of shit.

The curious thing is that there's no heat when they go up.

Mrs. Lancaster-Smith appeared on the landing as I climbed past her floor. Four more to go, thousands of us all over the city making the same or some similar climb now in suit, overalls, casual dresses, work clothes and jeans, coming home. "You forgot to lock up again," she said. Her voice pursued me up the stairs the way squeaky bedsprings carry through apartment walls. "Mr. Abib, from the next floor down?, was out on the landing, having a cup of whatever that is he drinks all the time, that always smells so sweet?, and heard voices. He walked up and found two kids standing outside your door. Another couple were on their way in." I thanked her and said I would be more careful, thinking all the time that *forgot* probably wasn't the correct word. At one level or another I was probably hoping someone would go in and strip everything out, carry off every trace of my previous life, give me permission to start over.

I climbed on, unlocked the door and went in. The logbox in the corner of the screen opposite the door registered four calls, three pieces of mail, a couple of bills paid as of nine this morning. "Hello, Annette," I said. *I'm home*, I thought. The screen itself showed prospects of blue sky, white clouds moving through them calm and slow as glaciers.

She'd gone up sixteen days before. We were sitting on a bench by the river downtown, the river they'd spent so much controversial taxpayer's money building. A plaque on the back of the bench read The Honorable Lawrence Block. All the benches were named for Senators who, having called in favors to finance creation of the river, couldn't leverage further funds from the House and finally elected to pay for benches, walkways and riverside amenities personally. Annette and I had had dinner at a Vietnamese restaurant, huge bowls of soup into which we threw sprigs of cilantro and mint, dollops of hot sauce, sprouts, then gone for a walk. The sunset was splendid, as days now, sunsets being dependent upon such things as p indexes, dust, and particle content. We sat watching as clouds fil with pink, as purple began seeping up like a dark, beautiful ink off the horizon, staining the sky.

"I'm so happy," Annette said beside me. I'd brought along a cup of Vietnamese coffee laced with condensed milk. I had it halfway to my mouth when she went up.

Then there was only that faint gray outline of a body on the bench beside me, that bare footprint of ash. After a moment, I drank.

"Hungry?" I said now, coming into the apartment. "I'm starved." Hard day at the office and all that. God knows why, but I'd gone on talking to her all this time. I came home, asked about her day, poured two glasses of wine, chatted as I cooked. This is what people, what couples, families, did. They made the climb in suit, overalls, casual dresses, workclothes or jeans. They came home, inquired after the children, asked how the day had gone, if there had been any calls. Sometimes the meals I fixed were inspired. Often they were common-place, barely edible; I could never discern what made the difference. Sometimes when I spoke to Annette, confused as to whom I might be addressing, the computer tried to respond.

The parent chosen for me by lottery was Mimi Blodgett: a name that, when I first heard it, made me wonder if I'd not somehow fallen through cracks in reality's pavement directly into a Dickens novel. But no, that was indeed her name, and she lived up to it. A barrel-shaped woman, foreshortened everywhere, arms, legs, neck, intellect; hair dyed brown and set each week at Josie's Cool Fixin's, Friday, three p.m., in curls that defied not only age but gravity as well; an armory of polyester pants, shirtwaists, and pullovers in the rickety closet, stacks of Reader's Digests in the bathroom, of her trailer. Mimi's love for me was like that trailer, never intended to be permanent though it turned out that way, and as durable basically (if also as unlovely and plain) as her rack of polyester. She worked at Billy's, the local drugstore, stock-ing shelves, hauling boxes out of the backs of trucks, helping at the register when once or twice a week, mostly Fridays, things got busy.

91

ntinued merchandise for me, packets of candy,
Christmas toys initially (including a submarine
ing soda tamped into ballast tank, sank and rose,
on shaving lather, razors, cheap aftershave I told
never used.

ong time to die. None of those hundreds of movies
ou how long it can take people to die, and none
give you any idea how death smells, the sweat that soaks into sheets
and mattress and won't be expunged, the ever-present tang of urine,
blossom of alcohol over it all, earthy, garden smell of feces under.
Dying people themselves begin to stink. They stink in ways that go far
beyond the unmistakable, sweetish smell, a smell you never forget, of
the cancer itself. They know this: you can see it in their eyes. Toward
the end, you see little else there. The sickness is eating its way out of
their body, like an insect. They've *become* the sickness. And so, for
a while, as caretaker, do you. As all the while, leaving us, they rise
higher and higher, air ever thinning.

The best part of the day was always when we came home, that first
hour or two. Annette wrote code for an insurance company, I wrote
advertising copy. Our arrivals never varied more than ten minutes.
This was before I switched to buses, when I still took the sub-t, and
sometimes we'd come up from opposite ends of the station simultaneously, pink flowers with dark stems blooming from the ground. We'd
walk the six blocks to our apartment, I'd loosen my tie, she'd slip
out of her shoes. And we'd sit there, young professionals in grownup
clothes, part of the glue that held it all together, two people very much
in the world as Heidegger would say, over glasses of wine and eventually, maybe along about the second glass, a plate of cheese and olives.

Thing is, no glue holds forever, and once Annette was gone,
veneers started peeling away everywhere: I saw the world's furniture
for the shoddy goods it was. Shortly thereafter I began to notice how
many were going up.

They'd been doing this for some time, of course; I knew that. I'd
just never taken much notice. It had little to do with me, after all, little
to do with *my* life of gourmet coffee, clients, spreadsheets, presenta-

92

tions. Packaging is what I was about, what I did: my genius, if you will. *Another sort of veneer*, I thought at first with Annette's departure—then realized it was in fact far more central. I had been instrumental in helping create nothing less than a new language, a house of words and image that, progressively, we'd all moved into to live. And now we couldn't get out.

Having realized this, I began to stutter. No longer could I begin sentences effectively or find my way easily to the end of them. Glibness, once gone, rarely can be regained.

The first one I witnessed go up was during *The Barber of Seville*. We'd bought season tickets almost a year back when life was casually on course, glibness intact, and $480 didn't have to be thought about; the tickets, at least, were still good. Ah, sweet irony. I couldn't pay my rent, but I could attend the opera. Sat there with the empty chair next to me fuller than most, watching beautiful women file in fawning over men in ugly coats and ties.

In the row behind me, six seats down, one of these men repeatedly fell asleep, to be, at first, whispered, then, irritation growing, elbowed awake by his companion. Said companion wore a gown artfully contriving to push her sagging bosom back towards cleavage and conceal a thickening middle. His suit, by contrast, had come right off the rack, coat 44, slacks 40 x 32, and was cinched like a saddle by a Western belt, its buckle the size of demitasse saucers and so shiny that lasers might have been bounced off it.

Halfway into the first act, Rosina pondering the voice she's heard below her balcony, the woman prised him awake for the fifth, sixth time. He came round groggily this time, slow to surface, to come to knowledge of where he was. He looked at his companion for a moment with brimming eyes, took a deep sigh, and went up.

Those in seats close by leaned away from the sudden, intense light and coughed apologetically.

Another empty seat then, like the one beside me. As this silliest of the great operas rolled on.

That evening, *après* opera, I created a sauce of porcini mushrooms, stock, red wine and roux, serving it over fresh polenta. I ate my own portion slowly, with half a bottle of a good Chardonnay, then scraped Annette's into the disposal. She had little appetite these days. Someday soon, I suspected, my own would fail. Afterwards I retrieved a favorite volume of Montaigne from the shelf and settled into bed with same, but found myself unable or unwilling to follow the scurry of his mind from notion to notion—the very quality for which I revered him.

On the bus the next morning I found my gaze drawn back again and again from observation of the world about me—drawn back, that is, from simple witness of those waiting at curbside and the ones who clambered aboard, corpuscles streaming through the city carrying nutrients and oxygen, keeping it alive—to billboards set in place above the train's windows. The windows themselves were scored amateurishly, tags and incomprehensible messages scratched roughly into them. While, above, pros had *their* say. Public service announcements, some, for clinics and the like, and in a variety of languages. The bulk of them, however, were ads of one sort or another, samples of that dialect, the idiom of American commerce, that's rapidly becoming our only language. Like any other native tongue, we learn it without direct intent, simply by exposure, absorbing it; after which, it governs not only the way we think, but what we're able to think.

I became silent that day. Not with the silence of Quakers, opening a space for whatever voice might come into it, God's perhaps, or that of my own conscience; nor with Gandhian silence, adopted in the knowledge that utterance itself is a kind of action, all action a species of violence; rather, with a silence akin to the silence of the world itself, and that of the things within it. I spoke only when necessary, only when there was information, *real* information, needing communication—that kind of silence. A silence all but lost to the murderous din of our materialism. As though if there were not this continuous noise, there would be nothing to hold us up, nothing for us to stand upon.

That day, as well, I began keeping a notebook in which I recorded all I could discover about those who went up in my presence. Often the page held little more than date, time and place. Occasionally a fact or two some momentary neighbor could recall when questioned: where the client came aboard the bus, what the client had carried with him. Upon occasion, comments from a driver who remembered the client from previous days. Sometimes, if I had nothing else, a sketch: stick figures ensconced in rear seats; bundles left behind.

Suddenly, then, it was fall. One morning, having come out in suit and tie as usual, I looked around in surprise at fellow passengers in coats and, as they stepped from the heated bus stop into that small band of open world before boarding the bus, the plumes of their breath. People had bulked up in dark colors; each leaf on each tree was a different blend of brown, yellow, red, rust, cinnamon, gold. Winds flew like great, silent birds through the caverns and canyons of the city.

That evening I sat in my apartment with Jorge, who brought with him a twelve-pack of South African beer. Jorge was virtually the only friend I had left. I'd run off the others, who grew tired (though a few, from loyalty or brute force of will, clung on till the end) first of reminiscences of Annette, then of unending discourse on this thing one did not speak of, all those going up around us. We were watching a movie I'd dialed in on the phone line, a Chinese comedy whose tags and markers were absolutely impenetrable to us. From time to time Jorge or I laughed, looking to the other to see if possibly we'd guessed correctly. An hour or so in, I set it on pause and did a quick stir-fry: carrots, celery, apple, tofu, lots of soy sauce. Rice being in short supply that month, I served it over couscous.

We moved onto the balcony to eat. Said balcony comprised a scant yard or so of floorspace extended out from the apartment and cut off by railings, of which the rental agents were nonetheless inordinately proud. Whenever I went out there, I felt I'd been set to walk the plank.

Jorge was never much for talking. We'd sat together through entire evenings during which he released, like bubbles floating slowly to the surface, perhaps a total of ten words. My own conversation, predictably enough, soon swerved from discussion of the movie (there was little enough to discuss, after all) to the folks I'd seen go up recently.

Jorge nodded from time to time. Then, miraculously, he spoke.

"There's never a morning I don't wake up thinking about it, wondering if this is the day I'll finally get down and do it. You want to know why I never have?" He took a swig of his beer. The label was all bright colors and zigzags, like a poisonous snake. "Cause I look like shit in gray, man." He laughed. "Besides, anyone hauls my ashes, it's gonna be me, you know?"

This from a man I would have considered the most undisturbed, the most untouchable (if also, or likewise, the most unimaginative), I knew. Scratch the veneer of a life, anyone's life, I suppose, and there's little beneath but cheap wood or pressboard, pain, despair.

No wonder they go up so fast.

Jorge and I never got back to the movie. We sat wordlessly there on the balcony as buses stopped running, as one by one streetlights and lights in all but government, emergency and residential buildings went out.

"Best get along," Jorge said.

Together we looked down towards the city's dark floor, far below.

"What about curfew?"

My friend shrugged. "It's a short walk. Skin like mine, who's to see me? I'm a moving shadow."

"You could stay over."

"Course I could. But you out of beer, man."

I smiled, immediately wondering when I'd last done so. "Take care, my friend."

He left without responding, without any show of leave-taking as always; part of that silence of the world and its things that I'd come to embrace; I suppose this was why I so valued his company. I gathered up dishes, bottles, utensils, took the movie off pause and shut it down, swished and gargled mouthpaste, smeared on cleanser and, looking in the mirror, wiped it off.

"Goodnight, Annette," I said quietly.

This was one of the times the computer grew confused.

"Excuse me."

96

"Yes?"

"Would you please repeat your last command?"

Realizing what had happened, I told it to delete.

"Are you sure?"

"Yes."

"Good night, then."

The next morning I slept late. Near noon, still in jeans and sweat-shirt reading *What? Me Hurry?*, I went down into the street. I had no intimations of higher directives, no wisdom, to bring down to them. Not anymore. I was done with all that. But I could join them in their sadness and pain.

At the Cheyenne Diner two blocks up, where occasionally I had breakfast, less occasionally dinner, I sat on a red-upholstered stool at the counter, as always, and attempted to draw the man seated next to me into conversation. With the first couple of remarks, on weather and a purported loosening of the curfew as I recall, he grunted or nodded noncommittally. Then, when I persisted, he glanced at me strangely. So did, in train, the waitress Maria and (I'm reasonably sure) the cook mounted at his console behind the pass-through, fingers poised over keys.

Next I progressed to the bus stop. Here, again, they all regarded me strangely: a surrogate mother with child slung between sagging breasts, two gentlemen in the orange uniforms of city sanitation, another in the pink uniform indicating a prisoner released to day work, a handful of hangers-on, outriders, in the current frontier gear of snug unbleached canvas pants, white rayon poet's shirt, Chinese cloth shoes. At the sub-t stop I'd frequented for so many years when Annette and I were together, the situation was little different. A different clientele, but that same strange regard. And much the same response to overtures of conversation.

When had people stopped talking to one another?

Entering the apartment, I stood for a moment before the screen, watching those familiar prospects of blue sky and white clouds roll across, as though a tiny portion of what used to be called *the heavens* had been caged here.

"I'm home," I said.

Choosing this occasion for discernment, the computer paused before responding. "You are addressing me?"

"Yes."

"Excellent. Would it be appropriate for me to remark that you are home early?"

"Listen. People are giving up, people everywhere. They look around them and just . . . let go. Go up, we call it."

"These people are no longer alive, you mean."

"They no longer even exist."

"I see. Why are they doing this? Or—to employ the second-person plural, as would be appropriate in such an instance—why are *you* doing this?"

"I don't know."

"Who does know?"

After a moment, when I said no more, the computer asked: "Will there be anything else?" and when still I failed to respond, shut itself down.

Leaving me suspended there in eternal mid-morning.

Day stretched out before me glacierlike, a white, featureless plain. No end to it, to any of it. Stepping out onto the balcony, from this posthistoric cave onto the cliff, I had a sudden flash, whether of intuition or some form of daydream terror I've no idea. I saw myself alone in absolute silence, all the others gone, surrounded by shelf after shelf of notebooks, hundreds upon hundreds of them, thousands, looming about me: all that remained of what had once been my race, my species, my people, mankind.

HOME LIBRARY

The Library: 2: HOME LIBRARY
Zoran Zivkovic

I UNLOCKED THE mailbox.

All I ever found in it were bills at the beginning of the month, but I still checked it regularly when I returned from work. I checked it on Saturday and Sunday, too, the same time as the other days, even though the postman didn't deliver on those days. Just in case. In addition, on Tuesday I always took a handkerchief and wiped out the dust that had collected inside, although you couldn't see the dust from the outside. We have to take care of such places, perhaps even more than those that are visible to the eye. People usually neglect them, even though they are actually the best reflection of tidiness.

There should not have been anything in my mailbox because it was only the middle of the month. But when I opened the wooden door, I saw a large book, hardcover bound in dark yellow. It almost filled the entire mailbox. Someone else in my place would probably have found many reasons to be surprised by this sudden apparition. First of all, who had sent it to me? No one had ever sent me a book before. Why would anyone, anyhow? Plus, it wasn't even wrapped, and nothing on it indicated it was intended for me. So why had the postman put it in my mailbox? And finally, how had he managed to fit it inside? The book was a lot thicker than the narrow slit through which he inserted bills. It certainly could not have got in through the slit.

I, however, wasn't surprised at all. I didn't let any of these annoying questions upset me. Long ago, I realized that the world is full of unexplainable wonders. It's no use even trying to explain them. Those who try anyway just end up unhappy. And why should a person be unhappy when he doesn't have to be? Unusual things should be accepted for what they are, without explanation. That is the easiest way to live with them.

Before this became clear to me, various inexplicable phenomena had made my life miserable. For example, the number of steps between my second-floor apartment and the ground floor. I'm used to counting steps, half out loud, everywhere and on all occasions, even when I already know the number of steps. When I climb up to my apartment, there are always forty-four steps. Whenever I walk down to the ground floor, there are only forty-one. For a while after I moved here, I found myself in some discomfort because of this difference. I tried just about everything to figure out what was wrong.

I first tried to outsmart the stairs. I counted them to myself while keeping my mouth firmly shut, so there was no way to know what I was doing. It didn't work. On the way up there were still persistently three more steps than on the way down. Then I counted them while walking backwards; although I walked carefully, this was not only hard to do and dangerous, but for some reason also drew confused and suspicious looks from my neighbors. Despite my polite greetings, raising my hat and giving a nod, they would just mumble in reply, heads down. People can really act strange at times.

Finally, it occurred to me to count the steps in the dark. I would leave the apartment after midnight wearing light, rubber-soled shoes so my footsteps wouldn't wake anyone. Without turning on the light in the stairwell, I walked down to the ground floor, then climbed back up to my apartment, down and up, up and down, until dawn. It wasn't hard, despite the murky darkness, because I knew the exact number of steps in either direction. I would have had a hard time—stairs can be dangerous even when you can see quite well, let alone like that in the pitch black of night—if I had stuck to what common sense told me: the number of steps must be the same going up and coming down.

That's when I gave up trying to find an explanation for everything no matter what the cost. Hats off to common sense, but you can't always rely on it. Sometimes it is much more advisable and useful to accept a wonder. It might even save your neck, and that's no small thing. Not only did I survive the dark stairwell, I quickly regained my peace of mind. As soon as I stopped burdening myself with superfluous curiosity, I slept better, my appetite returned, and I was no longer depressed all the time, apathetic and anemic. It's amazing how one simple decision can make a new man out of you in no time at all.

So now, instead of wasting time being amazed, I took the book out of my mailbox and examined it. The title was written in large, ornate black letters: *World Literature*. There were no other words on the cover, not even the author's name. I was not surprised, for how could anyone truly be the writer of such a work? I quickly leafed through the book and discovered there were even more pages than the size indicated because the paper was very thin, like onionskin. This suited the title: a limited scope would certainly not be exemplary. The edition seemed quite splendid in all respects. It even had a brown ribbon to mark the place where you had stopped reading.

I put *World Literature* under my arm and headed up to my apartment. I reached the twentieth step, then stopped short. Today was Tuesday! That fact had slipped my mind owing to the unexpected appearance of the book. I had no choice but to walk back down. One should not let anything interfere with carrying out one's duties, not even an unforeseen event. Descending to the ground floor, I took from the inside pocket of my jacket the green silk handkerchief, used exclusively to clean the mailbox.

When I opened it, another surprise awaited me: another thick, dark yellow book with the same title. Someone unaccustomed to wonders would probably have been amazed. Such a person might have stepped back, heart racing, a shudder going down his spine. When he collected his wits, he would begin feverishly searching for an explanation, but it would be hard to come up with something coherent. I hesitate to think of what he might do afterwards. Maybe even attempt suicide.

But I, of course, remained perfectly calm. There was no reason to get upset. I simply took out the second volume of *World Literature*, put it under my arm with the other one, and wiped out the mailbox. I only needed one hand for that, thank goodness. As usual, I concentrated on the lower corners, from which it was hardest to remove the dust and yet it collected there the most, as if out of spite.

I locked the mailbox door once again and headed for the second floor. This time I did not get very far: I'd just raised my foot to the first step when a thought struck me and brought me back to the mailbox. As I opened it, a surge of excitement flowed through me. Everyone enjoys having premonitions come true, particularly if they are auspicious. Had one of my neighbors walked by at that moment, he would have seen my face light up when a third dark yellow book appeared behind the door.

I can't explain how I suspected it would be there. Intuition, I guess, but not only that. An idea like that would never occur to a person who was unfriendly to wonders. That's another advantage of not giving in to prejudice. I took the new *World Literature*, but didn't put it under my arm. I couldn't hold three thick volumes. Instead, I placed the books in the crook of my left arm. Then I locked the door again, but this time I waited in front of the mailbox. I stood there for several moments, trying not to appear too impatient, then opened the mailbox a fourth time. Even though glad to see it filled once again, I found my previous excitement was somehow missing. Self-satisfaction is in bad taste. Or, at least showing it openly.

After the thirteenth book, I had to stop, mostly because of the weight. In my fervor, I'd forgotten that books, contrary to widespread belief, are not light, particularly when gathered in a pile. They had to be carried up to the second floor. I certainly would have had an easier time taking them down the stairs rather than climbing up, because, inter alia, there were three fewer steps going down. In addition, the load turned out to be quite awkward. I had to stretch my arms almost to my knees to hold the books piled one on top of the other, while my chin on top secured this unstable arrangement, my head forced back. I looked around uneasily. It wouldn't be good for one of my neighbors to see me carrying too many of the same kind of book. Who knows what they might think? People tend to jump to conclusions.

When I finally got home, I was gasping for breath. I had a hard time unlocking the three locks, the armload of books briefly supported by just one hand. The bottom lock, next to the threshold, gave me a particularly hard time. I had to squat, barely keeping my balance. If any other title had been involved, I might have had to put them down on the floor. Because I fastidiously clean the area around my front door, the books would not have gotten dirty, but the thought of *World Literature* against cold tile seemed somehow unbecoming. Almost a sacrilege.

Once I entered the apartment, I was confronted by the problem of where to put the books. I hesitated and stood next to the door for a time, not knowing what to do with them. In the end, I put them on the table until I could give it some more thought. The best solution would have been a bookshelf. That's the right place for books. Unfortunately, I didn't have one. What did I need a bookshelf for when I didn't own any books?

Since moving to the apartment, I had not kept a home library. My apartment is small—just a studio. One little room, a vestibule, a kitchenette, and a bathroom. You can't even turn around without banging your arms against the walls. And it is a well-known fact that books devour space. You can't reverse this law. However much space you give them, it's never enough. First, they occupy the walls. Then they continue to spread wherever they can gain a foothold. Only ceilings are spared the invasion. New books keep arriving, and you can't bear to get rid of a single old one. And so, slowly and imperceptibly, the volumes crowd out everything before them. Like glaciers.

But now I had no choice. The books were already in my apartment and they had to be put somewhere. I couldn't just leave them in the mailbox. After all, I'm a mature, responsible man. How would it look if I pretended, ostrich-like, that they weren't there? If nothing else, inaction on my part would arouse the postman's suspicions the next time he tried to insert my bills and couldn't because the mailbox was full. He would wonder why I hadn't picked up my mail. He might even come up to ask me about it. And what could I tell him? No, ignoring the books was out of the question. I had to bring them to the apartment. Later I would figure out what to do with them.

Now the question became how to carry the rest of them up, assuming there were more. I couldn't do what I had done the first time. That was too inconvenient. I had to find something suitable in which to carry the books. I looked around the room, and finally remembered something that would suit the purpose, although it was not within my field of vision. I took a large suitcase with brass reinforcements on the corners out of the double-door wardrobe. Lots of books could fit inside, which was good. However, once filled, it would be extremely heavy. Sometimes you can't have your cake and eat it too.

Bringing up fifty-six volumes of *World Literature* all at once to the second floor was no easy matter. I had to hold the suitcase handle with both hands. On the twenty-eighth step, I realized I shouldn't have loaded myself down so much. However, if I'd taken fewer books, I would have had to make the climb several times, actually gaining nothing. Only an elevator would have made any difference, but unfortunately the building didn't have one. Not a single shortcut could be taken if I wanted to bring the books up to my apartment.

While I started to take out the books and put them next to the first thirteen, I realized I had another problem. One more full suitcase and the thin legs of the little table would give way under the weight. And then what? Before continuing, I had to devise a plan. Something like this couldn't be approached haphazardly. I had no idea how many more volumes would appear in my mailbox. Maybe just a few, maybe hundreds. Most likely the latter. This was world literature, after all, and had to be enormous, even when printed on onionskin. I had to prepare for the worst.

The furniture in my only room was sparse, which now turned out to be a blessing. Along with the table and wardrobe, I had four chairs, a bed, a dresser, and a night table. I pushed them all into a corner, freeing up about two-thirds of the available space. Naturally, this had an equal and opposite effect: the area to the right of the door was now cramped and crowded. That didn't bother me. Exceptional circumstances require a man to make sacrifices without complaint. Besides, I never cared much for comfort.

I spread newspapers across the floor in the empty part of the room. It was spotlessly clean, of course, but this way seemed more appropriate. Then I started to move the books. This required some planning. I began by arranging them in the corner farthest from the door—the same place I would have started if polishing the floor, for example. A stack of exactly forty volumes fit from floor to ceiling. In order to place the last seven, I had to climb onto a chair. The tall yellow column would probably have toppled if it hadn't been leaning against two walls and secured firmly from above by the last book that I barely wedged in. I got down from the chair, took a step back, and admired the scene.

With my strategy established, all I had to do was get down to work. There could be no hesitation. Who knew how long the whole thing would last. I took the empty suitcase and headed downstairs. I had simplified the operation, so now I could act more quickly. After taking one volume out of the mailbox, I would just close the door briefly and then open it again. I didn't need to lock and unlock it. A new volume was already waiting inside. I became skilled at arranging the books in the suitcase, managing to fit fifty-eight volumes inside.

My neighbors passed by several times, but no one paid attention to me. All they did was look away and quicken their steps. It's hard to understand people sometimes. I don't mean to suggest that this lack of interest didn't suit me—I didn't want to explain my actions, even though in point of fact I didn't have to answer to anyone—but such indifference was nonetheless inexcusable. What if someone with suspicious intentions, or even worse with questionable sanity, had been there instead of me? These days, all kinds of disturbed people loiter around respectable apartment complexes.

As time passed, exhaustion inevitably crept up on me. After the twenty-seventh suitcase, I could no longer reach the second floor without a short break. The most logical idea was to take a break in the middle, after the twenty-second step, particularly since it was on the first floor. But I ran into trouble after the forty-ninth suitcase, at which time I decided to take a second break. Forty-four steps cannot be evenly divided into three parts. I was forced to resort to an inelegant solution. The first time, I stopped briefly after the fifteenth step, the second time after the thirtieth, with only fourteen steps left in the third part of my journey. The dissonance of the solution bothered me until the sixty-third suitcase, when the need arose for one more rest. Forty-four is divisible by four, thank heavens, so I was able to stop after every eleventh step, i.e., on the landings and on the first floor.

When I brought up the ninety-second suitcase, its contents filled the area I had emptied. Before me rose an enormous dark yellow wall. To behold world literature in this way revealed its true majesty. Night had fallen long ago, but I was still surprised when I looked at the clock and realized it was 2:17 a.m.

I could work deep into the night without bothering my neighbors because I didn't have to turn on the light in the stairwell. I also took special pains to be as quiet as possible. I even took off my shoes. The entrance to the bathroom, where I kept my lightweight shoes, was blocked by piles, so I stayed in my socks, but the warm weather meant I was in no danger of catching cold. I probably should have changed into something more appropriate, but in my rush I failed to do so. All the hauling had completely wrinkled the suit I wore to work, my shirt soaked in sweat and my tie loose. At least I had taken off my hat.

An end to my torment, however, did not seem likely. Regardless of how many times I emptied the mailbox, it was full the next time I opened the door. I had no other choice but to find space for the new books. I hesitated several moments about which piece of furniture I could best do without. I finally decided on the bed because it almost certainly would not be needed that night. I would have trouble finding time to take even the shortest break. Although small, the bed was heavy. As I carried it down, I was consoled by the thought that it would have been much heavier carried in the opposite direction. I took it to my basement storage space. The space was small but empty because I had nothing to store inside it. I pulled the bed upright, anticipating that sooner or later I would have to put something else inside.

Shortly before 5:00 a.m., after the one hundred and nineteenth suitcase, my fears became reality. The space vacated by the bed was now filled to the ceiling with dark yellow volumes. I agonized over what to take to the basement next, and then realized that it didn't matter. There was no sense in fooling myself. Each piece of furniture would have to be removed in its turn, so the best thing was to take it all at once. Now was the right time, while everyone slept. It could be done inconspicuously and not under the inquisitive gaze of the neighbors.

I had no trouble moving the table, chairs, dresser, and night table, but the wardrobe gave me a real headache. Not just because it was heavy, but because it was bulky. I staggered and swerved underneath it, struggling to keep my balance. On two occasions, I almost fell. I carried it on my back most of the time, trying to make as little noise as possible, although I couldn't help some squeaking and cracking. Hopefully, I hadn't woken anyone up. In any case, no one came out to see what was going on.

Once I reached the basement, all my efforts almost went for naught. It took considerable ingenuity and maneuvering to get the wardrobe through the narrow door. Not only was my storage compartment crammed, but I didn't see how anything could be removed without breaking down the partition wall.

As dawn approached, the rest of the free space in the room filled up. Before blocking the bathroom entrance with books, I spent several minutes inside. It was either then or never. I came out a bit more refreshed and tidy. I hadn't been able to remove all the traces of a night's hard work, but I hoped I wouldn't look too shocking when I began to meet my neighbors in the stairwell. In order to improve the impression I made, I put on my hat and shoes.

When it came time to cover the door to the kitchenette with books, I thought I might take at least the refrigerator and little stove out of there, if not the dishes and cutlery. But I had to abandon that idea. I didn't know what to do with those bulky things. There wasn't any room left in the basement and I couldn't leave them by front door. No, they could stay inside; even though inaccessible, they weren't in the way.

At 8:26 a.m., after the one hundred and forty-third suitcase, I had finally packed the room. Eight thousand three hundred five books! It was truly an impressive sight; after wedging in the last volume, I stood in the solemn silence, looking on in admiration. Had anyone anywhere ever had a chance to see all of world literature crammed into such a small space? It left me breathless. The enormous effort had been worth it in the end.

I didn't have much time to admire the sight, though. I had to leave for work. In all my years on the job, I have never been late. I would be able to enjoy the books to my heart's content when I returned home in the afternoon. I would sit in the vestibule in front of the open door to the room and just stare at the dark yellow treasury before me. What else did a man need? A chair, perhaps? No, I didn't need a chair. My needs have always been modest. Since I'd already done away with all the other things, I would make do without a chair. In any case, I would not be sitting on the bare floor. I had a rug made of pure wool.

Descending to the ground floor, I unlocked the door to the mail-box once again. Even though it was only Wednesday, I took the green handkerchief and wiped the inside, although in my rush I was not as thorough as usual. Books are clean, particularly new ones, but after so many volumes passing through the mailbox, there must have been some dust left behind.

A SEASON WITH DOCTOR BLACK
Brendan Connell

I have heard that Aconite
Being timely taken hath a healing might
Against the scorpion's stroke.
—Ben Jonson, *Sejanus, His Fall*

I.

DOCTOR BLACK, AT four feet, eleven inches, was taller than a midget. His neck, equal in circumference to that of the average bull-dog, supported a cranium of vast ability, a thinning corruption of growth combed back, over its surface; a black and frothing monument adhered to his chin. The eyes of a priest or judge. The head of a buffalo. Legs absurdly svelte. A torso profound in its girth.

Mr. Clovis drove the car with arms taut, motions mechanical; the decorum of the well paid servant. His eyes followed the curvature of the road, the play of light patching through the apple trees, and the cows, to his left, which bent over green pasture. Occasionally he glanced in the rear-view mirror, more to ascertain the well being of the Doctor than to appreciate the lack of approaching traffic.

"Eyes on the road, Dick," the Doctor grunted.

"Yes Doctor."

The car, like the shadow of some imperious, savage bird, drifted across the countryside, shaping itself to the protuberances and declivities that lay in its way, its presence, and the presence of its adherents, strangely out of place amongst the wealth of life that painted the landscape . . . At the dirt drive it turned in, to the left. Mr. Clovis, briefly removing himself from the vehicle, opened the rustic, corral-style gate. The tires ground along the narrow and arbored way, the thick neck of Doctor Black turning from left to right, in observation of the springtime of his estate.

The mansion, a structure built some two hundred years earlier by a wealthy and retired merchant, stood quaint against the backdrop of orchard and blue, cotton-spotted sky. Mrs. Clovis, brought down some three days earlier to get the establishment in readiness, stood arms akimbo on the front steps, her healthy chest and stomach thrust forward by way of greeting.

"It's about time you got here," she said to her husband as he extricated the valises from the trunk of the car. "His tomato soup has been ready for thirty minutes."

II.

The doctor enjoyed his tomato soup very much and the next day requested that a plate of the same fruit be brought to him, fresh and seasoned with balsamic vinegar, salt and fresh basil.

"Alfred brought me a whole box of these yesterday when he heard you were coming," Mrs. Clovis said, setting down the plate. She expounded on the hospitality of country folks as opposed to city dwellers and then, seeing the Doctor's attention drift decidedly toward his meal, commented: "He has a greenhouse-full over at his place. He seems to have it in his mind to make money off of them."

Doctor Black slightly rotated one of the ruby red disks with his knife and fork before slicing off a portion. Lifting it to his mouth, he noted a sunken lesion, which marred a small area of the skin.

"Anything wrong?" Mrs. Clovis asked, seeing his eyebrows contract and fearing she had made some careless mistake in her culinary preparation.

Without reply, he examined the tomato more carefully and then finished his lunch, his appetite apparently unhindered.

Later that afternoon he made his way over the field of new alfalfa, which lay beyond his own back yard, and along the creek-side until he reached Alfred's residence. It was obvious at first glance that the man had been busy since the year before. A long stretched out greenhouse lay on the side of the old farmhouse and others, in mid-construction, skeletal forms of plastic sheeting and pipe, were stationed in the near vicinity. In front of the house was a dusty yard strewn with tired discord: a roll of chicken wire, some rotted lumber, a wheelbarrow settled with rainwater and lively with nesting mosquitoes. The barn was on the other side of the yard, the door open. A man sat in the hay-strewn dirt, his body half in and half out of the structure, tinkering with a fishing rod and reel. He looked up and the Doctor could not help but notice the low forehead and rather broad zygomas—a skull structure not necessarily of the most advanced variety. With a certain degree of disgust Doctor Black considered that, after all, this specimen before him might be decisive proof that mankind descended from the hippopotamus rather than the agile ape.

A dog, of the miniature and hairless variety, impeded the Doctor's grim meditation with its bark and snapped at his legs. As his foot lifted the creature up, making it temporarily air-born, he considered how right Galileo was to disprove Aristotle's theory about a heavy body descending faster than a light one, for, as a projectile, the dog acted verily the same as any stone shot from a catapult.

The two men exchanged greetings. Alfred, showing the hospitality of a country man, invited his guest into the house for a glass of cider.

"No, thank you," the Doctor said firmly and explained his mission: "Though I do indeed owe you a social call, at present I have come regarding your tomato plants—A predicament which I am sure, in the long run, you will find much more beneficial than any unguided table talk we might share."

"So you don't care for a glass of cider?" Alfred asked with a bewildered expression.

"No my friend, I have come to see your tomato plants," the Doctor continued undaunted. "You brought me my breakfast which, to use the local colloquy, was 'right neighborly' of you, and I intend to repay the favor. You reportedly have the notion to subsist, at least in part, off of the proceeds of your crop. I will not venture to comment on the practicality of this projected means of livelihood, but merely wish to visit your greenhouse."

Scratching his head, Alfred led the way.

For a half an hour the Doctor examined the plants, now turning over the leaves of one, now caressing another's filamented stem. Alfred stood silent, with arms crossed, awaiting the unasked for verdict.

"I am afraid your entire greenhouse is suffering from the early stages of anthracnose," Doctor Black said gravely. "As you can see, the fruits are infected with these small, water-soaked indentations. On some of the lesions there are even masses of blooming fungus. As the situation progresses, the mildew which feeds on this decaying matter will undoubtedly penetrate the fruit and completely destroy it."

"I see a few little spots on a tomato or two," Alfred said with a surly twist of his lips, "but I'm not so sure it's such a big problem." The presence and threatening tone of this hunkered down, big talking city dweller put him on his guard and he was not immediately ready to accept his prophecies.

"The fruit may be infected when small," the Doctor persisted. "At this stage its appearance is relatively benign, the lesions not appearing until they begin to ripen. The tomatoes you brought me were not seriously wounded, but, from my observations, I can guarantee you that your entire crop is extremely susceptible; and as this harvest approaches maturity . . . Trust me my friend, a preventative fungicide is in order as well as an entire restructuring of the soil so as to allow adequate drainage. And crop rotation, possibly with basil—this is your only hope."

III.

Caparisoned in a smoking jacket of hue to match his name, Doctor Black sat in the library, eyes journeying back and forth between the pages of *The Journal of Mixoscopic Introversion* and the promontory of his pipe, which exuded a sleepy blue coil that rose and mated with the high rafters of the ceiling. These were the leisure hours, when his mind might sponge up information according to its own whim, while darkness coated the trees and fields, and his digestive organ slowly processed the repast of the hour previous. This organ, assisted by the occasional ablutions administered from a goblet of brandy, seemed, on this occasion, to be uttering slight grunts of dissatisfaction. The Doctor listened, his face assuming the annoyed expression of a judge tolerating the introduction of a surprise witness . . . There was sound indeed . . . He examined its mode of resonance, the bubbling and protruding cantata, its irregular scramble . . . It appeared, on more subjective discernment, to be generating from outside his intestinal scope . . . Yes, there was little doubt that its source lay not only beyond the ramparts of his belly, but beyond the very walls in which his entire composition abided.

"Go in and tell him," were the half-muted words that came from the hall.

"But you were the one that said she could stay!"

"Don't be a coward; tell him!"

After a few whispers and whines of uncertain phrase, a tap sounded at the door, which forthwith creaked open, revealing a quarter slice of Mr. Clovis, his mien especially grave, a pallor whiting his temples.

"Yes?" the Doctor asked, setting down his intellectual equipage.

The door opened further; Mr. Clovis stepped in.

"You know the road?" he asked meekly.

"The one at the end of the drive?"

"Exactly."

"Well?"

"You know the road?"

"Where cars go?"

"That is my point entirely Doctor!"

"That there is a road?"

"Yes, and that cars go along it . . . and . . . "

"And?"

"And . . . and sometimes they break."

"So, our car broke?" the Doctor asked rather curtly, flinging back his head.

"No, not ours."

"Then?"

"Hers, Doctor."

"Your wife—A car?"

"No."

"Pardon?"

"The young lady."

"Yes?"

"Yes."

"And this young lady is?"

"She is sitting in the dining room."

"And what is she doing in the dining room, might I ask?"

"Eating a sandwich, Doctor."

"So?"

"It is ham and cheese."

"And . . . So?"

"So . . . You refuse to have a phone line put in!"

"And where there is smoke there is fire?"

"Exactly."

"Which means?"

"Which means that Georgia is preparing the spare bedroom at the end of the hall."

"And you are asking my permission, or demanding my compliance?"

"Your permission, Doctor."

At that moment, the Doctor could not help but pity the broad range of mortals who suffer from the disease called marriage.

IV.

Nocturnal pollution to the image of a wallowing swine, erotic zoo-philia; or, for a certain nun, the sight of an ape, contact with a priest's hand, contemplation of the crucified Christ, or demon (such as with the head of a fish, or serpentine, pronged member—hell being a river of asps—coupling with the horns of the bull moose), the presence of flies in contact—The other boys hunting raccoons and opossums (to deliver, sell at the black cabins that which they themselves would not eat); him, alone, pursuing the mysteries of the Alabama cane break pitcher plant (mouths agape, bodies waxy, sinister without thought or particular will),—Others which might imbibe small reptiles, scorpions and frogs—pasty mucilage—(Francis Darwin growing his two colonies of sundews), Doctor Black thinking of the garden of the retired savant: Drosera rotundifolia, Drosera binata, and the great staghorn sundew with its twenty-three-inch leaves, or the Brazillian Drosera villosa, or the beautiful black-eyed sundew, and the tree-like giant sundew . . . A malicious hothouse: The huntsman's cup, the king monkey cup, Nepenthes ampullaria which, with no difficulty, could digest rats—White trumpet, hooded trumpet, yellow trumpet, sweet trumpet; and maybe a small pond of pisciverous plants—bladderworts; dropwort wreathing the water's edge, hemlock, you umbelliferous wonder, dead tongue, the silence of Socrates; or in cultivating some poisonous patch, take, as Hecate did, the foam of Cerberus (thrust upon the aged men of Ceos when their usefulness had expired), that fleshy, spindle-shaped root: monkshood; the juice of which, applied to an arrow's tip, was mentioned by Diocorids as being used to kill wolves, Aconitum lycotonum; thus wolf's bane; tongue and mouth tingling, ants madly crawling over flesh, pains epigastric, lightness of head, staggering, breath labored, halted.

Science: The art of intellectual cannibalism.

* * *

He sat with his back against a well-measured past, an intricate codex memorized by rote (his own mythology being more strange and dangerous than any of Hercules' tasks). There were experiences wrought, and discoveries, beneficial as locusts, piled up along the semi-material trail of his person, made apparent by hints and feelings and effects and after effects that might not be felt in their full measure till one hundred years hence.

V.

The next morning brought with it, aside from the Doctor's fried egg and half a cantaloupe, an image jointly stirring and fantastic.

She appeared in the door of the dining room wearing a pair of rather sheer pajamas, which, together with the early rays of light, accented her figure in a provocative manner. She stretched her long limbs and yawned; ran a hand through a spume of wild golden strands; blinked (robin's eggs on an outstretched sapling limb); and laughed.

Doctor Black rose from his seat, a spoonful of melon frozen in one hand, and greeted her with a rather severe degree of decorum.

"Oh, thank you so much for the bed," she replied, rushing forward and seizing the free hand of her host. "It would have been so awful to have had to sleep in my car all night!"

"Apparently it was my pleasure," he replied in a gruff voice. "You may sit down if you wish."

She did wish, and sat directly across from him.

"Do you like eggs?" he asked, eyebrows inclining darkly.

"If they are poached . . . If they are poached I like them."

"And might I ask the name of my guest who likes poached eggs?"

"Tandy," she replied, her face opening up into a fresh smile.

"Georgia!" the Doctor bellowed, turning his head toward the kitchen door. "A poached egg for Miss Tandy!"

He then lowered his visual apparatus, and resumed operation on the half cantaloupe.

Mrs. Clovis brought Tandy two poached eggs, two slices of buttered wheat toast, and a cup of creamed coffee, which the young woman consumed with an appetite.

VI.

She observed his activities with discretion, timidly circumambulating his vicinity. Occasionally he would raise his eyes from the tome before him and observe the shadow flit by the door, the sweep of golden hair that moved past the window.

Mr. Clovis was convinced that they need not commandeer a tow truck. He had offered his services as mechanic and could be seen in the drive, buried from waist to head in the hood of the car, or sucked beneath it, feet wagging under the bumper, the sound of grunts and thrash of wrench echoing from that region.

"You just make yourself at home," Mrs. Clovis told Tandy. "Don't mind the Doctor's ways. He seems rough on the outside, but I can tell he doesn't mind one bit having a pretty young lady like you around."

Tandy gave a cute shrug of the shoulders and demonstrated how naturally her lips could pout. She turned and walked toward the apple orchard (wearing simple shorts, a blouse, elegant summer apparel). A few soft clouds hung above the trees, and a few globes of unripe fruit beneath, or from. A blue jay rocked on a branch and then, at her approach, flew off to a more discreet location . . . Something else fluttered aside from those wings. She sighed, the subdued cursing of Mr. Clovis painting a shadowy backdrop to that article, like a landscape by Leonardo de Vinci, or Giorgione (serration and mystery of cold mountains making the valley's tranquil tints all the more profound, endowing the stationary female figure with a kind of kinetic energy).

"Place your foot upon me, your slave," she whispered, and let the sound dissipate in the still air, while the quivering of her lips by no means cut short the rose that blossomed within her, a dark maroon, with glistening thorns.

VII.

"It is amazing that they could sit in the same room for so long without either one speaking hardly a word," Mr. Clovis observed, shoveling a forkful of apple pie into the damp cave of his mouth.

119

"Either one?" his wife chirped. "The poor girl has tried, but he is so stone cold, it scares her. She thinks he wants her to leave."

"Well, maybe he does."

"Dick—Sometimes you amaze me. For a man, you know so little about men."

"You don't amaze me, Georgia. Women always think they understand men, and when they realize that they don't after all, it's too late."

"Is it too late for me, Dick?" Mrs. Clovis asked with intimidating drollery.

He shoveled another forkful of apple pie into his mouth.

* * *

Her sole occupation was the observation of the ash at the end of Doctor Black's corona. It grew, millimeter by millimeter, in train of the smoldering cherry, and then, all at once, was dislodged with a powerful gesture of its master's wrist. He read. He cleared his throat. He wet it with brandy. She watched. She waited. With the red of her tongue, she navigated the fullness of her lips. He did not look up. She did. He turned another page. She threw herself back into the unsympathetic luxury of her chair. He crossed one svelte leg over the next.

"Do you always read?" she ventured.

His eyes consummated the paragraph at hand, and he then slowly looked up, with an expression both sharp and languid, or annoyed.

"Do I always read?" he mirrored. "Do you never read?"

"I like to read *Cosmopolitan*," she replied, tucking her legs under her and curling, retreating into a corner of the chair. "Sometimes I also read books. I read F. Scott Fitzgerald."

"F. Scott Fitzgerald you say? . . . Do you also enjoy walks on the beach in the moonlight, foreign films, and horseback riding by candlelight?"

"Why, yes! How did you know . . . I mean, all but the horseback riding by candlelight. I haven't had that pleasure yet." She smiled.

He book-marked his literature. "Oh, I am sure you will," he said,

120

laying it aside.

His composure impressed her. The very immobility of his bearing carried with it a certain audacious element that made her feel as if she were in the presence of one much more powerful than herself; a lichen coated stone or petrifying, oxidized log of ancient redwood which, once dislodged from its precarious ledge, could very well break her tall, thin form—smudge its submissive fragility—The fragility of living flesh.

For several minutes he looked at her in grave silence while she pursed her lips prettily. It was obvious that he was positioning his rooks and knaves, lowering the bucket of his will into the deep and chilly well of his intelligence.

He got up.

She angled back her head upon its stem and cast out the blue petals of her eyes. The emotion she felt, when he chucked her under the chin, straddled the territory of both danger and longing.

VIII.

Web of skin,
Network of bones,
coated pliant,
quivering,
pleading negative taut as the drum of some animistic peoples, who stare into the wild of night, absorbed by the ancient and slowly-moving glacier of birth feeding on birth, the statue marble, Venus ground to dust, mixed with the humus within which he could stretch his roots, absorb the nutrients to feed those sticky tentacles.

"No?"

"Yes."

"No?" he laughed.

"Yes, yes, yes!"

Later, running one hand through the axe of his beard, he remembered the words of Baudelaire: Cruelty and sensual pleasure are identical, like extreme heat and extreme cold.

IX.

"Well, it's none of your business."

"I never said it was," Mr. Clovis replied, watching his wife dice a red onion. "It was an observation, that's all."

"What, you don't think I have ears as well?" She scowled, turning, the knife flashing in one hand and tears rolling down her cheeks. "I have eyes and ears just like you. I simply choose to keep them in their place."

"Yes . . . Yes, Georgia."

"You should be happy for him," wiping the tears from her eyes. "Find a little companionship . . . Man doesn't always have to be alone."

"No Georgia . . . Apparently not."

"What did you say?"

"I said yes Georgia . . . I'm going into town; to the auto shop."

"You're trying to hurry the job, aren't you?"

"No, Georgia; I'm taking as long as I possibly can."

"Well . . . Fine . . . And remember to pick up some chives while you're out."

She continued to dice the onion, which was destined to animate the body of a tuna fish salad. Ten minutes later, Alfred knocked at the screen door which was situated so as to give access to a small back porch where firewood was stored. He stepped in, his left hand gripping the neck of a duck which hung limp, its tail feathers almost touching the ground.

"I brought this for the Doc," Alfred said, holding up the fowl. "I wanted to leave it for him for thanks. Shot it this morning . . . He was right you know. He was pretty right about that fungus."

"He usually is," Mrs. Clovis said. "Wonderful!" she cried, taking up the bird in her plump hand. "Sit down and let me get you a glass of something . . . Some nice red."

Alfred took hold of the back of a chair, knit his brows, and then plunged his buttocks down on the seat, obviously unused to stationing himself upon furniture.

She did most of the talking, Alfred only occasionally articulating a few words between sips of his wine. He was hesitant with his speech, as are many men used to being alone, not fully trusting their tongues to act in strict accordance with the wills of their brains. As much as he liked the occasional caress of human contact and the light, comfortable kitchen filled with appetizing aromas, there was no question that he would have been relieved to be back home in the company of his dog and tomato plants.

The door that led to the dining room opened and Tandy stepped in. She wore tight jeans and red leather boots. Her t-shirt was stretched over her full bosom.

"I came to get the Doctor a cappuccino," she said. And then, turning to Alfred, she raised her hand and said, "Hi, I'm Tandy."

Alfred rose from his seat and muttered something inarticulate.

X.

The single grain of millet sat poised on the lip of the porcelain dish, which, in its turn, rested upon the tabletop in the back yard. Doctor Black stood at his study window, his hands wrapped around a pair of binoculars. He watched with earnest patience as a group of sparrows hopped around a section of the lawn, following the line of birdseed. One, more eager than the others, made a brief foray up to the sprinkled tabletop, pecked a few morsels, and then descended once more to the grass.

"Damn him," the Doctor breathed.

His vexation, however, was soon appeased. Another sparrow, less cautious, took its colleague's place, eating the scattered seed and turning with clipped motions around the shore of the dish. Doctor Black raised the binoculars to his eyes, adjusting the focus. The grain of millet sat alone on the porcelain lip. The bird observed it briefly, and then pecked it up and into its little beak.

"Good," the Doctor said, with composed excitement, removing the watch from his breast pocket and noting the exact time.

The sparrow chirped pitifully, took a hop, and then flew off the

123

table's edge. In mid air, approximately two meters from the earth's surface, it plummeted, and briefly palpitated on the grass.

"One fifteenth grain in fifteen seconds," Doctor Black said. "I will get Mr. Clovis to fetch it for weight."

The room above the study was that which harbored Tandy. She too was framed by a window, the slight shiver that coursed through her nervous system juxtaposing a dampness that arose from her skin; a languid and uncertain horror, desire.

The apparatus (well oiled, diabolic, a veritable stallion of cast iron, Trojan in its mythopoeic tragedy) roared, rhythmically, flywheels turning, pistons playing in and out of cylinders; the deliberate thrust of machination: Lameness, squinting, pedophilia, necrophilia, presbyphilia, pygmalionism—These under the heading *Abnormal Attraction*—and—and algolagnia; he could not forget that.

Through diverse experience he had found that to use his own self as the substratum for experimentation was, though dangerous, the best method by which to observe the psychological, even psychophysical, effects of morbid positionings and affinities. The true way to determine the effects (microcosmically) of thieving was to thieve: in order to clarify the impact of murder, one must turn murderer. Criminal behavior was a mildew; the latent need for incision, humiliation, consumption of still bleating sauce of flesh, vertigo of deviations resembling a tribe of monkeys springing through the trees: This binary space on which all combinations were transposed (even if subtly) aroused the Doctor's attention.

XI.

The day was especially nice and the air was still and quiet, sometimes stroked by the sound of a large fly descending on some small and rare spot of filth. Mr. and Mrs. Clovis were at the town which lay a few miles away, her buying provisions, him a few mechanical items.

The full afternoon light fell on Tandy's back. Her knees and hands pressed against the twig-covered earth, the raiment of maize-colored hair falling over her face. She twitched in anticipation, in the distance the hills, some areas covered with small forest, rolled away, seemingly shy to witness that human episode. Then the extent of the cane played in the air, described a few delicate, spiraling circles before descending, rattan cutting, whistling, giving the donation of localized, bodily suffering—And nature hid her face; the spirit of trees, oceans and wind recoiled at the sound of irreverent snarls, blaze of tormented lust, and pule of hammering detumescence.

Later, the western light solemnized the patch of ground, like the sleeping place of a dog, rubbed raw as an infected and itchy wound.

* * *

There were flashes, glimpses of life through a horrific, existential lens: the two of them, as if painted by Arcimboldo; her, a haunting, beautiful form, hair the flowing of an orange sulfur, face a cabbage white splayed over an orange jezebel, the brush feet of the Marpesia marcella marking her slim eyebrows, eyes themselves denoted in the blue eyespots of the Australian Tisiphone abeona morrisi—Let her exoskeleton be that of a giant swallowtail, veins of the pearly eye (the cute little proboscis of a Coenonym phadorus raised in the air) . . . For him, his head the Callipogon barbatus beetle, a Metrius contractus representing his beard, the longhorn, California prionus, that North American spiny necked giant would constitute his forearms, hands and fingers, the menacing jaws of the Dorcus titanus his mouth, the violent pincers of the Taiwanese male Dorcus sika his extended feet, cruel, prehensile—torso the two-tone Golianthus regius of the Ivory Coast, elytron, forewings extended, like a flapping, open blazer.

XII.

He projected, logic somewhat anaesthetized, his own vision of the future, its possibilities—those delights sitting beneath a playful veil, the hand of the tamer needing to merely tug it away . . . Of course, bearing within his person a rather granite streak of genius, he was not altogether unaware of the folly: Metaphorically, he slept with one eye open—or the lid slightly elevated at least.

Our first impressions of people may or may not contain a degree of accuracy; but our perceptions, meted by familiarity, certainly relay a far different signal. A man's silence we might initially judge as gravity, only later to denounce as mere stupidity; after acquiring a taste for snails, they are much enjoyed—to juxtapose the idea that familiarity breeds contempt, let it be said that familiarity has the ability to add entrancing gloss (and contempt is the bread eaten by the subdued, the infatuated).

The notes that he kept on their relations began to have hints of poetry—the pedantic stiffness of his style often reflected whispers, shimmerings of something not unlike the *Remedia Amoris* of Ovid. At first Tandy was referred to simply as "my subject." Later however he began to jot down her actual name—An aberration, unprofessional to the highest degree, which he had never before permitted himself. After having made the blunder a number of times he drew his attention to the subject and filled a page full of observations, in his close, spidery hand on what he believed to be the cause . . . Still the trick persisted. But, instead of breaking himself of the habit, he indulged further, finding it easier to trust in his eventual triumph than deal fully with those minute discrepancies of reason as they arose.

* * *

They walked in silence, Tandy a few paces behind him. Though her legs were the longer, they were kept in check due to a certain wariness, subjugation. She had many things to say, but emotions, tending towards awe, stitched her swollen lips shut—Fear (nocturnally applied) could lubricate those bands of flesh, split them into a punctured heart and drag forth the howl, scream of tortured ecstasy. And wax (soft yellow substance of bees, honeycomb cells), remembered, as it flowed over her breasts, stiffening in combination with the rosette petals to be traced by the grim fascination and tapering muscle of a dwarf.

He walked on with deliberation, eyeing the ground and noting

126

the grasshoppers as they propelled from the weeds along his path. As a boy he had made study of such insects, dislodging their jack-knifed legs and caressing their quivering and tragic antennae. Butterflies skewered, set upon cardboard sheets and beetles snatched from their gentle perambulations to be labeled, categorized, brooded over. And, it is said, men are simply boys of a larger dimension (that cranium swollen with incubating theories, gut blooming like a near-hatched egg). Aware of the apparition behind him, he walked on, blind to the incoming clouds as they blotted out the afternoon sun.

Respecting his abstraction, Tandy kept quiet, even as they mounted the low hill covered with a thin maple forest which rose up like a fallen mantle of rusty green above the rich knot of the valley, drops of rain ticking against the network of leaves. The drops came at first scattered and pleasant, then, as Tandy and the Doctor achieved higher ground, advanced in distance, the shower fell melancholy, heedless, plastering down the hair of the man's head and beading through the frothing monument which adhered to his chin, the female's hair gained depth of tone; her clothing, saturated, did what could only be described through cliché, the descending liquid dispelling any loose folds of silk or cotton. Doctor Black's svelte legs became pronounced, comic, ridiculous beneath that mammoth torso which was, in turn, capped by a bony and throbbing mass, bridge of genius.

"Should we turn back now?" his companion asked timidly.

The Doctor gave no indication of having heard. The ends of his trousers dragged through the mud; unsure, noir, the parallel bands of his legs advanced the grimly ludicrous man to the hill's summit, where he stopped, legs bowled, straddling the very earth.

"Come here," he sniffed, and turned, producing a length of cord from the breast of his jacket.

"Where should I go?"

"Over here—up against the trunk of this tree."

"But you don't seem to be in any state—"

"Move, slave!" he wheezed, blinking away the drops of water which rolled over his eyelids.

"Are you sure?" Tandy asked quietly. "Wouldn't you rather go back and have me make you a cup of tea with lemon and honey?"

He moved towards her with a kind of knotted exasperation. It was a bit too much—A bit too much to have to hear of the acid juice of a pale yellow fruit infused with the sticky sweet nectar of bees—She could stand prone and helpless, without the will to say no, yet the other would need the stamina to say yes. The rain came, heavy, morphing, its gloom washing away the stoic armor, that layer of grease which sealed out the cold.

"You're mine," he said, trying to operate.

A cryptic utterance of desperation.

XIII.

"He is normally so healthy—just like a rock."

"Yes," Mr. Clovis replied.

"I can tell you have your own opinions on the subject," his wife said, ladling out a bowl of steaming chicken soup patterned with celery.

"I still have a right to my opinions I suppose."

"Do you? . . . Well, you don't have any right to dislike her."

"I never said I disliked her."

"Well, you are jealous then."

"No, just a little worried—worried that he is getting carried away. He is not a young man you know."

"And he is not an old man—he is two years younger than you."

"But I don't chase after barely legal women."

"Do your job and take up this soup," Mrs. Clovis concluded, shaking her head—a motion that did not terminate with the departure of Dick and the broth, but accompanied her solitude (the solitude of a woman confident in the truth, the accuracy of titles, labels and their inherent reliability—the solitude of a woman who does not mind viewing her husband's opinions through the bars of a cage, but would prefer not to see them clawing clumsily over foreign soil and likely to cause localized regret).

XIV.

With catarrh of both nose and throat (flow of liquid; dulling, dimming of the mental organ) he lay, incarcerated by his bed—the lukewarm bed of a single man, not much regretted when born as the only possible sphere of normal rest, but gravely lamented and seen as cold comfort to the alternate animal (substantial, primal, void filling) heat that raised him from being not only a man in name, but a man in function. So one might try the narcotic drug heroin once for the experience of it, and try it a thousand times again, still claiming the experience while the underlying reality exists, in nomenclature akin to fact, as little more than the stereotypical junkie—though in the Doctor's case he was far past the frontier of stereotype, and the symptoms of addiction from which he suffered were not brought on by any sap of glorious poppy, were injected by modes other than those intravenous (that warm, kind *brutal* feeling of fondness *suppurating or carbonized lust* graspable as ghost; melting point of a phantom)
because when lay that way could see and see could feel soft substance between bones skin pulpy feel with upper limbs shoulder to hand palm. fist. finger an anatomist stepping from star to star of that body of that body breath through the trachea see diaphragm move take up the science. chain up the notes all while not knowing but being realizing cannot really both know (formulaically—pragmatically) and feel too quick you writhing snake—if mastery not much more than a diurnal offspring of villainy disguised in garments or raging genius, plethora of zigzagging appellations, well furnished dungeon of fence or chicken wire, thought trail of breadcrumbs or candy all children really fear to be eaten alive, for what is creature woman (leveling all pyramids of intellection), step on me kick my rib and there and there (pressure of heel, retrograde of calf) strappado oh you condiment you condiment for my hot meat

XV

His flesh was alive with cold shivers. An obnoxious taste, almost herbal, lined his nostrils. He was aware that the order of his mind was disturbed and he mentally applied himself to a few relatively basic mathematical equations, with unsatisfactory results.

"Poor dear," Tandy said, petting his forehead. She ran her hand over his chest, letting her nails trace furrows in the skin, breaking the elastic substance in the last lingering pressure.

"Another mouthful of soup . . . Go on."

He tilted up the bulk of his head and let the spoonful of soup be inserted above the growth of his beard, beneath the arch of his moustache. He knew very well that a damaged constitution often arose from causes hyper-mental rather than strictly physical, but lacked the energy, the dynamism of will required to trace and track the origin of the current unsettling of his system. There is an inherent difficulty in being both doctor and patient, just as an executioner is not so good at simultaneously playing the part of the very man he executes, the condemned.

Verily a Danae of Corregio (for she was no plump Ruben's or stomachy maiden of Boucher), and if she lacked the ability to go beyond simple premise, basic syllogism, she was still loaded with instinct and could appropriate more with an erotic smirk than another might with the composition of compendious volumes or years of astounding revelation. So, if he recklessly crawled on all fours:

"Just go ahead and whip me!"

"I don't feel like it."

"Oh God!" scratching at her nadir, wetting with tears the sole of her foot—And her:

Laughing, turning, walking away, not a follow me hither so much as knife twist of growing disdain, as if he were some crude though rich morsel which found its way to the pharynx, pushed through the esophagus, and then sat troublesome at the pit of her stomach, refusing to either advance or retreat, suddenly ugly as a court jester, she, amused as a low bred woman observing a show of most unusual persons of abnormal form, towing with chains still violent for all their lack of visibility, a savant or buffoon, great sir or midget stumbling, slithering in her wake—And he:

Perversely relishing his new role—the lush drums of desire beating in the curtained epicenter (punctuated by the spine traversing trilobite of fear, more ancient than the sea dwelling stramatolites), a variety of panic ensuing, destructive as locust or berzerking gypsy moth, he negotiates, like a subterranean rodent, the symbiosis of man (glint of steel restrained by scabbard), and woman (jellyfish), primordial vestment, as the bound marsupial is born still half embryonic to wallow in the temperate pouch.

XVI.

He had been sedulously avoiding all serious intellectual pursuit, all labor. Tandy insisted that he not alter his habits because of her presence. She said it would make her feel bad. He attempted to comply, locking himself in his study for a regulated period each day.

Tandy, who was an energetic young homosapien, went for walks on these occasions:

She walked along the country road, the colors all around vivid, hues as pure as paint. The lines of the tree trunks rose up, leading the eye into their clouds of pale, rustling green. The cows in the meadows were a chocolate brown and the perfume of the grass they chewed was delicious.

Tandy sucked in the air through her small, elegant nose.

The purr of a motor sounded from behind her and, as she proceeded, grew into a low roar. She turned and watched the tractor slowly bounce along the road and advance towards her. She waved at the approach.

"Hi!" she shouted.

The tractor slowed and halted quite near her. A low forehead sat beneath the straw hat; two blinking eyes appeared above those rather broad zygomas.

"How do you do, ma'am," Alfred blushed.

"I love your tractor!"

Swallowing: "Thank you ma'am."

"Where are you going?"

"Taking these tomatoes to town."

A trailer of tomatoes was in tow, the fruits red as blood.

XVII.

"She took the car and left."

"She did not say why?" the Doctor said with concern.

"I didn't ask."

Later, that evening, when he saw her at the dinner table, he thought her countenance looked particularly bright.

"You look very beautiful tonight," he remarked.

"Thank you." She put a shrimp in her mouth.

"Where were you today?"

She did not answer, but proceeded to serve herself a portion of tossed salad.

"What a wonderful salad. I love the spinach."

"Where were you today?" he repeated, setting down his knife and fork.

"Oh . . . I had to . . . Go . . . To the doctor."

"Is something the matter with you?" he asked with concern, his brows corrugating. "Are you not aware that I have a license to practice medicine?"

She stopped chewing, swallowed, and took a sip of the white wine that sat by her side.

Her eyes opened wide.

"I'm pregnant," she said.

Doctor Black was stunned. This was far more momentous than the growth habits of any Byblis gigantea or Utriclaria. Quarks and neutrons were indeed small things, as were the expanding and contracting spasms of the universe, compared to this tidbit of information.

He arose from his seat, approached her with solemn strides and, leaning over, applied a kiss to her forehead.

* * *

During the days that followed, he doted on her. She was moody. He was gentle. He began to wear a yellow tie and print shirts. Her breasts appeared especially full, her lips especially lush.

XVIII.

She suggested that they go down to the basement.

"May I ask why?"

"Oh, you know how I am," she replied. "I like things to be dark and cool."

The note of mockery in her voice, so it seemed to him, was one of flirtation. He followed her down the steps and noticed with distaste the untidy state of the basement. A single unshaded bulb, which was the only source of light, vaguely illumined a dusty chamber scattered with various useless items: a few broken pieces of sheet rock, wine bottles, a large oaken barrel, probably a century old, a coil of rusted chain, etc.

It had always been the Doctor's intention to have the place put in order and made use of.

"I will get Mr. Clovis to begin cleaning down here tomorrow," he said and kissed Tandy's hand.

She smiled as she looked down at the bald spot on the head before her.

She gripped his hair with her five free fingers and then let them drop to the back of his huge neck, which she stroked.

"Oh, you beauty," he thought and clung to her.

She made a suggestion which somewhat startled him.

"Blindfolded?" he said. "With what?"

A pair of sleeping patches dangled from her poised thumb and forefinger.

"You would like that?" he asked, rising to his feet.

"And why not?" she counter questioned haughtily. "Are you telling me you wouldn't?"

"I would," he replied quietly and stroked his beard.

Laughing, she put the blinds over his eyes and slapped him on the face. He was in darkness and heard her movements with amorous anticipation. The familiar rattle of chains met his ears.

"What is that dear?" he asked, knowing full well the answer.

"You'll find out," Tandy replied.

He felt weight applied to his shoulders, snake around his chest, and then bind his hands.

"You little vixen," he chuckled with the slightest hint of excitement.

"Are you my slave?" she asked.

He tried to move his arms but could not.

"I suppose, being bound to serve you," he replied, "I am your personal property—But I must say, my higher reason objects . . . Proceed."

He felt an immense crack to his jaw, which sent him reeling two steps back, where he knocked his head against the wall.

"Tandy!" he yelled. "Not so rough!"

"This is better than horseback riding by candlelight," she giggled, in her most silvery voice. "On your knees, dear."

He felt himself gripped and pushed down and experienced a mingling of fear and admiration for this previously unknown strength of hers.

"Oh, you beauty," he thought and then groaned as blow upon blow fell on his back.

"Take it off," he cried. "I want to see you in action. My God, but it hurts!"

The blinds were removed. To his horror, it was not Tandy who stood before him, but Alfred, with shirt off and bare, virile chest, strongly reminiscent of the cave dwelling ancestors of man.

"Alfred!" the doctor gasped.

A female laugh came from one shadowed corner of the basement. Her outline could be seen, bow shaped, with pale highlights and seemingly quivering.

"I hate to do this, Doc," Alfred said, taking him by the chain that bound his hands and yanking him to his feet.

The aperture of the wooden barrel enveloped him just subsequent to the painful kick he felt applied to his backside. His head knocked against the inside of the barrel and then, as it was heaved upright, he contacted the bottom, limbs tangled. The lid was applied and nailed shut, throwing him into complete darkness. Those familiar, erotic giggles came to him, pricking like thorns.

"What should we do with him?" she laughed.

"I guess that's up to you ma'am."

"Why don't we roll him down a hill, like in the cartoons?"

"It's whatever you want," Alfred replied. "But . . . "

"But? You have reservations? You don't want to obey me?"

"It's not that I don't want to obey you ma'am—It's just that his advice, honest to God, probably saved my tomato plants. They weren't getting proper drainage."

"You're such a good boy, aren't you?" she sighed.

Then there was a silence, one which the Doctor could hardly be grateful for, and noise, which sickened him.

XIX.

He stood, mute and abject in his study, the sound of her laughter filtering through the book laden walls. She was speaking to Mrs. Clovis, telling her how grateful she was about Dick and the car, the work he had done—the helpfulness of them both. There is little more cruel than to flaunt kindness to others before the despised, to parade aloof smiles before the dejected who feel a marked claim to affection.

His short stature swayed. He stepped to the window and leaned against the sill. He could hear the click of her heels on the parquet floor of the hall. Her fist knocked on the door.

The Doctor cleared his throat. "Come in," he said.

Turning his head, he saw her, sheathed in a leather jacket and trousers, heels, high, ominous, like balancing daggers. Her yellow hair swept over her shoulders and her face was the blank plastic of a doll's.

"Well, the car is running fine," she said.

"I see," with a slight tremor in his voice.

"Mr. Clovis did a wonderful job."

"Yes." The Doctor stared out the window. A brown leaf fell from a tree, floated slowly to the ground with pendulous motion. "He is an excellent mechanic."

Silence.

"So, I guess this is goodbye," she said lightly.

Doctor Black spun around and advanced a stride. "Why?" he groaned. "I don't see why it has to be that way."

"Because."

"Don't you think you are being a little too cruel my dear?"

"For a man who poisons small birds, that statement seems out of place."

"I . . . I am a scientist."

"And I am a woman."

He had to bend his neck back in order to meet her eyes, which glowed, dominant, a foot above his own.

"Oh God!" he moaned, burying his head in the palms of his hands.

Later, he heard the car door slam, the wheels grind out the driveway. His hazy sockets watered with a flash of self pity, and then contracted, lids half lowered, iris, pupil, like rosary peas, Abrus precatorius, shiny red and black; toxicity at fifteen ten-thousandths a human subject's bodily weight; the drear of the book-laden study slithering over the cornea, penetrating the optic nerve. Indeed, to be strangled with strands of silk was more painful than with a rusty circlet of strong wire. All the facts, the weight of his intellect suddenly crushed him like so much baggage of granite and marble; and pinched, as a swamp of dull scissors might; ego under the strain of rejection, cast off from the clouds into the worm infested soil, to sharpen its fangs and lash out, gaining nourishment by whatever means it might. His lips curled with bitter amusement and quivered, the flavor of abasement still coating his tongue. There were those memories, like frescoes of hell; her leg raised, the ball of her foot balanced on his bowed head; and fantasies, what should have been   *him crucified on an obscene gesture of her hand, the nail, like a sharpened spade, piercing the back of his neck, slicing through his brain, which is dulled to the state of a mollusk, a limpet, while his arms are stretched, broken on her protruding and strained knuckles   naked, manacled, restrained in a dungeon, head pushed against antique stone secreting liquid filth, back lashed by her hair done up in a vicious and snapping braid   imprisoned in a minute and frigid cage, his ample flesh pushing through the tight constraint of bars—she sits atop the grill and laughs musically, her naked buttocks press through to his palpitating   whinnying form; he pushes a tremendous ball of near molten iron (glowing orange and orchestrating sizzling sounds upon his skin) up an almost perpendicular hill, her in the rear—she pokes him with her toe, teases his sparse head of hair, makes lisping promises as fire hiccoughs from the earth   him, hands and feet stapled together in the position of a roped calf, her searing, branding his side with the seal of her perversion   violent and abrasive amphibians gnaw at his limbs, entwine them with their tails, as she giggles, rocks with liquorice merriment, naked, one leg draped over the next   skewered, secured upon a red hot metal spit which she turns with a single outstretched finger, orange and blue flames crackling below, a squadron of meat hungry, burly and stupid men form a semi circle around the scene, licking their chops.*

XX.

The weather grew cooler and the wooded hillside began to gain tints of yellow and a deep, sad red. The creek was almost dry and its banks of smoothed stones and coarse sand took on a rich, golden color in the early fall light.

Alfred could be seen across the field of ripe, mellow alfalfa, busy

137

with his tomato plants, which were prospering and bursting with fruit. The dog, a mere spot at his heels, turned and barked at the house opposite, the sound carrying through the still air, shrill, defiant.

Mrs. Clovis sat on the passenger side of the front seat and watched as her husband transported the luggage down the steps and loaded it in the trunk of the car. The forest of apple trees sat to her left, the fruit ripe, and much of it damaged by the society of crows and other birds that rattled in its branches. She had a small bag of deep red spheres at her feet, and another of granny smiths, green and slightly bitter, which she would transform into a set of pies once they returned home.

The Doctor walked out the front door, steps somewhat unsteady, his head covered by a black felt hat which, due to its newness, was strangely incongruous with the gray batch of face beneath it, beard draping somberly to his chest. He locked the door and strode down the steps.

"Everything in order?" he asked.

"All gassed up and ready to go," Mr. Clovis replied, slamming the trunk of the car shut. His manner had a sort of tight joviality to it, consistent with what was unsaid but was undoubtedly thought.

Both husband and wife had always viewed the Doctor with a mixture of awe and indulgence: Awe due to his obviously superior intelligence, social standing, and the fact that he paid their wages and therefore, to a certain extent, held their lives in his hand. There was however the other side of the coin: Doctor Black was a man so absorbed in his mental world that he might very well starve to death without someone to cook for him, and would undoubtedly be condemned to go about on foot without Dick there to perform the mundane but necessary task of keeping the car with gas and oil.

At the moment, the moment of crisis, they felt, to some extent, superior to the Doctor who had let himself be jostled by a common emotion; an emotion Mrs. Clovis had previously felt, if he was ever susceptible to, would certainly be in the position of commander-in-chief, not cast aside subordinate.

"It's disgusting," Mr. Clovis had said to her when the situation became obvious.

"Yes," she had replied, "it is disgusting to see a man let his spine be plucked out when a woman is just begging to be made to feel like a woman!"

The wild, predatory look in his plump wife's eyes had made Mr. Clovis hasten to the nearby woods, where he spent a good deal of time gathering kindling for the evening's fire.

Now the season was over. The Clovises awaited him, both positioned in the front seat of the large, American car; Mr. Clovis upright behind the steering wheel, his wife across from him, her eyes peering out the window. With a sigh the Doctor took a farewell look at his country property, with its calm fall beauty. The city and a good deal of labor awaited him, which might very well be the balm he so needed for his gored vanity. He breathed in deeply through his nose, letting the intake expand the oxygen loving organs of his chest, and then, firming up the musculature of his face, opened the door of the car and climbed in the back seat.

Mr. Clovis started the car, let it idle for a moment, and then pulled out of the driveway. The soft light filtered through the trees and patterned out over the car seat and Doctor Black's trousers and jacket. The car hit pavement, turned to the right, and purred down the road, off into the hills, a long, dull shadow stretching behind it and seeming to remain a great while, even after the vehicle had disappeared around the bend. Gravely, the sound of the motor withdrew into the distance.

THE CAMUS REFERENDUM:
A Jerry Cornelius Story
Michael Moorcock

In Memorium: For Douglas Oliver.

WAHAB
Farther Down The Line

All of a sudden, then, I found myself brought up short with some though not a great deal of time available to survey a life whose eccentricities I had accepted like so many facts of nature. Once again I recognised that Conrad had been there before me . . . I was born in Jerusalem and had spent most of my formative years there and, after 1948, when my entire family became refugees, in Egypt.
Edward Said,
London Review of Books,
7th May 1998

Jerry took the July train out of Casablanca, heading East. There was a cold wind blowing. It threatened to pursue them to Cairo.

"It's like you've been telling them for years." He was leafing through *Al Misra*, thinking it could do with a few pictures. "They're academics and politicians mostly, debating whether or not flight is possible or if it is whether they should allow it, and everywhere above them the sky is full of ships." He frowned. "Is that a quote? If we're living on the edge of the abyss, Mrs. B, I think we should make the best we can of it. Love conquers all. A bit of vision and we'd all be more comfortable."

"I have had visions since I was a child." With prissy, habitual movements Miss Brunner arranged her *hadura*. She was calling herself General Hazmin but her old, green fundamentalist eyes still winked above her yashmak. Her accompanist, Jerry's current lover, snored lightly in the corner chair while the grey, flat roofs of Casablanca began to flash past faster and faster. "Originally of the Prophet, but later of ordinary people from history, or people I did not recognise, at least. I always felt very close to God."

"Me, too." Jerry settled himself into his deep chair as the train torqued up to sound minus ten. "With me, of course, it was Jesus. Then the middle ages, mostly. Then the nineteenth century. Now we're somewhere between the end of one millennium and the beginning of another. The blank page between the Old Testament and the New. I had no idea what it was all about. These days I just see things in shop windows. They always turn out to be something ordinary when I examine them. Maybe it was the dope in the sixties? They sell you any old muck now." He patted his heavy suitcase.

"This is the age of the lowest common denominator. I blame America."

"Don't we all?" She stared vacantly at the blurred landscape. "A ram without a brain, a ewe without a heart."

He blushed. "Impossible!"

She looked into the whispering corridor. "Flight is so unfashionable, these days."

DOS
American Tune

His life was dedicated to the United Kingdom, and he always spoke for all the people of this fair land. Enoch warned us about Europe, about excessive immigration, and he reminded us of our heritage and history. If only we had all listened . . .

Stuart Millson,
This England, Summer 1998

"A mature democracy is surely a democracy which orders its affairs by public debate and reasoned agreement. An immature democracy is one where affairs are settled by conflict, by adversarial court cases, authoritarian laws resisted by civil liberties groups. Didn't America lead the way in this appalling devolution? Why would any democracy want to repeat that mistake?" Prinz Lobkowitz looked at his dusty drawers and coughed as if embarrassed.

"Immature or corrupted, the body counts are the same. They were almost up to the 100,000 target last year. It's a big market, major. A lot of citizens. A lot of good gun sales. All I need is for you to give me the slip." Jerry took dust from his eyes with a fingertip, glaring at the disturbing fan above. "And if you could spare a little something for the journey . . . "

"Of course." Lobkowitz found his documents. "Ugh!"

"That was probably me." Shaky Mo Collier spoke from the shadows where he had been posing with his new ordnance. Lazily he flipped and zipped. "You had marmite or something in there. I thought it was resin or ope but I couldn't get the lid off without using my knife. Sorry. You'd know if I was *trying* to make a mess."

"Thanks." With insane deliberation Lobkowitz began to whistle 'Dixie'.

DREI
Valentine

I dreamed I was in England
And heard the cuckoo call,
And watched an English summer
From spring to latest fall,
And understood it all.

Enoch Powell,
The Collected Poems of Enoch Powell

"The land of cotton." Major Nye took Una her gin sling. She was hypnotised by the waters of the Nile white against the steel grey rocks. "The river runs a merrier course nearer to her source than her destination. What?" He sat down in the other chair as she turned, uncrossing her legs. She wore Bluefish, longing for authenticity in pastel luxury. And elegant beyond understanding, he thought. She was unassailably beautiful these days. They sat at their old table on the terrace of the elegantly-guarded Cataract Hilton. Fundamentalists had made tourism a luxury again. It was wonderful. Indeed the fundamentalists were very popular in America now because they had successfully prepared for Western business and attendant human rights legislation by reducing their national economies to zero and attracting the benign authority of the democratic corporations.

Una and the Major were surveying neighbouring Elephant Island for an EthicCorp™ which had already done miracles in Egypt. And everyone admitted *DisneyTime*™ had turned Alexandria into the thrusting modern metropolis it was today. They had even removed the original city to the Sinai between *Coca Cola*™ University and *Sinbad's Arabian Fantasy*™, in a successful effort to improve trade, tourism and education in the region. Who could complain? In *LibraryWorld*™ the scrolls could almost be real.

"Of course." Una concentrated on a pleat. She shook her skirt again. "We are making a rod for our own backs, major. Or, at least, putting all this tranquility in jeopardy."

"It's share and share alike nowadays, Mrs. P," Major Nye tipped his cap towards the river. "We all have to take a little less. Like the War, what?"

"What war?"

"Last one. Big one. What?" He frowned. "Are you joking, Mrs. P. Or are you in trouble?"

She reassured him. "Just a joke, major. In poor taste."

"I know exactly what you mean." He offered her a bowl of cherroids. "These are dreadful."

ARBA
Heartland

"If two quarrel, the Briton rejoices," has long been a proverb. In the course of centuries but few had seriously endeavoured to catch the measure of Mephistopheles, and none had succeeded. The wilder the turmoil in Europe, the more might England rejoice, for countries that had got their heads battered were afterwards easily the most docile."
Hindenburg's March On London,
Germany, 1913, Eng. Trs, 1916

"OK, Mr. C, so you never caught *The Desert Rats*. Then rely on me like an old-fashioned officer and I will get us through, okay? There isn't a World War Two movie I haven't seen at least twice and I've always been very fond of a wasteland." Mo's voice was muffled by his respirator, a black and belligerent snout. "Here we go!"

The half-track's caterpillars whistled impotently over the sand. Another shell made a neat, noisy crater only a few yards away. They wiped at their goggles with dirty gloves.

"Libyan." Sniffing, Shaky Mo paused in his busy handling of the gears and gunning of the engine. "You can always tell."

"But we're so far from the border." Bishop Beesley's camouflaged mitre oozed from the conning tower. "And a long way from the Basra Road."

"Never very far, bishop." Shaky Mo did something angry to the machinery and it lurched upwards, back onto the blitzed concrete of the road. "Not these days. Not ever."

PYAT
Across the Borderline

Then in the year 1870 something quite unheard of happened. About that time there all at once appeared in Europe in the foreground a youth in the fullness of his strength—young Germany! He was a sprig of the good, stupid old-German Michael, who had fared especially badly owing to his horizon bounded by the church tower, and his secluded mode of living. Michael had to sit very far behind in the European State class, and during the last five hundred years he was always several decades behind the others. Young Michael, however, the fair-

145

haired, blue-eyed fellow, was of a different mould! To the schoolmistress on the other side of the Channel he looked a very slippery fish!
Hindenburg's March on London.

"They've been chopping up children, mostly, as far as I can tell." General Hazmin had removed her yashmak and now wore a massive gas mask, designed to resist the most fashionable mixtures. She resembled a Hindu goddess, moving. She moved ponderously through the village. Every so often, when Jerry slowed down, she gave the rope a tug. He had begun to enjoy the sensation. His giggling grew louder as she dragged him, for a moment, through the gobs of bloody flesh. "Oh, Christ!" He shook. "So cold. Oh, fuck." General Hazmin was discovering the frustrations of trying to punish a creature that had either experienced everything or was grateful to experience anything. "You are no longer human, Captain Cornelius."

He shrugged. "I never was. Was I?"

"We are all born human."

"Somewhere back on the clone line, sure. It's the type, though, that's important, isn't it. Cromagnon, I mean, or Neanderthal. We should never have got mixed up. It's not their faults. You either got soul or you don't." He had a mood swing. He had begun to weep over the remains of a little girl whose throat had been slit and whose mother's hands had been cut off before she, too, had been killed. "Their brains can't make the connections most of us make. They look human. But they're not quite. Thirty percent of the population, at least? Genetics are so important these days, aren't they?"

Una Persson had taken the rope from General Hazmin's gloved hands. She swung her lovely hair as she looked back at him. "So which are you, Jerry, love?"

"Bingo bango bongo, I should never have left the Congo." Jerry sometimes wished he hadn't abused his homo superior status so frequently and so self-indulgently. "I used to be the world's first all-purpose human being. I was really happy in the jungle. Just like Derry and Toms. A new model of the multiverse. But it all turned back to shit. Africa should have negotiated new borders for herself. That's where the trouble began. I should know. I started it."

"Yes, right. You and bloody Sisyphus. " Una exchanged some enjoyable glances with General Hazmin. "What shall we do with him this time?"

SIX
She's Not For You

Successive generations of our politicians have failed, or in some cases actively betrayed, their country's interests. Now only the ordinary people can hope to reverse the tide of bureaucracy and centralised control which is already engulfing every participating nation in Europe. Are there enough people who care or dare to do something about it? Or is *Land of Hope and Glory* finally to be replaced by *Deutchshland Uber Alles*?
Letter, This England, Summer 1998

"I'd like to stop off in Algiers as soon as possible." Una had slung Jerry over her best pack camel. He rubbed his face on the animal's hide. He moaned with tiny pleasures. "I had a wire from my agent. We're doing a revival of The Desert Song in Marrakesh next month. I promised them I'd get you to sing."

"Blue heaven and you," croaked Jerry as he bounced. "One alone. We are the Red Shadow's men. One for all and all for one. Or is all one, anyway? One or The Other? Never more than two? I can't believe in a simple duality. The evidence is all against it. Once a clone . . . Clone away, young multiverse. Clone away. Oops. Oh! Oh! Yes! Watch it, Stalin. The cells are out of control."

"Damn!" By accident, she had struck him full across the buttocks with her camel whip. She took some rags and a bowl from the saddle-bags and tried to save the fizzing, strangely-coloured sperm running down the animal's flanks.

This amused him even more.

SEBT
What Was It You Wanted?

Sir: I have recently returned from a business trip to the Arabian Gulf and was immediately struck by the presence there of a British export which is rarely found

anywhere else in the world. Why is it that when we travel several thousand miles to somewhere as alien to us as Bahrain or Dubai we can still buy a pint of good English bitter, yet those closer to us (geographically and politically) never stock anything but lager and pilsner? One could tread the pavements of French towns for hours and never find even a smell of anything like traditional English Ale."
Letter, This England.

"Imperialism breeds nationalism and nationalism needs guns. America supplies both, just like ICI and Dupont make bullets and bandages. It's the trick the rubber trade learned early on. Condoms or rubber knickers. There's always a market."

Una signed the form and handed over the remains. In his tank, Jerry opened and closed his mouth. Tubes ran from all his other orifices. "What?"

"You'll be fine," she said.

The whole tribe surrounded him now. They seemed proud of their bargain. Discreetly, they pointed out the peculiarities of his anatomy. He was enjoying an unfamiliar respect.

"It is beautiful," said one of the young women. Like the other Berbers, she wore no veil. Her aquiline features were striking. Her green eyes were exceptional. "Some kind of cuttlefish?"

Una shook her head.

"Not nearly so interesting. Or intelligent. It's the light. See?"

OCHO
Getting Over You

I had allowed the disparity between my acquired identity and the culture into which I was born, and from which I had been removed, to become too great. In other words, there was an existential as well as a felt political need to bring one self into harmony with the other . . . By the mid-seventies I was in the rich but unenviable position of speaking for two diametrically opposed constituencies, one Western, the other Arab.
Edward Said, Between Worlds.

"You were monumental in Memphis." Shaky Mo was trying to cheer his exhausted chum. "What a tom, Jerry. What a comeback!"

"Too many." Jerry smiled sweetly into his restored reflection. "Too much."

Mo wasn't really listening. With a thumbnail, he scraped at a bit of hardened blood on his barrel. "It was a shame about Graceland. Could have been a crack. But nobody's got any money, these days. It had to go to a private buyer. Nothing like the smell of an old Vienna."

"Land of Song." Jerry slipped a comb through his locks. "Land of Smiles. Where there's a drug there's a way. Millions will pay through the nose to visit that historic toilet."

Mo put his gun down and carefully got out his maps. "Now all we have to do is find a drum."

"Boom, boom," said Jerry.

"I meant a gaff." Mo folded the filthy linen. "Sometimes I wonder about you."

ENIA
The Most Unoriginal Sin

Your paper talks about the balkanization of American society and the imminent train wreck we face. Any suggestions on what readers can do to help turn this around?

I urge your readers to become very aggressive in fighting for the enforcement of the nation's civil rights laws . . . The civil rights laws passed in the 1960s are, for the most part, not enforced or are weakly enforced. A white man like me can pretty well discriminate against Americans of color every day of the week—in housing, employment, public accommodations, schools—with no fear of being punished under the civil rights laws. For example, it's estimated there are 4 to 8 million cases of racial discrimination in housing each year, and yet very few whites are ever punished, even mildly, for this massive discrimination . . .
Joe Feagin, Southern Poverty Law Center Report, June 1998.

We don't have to worry about the Europeans. All the British and the French are waiting for is American leadership.
Bob Dole to Congress, 1995.

The American general had all the flaky wariness of his kind. He wasn't used to being in this position. Nobody spoke his language. He made complicated, aggressive movements with his cigar to show he was on top of things. His inexperienced lips trembled with frustration. His boy's eyes shifted uncontrollably, sensing the necessity of self-reliance but having no appropriate training, only the rhetoric. The Chlue were as mystified by him as the Sioux by Custer. But, like the Sioux, they had no problems with the idea of genocide. They had some sense of what his rituals meant and were wary of them. Perhaps they recognised the traditional American warm-up to a necessary action. When sentimental speeches failed, there was only the rocket.

The black tents were pitched all along the shallow valley. Sweat and animal dung, cooking fires, tajini, kous-kous. A noise of goats and ululating women. Horses. Metal. A subtle, pervading odour of cordite, a faint, blue haze of rifle-smoke. In the distance were the banners of the Rif and the Braber. All the Berber clans were assembling. Only Cornelius could have brought them here. He was one of them. Their cause was his. They asked little more than freedom to roam.

The general settled his plump bottom onto the director's chair, which he had brought with him. Everyone else sat on carpets.

"Tell these bastards that they're Berber-Americans now. They can vote. We've given them several choices."

In Arabic, which all the Berber tribes could understand, Jerry said:

"You have no choice. If you do not sell him your villages, he will have you all killed by fundamentalists."

This made sense. Sheik Tarak, their spokesman, gave it some thought.

"Tell them about human rights." The general was impatient. "War crimes."

"He will then kill the fundamentalists. So all but him and his corporation will perish."

"You will not perish, dear friend." Tarak's old eyes remained amused. "We'll sell him the villages. After all, it's only fifty years or so since our noble grandfathers wiped out the bastards who used to own them."

"They'll sell." Jerry turned to the general. "But they want a royalty."

"Royalty. Fucking royalty? Don't they know we've abolished all that in America." He began to roll up his plans. "This is going to be an eco-complex, not a fucking casino."

"They say there's no royalty on egos." Jerry responded to Tarak's inquiring eye.

"Good!" The handsome old sheikh understood perfectly. "Let them build their hotels. Then we will come back upon a great *harka*. And lay waste to everything. Thus it begins again."

"He's prepared to negotiate a lease," Jerry told the general.

TISA
Don't Give Up

Our passion for a city is often a secret one. Ancient, walled cities like Paris or Prague, or even Florence, are introspective, closed, their horizons limited. But Algiers, in common with a few other ports, is as open to the sky as an eager mouth, an unprotected wound. Algiers gives you an enthusiasm for the common-place: how blue sea ends every street, the peculiar density of the light, the beauty of the people. And, inevitably, amidst all this unprotected generosity, you scent a seductive, secret ambience. You can be homesick in Paris for breathing space and the whisper of wings. In Algiers, at least, you can sample any desire and be certain of your pleasures, your self, and so know at last what everything you own is worth.
Albert Camus, Algerian Summer

In Marrakesh, Jerry sat back at his café table and watched the German tourists boarding the evacuation buses taking them to their planes and trains. The Djema al Fnaa, the great Square of the Dead, had lost none of its verve. In fact, since the departure of the Germans a rather gay, lively quality had returned to the city. The storytellers were already drawing large crowds as they described the Rif's decision to drive the infidels from their territory. "There is a tendency to play to the lowest common denominator, even here." Prince Lobkowitz leaned to freshen Una Persson's cup. "Sugar?"

Mo Collier was bored brainless. He had set his vibragun on its lowest notch and was giving his back a massage. "You got to admit, Prince L, that they do a nice coffee. The krauts. I've never found this Turkish stuff much cop, even when you call it Greek stuff. Or Moroccan stuff. But your German, now, given half a chance, knows his Columbia from his Java and can brew a bean with the best. If only the rest of Fritz's food was edible, they could have become a nation of restauranteurs and we'd all like them now. They always meant well. But they shouldn't've brushed up on the old cuisine and not tried for the macho image. It doesn't suit them. It makes them even more ridiculous than most. They should have gone on laughing at the Prussians. Talk about the lowest CD of all, eh?"

"Bismarck was a great leveler," Prince Lobkowtiz agreed. "And so was Hitler, for that matter. An odd record, really, for so benign a race. They just want to bring the best they have to everyone else."

The tourists were squeezing themselves through the double-wide doors as hard as they could. There were no street boys on hand to push them in. Their proffered francs and marks lay on the ground where they had been thrown back by the crowd. The Rif had made examples of surrounding villas owned by German infidels. The Marekshis were in a jolly mood. The Germans had no power now. Their marks were a bad memory. Some of the Berbers had brought food and video-cameras and were filming the sweating Teutons, in their damp, grubby whites, as they silently embarked.

Una eyed the swollen bottoms with some interest. "Do you think they're growing into Americans?" she asked. "Or are Americans descended from them?"

"Hard to tell. What an aggressive gene, eh? The Germans used to think of themselves as undeveloped Englishmen. They had that in common with the Americans. Now, of course, they need no models. They are all king-size. They have their wealth instead."

"Some day." Mo was in a visionary mood. "People will hunt them. Not much sport, though."

"German?" Major Nye parted his lips in a silent laugh. His pale blue eyes were almost lively. "I thought they were all Scotch. You know—MacDonalds, Campbells, Murdochs. Those chaps own everything. The most aggressive people on earth. Devolution was the best idea the English ever had. Now, with nobody else to blame, the Scotch and the Irish can go back to fighting each other. We can just hope they won't start marching on London again. They drink too much. And then they decide to claim our throne. Those sectarian battles never cease. They're a tradition." The old soldier savoured the delicate mint. "When a few Yankee scrooges refused to pay for the army that protected their backsides, then borrowed a couple of old slogans from the London mob to offer a moral reason for welshing on their bills, they started a habit of always having moral reasons for not coughing up their fair share. No taxation without representation? Tell that to your green card residents. As for the victimised Irish, haven't you noticed how all the Federal soldiers who massacred Indians had Irish names. Kipling's Indian-killers had Irish names, too, come to think of it. And what about them Israelites? Federal soldiers who . . . "

As the muezzin began his electronic call from the Booksellers' Mosque, Una Persson bowed her head over her black cup. "That's progress for you."

"And Heinz," said Mo. "And Sarah Lee."

"What?" Jerry was distracted. He murmured the responses.

"General foods." Mo seemed to offer this as an explanation.

They allowed him a moment's time for himself.

"Nestles," he added.

"Mo?" said Jerry.

"I thought we were doing one of those guessing games. The seven most powerful food corps. Like the names of the seven dwarves. What's that?" Mo's ear ticked.

"Six," said Jerry. "Unless Private Murdoch doesn't count."

"It's like adding a Greedy. Seems there should be one. But there isn't. OK, no junk media. How about Pepsi?"

"Drinks mostly. And burger chains."

"That's food, too, though. Same with Coke."

"We should stick to, you know, general foods. Basics."

"Are we counting services?"

"No."

"Then you cut out MacDonalds."

"Okay. Three."

"Right," said Mo, narrowing his eyes. "Let's think of the rest."

The last prayer called, the square was filling with its evening population. A wash of deep scarlet and glittering gold raced out of the shadows of the surrounding market stalls—the acrobats had arrived. The fire-eaters and snake-charmers and conjurors called their audiences to them. Fortune tellers were busy with their cards and bones. A squeal of flutes. A mumbling of drums. Dark shapes moved boldly around the parameter and the Pakistani fakir, originally an engineer kicked out of Saudi, lowered himself onto hot coals.

There was a smell of roasting mutton, of chestnuts, of jasmine and warm wax.

Una sighed at the texture of it. Her relaxed fingers traced eccentric geometries over the china. She folded down the collar of her black car coat and unbuttoned. Her chest foamed, white flecked with red. It was her linen, no longer constrained. She hadn't had time to change. She had come straight from the theatre with Jerry. She reached to caress his cooling hand. She had no fear that she was setting a precedent. If it didn't exist now, it wouldn't exist.

She stroked his rapidly growing nails. Entropy and the Absurd. You had to love it.

Jerry raised his head. He smiled. He purred. A jaguar. "My brain's changed."

Major Nye beamed upon the crowd. He had not looked so dapper since the last time he was here, with Churchill, in 44. The prayer having ended, he returned his cap to his head.

"What a blessing religion can be."

Thanks to Willie Nelson and *Across the Borderline*.

THE VENGEANCE OF ROME
(Chapter 3)
Michael Moorcock

*I began the Colonel Pyat sequence after a number of experiences
came together. I watched a Leon Uris TV movie, which depressed
me with its terrible simplifications, I travelled on Russian ships, on
which I met many Russians and Germans and discovered that one
thing they still shared in common was anti-Semiticism. Travelling as
I did, I became interested in the "roots" of the holocaust, specifically
the 20th century ones, and I decided I had to try to write a novel
sequence which covered all the various factors leading to that ultimate act of modern horror, the Final Solution, in which we were all,
to some degree, compliant. However, I was not about to write anything close to the sort of thing Uris and others had already written,
which I believed to be almost as full of dangerous simplifications as
the Nazism it seemed to be challenging. We are seeing far too much
of that awful rhetoric coming out of Jerusalem and elsewhere at the
moment. Being a victim should not, I hope, give you the right to
create more victims, although we all know it is a common psychological response. The books also had to have a comic quality if they were*

going to offer exaggeration without, as it were, too much sensational-
ism. There are few ways of intensifying your material, one of which
is to make it fantastic and surreal. The best way I have found is
in comedy, even farce, which allows the same exaggerations but are
read in a different context. The character of Pyat, who is the emblem-
atic Jew-hating Jew often mentioned by Nazis as some sort of con-
fused wretch, was based on a near neighbour (actually Polish) whom
I knew for some years in Ladbroke Grove. The research has been
pretty exhaustive, largely depending on personal accounts, several
of which I have collected from first sources. I have used the reminis-
cences of disappointed Nazis "betrayed" during the Night of the Long
Knives, when Hitler rid himself of the left wing of his party. These
reminiscences, written before the start of World War II, *are often far*
more revealing that the later apologias published by repentant or even
defiant Nazis. Pyat's journey has taken him from Ukraine, through
Russia and the Civil War, through the Turkish upheavals immediately
following the first world war, through Europe, through an America
reeking of racism both in the rural south and the cosmopolitan cities
and where Pyat enjoys an intimacy with the Ku Klux Klan as well
as somewhat less flashy organisations symptomatic of the endemic
racism which runs through America and in my view did much to
allow, even encourage, the Holocaust. The books make up a brief
*statement—*Byzantium Endures/The Laughter of Carthage. Jerusalem
Commands/The Vengeance of Rome. *I see the roots of our present*
disputes very much founded in the common history referred to in
those titles. In the previous book, Jerusalem Commands, *we travelled*
through the Middle East to North Africa, so now Pyat has escaped El
Glaoui's insane Moroccan court, dumped his best friend, picked up a
new girl friend and finally made contact with old Italian companions
(from the first and second volumes) who are celebrating Mussolini,
their hero, and take the Colonel to Venice where he finds he has a
little trouble with a surfeit of masks . . . This work in progress is from
The Vengeance of Rome.—MM

I HAD BEEN sleeping and came awake suddenly with no notion of the time. I was alone. For some reason I experienced a rush of terror and then opened my eyes to see that a steward had brought me some tea. He seemed amused. My hand trembled badly as I accepted the glass. He told me that Signorina Butter and Doctor De Bazzanno requested that I urgently join them in the observation cabin.

Still conditioned to crisis, I quickly washed and dressed. I hurried out of my quarters, along the vibrating metal passage to the cabin where my friends were already seated staring out of the wide window at the approaching horizon.

"You seemed to need the rest, so I left you sleeping." Mandy Butter with a smile. Only then did I realise it was not morning but late evening. We were nearing our destination. That afternoon, while airborne, I had entertained Miss Butter in my quarters and then, evidently, fallen fast asleep.

"I didn't want you to miss this." De Bazzanno spoke with warm, proprietorial pride. "It is, after all, the birthplace of my ancestors!"

I took my seat beside him. The plane suddenly banked, levelling out close to the water, and as the horizon came up again I understood why De Bazzanno had wakened me so insistently.

Most of us see pictures of them from childhood and in some sense always know what to expect. Yet all the wonders of the world, the Pyramids or Niagara Falls or any of the others, have this in common: We are always prepared for them and yet never quite ready for their actuality. The actuality is always breathtaking, never disappointing, always better than any representation we have seen. The desert in that Lawrence film was a tawdry backdrop in comparison to the original. The Grand Canyon in *Cinerama* is still merely a cheap illusion. The reality is always too vivid ever to become truly familiar.

And so it was, of course, with Venice. Her sky was alive with gold and rose. Her olive domes were half-immersed in a ruby-coloured aura. Her smouldering bronze, silver stone, emerald tiles, her thousand shades of terracotta, her canals like mercury, all were woven together into one great carpet of colour whose tones faded or deepened with the setting of the sun, displaying the entire spectrum, containing such a variety of copulas and towers, curves and angles, she seemed to exist in more dimensions than our mere four.

Venice's confident beauty contradicted any conventional understanding of space, just as she revealed whole varieties of tints and washes, which, I could swear, I have never seen since. As her colours darkened, her lights made little pools of shivering copper and warm saffron refracted in water which diffused and enriched her so that the outlines of her buildings merged with sky and water and made it impossible to know where the reality ended and the mirage began. It was easy to believe that the whole vast scene was an illusion and to understand how she had for so many centuries resisted her would-be conquerors.

Again *La Farfalla Nero* banked steeply, lending my first sight of that fabulous city a further crazy unreality. We swept towards the vivid tapestry as if to be absorbed by it, then we banked again, making a pass at the water as we prepared to put down. There was a sudden loud bang, a series of sharp shudders, then a sense of bouncing gently forward until we at last settled. There came a massive roar from the engines steadying the ship as she came about, preparing to taxi towards the dark outlines of churches and storehouses, palaces and merchants' mansions, banks and museums, all built with that same enchanting combination of knowing magnificence and artless beauty which possesses no rival anywhere in the world. Odessa in her golden age could not begin to match the brutal and subtle glamour of that ethereal Queen of Ports whose influence has stretched around the world, whose style has so frequently been imitated and never successfully equalled, even by Hollywood. Venice's beauty set the standard by which all watery cities, be they Stockholm, Rouveniemi, Amsterdam, or Bangkok measure themselves.

"I'll send my orderly to the harbourmaster with a note," De Bazzanno told me. "They'll come and collect us in a decent boat. We shall be staying at my family home near La Fenice. I apologise in advance for the building's condition. I was only recently able to reclaim it from the people who occupied it since we lost it in 1797.

Their taste was typically bourgeois. I'm having the whole place redecorated."

I remarked that he had reached quite a height. Ten years ago, as an impoverished artist, he had only dreamed of the world he was now helping to create.

"It's crazy, isn't it?" My observation seemed to sober him. "Yet isn't there an emptiness about it? Doesn't it feel to you, my dear Max, as if it could all fade away tomorrow, like fairy gold? *This* is our time, Max. I doubt we'll have another. We must enjoy it to the full. When we wake up, we could be rotting in some prison or, worse, discover our real selves to be nothing but bank clerks and minor civil servants with cheap ambitions!"

I was a little surprised by this decided change of mood. Only a day or so earlier he had been describing the triumph of a New Rome which would rule the world for millennia. I said that I thought he was being both too self-deprecating and too pessimistic. This, I said, was only what he had honestly earned. "This is what you starved for. What you worked for. These are the rewards of the hard, dangerous, hungry years. Your Duce knows what you are worth."

He leaned forward and kissed me on the cheek. "Well, let us hope you are right. Meanwhile, I suggest you take my advice anyway. After all, what can you lose if I'm wrong? It is how life should always be lived, relishing the moment. Death steals everything but that moment from us. Everything."

Miranda Butter was clearly impressed by this profoundly Latin attitude which to me seemed to carry a certain cargo of self-pity, so unlike our own Slavic soul-searching which contains an intellectual element lacking in the Italian's fiery despair.

"But death," I said, " also presents us with that moment."

At this, my lovely companion almost gasped and placed her hand on mine. Her eyes were hot with tears. "That's so true."

De Bazzanno shrugged and ordered us more cognac. His normally droll face was suffused with emotion so that now he resembled a pantomime horse playing Ibsen. In silence, he became absorbed in the scene beyond the window.

159

"What does Venice mean to you, Prince Max?" The young American woman still habitually used the formal title when we were together in public, though I did not desire it. "Do you, too, have family here?"

I nodded. "In a sense. But what I see now, first and foremost, is one of the legendary unfallen bastions of Christendom, perhaps our last great shield against the Turk! The heroine of a hundred unsuccessful sieges." I looked across the black, jewelled waters to where the lights of gondolas and fishing boats came and went against the misty outlines of the quayside buildings, the queerly angled mooring posts. "She is a marriage of western and eastern civilisation. I believe under Mussolini she will now understand she must do penance for her betrayal of Constantinople in 1453 and take up the banner of Christendom as our defence against the Turk and his co-religionists. I look forward to knowing her better."

My admirer spoke softly. "We'll explore her together. But you must remain my spiritual guide and my teacher. I'm so ignorant of your history."

"Unfortunately for my family," I told her, "we are almost nothing but history." My smile was self-mocking. "And we are not known for our lack of spirituality, either. We are true Russians."

De Bazzanno, pulling himself out of his mood, laughed suddenly, displaying his huge, yellow teeth. "History! We want as little of the past in Italy as possible. Until now Italy has been picturesque ruins, memories of former glory. We have lived off nostalgia and spaghetti for centuries. The new Italy has a place only for the future—the history we ourselves are making today!"

We drank to the future in Krug. We drank to the city, to the nation, to the leader. We drank to the fulfillment of all our most wonderful dreams. In those days, our faith was in a fascism as yet untarnished by the actions of its less disciplined adherents. Real, idealistic fascists, like De Bazzanno, loathed everything that their movement became; a party divided by crude rivalries and guided by an orthodoxy which Mussolini himself always sought to discourage.

But then, in our happy innocence, we drank to our Golden Age.

A little later, a motor launch, carrying a small blackshirt guard of honour and the deputy mayor, came out to take us to the quay. Signora Sarfatti had joined us and sat across from me, every so often offering me a friendly wink. She was completely at ease and radiated authority. I felt uncomfortable, sitting, with my precious luggage, between two stern footsoldiers of the new Italy, but they were eager to oblige us in every way, eventually helping us disembark and carrying our bags to a waiting cart which they proceeded to steer at a trot, with loud whistles of warning, through San Marco's gathering crowds.

To my still befuddled mind, it seemed that somehow we were all shadows—substantial and colourful, perhaps, but nonetheless still only actors in some extravagant movie. This sense of unreality was added to by the expressions on the surrounding faces. The Venetian air itself heightened the contrasts. Grotesque, immobile, animated or familiar, all had a certain theatrical cast. The clothes, though of conventional or modish design, also had something of the quality of stage costumes while the buildings, even the canals and alleys, sustained the impression of enduring artificiality. Even the voices—the organ-grinders, the fiddlers, the jumping jack-sellers, the hawkers of tin toys and cheap scarves and whole ensembles of masks, seemed orchestrated for the stage. We crossed a couple of small, dramatically arching bridges, passed down a zigzag of twitterns, stumbled for a while on a cobbled path running beside a narrow canal over which gaudy washing hung like welcoming flags, and at last entered a small dead-end square smelling strongly of cat urine. Here the cart was brought to a sudden stop and the *fascisti* saluted. De Bazzanno returned their salute, took a bunch of keys from his pocket and inserted a large brass monster into the lock of a rather scruffy looking door made from ancient, iron-bound wood. Light spilled suddenly into the little square and a shrill voice cackled in happy surprise from within. *"Fiorello! Fiorello! Mi figlio!"*

In the doorway an old man appeared. His back was curved with scoliosis but his huge head beamed up at us, his vast mouth displaying his few brownish teeth. His amiable, short-sighted eyes were blood-shot mahogany and his jowls were covered in white stubble. He was dressed in a coarse, brown monk's robe and appeared to be a priest.

161

His resemblance to De Bazzanno was striking. If he lived long enough, no doubt my friend would one day exactly resemble his sire.

Hugging the old man tightly, De Bazzanno introduced us to his father, even as servants appeared, greeting us all with the same nods and grins and carrying the luggage into the house. With warm thanks and ample tips, De Bazzanno dismissed our guard of honour, informed the deputy mayor that he would be calling at the town hall as soon as he was settled in, shook hands, and closed the door on the street.

The house felt to me like a theatre's back-stage haven. I almost expected to find dressing rooms leading off the main passages. It was, in fact, a typical old Venetian house, built around an interior court-yard completely inaccessible and invisible from outside.

The high-ceilinged passages were lit by candles and oil-lamps. They threw our long shadows upon the walls and staircases and the ancient blackened beams. Our shadows continued to dance and shud-der as we followed the two Bazzannos, deep in happy conversation, through a house smelling strongly of the canals outside and for which, over his shoulder, De Bazzanno periodically apologised. His whole attention was focused on his father. I have rarely known two relatives to take such tremendous joy in each other's company. I felt a pang of loss for my own father, whose foolish radicalism had separated us. I assumed them to have been apart for months, but a fondly indulgent Margherita Sarfatti told me it had been only a couple of weeks since Bazzanno had departed. "It is a love affair that has been going on since he was born." She shrugged and offered me a droll wink. "How can I compete?"

Not by nature a discourteous soul, De Bazzanno remembered himself long enough to tell us that he had wanted the house to be ready for guests. "But we have almost a hundred and fifty years of neglect to cope with. They did nothing. They didn't spend a penny on the place."

"A Jewish family," said old De Bazzanno by way of explanation. He shrugged. "Very pleasant people. Nothing wrong with them. But you know how they hate to part with cash."

"We're having electricity, gas, water—everything piped in. And new sewers. And walls have to be repainted. Plastering . . . " De Bazzanno returned his attention to his father.

Old De Bazzanno added: "They were not real Jews. They went to the same church as my aunt. Everyone liked them. They were generous to the church, she said. But not to themselves. Or the house." His shrug was a distorted echo of his son's.

"What happened to them?" I asked Margherita, as we continued to penetrate the warren of tiny passages and rooms. But she shook her head. She had heard something, she said, but she wasn't sure if it was true. She had an idea they had moved to Austria where they had a son. She moved on ahead of us to inspect a faded tapestry.

"They weren't Jews at all, then," interposed Miranda Butter almost aggressively. "Were they? I mean, they were Christians."

"Once a Jew always a Jew," I told her kindly. "In America you have not had our experience of the Children of Abraham, I think."

I would remember those words some years later and understand their full significance only then. At that time, I did not pursue the subject as Margherita had rejoined us with a murmured apology and an enthusiastic diversion on the subject of 14th century Norman tapestry.

Eventually the passages opened out onto a gallery. We were on the first floor, looking down into a large hall where a table was being laid and a fire made. Clearly, the servants had not known when De Bazzanno would return. We crossed the gallery into another wide corridor. We discovered our bedrooms, our bags already there.

Again I felt as if I had entered some Hollywood historical extravaganza. The rooms had huge four-poster beds. Their iron-hard, nameless wood was carved with all kinds of dark animals and plants, with faded gold-leafing and heavy hangings greasy with age, the furniture preserved by the candle-wax, cooking fats and grime of centuries. Mysterious pictures, so dark it was impossible to tell the subject, clung to the walls. A small fire waved from my grate and fat copper lamps guttered in iron sticks mottled with oil and verdigris. My evening clothes had been unpacked and laid out for me. My few other clothes had been put away in a vast armoire. The rest of my possessions—my films and my plans—had not been touched. Nonetheless, I leafed through the rather dog-eared blueprints and notes to make sure no enterprising trainee spy had removed anything. I also checked that my cache of cocaine was in order. I soon discovered with a rush of gratitude that my cousin Shura, as a parting gift, had left me with ten large packets, sealed neatly in waxed paper like grocer's sugar, of the very finest *sneg*. A year's supply even if used with irresponsible abandon! To celebrate, I called Signora Sarfatti and Mandy Butter to my room, and we indulged in a small line or two before dinner, chopped out by Margherita Sarfatti under the gaze of an admiring Miss Butter who had only since our acquaintance become an enthusiast for the life-enhancing powder. De Bazzanno had, at least for the moment, renounced cocaine. I had every sympathy for him. From time to time a little fasting is good for the soul as well as the blood. But he did not like to be reminded of what he had given up, so Signora Sarfatti was delighted to join us in this innocent secret.

Later, we enjoyed a simple meal of tripe soup and fried shellfish while De Bazzanno the Younger, in graphic gestures and with wild laughter, detailed the problems they had had with the flying boat and De Bazzanno the Elder, devoting himself to his dinner in the manner of the aged, occasionally interjecting a polite exclamation. I was again reminded of two comic horses from the old *Funabile*, enjoying a gossipy manger of hay together. At one moment they might break into the mock-philosophical patter for which Ah-Ee and Eeh-Ah were famous when I was a boy in Kiev. The candle flames gave the faces of our female companions new angles and secrets. The servants all had that prematurely wizened appearance of a people with blood so ancient, so little diluted, that they appeared representatives of a different and earlier race altogether.

The Venetians, Signorina Sarfatti (a native of the city) would tell me, not only looked different and spoke differently, they also thought differently. They had, she said, antique minds, full of sophistications and experience unknown to the rest of us; full of strange, uncommon assumptions on matters of health, morality, politics, and even literature.

"What they value is not always what the rest of us value," she said. "The Venetians built their first houses on stilts above the swampy delta islets which in those days were already inhabited by a race whose skills and appearance were not at all human. The two species interbred. Some believe the Venetians are the only survivors of Atlantis. Their inhuman ancestors escaped the deluge which drowned that extraordinarily advanced civilisation. Venice is full of great cathedrals and churches, yet she is still as profoundly pagan as she is practical. Venice will survive any disaster and adapt herself to any changing conditions. She is a city whose principal trade is in illusion. For her, deception really is an art! And a saleable art, at that!"

De Bazzanno was familiar with his mistress's arguments and dismissed them with good humour. "My darling Margherita, the only art Venetians have learned is the art of good living. Everything else is imported. They will trade with anyone. That is the real secret of their enduring supremacy. They honestly believe that making money is a moral pursuit, that gold has an ethical and spiritual value, that a man without profit is a man without honour. These aren't the survivors of Atlantis, dear friends, but of Ur! They are the ancestors of all usurers and merchants. And good luck to them." He signed for her glass to be replenished.

"Fiorello," she crooned, "you tolerate everything and everyone." Her brunette waves tumbled fetchingly across her face.

"It is our greatest Italian virtue, my dear."

"It's the disease for which fascism is the remedy." She was sardonic. Her lips pretended sternness she could not feel towards her lover. "At least, that's what I hear you saying in public."

"One has to use stronger, simpler language in public than one uses in private, Margherita. Fascism balances and moderates our natural tolerance and binds all our qualities of manliness and femininity together in one strong bundle." There was an equally obvious note of self-mockery in his voice when he made such pronouncements.

"There does not," observed Signora Sarfatti dryly, "appear to be a very strong element of femininity bound into our Duce's bundle of faggots."

"You'd be surprised." That was all De Bazzanno would give us.

"These things surely are all a matter of interpretation." Miss Butter's Italian was not as good as her French but it was better than mine, so we had agreed to use French as our common tongue. "What, after all, do the words 'masculine' and 'feminine' mean?"

Such abstractions were too much for us, so we changed to a different subject and had Miss Butter tell us of her native Texas, its cowboys and wild Comanches. She had little direct experience of either, she said, having been educated in Atlanta and raised in Galveston, on the coast. "Which has rather more to do with commerce and shipping."

I had once had political connections in Houston but thought it inappropriate to mention them. Miss Butter was at the naive stage of her own political development, full of a sort of generalised sentimentality towards all lame ducks. Sometimes in private I laughed at her, telling her she could not nurse all the world's walking wounded. But I had no wish to revive arguments on subjects that still aroused my own passions. I wanted to put all my conflicts behind me and begin my career where the Bolshevists had cut it off some ten years earlier.

I reminded myself that I was not a politician but a scientist. Not an actor, but an inventor. In future, my contribution to the human race would be thoroughly practical. I would no longer talk of 'lifting the masses'—I would lift them through my deeds, by example. That was where my own idealism belonged. I think Miss Butter recognised this and it was these qualities in me rather than my political opinions which she found attractive. Aside from my admiration of Mussolini, fear that civil war must soon break out in France and Germany, a consciousness of the general causes of our European malaise and a notion of whom the chief villains were, I expressed few opinions. What my friends wanted to hear from me was not what they already knew. Instead, they wanted my vision of tomorrow where flying cities and vast engineering works brought peace and prosperity to all. A vision which I carried always in my head. I described my notion of a huge airliner which was entirely comprised of wing—a massive flying wing, some thousand yards wide! My steam car, I told Fiorello, on his

166

enquiring, was now a reality in California. My light aircraft were flying in the airforce of the Caid in Marrakech. In France, at a secret hangar near St-Denis, my airship yearned to be airborne, grounded by the squabbling greed of her investors. I had built flying infantry for the Turks and designed a secret weapon for Petlyura in Ukraine. Other ideas of mine, such as the autogyro and the ocean-based aeroplane staging platforms, were realities. It had never been my intention to get rich from these ideas. My first goal was to ease the human burden. Any profit I made was incidental. Again and again Fiorello and Margherita assured me that I was just the type Mussolini wished to recruit for his great army of scholars, scientists, soldiers and engineers. It was his willingness to give such men as myself a chance that made him so great.

My earlier sense of urgency, which had enabled me to sustain myself in Morocco and given me a persuasive motive for returning to Europe had been replaced by a quieter and, I believe, stronger emotion. I wished to take stock of myself as well as the country before I presented myself to *Il Duce*. What was more, I had fallen in love a little, with the delicious Miss Butter, and was soon infatuated, head over heels, with the Sublime Port!

Together, Miss Butter and myself visited Venice's museums and magnificent public buildings, gasping at her astonishing wonders and riches which we came upon often unexpectedly, when rounding a corner of an alley and finding, for instance, the white marble church of Santa Maria dei Miracolli, entering her relatively austere portals to discover a wealth of gold, a feast of murals and pictures and a towering altar which seemed to draw you directly up to heaven. Every square had a character of its own, every bridge opened onto a picture, every garden displayed the orderly beauty of centuries of cultivation, nurtured and shaped to gladden both the eye and the heart.

De Bazzanno had been right—in the daylight, with her bustling business life, her babble of voices, her washing lines and murmuring touts, Venice was nothing but reality. Even along the Grand Canal, where building after building spoke of a magnificent history, where baroque and gothic and Romanesque, Moorish and Byzantine styles stood shoulder to shoulder against any easy definition, there was a domestic ordinariness to her scenes, with people coming and going on a thousand different missions, crossing the bridges, taking the gondolas as others might take buses and taxis, striking bargains, chatting, quarrelling, even as they stood in the little boats which plied constantly between the quays. And yet, in my bones, I knew that at night these same people transformed into creatures that were not quite human. These same locations would be touched by Titania's wand to become scenes from fairyland where sorcery and magic were concrete realities.

Sometimes, when I look back, I feel that I crossed from one version of the world's history into another. At the time, it was clear that I had discovered myself at the nativity of a modern Renaissance, that I was privileged to live in the first years of a period which would be remembered as a Golden Age. Then something went wrong. But I could not anticipate that. I could not predict how the envious, venal and most banal forces of our century would force the planet into a prolonged nightmare: a nightmare from which there now seems no chance of awakening. Perhaps Venice is a gateway from one potential world to another. Perhaps, accidentally, I stepped through that gateway and became a prisoner here, longing for the just, safe, and orderly world I had lost. But in those early weeks I had no such gloomy ideas. My love affair with Miss Butter and with Venice remains amongst my happiest memories.

A city heavy with such a unique history is arrogant but far too well bred to show it. She is narcissistic—infinitely reflected in her own waters—and she is vain. Venice is interested only in herself. She possesses the haughty charm of antique tradition and ancient wealth. Her condescending tolerance is based on the sublime understanding that she has no natural enemies and that the rest of the world, even the Turks, share an instinctive desire to serve her and please her. Venice owns an elusive heart, a mysterious soul. Even in her silences or in the gay music of her many masques and concerts, her theatrical performances, you can sometimes hear the beating of a powerful prehistoric organ, the whisper of ancient arteries, the pulsing of forgotten veins.

Sometimes a faint drift of unnamable colour undulates across a square or passes you on one of the narrow canals. Shadows appear which owe nothing to the position of the sun or the moon.

Her history a mixture of glorious nobility and brutal greed, Venice is the crystallisation of the Mediterranean's fears and desires, offering all the satisfactions for which one ever dared and many which one never imagined. Moreover, with De Bazzanno's own brainchild, the Festival of Fascist Arts, she had become the Mecca for bohemians, especially Italians who found the new Rome a little too austere for their tastes. Cafés and cabarets had sprung up for their entertainment, attracting performers from Berlin, New York, and Athens, from Cairo and Paris.

For all that I despised much of their clientele I still found myself attracted to these places. I had spent my youth in them and received much of my education there, in the company of my cousin Shura or with my beloved friend Count Nicholai Feodorovitch Petroff—my Kolya. I will admit, indeed, that I was addicted to them. Soon Miss Butter was seeing a wholly different side of Italian life from the great public ceremonies of *Il Duce* and the Vatican. Every kind of sexuality was represented and catered for. Every kind of music, from the sweet, old tunes of Vienna and Prague, to the neurotic modern concoctions of Mahler and his arch-collaborator Schoenberg, from the bitter-sweet accordion to the wailing saxophone, harsh Berlin syncopation and syrupy English vibrato; all of which, I was assured, was untypical of Venice, which had been notorious for its lack of nightlife.

These places were also the meeting grounds for people of differing political persuasions and interests and, during that period, for arms dealers anxious that their negotiations be discrete. De Bazzanno informed me that all the big people came to Venice regularly and that no week passed without at least two or three South American governments sending their representatives to shop for guns. The air of the restaurants and cabarets where such transactions took place was very different from the rest of the city and few of the local people welcomed it. The Italian authorities, perceiving Venice as a kind of free port,

169

turned a blind eye to activities which, one way or another, were benefiting them.

In the course of a single evening I overheard plans for arming various Balkan factions and part of a negotiation in which an Algerian businessman was openly bargaining for a consignment of Martini rifles to be used against the French. I have never had any time for those who profit from others' misery and did my best to ignore what was going on.

Miranda Butter, on the other hand, was writing several stories a day and mailing them back to her paper because she was afraid to wire them. I was not sure that the secrecy or the urgency were necessary, especially since her editor in Houston was not greatly interested in the intricate corruptions of modern Europe. He wanted altogether more immediate scandals, with personalities and titles he had heard of.

Meanwhile she continued to interview me and had now decided to write a book about my exploits. "You are, dear Prince, the model of the modern hero."

One evening, in a place called *The Little Gigolo*, where the cabaret was amusing and not too raucous, I was attempting to dissuade her from this idea by insisting that I could not afford to tell her very much about my background for fear of implicating others who were still in Russia.

She was listening with her usual doting attention when our voices were suddenly drowned by a discordant chorus of some Bavarian folksong performed by a group of very drunken Germans over in a corner near the stage. They had been there all evening, engaged with one of the South Americans, and had been drinking heavily. Several of them were clearly homosexual and were openly kissing and cuddling to the amusement, rather than the disgust, of the other patrons.

As the Germans began the umpteenth chorus of their song, a newcomer joined them. He was large and effeminate in a fur-collared black overcoat and a homburg hat a size too small for his head. His back was towards me but was very familiar. I was trying to recall the man when I heard his voice raised in angry German which almost at once turned into near-hysterical Russian, then into Spanish and eventually into broken Italian, all on the same note.

My heart sank. There was no mistaking Sergei Andreyovitch Tsipliakov or his familiar complaints. Clearly his friend of the same sexual persuasion belonged to the German group but had not turned up. The group was far too drunk and careless to be of help in finding him.

I had no great wish to see Seryozha at that time. It was obvious that he was no longer with the ballet, unless as a choreographer, for he was getting fat. As his ruined face turned away, his self-indulgent jowls emphasising his lugubrious dismay, I tried to escape his eye, but he had seen me. A hand flew to his mouth. His expression changed to one of absolute joy and his voice rang through the room. "Dimka! Dimka, darling! Dear heart, they told me you had gone back to Peter and were working for the Okhrana! Are you really a secret policeman now, Dimka, darling? Were you one in Paris? Oh, the stories I've heard! What *ever* happened to you? Why did you abandon me? Dear heart, I was so good to you!"

My sole consolation was that my embarrassing friend spoke in Russian, one of the few languages Miss Butter did not understand.

He engulfed me. His wet lips met mine. A small-time Judas.

PHOCAS
Remy de Gourmont
Translated by Brian Stableford

THE PRAETOR HIMSELF gave the most precise instructions to the decurion charged with arresting Phocas. That magistrate, Aurelius by name, was a serious, honest, and intelligent man. A great legal expert, he would not abuse his science, nor statutes, nor edicts to crush with a uniform and traditional rigour the criminals committed to his tribunal. Entirely to the contrary—profiting from the freedom which judges then had to decide according to their conscience, he liked to forget the hardened imperative of the penal laws. More than once he subjected the miserly and inflexible rich to heavy fines, while admitting that he was himself guilty of theft, on the grounds that the need was extreme, declaring that "there is a certain degree of misery which authorises one who has nothing to take from one who possesses everything." Such judgments would seem scandalous to the refined morality of today, arousing indignation—but in the 4th century, at Sinope(1), in the province of Pont, where these events came to pass, men denuded of high principles freely accepted the kind of justice that Aurelius dispensed; annoyed, but fully convinced that to let a human creature die of hunger is as much a crime as to strangle him with clean hands, they would pay the fines—after which, to avoid further just thefts, they would give to the poor of their own free will.

Christian ideas had penetrated little by little into Sinope, as they had in the greater part of the Roman Empire, but not yet under their true name. The name of Christianity was still detested, and the new religion was widely regarded with horror, mixed with dread—but in advance of its dogmas, the principles of justice and pity had crept like lame beggars through the gates of the town, the words murmurously repeated by people taken by surprise.

Of true Christians, instructed as to the birth, death, and resurrection of the Nazarene, there were very few in Sinope, all of them among the weavers of the outlying districts, the peasants of the countryside, and the bondsmen of the great estates. It was rumoured that the chief among them—the most fully-instructed and, in consequence, the most dangerous—was a man named Phocas, a gardener by profession: a freeman who cultivated a smallholding and sold its produce at the town gate.

Thus, by a strange contradiction, the people of Sinope—who loved justice—hated those who were the living examples of justice. Even Aurelius, the helpful judge, lost his temper and swore by the infernal gods as soon as the name of Christ was pronounced in front of him. Meanwhile, edicts arrived from Rome which commanded the searching out and condemnation of all the followers of the new religion. Aurelius read the edicts that were sent to him by the prefect of the province and, for the first time in his life, found a certain happiness in reading an imperial edict.

* * *

Having summoned Amasius, the officer in charge of the decury of soldiers employed to search out criminals, Aurelius commanded him to seize Phocas and bring him to Sinope, alive or dead. These instructions were given to him, written on a tablet of wax: "Phocas, Christian, scorner of the Gods, enemy of the emperor and the Roman people. Notorious bandit and guileful conspirator, chief of a band of cruel rogues, he is also a very accomplished magician. He knows the mysterious art of killing at a distance, either by frightful combinations of elements, or by signs, or by a secret compact with infernal spirits. You must approach him carefully and deceptively; go there in danger of your life, but go with the salutation of the Republic."

Amasius considered these instructions, chose a few dependable men—veterans of the barbarian wars—and the little troop immediately set out (the police made haste in those days). They set out early in the morning, slightly uncertain of their direction because the exact location where Phocas conspired to water his salad-vegetables was unknown. They decided to make straight for the bottom of a small valley which hollowed out a clearing of grass within the forest, to make enquiries of the woodcutters.

Amasius, a brave decurion who had slain more Goths than he had teeth in his jaws, imagined that Phocas must be hidden away in a shadowy cavern or some other inaccessible lair, and he anticipated that his quest would be difficult and distressing—but the weather was pleasant and his men were brave. We shall be able to sleep in the open for as many nights as necessary, he thought, under the protection of the goddess with twelve breasts.(2)

Having followed a stream that flowed through the valley that divided the forest of Sinope, the soldiers found themselves, a little before mid-day, facing a small hut covered with roses, with a pleasant garden behind. Amasius saw no cause for suspicion; he knocked at the door in order to ask for hospitality.

The door opened and a man appeared. He was clothed like a peasant, in a short tunic which left his arms and knees bare. His hair was short and his beard long. His manner was tired and gentle. His eyes, behind their lowered lids, were blue and a little vague.

The man seemed to be about fifty years old, but his soul was certainly young, for he expressed great pleasure at the fact that Providence had brought strangers to his door.

"Come in, come in! Soldiers, are you? Have the Goths returned?"

"No," said Amasius, "but we seek a bandit more ferocious than the sons of the Amales(3): a Christian, a scorner of the gods"—he was quoting his commission—"a magician who knows the arcane art of killing at a distance . . . "

"There are no magicians around here," Phocas said, "but the country is full of thieves. They do not even wait until my vegetables are fully developed before they tear them up. They double my labour, requiring me to start planting all over again—but what can you do? If they take my vegetables from me, it's because they have need of them—perhaps a greater need than mine. I forgive them and I allow them to get away."

"You're too indulgent," said Amasius. "The Emperor, who is just, has resolved to punish the bandit-leader—for it must surely be their leader that I'm ordered to find."

"What is his name?" asked Phocas.

"His name?" Amasius consulted his tablets. "Phocas."

"Phocas!" said the poor gardener. "But I know him—he lives close by. He's a Christian."

"I must find him," said Amasius.

"Good," said Phocas. "A Christian, absolute and untamed! A scorner of the gods! I'll take you to him myself, before sunset. You're very welcome. Phocas! Never fear, he'll appear before your very eyes and be delivered into your hands. But in the meantime, while you're my guests, hospitality obliges me to give you a meal. Bread, and vegetables from my garden—those which Phocas has left in place."

"Is it Phocas who has stolen your salads from you?" Amasius asked.

"The very same," Phocas said.

"We shall not spare him."

"I certainly hope so," said Phocas. He went on: "And for guests, I keep a jar of Asian wine buried out there in the earth. I never drink it myself, because the water from the stream is so good . . . "

"We'll drink it!" the soldiers said. "I certainly hope so," said Phocas.

The soldiers and the gardener sat down at the table. Phocas, at the insistence of Amasius, drank a little wine and became a little excited.

"I love you, my friends," he cried to them, "You are my brothers, as all men are! Often, when I rest from my labour—when my lettuces, having been watered, fall asleep like all good little creatures in the peace of the night—I dream of the future happiness of humankind, the children of God. I often dream, too, of the immediate happiness that each of us can find within himself, if he lives in love, justice and charity. Do you love one another? If your brother is cold, do you give him a place at your hearth? If he is hungry, do you sit him down at your table? If he is ignorant, do you instruct him? If he is wretched, do you make him happy by being happy for him? The times are changing. I see a new age coming. Clad all in white like a morning sky, he is coming over the sea, and the clouds become calm as he passes, and the great birds which soar over the waters make a procession of love . . . He is coming; I see him! He has the clear eyes of a messenger bearing good news; he sings a hymn of joy; the beating of his wings has a calming influence . . . He is coming, I see him! The luminous archangel arrives among us . . . love, love, implacable will be the strength of love! Love men in spite of themselves, love them until your love tames them, transforms them and refashions them in the image of the One who, though all-powerful, chose to die . . . "

The soldiers were moved, although they did not really understand. Amasius would have liked to hear more of this talk of love, which was more intoxicating than the wine of Asia—but, faithful to the word of his command, he thought of Phocas the abominable bandit, and he made the effort to say: "Master, I will come to see you again, for your discourse has aroused me as I have never been aroused before by the most beautiful rhetoric . . . I shall never forget you. I have heard tell of a philosopher called Socrates, or Plato—I don't know which—that my centurion venerates like a god . . . You are my Socrates . . . Oh! your words have made me a better man . . . Never have I heard words like them . . . "

He trailed off before renewing his effort: "And this Phocas?"

The poor gardener rose to his feet and said: "I am Phocas."

"You? Master, has the Asian wine made your head spin?"

"I am Phocas."

By means of wax tablets, and a bronze plaque which affirmed the gratitude owed to him by the town of Antioch for his courage in a time of plague, Phocas proved that he was Phocas. Convinced, Amasius murmured some words of contempt for the stupidity of the Praetor Aurelius—and then he took Phocas away. The night was not far advanced when they re-entered Sinope.

* * *

On the following morning, Phocas was judged. The people, forewarned, gathered in a great crowd. At the sight of the bandit, the Christian, the blasphemer who hated the gods, they let out joyous cries:

"Put him to death! Put him to death!" cried the people.

Aurelius, after some minor tortures and an investigative hearing, during which Phocas had admitted his crime of being a Christian, pronounced his sentence: "Send him to the beasts!"

And the people repeated: "To the beasts with the Christian! To the beasts, to the beasts!"

Shortly before midday, the circus was opened and Phocas appeared in the arena. Careless of the howls of the happy crowd, without any thought of wild beasts or bulls, he cried in a loud voice: "I am a Christian!"

Then he fell to his knees in prayer, and waited.

It was a bull which came out of the subterranean cage. The beast descended upon its quarry, pierced him with a thrust of its horn, threw him into the air, then moved away.

Phocas fell back amid a rain of blood. He had not yet lost consciousness. Clutching the belly from which his entrails were dangling, he managed to resume his kneeling position and continued his prayer.

At that moment he saw, next to the door of the cage, Amasius and his soldiers. They had been posted there, swords at the ready, in order to chase the victim back to the centre of the arena if he sought to flee towards the cellars. Recognising his friends, he gathered his strength and raised himself up, lifting a heavy hand in order to send them a sign of love and farewell.

The soldiers, who had been touched by a desire for glory and mystery, looked at one another for a moment. Then, as one, they leapt forward and ran towards Phocas, crying: "We are the sons of Phocas! We are Christians!"

It made for a wonderful occasion, which the people of Sinope remembered for a long time. The lions and the panthers were let loose, and instead of a single victim a full dozen were done to death. The eyes of the women of the city drank in the sight of their blood.

NOTES
(1) Sinope was an important Greek colony on the north coast of Asia Minor. After a period of independence it became part of the kingdom of Pontus. Once absorbed into the Roman Empire—after long resistance—it went into a long decline. It was the native city of the renowned cynic philosopher Diogenes—which may help to explain its frequent occurrence in Gourmont's historical *contes cruels*. Its site is now occupied by the port of Sinop in northwest Turkey.

(2) The Roman goddess Diana, the equivalent of the Greek Artemis, was thus depicted at the famous temple of Ephesus (one of the Seven Wonders of the Ancient World), in order to emphasize her role as a symbol of motherhood. Diana was the patron goddess of the Roman plebeians, from whose ranks Amasius had presumably been recruited.

(3) The Amales were one of the "royal families" (or, more prosaically, tribes) of the Ostrogoths; the most famous of the "sons of the Amales" was Theodoric the Great, the founder of the Gothic kingdom in Italy, which inherited the ruins of the western Roman Empire in the fifth century.

THE EVENKI
Eugene Dubnov
Translated from the Russian by the author
and John Heath-Stubbs

I.

I OWE MY penetration into the enigma of the Evenki to the following comrades: comrade Rusalka, who set me the task of giving a talk
on the theory of evolution; the author of the article on evolution in
the Great Soviet Encyclopedia (and likewise to the authors of various
other articles and ethnological monographs which I read); assistant
lecturer Abramkina and my fellow students Sinelnikov, Vladimirov,
Abrikosov and Yosio Sato. I am also indebted to Engels-Marx and
Grandpa Lenin who clarified completely for me the profound ontological significance of the Evenki phenomenon in history and its impli-
cations for not only the destinies of the Party and Government but all
the Soviet people and mankind as a whole.

But let me not anticipate. It all began like this. I had been preparing the talk which I was to give at our next seminar on the history of
Marxism-Leninism. In this talk, Oktyabrina Ivanovna Rusalka, assistant lecturer in our Faculty of Philosophical Sciences, had directed

me to refute the fallacies of western reactionary pseudo-philosophers concerning the so-called divine origin of evolution. I decided, for a start, to acquaint myself with the general outlines of the subject and the bibliography appended to the relevant article in the Great Soviet Encyclopedia.

But turning over the pages in the 48th volume in my search for an article on evolution, I came across, on page 294, an article on the Evenki. The word "Evenki" in itself caught my attention immediately. The thing is, before comrade Rusalka—she of the fiery-red hair and inflammatory glance—had persuaded me to transfer to the Faculty of Philosophy, I had been studying in the Faculty of Foreign Languages where I was particularly interested in Celtic philology. Indeed, the very title of my dissertation there was "Some still unsolved problems of Old and Middle Welsh in the light of Celtic mythology, considered with reference to the class struggle, forces of production, and industrial relations." (I hope it's not too immodest to mention here that this opuscule of mine, although in many ways half-baked undergraduate work, was immediately published in the journal *Problems of Linguistic Science*; moreover, it was through it that the Rector of the University, the Secretary of the Young Communist League, the Party Representative, and comrades from an organization well-known for its concern for education, showed a special interest in me and designated Oktyrabrina Ivanovna to direct my destiny.)

And so, armed with a not-insignificant array of philological apercus, I straightaway began to ponder the etymology of the word "Evenki." Isn't there—I asked myself—a direct connection with the well-known Addanc of the Lake, the Black Serpent of the Carn in the Welsh mythological tales? (Of course, the double "d" in Welsh represents a voiced "th" sound, and this in Russian could easily become a "v".) And the further I read the article in the Encyclopedia, the more carried away I became with the subject under discussion.

How is it, thought I, that such a remarkable people, whose very name, originating as it is did in Celtic antiquity, bears witness to their deep roots and wide folk-wanderings, should still remain so little studied in our country? I, for example, had known virtually nothing about them until I by chance came across this article.

The religion of the Evenki—I read on—was shamanism, and the word "shaman" itself came into Russian from the Evenki language: the Evenki, therefore, had made their contribution to our language and literature. In the 19th century, almost all the Evenki living in the Russian territory became nominally Christian; this, too, was all very right and proper, being historically progressive in relation to shamanism. The use of the Latin alphabet was introduced among them in 1931 and was replaced in 1936 by the Cyrillic alphabet: that is to say, the Evenki people rejected western orthography, having decided for themselves, in the words of Bogdan Khmelnitsky, the 17th century Ukrainian leader, "forever with Russia, forever with the Russian people!" The fact that the noun in the Evenki language has 13 cases evinces the astonishing creativity of that people, whilst the multiplicity of the alternative names for the Evenki (e.g., Tungus, Orochen, Kile, Lamut, etc.) demonstrates their wide diffusion and ethnic diversity.

But gradually I began to ask myself: why should one people need so many names? Would it be such a good thing, after all? Wouldn't it create confusion when one had to fill in the "nationality" entry in official papers? Moreover, might it not be possible that this very wealth of nomenclature was aimed at misleading the relevant authorities? For instance, supposing a decree were to be issued forbidding the Evenki to leave their own Evenki Autonomous Region? "What are you doing in Moscow instead of being on the banks of the Nizhnyaya Tunguska—by all tokens you would seem to be an Evenk!"—"No, I'm not an Evenk—I've even got it written down in my passport—I'm an Orochen." Or else: in response to the wishes of the Evenki proletariat, peasantry and intelligentsia, it has been decided to allow the Evenki people to engage in permanent voluntary labor on the construction of a Magadan-Warsaw pipeline. "And you—why are you engaged in hare-coursing instead of laboring on the pipeline?"—"Because I'm a Tungus: here is my passport, see for yourself." You know what that sort of thing could lead to! Yes, there is definitely something fishy about it. And why does such a seemingly backward people want so many cases to its noun when even we Russians get along perfectly well with no more than six, while the so-called developed western nations, such as the English, have two at most? All this cannot fail to make one think. And, what's more, isn't it odd that first of all the Evenki adopted the Latin alphabet and a mere five years later switched to the Cyrillic? Obviously they were waiting to see which way the wind blew: by 1936 it had become clear to everyone that the Soviet State was here to stay, and even the Entente countries had ceased to hope for the success of an armed intervention. But were not these very countries, in 1931, wooing the Evenki with their Latin alphabet in order to create a fifth column? And if one were to dig deeper into history, might one not find that the adoption itself by the Evenki of Orthodox Christianity, as well as the infiltration of cult words from their language into Russian, represented a subtle attempt at a long-range subversive activity?

Forgetting all about my projected talk on evolution, I went straight from the faculty library to the Leninka and spent the rest of the day there until the Library closed. By that time, my first vague surmises had been completely confirmed (my intuition never deceives me—and later on the Kremlin comrade himself was to say that I possessed a good ideological nose). There was no possible room for doubt: the Evenki, a people unusually gifted and destined for great things, had taken a wrong turn.)

The rest of the week I devoted to a thorough preparation for my talk, which was due to be delivered in the third period on Monday morning.

The first period was devoted to language laboratory. It was during this that I came to understand the direct link between the supposedly far-off Evenki tribe and our own colleagues who are all around us every minute of the day. This discovery I made toward the end of the lesson, while Bella Izrailevna Abramkina, our teacher, was correcting Sinelnikov: "It's not 'boss' but 'both'; it's not 'puss' but 'purse'." All of a sudden, I noticed a strange resemblance between pupil and teacher. There could be no doubt of it—the author of that anthropological article I'd read was quite right when he stated that "their features are so characteristic that an experienced observer would almost always

184

recognize an Evenk."

I extracted from my bag a thick exercise book with the notes I had been taking in the Lenin Library and started to compare the description of the typical Evenki physiognomy with that of Abramkina and Sinelnikov.

"Hair and eye color dark"—correct. "Eyes remarkably expressive"—that tallied too. "Nose rather large, with quivering nostrils"—just so. "Lips frequently thick"—yes, indeed!

"Tolya," I whispered to Sinelnikov when he sat down, "admit it, I won't tell anybody, you are an Evenk, aren't you?"

He became extremely agitated, turned crimson, and began to stammer in reply. "I'm . . . n-nothing of the sort . . . my identity card shows me as . . . R-russian." "All right, all right," I calmed him down, "so Russian you are—forever with Russia, forever with the Russian people, as the saying goes—what has it to do with me—I merely asked out of curiosity." But things were becoming clear to me, and I decided to scrutinize closely my fellow students and teachers with a view to their possible Evenki connections.

In the very beginning of the next period—an introductory lecture on Psychology given by the Head of the Department, Leontyev, himself—I noticed something happening on either side of me.

To my right, Yosio Sato, scion of the Japanese proletariat, was taking an object from his pocket and presenting it to Yuri Vladimirov. It was a piece of foreign chewing gum. To my left Valeri Abrikosov was eagerly watching them, obviously hoping for a bit of it too. As the gum disappeared into Vladimirov's mouth, Abrikosov whispered to me to find out if Sato hadn't got one more bit. With an apologetic smile, Yosio said that this was his last. Then Abrikosov asked me to see if Vladimirov wouldn't let him have a go when he'd finished chewing. I passed the message on, and Vladimirov nodded in assent. This kind of toadying to western consumer goods cut me to the quick, and I was just about to tell Abrikosov off very sternly when, as if for the first time, I noticed his hair. I might have guessed!—I reproached myself, as this phase flashed into my memory: "curly-haired Evenki not infrequently occur."

"What would your nationality be, Valera?" I asked tactfully.

Like Sinelnikov before him, he became distinctly flustered and started to mutter something about "fascist inquisitions." Having done with him, I turned to look at Vladimirov and Sato. With Yura Vladimirov I wasn't at all sure: his nose had every appearance of being snub, his hair seemed smooth and of chestnut color, his cheekbones looked prominent, and his eyes gave the impression of being of a light hue, too. But having had a closer look at his hands, I noticed the thick dark hairs protruding from under his cuffs. Such excessive hirsuteness in a supposedly native-born Russian struck me as anomalous, and my lips, of their own accord, silently mouthed: "body hair tends to be luxuriant."

"Listen here, Yura." I leaned toward him and pointed to his wrists. "See how hairy you are—aren't you an Evenk—or at least half a one at least?"

"Wouldn't be surprised!" he was forced to admit, taking the gum out of his mouth and passing it on through me to Abrikosov.

Satisfied now, I began to scrutinize the Head of the Department's typically Slav features—and then it came to me that he was saying some very odd things.

"It should be clear to all of us that thought by its very nature is non-material," opined Leontyev, pacing up and down in front of the class. "But in that case, just what is it? And how can non-material thought be the product of the material brain?" "Yura," I turned to Vladimirov, "what is he saying things like that for? He'll get a rocket—and quite right, too!"

"Oh no, he won't," Vladimirov replied. "He's got a name, and besides, he's an old man, his eccentricities will be overlooked."

Everything now fell into place. It was a conspiracy. They, these Evenki, having misdirected their inventive powers in an ideologically erroneous way, had also drawn in other, purely Russian people like Leontyev—and who knows who else besides! This they must have done in order the better to conceal their ethnic ambitions, the better to act the shaman in our midst, the better to impose their cult on us and recruit for it ever fresh neophytes.

History itself had assigned me the task of unmasking them—and had given me, in my forthcoming talk at the seminar, an exceptionally favorable opportunity.

"A talk on the place of Evolutionary Theory in Marxist-Leninist doctrine will be given by Nikanor Khoroborenko," announced Oktyabrina Ivanovna, and I came up to the table without any papers or notes.

"Comrades," I began, "I would like first of all to speak my mind on the question of nationality. There are among us comrades belonging to a tribe whose homeland is somewhere else. I will name no names—everybody knows who they are, and here not even what is entered as their nationality on their identity cards will help them. By now each one of you should have understood what people I am talking about, and I won't drop any further hints. We, comrades, must make sure that the teleological forces of this people shall be directed creatively rather than destructively. It is with deep concern that I am obliged to reveal that representatives of the aforementioned nation are, under our very noses, endeavoring to curry favor with the West, appearing in the role of cosmopolitan peddlers of a way of life alien to us and in general attempting to bring into our frame of ideas their existentially subversive activity. Furthermore, they have already succeeded in winning over some of us—and even some of our teachers, who have become, as we all witnessed only a few minutes ago, the involuntary carriers of their shamanism. And, speaking of evolution—the subject about which I have been assigned to talk by comrade Rusalka—we all know, comrades, that ontogenesis recapitulates philogenesis, but is it clear to every one of us that ethnically, too, nations evolve in a cosmogonic manner. I ask each of you here present to look into your hearts and examine them in the light of the national standard of ethnogenesis."

I paused and turned to Oktyabrina Ivanovna. "And you, comrade Rusalka, with your, as it would outwardly seem, ideologically opulent body, ask yourself whether its depths do not serve as a receptacle and conductor for the ideas of a people who have betrayed the so-called comrade Leontyev might call their psychocratic essence?"

And would you believe me, the moment that I said this, Oktyabrina Ivanovna wrung her hands, gave a little whimper, and ran out of the room.

"That is the end of my talk," I said and, without looking at anybody, calmly returned to my seat.

After this events began to develop at a really phenomenal rate.

Vladimirov had hardly the time to say "Bravo!" when the door of the classroom opened and in walked our Party Representative. "Comrade Khoroborenko," he said, "can I have a word with you?"

II.

A car stood by the faculty entrance. Out of it stepped an officer who saluted me. "Colonel Evenkov," he said, "detailed to transport you."

He turned to our Party Representative and uttered a strange word that sounded like "munnukan." The Party Representative clicked his heels and replied, in the same crisp military way: "pagluk." After this he gave me a fatherly pat on the shoulder and went back into the faculty building.

I could not see where we were going, because the curtains of the car windows were drawn, but from the general direction and short duration of the journey I made a guess. And again my intuition did not let me down. The sentries at the Kremlin gates stood to attention and saluted, their eyes bulging with respect. And when we came to the grand staircase, who should be running down it but comrade Rusalka, all beaming with happiness and stretching out her hand. But I noticed that she was dressed rather oddly—in a gray tight-fitting costume with ears and a little tail.

"Here he is, our hero," she said, "quick, you're expected"—and already she was leading me by the hand up the stairs.

At the massive cedar wood doors she halted, looked herself over, adjusted her ears and tail, and knocked. "Welcome." From within came a voice that I immediately recognized: it belonged to the head of that same organization well known for its concern for education which I have already mentioned. I had often heard that voice on the radio.

And no sooner had we entered the huge salon than the owner of the voice himself came toward us, dressed in the same gray tight-fitting costume as Oktyabrina, only with bigger ears and fluffier tail.

"We have been watching you, comrade Khoroborenko, for some time," he said, "and your ideological acumen has made a very good impression on us. The fact that you on your own, without anybody's assistance, have discovered the Evenki phenomenon and penetrated to the heart of it, speaks for itself. The Party and Government, following my recommendation, have appointed you to the post of Evenkologist General of the Soviet Union. Comrade Rusalka, from now on exclusively at your disposal, in a minute will acquaint you with our Kremlin wildlife sanctuary. Are there any questions you want to ask?"

"If I may make so bold, comrade Kremlin-comrade," I hazarded, "I would like to ask about two unfamiliar words which colonel Evenkov and our Party Representative exchanged and which comrade Rusalka likewise uttered just as we came in."

"Comrade Khoroborenko, open your exercise book at the very beginning of its third section, where at 17:16 hours on Tuesday last, in the Lenin Library, you copied out a quotation from a book by General Dragunsky entitled *The Evenki*."

I took the exercise book out of my briefcase, found the right page, and read there: "The hare ('munnukan,' 'pagluk') was hunted mainly by the Evenki who dwelt around the headwaters of the Nizhnyaya Tunguska . . . "

"Is everything clear now?"

"Almost," I said, "but why the hare, of all creatures?"

"To this question you will shortly receive a reply." He smiled and led Oktyabrina and me up to a curtained wall. As soon as we approached it, the curtains parted, revealing large glass doors and beyond them open fields, gardens, and woods.

Oktyabrina again took me by the hand, and we went out through the doors to the top of a staircase, at the bottom of which the woodland track began.

And then, all of a sudden, a few yards ahead, a hare jumped out of the bushes, skipped onto the pathway and stopped, as though waiting for us.

We came up to it. "Well, who is this?" asked Oktyabrina.

I gave the hare a closer look, and its face seemed familiar—especially the beard and moustache. "Give me a clue," I begged her.

"This is Friedrich Karlovich," she prompted, and I completed the name gleefully: "Marx-Engels!"

She wagged a roguish finger at me, and the hare likewise shook its head, half in jest, half in reproach. I had another look at its beard and corrected myself: "Engels-Marx!" It smiled benignly, made a gesture of greeting with a forepaw and said: "When your youth and inexperience, comrade Khoroborenko, are taken into account, your initial confusion is forgivable. We also know what brought you here—and your comrade-superiors have done the correct thing in directing you to the Socialist Classics. Allow me then to quote an excerpt from my letter to Karl Friedrichovich on the Evenki question, written in May 1853: 'The Evenki are essentially a small nomad tribe, and it is now clear to me that the so-called sacred writings of the Evenki are nothing more than the record of their ancient tribal traditions, modified by the early separation of the Evenki from their ethnically related neighbors.' And apart from this, as I wrote in my letter to an unknown correspondent on April 19, 1890, 'we owe too much to the Evenki. To say nothing of Heine and Borne, Marx was of pure Evenki stock; Lassalle was an Evenk. Many of our best people are Evenki. My friend Victor Adler who is at present in a Vienna prison paying for his devotion to the cause of the proletariat, Eduard Bernstein, editor of the London *Sozial Demokrat*, Paul Singer, one of the best men in the Reichstag— people of whose friendship I am proud, are all Evenki! Have I not been turned into an Evenk myself by the baiting of the press?"

He paused and gave me a quizzical look.

"Of course you have!" I hastened to reply, and only at that point did the meaning of what had been said begin to dawn on me.

"Then, that is to say that both you, Friedrich Karlovich, and you,

Karl Friedrichovich, are . . . " I muttered with a faltering tongue. But the creature did not stay to listen: it gave a leap and a bound and vanished into the tall grasses.

"Come back!" I shouted, but there was no answer.

"What is going on here, comrade Rusalka, and where have the Socialist Classics hopped away to?" I asked querulously.

"Now, now," she smiled her enigmatic smile and waggled her ears, "come and you shall see." And indeed, the moment we got to that spot where the hare had vanished into the grass, it jumped out again—and there it was, on the path in front of us.

"Comrade Engels-Marx." I was overjoyed. "So you're back!"

"Have a closer look," said Oktyabrina, "and stop making mistakes—or you'll go ideologically blind."

Of course—it came to me in a flash—to whom else could this twinkle in the eye, this bald pate and this little pointed beard belong!

"Grandpa Lenin," I whispered with awe.

"He it is, in his very person, Vladimir Ilyich," Oktyabrina confirmed, proud of my achievement, while Grandpa was already proclaiming in the voice of a railway station announcer: "Citizens Evenki leaving for the Middle East! Your train 'Moscow-Siberia' is waiting at the platform."

My bewildered look must have struck him as comic, for he burst out laughing. "Don't worry, comrade Khoroborenko, you'll understand eventually. As early as 1903, I write that 'unity between the Evenki and the non-Evenki proletariat is necessary for a successful struggle against anti-Evenkism, that despicable attempt of the exploiting classes to exacerbate racial particularism.'" He paused and asked: "Any questions?"

Feeling diffident, I glanced at Oktyabrina, but she nodded encouragement. "If I may presume, Vladimar Ilyich, I would like to know why all the comrades here look so . . . not your usual selves but as if you were hares?"

"Hasn't this been explained to you yet? Don't the words 'munnukan' and 'pagluk' mean anything to you?"

"They are the Evenki names for the hare," I said. "But the direct connection between them and your masquerade costume—if I may so term it—still escapes me."

His eyes twinkled still more. "Tell me now, comrade Nikanor—I can call you by your first name, can't I?—which Evenki tribes hunted the hare—whose territory marched with theirs?"

"Why," I immediately recalled the notes in my exercise book, "their neighbors were the Russians on the Nizhnyaya Tunguska."

"And on what other river?"

"Excuse me, I'll just look it up. I've got it all written down." I hastily produced my exercise book and read out: " . . . hunted mainly by the Evenki who dwelt around the headwaters of the Nizhnyaya Tunguska and the Lena."

"There you are, you know it yourself. And what's my alias?"

"Comrade Lenin!"

"That is the connection. I adopted this alias in memory of my Evenki mother who hailed from the headwaters of the Lena."

"So you, comrade Ulyanov-Lenin, are yourself half-Evenki," I blurted out. "And Marx is an Evenk, and Engels has been turned into an Evenk by the press!"

But he was already far away, full pelt, only his little fluffy scut flashing among the ripened ears of corn.

Everything swirled in front of my eyes, my legs gave way, and I collapsed onto the path, having involuntarily (this is the last thing that I remember) butted comrade Rusalka in the stomach with my head.

III.

At present I am resting, recuperating and waiting until the international situation changes for the better. Oktyabrina Ivanovna, dressed as a nurse, visits me twice a week and asks me how I'm feeling. Once a month she takes me to see the Kremlin comrade who himself wears, on these occasions, a doctor's white gown. He asks me whether I have met any more hares lately, whether I am thinking a lot about the Classics of Marxism-Leninism or about the Evenki and whether I dream about the rivers Lena and Nizhnyaya Tunguska. If I happen to ask him or Oktyabrina Ivanovna when I shall be able to take up my post of Evenkologist General, they change the subject and begin talking about the weather or nature. In fact, I haven't met any more hares, although I take a stroll around the grounds every day. As far as I can tell, I am quite alone in this Kremlin wildlife sanctuary: although sometimes I seem to see around me the silhouettes of people, they vanish into thin air before I have time to come up to them.

My room is sunny, the food is good and rich in vitamin content, and my sheets are changed regularly.

My own explanation for this peculiar alteration in my fortunes and in the behavior of Oktyabrina Ivanovna and the Kremlin comrade goes like this. They must from the start have overestimated my psychological resilience, failing to foresee the traumatic effect my conversations with Engels-Marx and Grandpa Lenin would have on me. Moreover, the international situation has become graver. This was made clear to me from a copy of a newspaper left as if accidentally by Oktyabrina Ivanovna and open at the foreign news page. Reading there an article about the whipping up of tension in the Middle East, I could not fail to recall Vladimir Ilyich's words about the Evenki supposedly leaving for that area. I haven't yet completely got everything straight, but one thing is clear to me: we cannot afford to let our Evenki out until the situation there stabilizes. In the meantime, as Vladimir Ilyich prophetically indicated, all our Evenki migrants shall be gathered together and returned to their own Autonomous Region.

I don't lose hope nor let my spirits become dejected. I am confident that my post is waiting for me, and as soon as I have fully recovered and the international situation has improved, I shall be called upon. One day comrade Rusalka before my very eyes will tear off her fancy dress—and underneath her silly nurse's cap will be those familiar ears, and underneath her uniform, all the rest of the hare costume. And the Kremlin comrade to whom she will conduct me, in his turn, will stop pretending to be a doctor but will instead show me his silky little scut and say: "Pagluk-munnukan, your time has arrived, comrade Khoroborenko, the Evenki question can wait no longer."

NIGHT LIBRARY

The Library: 3: NIGHT LIBRARY
Zoran Zivkovic

I SHOULDN'T HAVE gone to the movie first. If I'd known it would last almost two hours, I'd have gone to the library beforehand. I might have felt silly with several books on my lap during the movie, but I doubt anyone would have noticed. As it was, around 7:30 p.m. I began to squirm in my seat. I kept turning my left wrist towards the screen so I could see my watch. Although gripping, the plot seemed longer than it should have been. I was tempted to leave before the end, but since I was sitting in the middle of the row, it would have been too awkward.

When the movie finally ended at ten to eight, I hurried out of the theater. I received several reproachful glances and heard muffled complaints as, apologizing, I cut my way through the moviegoers who were closer to the exit. If I quickened my pace, I might still make it. The library was not far from the movie theater. It closed at eight, but I was a frequent visitor. I could probably count on a bit of forbearance from the employees.

Everything would have been different, of course, if it hadn't been Friday. Saturday and Sunday, the library would be closed, meaning that if I failed, I would have nothing to read over the weekend, a possibility that wasn't at all pleasing. Since I live alone, I am inevitably faced with an abundance of free time that has to be filled with something. Long ago I discovered that reading was much more useful and pleasant than dulling my senses in front of the television.

The threat of spending the next two days in front of the television, filled with frustration and self-reproach, forced me into a run. Running wasn't easy, however, because it had started to snow while I was at the movie. Driven by the wind, the large, thick flakes fell at a slant, hitting me in the face as I rushed forward. I finally had to open my umbrella, holding it in front of me to ward off the snow. This slowed me down since I couldn't see where I was going. Luckily, I knew the way and in such weather there weren't many people in the street.

I reached the library at three minutes after eight. Looking through the glass door, I read the time on the large clock hanging from the ceiling in the foyer. The lights were still on, but if the door was locked not even my close relationship with the librarians would be of any help. I grabbed the cold doorknob apprehensively and pushed. I couldn't help but sigh in relief when the door opened. I entered quickly, turned to shake off the snow coating my umbrella, and then closed the door behind me.

I spent a few moments in the foyer cleaning the snow from my hair and stamping my feet on the doormat to remove bits of slush. I also took out a handkerchief and wiped off the water streaming down my glasses. I put my umbrella in the brass stand next to the door, then rushed up the narrow staircase to the main library area.

It was quite warm in the building, causing my cold glasses to fog up as I climbed the stairs. When I entered the large room illuminated by neon lights, I had to take them off again and wipe them. Even though I am extremely near-sighted, I could move forward as I wiped my glasses since there were no obstacles on the wide, dark-red carpet before me. The tables and chairs were to the left, next to the tall windows. Holding my glasses and handkerchief, I took long strides towards the counter at the opposite side of the room. To the right rose shelves full of catalogues and various reference books which, owing to my blurred vision, looked like dark, overhanging masses.

I put on my glasses the moment I reached the counter. I had already thought of an apologetic excuse I could make for being late, one that, accompanied by a suitable smile, would put the librarian in a good mood. Unless ill-tempered by nature, people are usually obliging in such circumstances, even when they consider the request excessive— probably so they can take pride in their kindness afterwards. However, I had no one to give my excuses to. There was no one sitting behind the counter. Had my glasses been in place, I would have noticed this earlier.

I turned around in bewilderment. Perhaps, preoccupied with wiping my glasses, I had passed by the librarian without noticing him. But there was no one behind me; the long room was yawningly empty. There was actually little chance that we had passed each other. I might have missed him but he wouldn't have missed me, and the librarian would have been certain to address me. Hesitant, I turned towards the counter once again. Then I realized what had probably happened. Since no one was expected, the personnel had retired to some back room in anticipation of going home.

I coughed loudly, but no one appeared at the half-opened side door that was the main entrance to the area behind the counter. The light was on in the room behind the door, but no sound came from that direction. "Good evening," I said, and waited a bit, then repeated it in a louder voice. Still no response. Silence reigned in the library.

As I stood there, not knowing what to do, the lights suddenly went out. All at once I was surrounded by darkness. The windows that had been dim rectangles a moment before were now the only source of light. Through them came the orange glow of the streetlights, muted by a coating of snow. As my eyes adjusted to the darkness, I looked around, trying to figure out what might have happened and having no easy time of it.

Then, from somewhere downstairs I heard a sharp metal sound, like a key turning in a lock. That same moment, I realized what was going on. The personnel did not have to go through the main room to reach the ground floor. As I had waited in front of the counter, they had reached the stairs some other way, or had taken the elevator. On their way out, they had turned off the building's power from the central switch. That was a reasonable precaution for an institution such as a library.

"Wait!" I shouted, running across the room. In the darkness the carpet became a straight, black strip, allowing me to move quickly even without light. But when I reached the stairs I had to slow down. It was considerably darker in the windowless foyer. The only bit of light came from the glass door at the entrance. I groped for the handrail on the right, grabbed hold of it, and started downward, even though I was already too late. There was no one by the door.

Turning the doorknob and pushing brought anger this time, not relief. I was most angry at the librarians. How could they just lock up and leave, without checking whether anyone was still inside? True, I had entered after working hours, but even so. What if a thief had entered instead of me? The library security system clearly left much to be desired. But I was also to blame, quite honestly. I have never had a high opinion of people who leave everything to the last minute, and that is exactly what I had done in my haste. All because of a movie that I could have seen another time. In fact, nothing would have been lost if I'd never seen it at all.

Well, agonizing over it now wouldn't help. I had to devise a way to get out of the building. The thought of staying locked in the library until Monday morning made me shudder. That would not do at all, even though I certainly would not be bored surrounded by so many books. The heating might have been turned off with the power. The building might become colder and colder with each passing hour; they might find me frozen in two and a half days, in spite of my warm coat. There were other problems, too. I would not die of thirst—the restroom was probably in working order—but how could I survive sixty hours without food? And where would I sleep? I couldn't just sit and read the whole time. I shook my head, still holding onto the doorknob, as though expecting the door to budge. There had to be a solution.

What would I do if I really were a thief? A thief would not wait until Monday to be let out. What would someone like that do in my place? I thought about it for a moment, but everything that crossed my mind was either too violent, too dangerous, too hard to carry out, or required tools that I did not have at my disposal. All in all, it seemed I could not depend on any latent aptitude for thievery.

Then it dawned on me—a simple solution, but one a thief would never think of even in his dreams. All I had to do was return to the counter and use the phone there. Telephones work when the power is off. I would simply call the police and explain my predicament. They might think it was a crank call, but even if they didn't believe me right away, I would keep on calling until they checked on me. Everything would be easy after that. They would probably take me to the police station to make a statement. Even a run-in with the police was more acceptable than languishing in the library for two and a half days.

Stepping with care through the pitch black that engulfed me when I turned my back to the entrance, I walked up the stairs, my hand on the rail. Even though I could see nothing, climbing was not difficult, particularly since I no longer had to hurry and everything would be better as soon as I reached the room. And it truly was better, but not just because of the meager light that poured in through the windows. Although weak and dimmed by the plastic green shade, the desk lamp at the counter seemed strong as a floodlight to me.

I stopped at the entrance to the main room and stared straight ahead. How could that lamp work if the power had been turned off in the whole building? Maybe I had come to the wrong conclusion. On their way out, the librarians had probably just turned off the ceiling lights. There could be no other explanation. But even so, someone had to turn on the lamp. When I'd left the room, it had not been on, and no one in the library but me could have turned it off. Or was I wrong about this as well?

As if in answer to my question, the door leading to the back room opened wide and someone entered the area behind the counter. I was rather far away, but I managed to make out a tall, thin, middle-aged man in a dark suit. He headed for the librarian's chair and sat down in it, turning his attention to something in front of him. He did not raise his head towards me. Even if he had looked in my direction, he would have had trouble seeing me since I blended into the darkness around

201

me.

I remained hidden, trying to figure out the man's function. It did not take long: he was the night guard, of course. Why hadn't I thought of it before? I sighed in relief. My troubles were at an end. I wouldn't have to call the police. I would tell the man what had happened; he would have no reason not to believe me. Anyway, he could easily check the library's records and see that I had been a member in good standing for many years.

Even so, I had to adjust my approach to the circumstances. The night guard certainly did not expect someone to jump out of the darkness at him. Who knew how he would react? He might even aim his gun at me, and that was all I needed. I coughed and walked towards him slowly. After several steps I said in a mild, well-intentioned voice, "Good evening."

I had assumed he would stand up, perhaps even jump up, from his chair. I would stop in that case and let him walk towards me, giving him a chance to collect his wits. Any sudden movement, even just walking toward him, would be inadvisable, since it could be interpreted as a threat. But, contrary to my expectations, the guard just raised his eyes towards me and returned my greeting, not the least bit surprised, as though my sudden appearance was quite natural: "Good evening. May I help you?"

I walked up to the counter. The man had a nicely trimmed, thick black moustache, but his hair was already turning gray. The suit he wore seemed of high quality. The handkerchief peeping out from his breast pocket was the same shade as his tie. I am unfamiliar with the dress code for library night guards, but I certainly hadn't expected this! The director of the library might as well have stood in front of me, wearing his best suit.

"You see," I began, "I'm a little late . . . "

"You're not late at all," said the man behind the counter, interrupting me. "We work at night. This is a night library."

I stared at him in bewilderment. "Night library? I didn't even know they existed."

"Yes, they do. And have for a very long time. Although very little is known about us. Were you interested in a book?"

"Yes, if possible. I really enjoy reading on the weekend. I was already afraid I would end up empty handed this time. It's really nice that books are available at night, too."

"Of course they are. Although the selection is different than during the day. We only have books of life."

I thought I had misunderstood. "Excuse me?"

"Books of life. You haven't heard of them?"

I shook my head. "I'm afraid not."

"Too bad. I certainly recommend them. Quite interesting reading. Contrary to widespread belief, real lives are often considerably more exciting than those that are invented."

"Which real lives?"

"Everyone's."

"What do you mean—everyone's?"

"Literally. The lives of all the people who ever existed."

I studied the man on the other side of the counter in silence for several moments. "There must be a lot of them."

"Yes, there are. One hundred nine billion, four hundred eighty-three million, two hundred fifty-six thousand, seven hundred and ten. As of the moment you entered the library."

I did not reply at once. I hoped that he interpreted my silence as an expression of amazement at the information he had just given me. What was going on here? Who was this man? He wasn't the night guard—that was quite certain. I also doubted his claim to be the night librarian. Whoever he was, I had to be careful. I was locked in a dark, deserted library with him. I had to avoid any conflicts, not deny anything, not contradict him, not enter into unnecessary discussion. Just wait for a chance to get out of there with the least difficulty. Suddenly, I wasn't interested in books anymore.

"You don't say!" I said finally, trying to appear properly amazed.

"Yes, but don't let this enormous number give you the wrong impression. Even though there are so many lives, each one of them is unique and unrepeatable. Precious. That is why they deserve to be recorded. Thus the books of life."

"So, more than one hundred billion of them. That is truly a gigantic library!" I figured a little flattery wouldn't hurt.

"Yes." A proud smile appeared on the stranger's face. "And constantly growing. A daily update is made of books on the people who are living now. And there are more than six billion of them! With new additions arriving all the time. Mankind is multiplying unchecked."

I nodded in admiration. "If I understand you correctly, the books of life are some kind of diary."

"You might call them that. But they are very objective diaries. That is their main attraction. Nothing is left out, nothing is hidden, nothing is shown in a different way. They are perfectly true. Which is only fitting. Like documentary films. You'll see for yourself when you read one of the books of life. Which one would you like?"

I thought it over. "I wouldn't know. It's not easy to decide when there are so many to choose from. What would you recommend?"

"Almost everyone chooses the book about himself first. Which is a little unusual since they have already read that book, in a way. But many still find it full of surprises and revelations. People are mostly inclined to forget things or suppress them."

"Do you mean to say there is a book about me, too?" My surprise was not exactly feigned.

"Of course. Why should you be an exception?"

I hesitated briefly. "All right. I'll take the book about myself."

"Fine," replied the man in the dark suit. "Wait here, please. I'll bring it to you at once."

He got up and headed for the back room, leaving the door ajar behind him. I stood in the small circle of light around the counter. I started to feel warm. I still had no idea what was going on, but asking for the book would let me end the whole thing calmly. I would take the book he offered, thank him, and leave. Everything would be much simpler once I left the library.

What the man brought me several minutes later was not exactly a book. It resembled a large binder. A thick sheaf of pages stuck out from between brown cardboard covers. Noticing my puzzled look, he hurried to explain. "This is the only way to add new pages during the update. The book will only be bound when there is nothing more to add." He smiled at me again. "Luckily, in your case that time has not yet arrived."

I returned the smile and took the binder. It was quite heavy. My name and date of birth had been printed in large, blue letters on the cover. The place for the other date was blank. I put the binder under my arm, reached into my jacket pocket, and took out my library card. "Is this valid for the night library, too," I said, handing it to him, "or does it require separate membership?"

"No need. We do not stick to formalities here. You are already a member by virtue of the fact that our holdings contain a book about you. In any case, we don't lend books, so there is no need to keep records."

"You don't lend them?" I asked, confused. "Does that mean I can't take this with me?"

"Unfortunately, that's impossible. It's the only copy we have. Something might happen to it outside the library, and that would be an irreparable loss. All traces of you would be lost, everything kept inside. It would be as though you'd never lived. We cannot take such a risk. But you can read it here at your leisure." He pointed to the tables to the right. "Make yourself comfortable and turn on the lamp. You can have as much time as you need."

I shouldn't have accepted it. I should have thanked him for the offer, told him it was late, I was tired, promised to return another time, and left at once. But I didn't. Vain curiosity won out. It isn't every day you get to read a book in which you are the main character. I wouldn't keep it for long, just leaf through it, I told myself. I sat down at the closest table, pushed the button on the table lamp, and put the binder in front of me. The stranger at the counter bowed his head, engrossed in his own work.

If I hadn't been in a hurry, I would have started at the beginning, although I wouldn't have been able to testify to the accuracy of the account. Who still remembers their earliest days? I turned the binder face down and opened it from the back. I wanted to see how up-to-date it was. This all seemed like a lot of fun, of course, but a flicker of apprehension rose somewhere in the back of my mind. I felt like someone who doesn't believe in fortune telling, standing before a clairvoyant who is about to tell him his future.

The last page had been filled with tiny writing. A heading with today's date straddled the middle of the page. I started reading from that spot. Somewhere towards the bottom I reached into my coat pocket and took out my movie ticket. I compared the row and seat numbers with the ones cited in the book of life. A lump formed in my throat. The last sentence brought vividly to memory the clock in the library foyer whose hands showed three minutes after eight.

I glanced at the man sitting in the librarian's chair, his position unchanged, and then looked around uncomfortably. I suddenly got the impression of invisible eyes piercing the darkness, staring at me from all sides. This sensation made it hard to concentrate on my reading. But I had to continue despite an overpowering feeling that I would certainly not like what was to come next.

I began to turn the pages impatiently, leaving the end of the binder, heading towards the past. I searched for special dates in my life, dates when something had happened that no one else would know about except me. Or should know. Or had a right to know. And yet they still knew. Everything was written down there before me, all the dry facts, like a court indictment. Every secret that I had hidden not only from others, but often from myself. I felt hopelessly naked, like a hardened criminal whose crimes have suddenly been disclosed to the public.

I closed the binder. Beads of sweat streamed down my forehead, and not just because I was wearing a coat. I sat there a while longer, not moving, eyes empty. Then I turned out the lamp and slowly went up to the counter. I put my alleged book of life on it. The stranger smiled at me again, but I remained serious and dejected.

"This isn't a night library, right?" I said in a hushed voice. "This isn't a book of life, either. It's my dossier. And you are some kind of secret police, a service that spies on the people, or whatever you're called. I don't know much about such things. Congratulations. You've done a wonderful job. I had no idea that such surveillance was possible. Truly unbelievable. And terrifying. All right, now what? You know literally everything about me. There's nothing you can accuse me of, but you've collected more than enough to keep your hands on me. So you can blackmail me. That's what you're up to, right? The only thing I don't understand is why you had to invent that fantastic story about the billions of life stories since time immemorial, when you could have done perfectly well without it. Particularly since it's not the least bit convincing."

"Nothing has been invented, although I don't blame you for thinking so. Almost everyone who reads his own book of life reaches the same conclusion as you. It's quite understandable."

"But the story has its weak spots. You overlooked some details. How, for example, did you know which binder to bring? I didn't introduce myself beforehand."

"We knew. Everyone goes to the night library sooner or later. It was your turn today. We were waiting for you."

"Really? Are you waiting for someone else after me, perhaps? If you are, I've got bad news for you. The entrance is locked. No one else can come in. And what kind of a night library is it that's locked at night, huh?" I hoped I sounded caustic enough.

"You're mistaken," replied the man behind the counter softly. "It's open. You'll see for yourself when you go downstairs."

We looked at each other several moments in silence. The smile stayed on the stranger's face.

"Do you mean to say," I said in the end, "that I am free to go?"

"Certainly. How could you be stopped? Libraries are free to enter and exit as you like. That's how it's always been. Night libraries are no exception. Unless there's something else you would like to read, nothing prevents you from leaving."

I didn't think twice. "I don't think I care to read anything else. Thank you."

"You're welcome. We are pleased that you visited us. Good night, sir." He took the binder, stood up, nodded to me, then walked into the back room.

"Good night," I replied, when he was already on the other side of the door.

I stayed in front of the counter a little while longer. The silence began to thicken around me. I could feel the ghostly eyes from the darkness stabbing me in the back. The man did not return. I turned and headed down the long, dark carpet at a faster pace than I had intended. I stopped at the end of the room and turned around briefly. The lamp had been turned off.

Holding onto the rail, I walked down to the ground floor. I grabbed the doorknob, but didn't twist it. For the third time, the outcome of this simple movement filled me with apprehension. The previous times had been easier. I would not have been in any serious trouble if the door hadn't opened. It would just have caused minor problems. I would have been without anything to read over the weekend, or I would have had to call the police to come and get me out.

Now, however, I didn't dare think about my fate if the door turned out to be locked. I would be trapped with no way out. But I couldn't hesitate forever. The doorknob slowly turned. When I pulled the door, it glided smoothly towards me and wrapped me in a whirlwind of large snowflakes. I quickly went out and took in a deep breath of cold winter air. The door closed automatically behind me.

I stood in front of the library, hands in my pockets, collar raised. I had no reason to stay there, but somehow I didn't want to leave. Before I finally left, I turned once more towards the entrance. Not much could be seen through the glass. Just beyond the door rose an opaque wall of darkness. The clock hung from its very edge; the rod that attached it to the ceiling could not be seen in the darkness, so it seemed to float. My gaze passed fleetingly over that round, white surface with its numbers and hands. At first, I didn't realize the problem.

The nature of my new distress only became clear after I had taken a few steps away from the library. I stopped in my tracks, then rushed back to the entrance. I pressed my face against the glass and sheltered my eyes with my hands. A shiver ran down my spine. I stood back from the door, took off my glasses, and raised my left wrist. The conviction that I would see something different was fragile and unstable, but what else remained? The feeling disappeared instantly, which is what happens to futile hopes. Both clocks, the one inside and mine outside, showed the same time: three minutes after eight.

I shook my head in disbelief. This simply could not be. I had spent at least an hour in the library. Maybe even an hour and a half. That was quite certain. Every moment was still vivid to me. My experiences could not have been an illusion or my imagination. On the other hand, time cannot stand still. Regardless of their power, the secret police still cannot stop time. So what had happened? There had to be an explanation.

There was only one way to find the answer: by entering the library a second time. The thought did not appeal to me at all, but reliving an impossible mystery for the rest of my life would have been even harder. A shiver went through me when I reached for the doorknob. I pushed the door but it didn't move. I tried once again, harder, but it did not budge. The library was locked, just as it should have been. Libraries don't stay open at night. There are no night libraries. Working hours were over and the personnel had gone home. I was too late.

I had to resign myself to the situation, particularly since I didn't know what to do. I couldn't break into the library, of course. Even if I'd wanted to, how could I have done it? I was no burglar, I hadn't the talent for it. I hushed the voices inside me that opposed my withdrawal. What else could I do? What was the point of standing there in the darkness and the snow? I would only catch cold needlessly or appear suspicious to some cop on his beat. I put my hands back into my pockets, hunched my shoulders, and headed down the street through the thick swarm of snowflakes.

I didn't get very far this time, either. I stopped in mid-step, next to the nearest lamppost, although I couldn't figure out why at first. The vague feeling came over me that I had missed something. I had overlooked some detail. I racked my brain, but it was just out of reach, like a word on the tip of your tongue that you can't remember. I looked toward the sky. The wide, orange beam of light from the street lamp was dotted with innumerable flakes, slowly floating downwards, carried by the wind. The moment they started to fall on my face, it dawned on me.

I turned and hurried back to the entrance to the library, almost slipping in the slush. I no longer needed to shield my eyes from the outside light. I no longer really needed to even look inside because, even before I did, I knew what I would see, in spite of the darkness inside the library. The handle of my umbrella was sticking out of the cylindrical brass stand.

KAFKA IN BRONTËLAND
Tamar Yellin

MY PARENTS BELONGED to the lost generation, and when I was growing up their drawers were full of old letters, stopped watches, bits of broken history: a Hebrew prayer book, an unblessed mezuzah, nine views of Budapest between the wars. I drew pictures on the prayer book, mislaid the mezuzah, swapped the postcards for Peruvian stamps; and when my parents were dead and I was fully grown I looked at the hoard and saw it was nothing but junk. Then I hired a skip and threw the lot—watches, pictures, letters and prayers—onto the heap of forgotten things, and came up here to start a new clean life; but I rattled the cans of the past behind me willy-nilly.

* * *

There is a man in the village, they call him Mr. Kafka. I do not know if that is his real name. He does not often speak to people. He is very old. Every day he walks down the village in the company of an elderly and asthmatic wire-haired terrier.

He does not speak to people. But he smiles occasionally: a faint and distant, somewhat dreamy smile. In this respect, but in no other,

211

he resembles a little the Kafka of the photographs.

Derek the builder says that he is Dutch. Kafka is a Dutch name. No, no, I tell him, it is Czech, it is the Czech for jackdaw. It is like the writer Kafka, who was born in Prague. Who? The writer. Kafka the writer. The one who wrote *The Trial*.

Well, you never know, says Derek. And he tells me a story of how people die and come back to life. How young Philip Shackleton, who used to work at the quarry over Dimples Hill, fell into the crusher one day and disappeared. "Never found his body. Just traces of blood in the stones. Next year he turns up in Torremolinos."

The main question, however, is whether there are beams behind my cottage ceiling. Derek taps the plasterboard with his implement.

"Yes, I should think you've got a nice set of beams under there. Pine. Shall I go whoops with the crowbar?"

I say we had better wait a little.

When he has gone I dart across to the Fleece for a box of matches. Mr. Kafka is sitting in the corner over a pint of dark beer. He wears a dirty mackintosh and a buff-coloured hat like James Joyce, and he stares into his beer as though time has ended for him. I consider making conversation, but I haven't the courage.

* * *

When I was a girl I wanted to be Emily Brontë, but this summer I am reading Kafka with all the new enthusiasm of an adolescent. I walk the moors with a book, utterly entranced. I have fallen in love with him. Sometimes I imagine that I am him.

These literary obsessions are hardly innocent. My urge to be Emily, for instance, has altered my entire life. That is why I am here, alone in Brontëland. I grew up determined to live in passionate isolation. Only recently did I realise I had been misled: that she never spent a single day of her life alone in Haworth parsonage.

And now I have chosen to fall in love with Kafka. Kafka, child of the city. Kafka the outcast, Kafka the Jew. He wasn't inspired by spaces, he didn't belong in the hills. He didn't care for weather. He would have hated it here.

* * *

Emily Brontë called these mountains heaven. Today they are referred to as the white highlands. Down in the valley, in the poor town, live the Asians, Pakistanis, Muslims from Karachi and Lahore.

Derek tells me about the first time he ever laid eyes on a Black man. "I just stared." It was in the next village. "Nothing so exceptional now." "Yes," nods Hilda. "You don't see that many here still; but they're creeping up the valley road."

Hilda is a Baptist, Derek a Wesleyan; or it might be the other way round. They are always sparring. When she hears that I play the piano, she lends me a copy of *The Methodist Hymn Book*. "You're not the only Jew round here, you know. Mr. Simons who runs the off licence, I think he's half-Jewish."

I ask about Mr. Kafka. Kafka, I say uncertainly, is a Jewish name.

"I thought he was Polish. Isn't he Polish, Derek?"

"Dutch," says Derek, with conviction. He lights his pipe. "Some sort of a writer fellow, so I've heard."

Then he tells a story about the Irish navvies who helped to build the reservoir. One of them, who was in love with the same lass as his neighbour, took the brake off one of the carts one day and ran him over, and they carried him up to the village, dead. "They said it was an accident," he concludes, "but you ask Ian Ogden and he'll always tell you, murder was committed in this village."

The Greenwoods and the Shackletons all have Irish blood. Derek's great-grandfather was a Sussex landlord. Hilda's used to make boots for Branwell Brontë.

* * *

Twice a week I ride down from the white highlands to the black town. In fact it is more of a grey colour. It has a shopping centre, a cenotaph and a community college. I am learning Urdu.

Ap ka nam kiya hai?
Mera nam Judith hai.

On Tuesdays I teach English to a young woman from Lahore. She is recently married: at the moment she seems to spend most of her time rearranging the furniture in the lounge. Every time I visit we sit somewhere else.

As a matter of fact her English is rather more advanced than my Urdu. She has a degree in Psychology. I decide we will read *Alice in Wonderland* together.

Mrs. Rahim has lovely tendrils of hair at the nape of her neck, and I spend much of the lesson watching her play with them. I also stare at a framed picture of the Ka'ba done in hologram. The mad dream of Wonderland, taken at such protracted length, makes no sense whatever: we might as well be reading Japanese.

Mr. Rahim pops his head around the door: a cheerful face, a white kurta. He is carrying a live chicken by the legs. Shortly afterwards I hear him killing it in the kitchen.

As I leave the house at five the children are making their way to mosque to learn Koran: boys in white prayer caps, solemn little girls in long habits. I remember that a Jew should not live more than half a mile from a synagogue, to prevent the desecration of the sabbath; nor can he pray the services alone. Ten men are required for a congregation; though they do say that a Jewish woman is a congregation in herself.

It is getting dark, and all the shops, the Sangha Spice Mart, Javed Brothers, the Alruddin Sweet Palace, are lit up like Christmas. I am filled with nostalgia for something I never had.

* * *

Today I read the following lines in my *Introduction to Kafka*:

214

> More than any other writer, Kafka describes the predicament of the secular alienated Jew. Yet his work, so personal on one level, remains anonymously universal. He has no Jewish axe to grind. Nowhere in any of his fictions does Kafka mention the words Jewish, or Jew.

This seems to me remarkable. Can it be so? I resolve to make a thorough survey. There must be the odd Jew somewhere that my commentator has missed.

I cannot escape the impression that this is a pat on the back for Kafka. Yet they seem rather a sad conjuring trick, these disappearing Jews. A bit like that author who composed an entire novel without using the letter e.

The Brontë sisters did not recoil from mentioning Jews. I know all their references by heart. *Villette* has an "old Jew broker" who "glances up suspiciously from under his frost-white eyelashes" while he seals letters in a bottle; but at least he does a satisfactory job. Charlotte describes her employers, "proud as peacocks and wealthy as Jews," but I have never liked Charlotte much. There is a "self-righteous Pharisee" in *Wuthering Heights*, and in some ways I am grateful Emily did not live to finish that second novel.

The Brontës, of course, are often praised for the universality of their work. Especially *Wuthering Heights*, which is extremely popular in Japan. All of which goes to disprove our professor's thesis: in order to be universal you don't have to leave out the Jews.

* * *

I may change my mind about ripping down the ceiling in my cottage. It is a perfectly good ceiling, after all. A little low, perhaps—it gives the room a constricted feeling—but it covers a multitude of problems. Exposed plumbing, trailing cables, not to mention the dust, the spiders. And there may not even be any beams behind it.

"Can you assure me categorically that the beams are there?"

"Put it this way, I'm ninety-nine percent certain." Then Derek tells me how once, when he was pulling down a ceiling at Egton Bridge, he found a time capsule hidden in the joists. "One of those old tin money boxes with a lock. But it wasn't mine, so I gave it to the owner and he broke it open." What did they find? "A bit of a newspaper, five old pennies, and a picture of a naked lady."

I say we will hold off on the ceiling for the time being. I ask him to tell me more about Mr. Kafka. Has he lived in the village long?

"I can't rightly say. Have you seen his place? That cottage on the back lane with the green door: looks like a milking shed. The one with thistles growing out of the doorstep." In winter the thinnest trail of smoke came from the chimney. Sometimes the children played round there, but their parents didn't like it. Sometimes the old man tried to give them sweets.

No doubt the council were trying to get him rehoused. But, though he was a foreigner, he had Yorkshire tenacity: he wasn't moving for anyone.

I stop asking questions about Mr. Kafka. I am suddenly embarrassed, as though by taking a special interest I have linked myself to him. It is a kinship I would prefer not to acknowledge.

* * *

Not long before she got married, Mrs. Rahim's father died. She nursed him herself for three months before the wedding. When he died she felt a great peace in her heart, as though she could sense him entering the gates of paradise.

Even so, he was always very close. Sometimes she was certain she could hear him talking in the next room. When she opened the door there was nobody there, but the room was filled with a feeling of warmth and love.

We are talking about death, and we are not making much progress with *Alice in Wonderland*. Death is less perplexing: we share many certainties regarding it.

"I think they are still here: I think they are listening," says Mrs. Rahim. "My father suffered very much. But he is happy now."

Mrs. Rahim reaches for her big torn handbag and brings out a man's wallet, worn, old-fashioned, foreign-looking. It is stuffed with papers covered in tiny handwriting. She clasps the wallet between her palms and holds it to her nose: sniffs deeply as though it is some redolent flower.

"I always keep it with me. It is like him."

I have a cold. She makes me milky tea boiled with cardamom, ginger and sugar. She slips a dozen bangles up my arm. Later, in an aura of almost sacred comradeship, we look at the Koran, which she carries to the table wrapped in a silver cloth.

She cannot touch it, she explains, because she is menstruating. Nevertheless I turn the pages for her reverently as she reads. She reads beautifully. I dare not tell her I am menstruating too.

* * *

"Kafka. K-a-f-k-a. Kafka."

"What sort of a name is that, then? Is it Russian?"

"No, it's Czech."

"Have you tried under foreign titles? I don't think we have any books in Czech."

"He wrote in German, actually. But he's been translated."

"Oh, look, it's here, Jean: someone must have put it back in the wrong place."

A robust copy of *The Trial*, wrapped in institutional plastic: they leave me to it. Avidly I check the date stamps and the opening page.

Why do I do this? It's a symptom of the literary obsessive: merely the desire to see the cherished works in as many editions as possible. As though one could open them up and discover new words, new revelations. I myself possess four different copies of *Wuthering Heights*. With Kafka, it is something else. I need to see which translation it is. This I can tell immediately, from the first sentence. "Someone must have traduced Josef K., for without having done anything wrong he was arrested one fine morning." I don't like 'traduced.' It's an immediate stumbling block. A lot of people don't know what it means. "Someone must have been telling lies about Josef K., for without

217

having done anything wrong he was arrested one fine morning." That's better. Comprehensible. This copy is a traduced.

I didn't expect the people of Brontëland would have much call for a book like *The Trial*. There would be a few lonely borrowings, half-hearted attempts, defeated best intentions. But I get a surprise. The label is a forest of date-stamps, repeated and regular, going back years: there are even a couple of old labels pasted beneath with their columns filled. I pick up *The Castle*. That will be different, I think: everybody reads *The Trial*. *The Castle* is, if anything, just as popular. There is a kind of frenzy in the frequent date-stamps which suggests, even, a profound need for Kafka in Brontëland.

It could all have been the same borrower, of course.

I leave the library with a strange reverence. It is as though the town and its cenotaph carry a peculiar secret, which I have stumbled on in the pages of a book. I see them for a moment with different eyes.

* * *

Having soaped my arm to remove Mrs. Rahim's obstinate bangles, Hilda has lent me another book, *John Wesley in Yorkshire*. I thank her politely. I have not yet learnt any of the pieces in the *Methodist Hymn Book*.

My front door is open. Derek strides in, a big rangy man, and without a word he buries his pickaxe in my smooth white ceiling. It smashes up like papier-mâché. He grins a long sideways grin.

"By heck, I hope I'm right about this."

He heaves at the plasterboard with all his strength and it comes crackling down, along with a shower of dirt and beetles which covers us both.

My beams are there. My revelation. The double crossbeam, backbone of the house: the ribwork of joists between. One has a blackened bite taken out of it where the oil lantern used to be. All are hung with a drapery of webs. Not so beautiful just now, perhaps: but when I have scrubbed them and scraped them, sanded and stained them, varnished

218

them three times with tender loving care, they will be magnificent.

Derek stoops and picks out something from the heap of dirt: a piece of metal wrapped in a strip of cloth. "Old stays," he mutters. He raises his eyes to the ceiling. "Lady of the house must have been dressing herself up there," he says, "and dropped 'em through the floorboards. An heirloom for you."

He hands it ceremoniously to me. I use it as a bookmark.

* * *

When he has left I go for a walk on the moors. The sun is setting: lights are coming on in the valley. Someone is walking towards me down the moorland track.

It is Mr. Kafka. He is following his slow dog down the hill to the village. He has nearly finished his walk, and his head is bent, contemplatively.

I wonder whether to acknowledge him. I am afraid to disturb his silence. He does not often speak to people. Sometimes he nods a greeting to those he knows.

As we pass each other my voice chokes in my throat, I can say nothing; but I manage a smile. Our eyes meet; he smiles back at me.

It seems a smile of recognition, and for the briefest moment he resembles once more the Kafka of the photographs.

THE WEIGHT OF WORDS
Jeffrey Ford

I.

BACK IN THE autumn of 57, when I was no more than thirty, I went out almost every night of the week. I wasn't so much seeking a good time as I was trying to escape a bad one. My wife of five years had recently left me for a better looking, wealthier, more active man, and although she had carried on an affair behind my back for some time and, upon leaving, told me what a drab milksop I was, I still loved her. Spending my evenings quietly reading had always been a great pleasure of mine, but after our separation the thought of sitting still, alone, with nothing but a page of text and my own seeping emotions was intolerable. So I invariably put on my coat and hat, left my apartment, and trudged downtown to the movie theatre where I sat in the dark, carrying on my own subdued affair with whichever Hepburn had something playing at the Ritz. When it was Monroe or Becall, or some other less symbolically virtuous star featured on the marquee, I might instead go for a late supper at the diner or over to the Community Center to hear a lecture. The lecture series was, to be kind, not remarkable, but there were bright lights, usually a few other lonely

221

souls taking notes or dozing, and a constant string of verbiage from the speaker that ran interference on my memories and silent recriminations. Along with this, I learned a few things about The Russian Revolution, How to Care for Rose Bushes, The Poetry of John Keats. It was at one of these talks that I first came in contact with Albert Secmatte, billed as a *Chemist of Printed Language*.

What with the drab title of his lecture, "*The Weight of Words*," I expected little from Secmatte, only that he would speak unceasingly for an hour or two, fixing and preserving me in a twilight state just this side of slumber. Before beginning, he stood at the podium (behind him a white screen, to his side an overhead projector), smiling and nodding for no apparent reason; a short, thin man with a slicked back wave of dark hair. His slightly baggy black suit might have made him appear a junior undertaker, but this effect was mitigated by his empty grin and thick lensed, square framed glasses, which cancelled any other speculation but that he was, to some minor degree, insane. The other dozen members of the audience yawned and rubbed their eyes, preparing to receive his wisdom with looks of already weakening determination. Secmatte's monotonous voice was as incantatory as a metronome, but also high and light, almost childish. His speech was about words and it began with all of the promise of one of those high school grammar lectures that insured the poisoning of any youthful fascination with language.

I woke from my initial stupor twenty minutes into the proceedings when the old man sitting three seats down from me got up to leave, and I had to step out into the aisle to let him pass. Upon reclaiming my seat and trying again to achieve that dull bliss I had come for, I happened to register a few phrases of Secmatte's talk and for some reason it caught my interest.

"Printed words," he said, "are like the chemical elements of the periodic table. They interact with each other, affect each other through a sort of *gravitational* force on a particulate level in the test tube of the sentence. The proximity of one to another might result in either the appropriation of, or combination of, basic particles of connotation and grammatical presence, so to speak, forming a compound of mean-

222

ing and being, heretofore unknown before the process was initiated by the writer."

This statement was both perplexing and intriguing. I sat forward and listened more intently. From what I could gather, Secmatte was claiming that printed words had, according to their length, their phonemic components and syllabic structure, fixed values that could be somehow mathematically ciphered. The resultant numeric symbols of their representative qualities could then be viewed in relation to the proximity of their location, one to another, in the context of the sentence, and a well-trained researcher could then deduce the effectiveness or power of their presence. My understanding of what it was he was driving at led me to change my initial determination as to the degree of his madness. I shook my head, for here was a full-fledged lunatic. It was all too wonderfully crackpot for me to ignore and return to my trance.

I looked around at the audience while he droned on and saw expressions of confusion, boredom, and even anger. No one was buying his bill of goods for a moment. I'm sure the same questions I presently entertained were going through their minds as well. How exactly does one weigh a word? What is the unit of measurement that is applied to calculate the degree of influence of a certain syllable? These questions were beginning to be voiced in the form of grumblings and whispered profanities.

The speaker gave no indication that he was the least aware of his audience's impending mutiny. He continued smiling and nodding as he proceeded with his outlandish claims. Just as a woman, a retired Ph.D. in literature, in the front row, a regular at the lectures, raised her hand, Secmatte turned his back on us and strode over to the light switch on the wall to his left. A moment later the lecture room was plunged into darkness. There came out of the artificial night the sound of someone snoring, and then, click, a light came on just to the left of the podium, illuminating the frighteningly dull face of Secmatte, reflecting off his glasses and casting his shadow at large upon the screen behind him.

"Observe," he said, and stepped out of the beacon of light to fetch a sheet from a pile of papers he had left on the podium. As my eyes adjusted, I could make out that he was placing a transparency on the projector. There appeared on the screen behind him a flypaper yellow page, mended with tape and written upon with a neat script in black ink.

"Here is the pertinent formula," he said and took a pen from his jacket pocket with which to point out the printed message on the transparency. He read it slowly, and I wish now that I had written it down or memorized it. To the best of my recollection it read something like—

Typeface + Meaning x Syllabic Structure - Length + Consonantal Profluence/Verbal Timidity x Phonemic Saturation = The Weight of a Word or The Value

"Bullshit," someone in the audience said, and as if that epithet was a magical utterance that broke the spell of the Chemist of the Printed Word, three quarters of the audience, which was not large to begin with, got up and filed out. If the esteemed speaker had looked more physically imposing, I might have left, myself, timid as I was, but the only threat of danger was to common sense, which had never been a great ally of mine. The only ones left beside me were the sleeper in the back row, a kerchiefed woman saying her rosary to my far right, and a fellow in a business suit in the first row.

"And how did you come upon this discovery," said the gentleman sitting close to Secmatte.

"Oh," said the speaker, as if surprised that there was anyone out there in the dark. "Years of inquiry. Yes, many years of trial and error."

"What type of inquiry?" asked the man in the front row.

"That is top secret," said Secmatte, nodding. Then he whipped the transparency off the projector and took it to the podium. He paged through his stack of papers and soon returned to the machine with another transparency. This he laid carefully on the viewing platform. The new sheet held at its middle a single sentence in typeface of about fifteen words. As I cannot recall for certain the ingredients of the aforementioned formula, the words of this sentence are even less clear to me now. I am positive that one of the early words in the line, but not the first or second, was "scarlet." I believe that this color was used to describe a young man's ascot.

Secmatte stepped into the light of the projector again so that his features were set aglow by the beam. "I know what you are thinking," he said, his voice taking a turn toward the defensive. "Well, ladies and gentleman, now we will see . . . "

The sleeper snorted, coughed, and snored twice during the speaker's pause.

"Notice what happens to the sentence when I place this small bit of paper over the word 'the' that appears as the eleventh word in the sequence." He leaned over the projector, and I watched on the screen as his shadow fingers fit a tiny scrap of paper onto the relevant article. When the deed was done, he stepped back and said, "Now read the sentence."

I read it once and then twice. To my amazement, not only the word "the" was missing where he had obscured it, but the word "scarlet" was now also missing. I don't mean that it was blocked out, I mean that it had vanished and the other words which had stood around it had closed ranks as if it had never been there to begin with.

"A trick," I said, unable to help myself.

"Not so, sir," said Secmatte. He stepped up and with only the tip of the pen, flipped away the paper covering "the." In that same instant, the word "scarlet" appeared like a ghost, out of thin air. One moment it did not exist, and the next it stood in bold typeface.

The gentleman in the front row clapped his hands. I sat staring with my mouth open, and then it opened wider when, with the pen tip, he maneuvered the scrap back onto "the" thus vanishing the word "scarlet" again.

"You see, I have analyzed the characteristics of each word in this sentence, and when the article 'the' is obscured, the lack of its value in the construction of the line creates a phenomenon I call *sublimation*, which is basically a masking of the existence of the word 'scarlet.'

That descriptive word of color is still very much present, but the reader is unable to see it because of the effect initiated by a reconfiguration of the inherent structure of the sentence and the corresponding values of its words in relation to each other. The reader instead registers the word 'scarlet' subconsciously."

I laughed out loud, unable to believe what I was seeing. "Subconsciously?" I said.

"The effect is easily corroborated," he said and went to the podium with the transparency holding the line about the young man's ascot only to return with another clear sheet. He laid that sheet on the projector and pointed to the typeface line at its center. This one I remember very well. It read: The boy passionately kissed the toy.

"In this sentence you now have before you," said Secmatte, "there is a sublimated word that exists in print as surely as do all of the others, but because of my choice of typeface and its size and the configuration of phonemic and syllabic elements, it has been made a phantom. Still, its meaning, the intent of the word, will come through to you on a subconscious level. Read the sentence and ponder it for a moment."

I read the sentence and tried to picture the scene. On its surface, the content suggested an image of innocent joy, but each time I read the words, I felt a tremor of revulsion, some dark overtone to the message.

"What is missing?" said the man in the front row.

"The answer will surface into your consciousness in a little while," said Secmatte. "When it does, you will be assured of the validity of my work." He then turned off the projector. "Thank you all for coming," he said into the darkness. A few seconds later, the lights came on.

I rubbed my eyes at the sudden glare and when I looked up, I saw Secmatte gathering together his papers and slipping them into a briefcase.

"Very interesting," said the man in the front row.

"Thank you," said Secmatte without looking up from the task of latching his case. He then walked over to the gentleman and handed him what appeared to be a business card. As the speaker made his way

226

down the aisle, he also stopped at the row I was in and offered me one of the cards. I rose and stepped over to take it from him. "Thanks," I said. "Very engaging." He nodded and smiled and continued to do so as he walked the remaining length of the room and left through the doors at the back. Putting the card in the pocket of my coat, I looked around and noticed that the woman with the rosary and the sleeper had already left.

"Mr. Secmatte seems somewhat touched in the head," I said to the gentleman, who was now passing me on his way out.

He smiled and said, "Perhaps. Have a good evening."

I returned his salutation and then followed him out of the room.

On my way home, I remembered the last sentence Secmatte had displayed on the projector, the one about the boy kissing the toy. I again felt ill at ease about it, and then, suddenly, I caught something out of the corner of my mind's eye, wriggling through my thoughts. Like the sound of a voice in a memory or the sound of the door slamming shut in a dream about my wife, I distinctly heard, in my mind, a hissing noise. Then I saw it: a snake. The boy was passionately kissing a toy snake. The revelation stopped me in my tracks.

II.

Having been a book lover since early childhood, I had always thought my job as head librarian at the local Jameson City branch the perfect occupation for me. I was a proficient administrator and used my position, surreptitiously, as a bully pulpit, to integrate a new world view into our quiet town. When ordering new books, I set my mind to procuring the works of black writers, women writers, the beats, and the existentialists. Once I had met Secmatte, though, the job became even more interesting. When I wasn't stewing about the absence of Corrine, or imagining what she must be doing with the suave Mr. Walthus, I contemplated the nature of Secmatte's lecture. Walking through the stacks, I now could almost hear the ambient buzz of phonemic interactions transpiring within the closed covers of the shelved books. Upon

227

opening a volume and holding it up close to my weak eyes, I thought I felt a certain fizz against my face, like the bursting bubbles of a Coke-a-Cola, the result of residue thrown off by the textual chemistry. Sec-matte had fundamentally changed the way in which I thought about printed language.

Perhaps it was a week after I had seen his talk and demonstration that I was staring out the large window directly across from the circulation desk. It was mid-afternoon and the library was virtually empty. The autumn sun shown down brightly as I watched the traffic go by outside on the quiet main street of town.

I was remembering a night soon after I was married when Corrine and I were laying in bed, in the dark. She used to say to me, "Tell me a wonderful thing, Cal." What she meant by this was that I was to regale her with some interesting tidbit of knowledge from my extensive reading.

"There is a flower," I told her, "that grows only on Christmas Island in the Indian Ocean, called by the natives of that paradisiacal atoll, the Warulatnee. The large pink blossom it puts forth holds a preservative chemical that keeps it intact long after the stem has begun to rot internally. From the decomposition, a gas builds up in the stem, and eventually is violently released at the top, sending the blossom into flight. As it rapidly ascends, sometimes to a height of twenty feet, the petals fold back to make it more streamlined, but once it reaches the apex of its launch, the wind takes it and the large soft petals open like the wings of a bird. It can travel for miles in this manner on the currents of ocean air. Warulatnee means the sunset bird and the blossom is given as a token of love."

When I was finished, she kissed me and told me I was beautiful. Fool that I was, I thought she loved me for my intelligence and my open mind. Instead, I should have held her more firmly than my beliefs—a miasma of weightless words I could not get my arms around.

Memories like this one, when they surfaced, each killed me a little inside. And it was at that precise moment that I saw, outside the library window, Mr. Walthus' aquamarine convertible pull up at the

228

stop light at the corner. Corrine was there beside him, sitting almost in his lap, with her arm around his wide shoulders. Before the light changed, he gunned the engine, most likely to make sure I would notice, and as they took off down the street, I saw my wife throw her head back and laugh with an expression of pleasure that no word could describe. It was maddening, frustrating, and altogether juvenile. I felt something in my mid-section crumple like a sheet of old paper.

Later that same day, while wandering through the stacks again, having escaped into thoughts of Secmatte's printed language system, I happened to pass, at eye level, a copy of the letters of Abelard and Heloise. At the sight of it, a wonderful thought, like the pink Waru-latnee, took flight in my imagination powered by effluvia from the decomposition of my heart. Before I reached the coat closet, I had fully formulated my devious plan. I reached into the pocket of my overcoat and retrieved the card Secmatte had given me the night of his lecture.

That afternoon, I called him from my office in the library.

"Secmatte," he said in his high pitched voice, sounding like a child just awakened from an afternoon nap.

I explained who I was and how I knew him and then I mentioned that I wanted to speak to him at more length concerning his theory.

"Tonight," he said and gave me his address. "Eight o'clock."

I thanked him and told him how interested I was in his work.

"Yes," was all he said before hanging up, and I pictured him nodding and smiling without volition.

Secmatte lived in a very large, one-story building situated behind the lumberyard and next to the train tracks on the edge of town. The place had once held the offices of an oil company—an unadorned concrete bunker of a dwelling. There were dark curtains on the front windows, where, when I was a boy, there had been displayed advertisements for Maxwell Oil. I approached the non-descript front door and knocked. A moment later, it opened to reveal Secmatte dressed exactly as he had been the night of his lecture.

"Enter," he said, without greeting, as if I were either a regular visitor or a workman come to do repairs.

I followed him inside to what obviously had once been a business office. In that modestly sized room, still painted the sink cleanser green of industrial walls, there was an old couch, two chairs, stuffing spilling out of the bottom of one, and a small coffee table. Next to Secmatte's chair was a lamp that cast a halfhearted glow upon the scene. The floor had no rug but was bare concrete like the walls.

My host sat down, arms gripping the chair arms, and leaned forward.

"Yes?" he said.

I sat down in the chair across the table from him. "Calvin Fesh," I said and leaned forward with my hand extended, expecting to shake.

Secmatte nodded, smiled, said, "A pleasure," but did not clasp hands with me.

I withdrew my arm and leaned back.

He sat quietly, staring at the tabletop, more with an air of mere existence than actually waiting for me to speak.

"I was impressed with your demonstration at the Community Center," I said. "I have been an avid reader my entire life and . . . "

"You work at the library," he said.

"How . . . ?"

"I've seen you there. I come in from time to time to find an example of a certain style of type or to search for the works of certain writers. For instance, Tolstoy in cheap translation, in Helvetica, especially the long stories, is peculiarly rich in phonemic chaos and the weights of his less insistent verbs, those with a preponderance of vowels, create a certain fluidity in the location of power in the sentence. It has something to do with the translation from Russian into English. Or Conrad, when he uses a gerund, watch out." He uncharacteristically burst into laughter and slapped his knee. Just as suddenly, he went slack and resumed nodding.

I feigned enjoyment and proceeded. "Well, to be honest. Mr. Secmatte, I have come with a business proposition for you. I want you to use your remarkable sublimation procedure to help me."

"Explain," he said, and turned his gaze upon the empty couch to his right.

"Well," I said, "this is somewhat embarrassing. My wife left me

230

recently for another man. I want her back, but she will not see me or speak to me. I want to write to her, but if I begin by professing my love to her openly, she will crumple up the letters and throw them out without finishing them. Do you follow me?"

He sat silently, staring. Eventually, he adjusted his glasses and said, "Go on."

"I want to send her a series of letters about interesting things I find in my reading. She enjoys learning about these things. I was hoping that I could persuade you to insert sublimated messages of love into these letters, so that upon reading them, they might secretly rekindle her feelings for me. For payment of course."

"Love," said Secmatte. Then he said it three more times, very slowly and in a deeper tone than was his normal child voice. "A difficult word to be sure," he said. "It's slippery and its value has a tendency to shift slightly when in relation to words with multiple syllables set in a Copenhagen or one of the less script influenced types."

"Can you do it?" I asked.

For the first time, he looked directly at me.

"Of course," he said.

I reached into my pocket and brought out a sheet of paper holding my first missive concerning the Column of Memnon, the singing stone. "Insert some invisible words relaying my affection into this," I said.

"I will make it a haunted house of love," he said.

"And what will you charge?"

"That is where you can assist me, Mr. Fesh," he said. "I do not need your money. It seems you are not the only one with thoughts of putting my sublimation technique to work. The other gentleman who was at the lecture on the twelfth has given me more work than I can readily do. He has also paid me very handsomely. He has made me wealthy overnight. Mr. Mulligan has hired me to create ads for his companies that utilize sublimation."

"That was Mulligan?" I said.

Secmatte nodded.

"He's one of the wealthiest men in the state. He donated that community center to Jameson," I said.

"I need someone to read proof copies for me," said Secmatte. "When I get finished doctoring the texts they give me, playing with the values and reconstructing, sometimes I will forget to replace a comma or make plural a verb. Even the Chemist of Printed Language needs a laboratory assistant. If you will volunteer your time two nights a week, I will create your sublimated letters one a week for you. How is that?"

It seemed like an inordinate amount of work for one letter per week, but I so believed that my plan would work and I so wanted Corrine back. Besides, I had nothing to do in the evenings and it would be a break from my routine of wandering the town at night. I agreed. He told me to return on Thursday night at seven o'clock to begin.

"Splendid," he said in a tone devoid of emotion and then rose. He ushered me quickly to the front door and opened it, standing aside to ensure I got the message that it was time to go.

"My letter is on your coffee table," I turned to say on my way out, but the door had already closed.

III.

My evenings at Secmatte's were interesting if only for the fact that he, himself, was such an enigma. I had never met anyone before so flat of affect at times, so wrapped up in his own insular world. Still, there were moments when I perceived glimmers of personality, trace clues to the fact that he was aware of my presence and that he might even enjoy my company on some level. I had learned that when he was smiling and nodding, his mind was busy ciphering the elements of a text. No doubt these actions constituted a defense mechanism, one probably adopted early on in his life to keep others at bay. What better disguise could there be than one of affability and complete contentment? An irascible sort is constantly being confronted, interrogated as to the reason for his pique. Secmatte was agreeing with you before he met you—anything to be left to himself.

The work was easy enough. I have, from my earliest years in school, been fairly good with grammar and the requirements of proof-reading came as second nature to me. I was given my own office at the back of the building. It was situated at the end of a long, dimly lit hall-way, the walls of which were lined with shelves holding various sets of typefaces both ancient and modern. These were Secmatte's build-ing blocks, the toys with which he worked his magic upon paper. They were meticulously arranged and labeled, and there were hundreds of them. Some of the blocks holding individual letters were as large as a paperback book and some no bigger than the nail on my pinky finger.

My office was stark, to say the least—a desk, a chair, and a stand-ing lamp no doubt procured at a yard sale. Waiting for me on the desk upon my arrival would be a short stack of flyers, each a proof copy of a different batch, I was to read through and look for errors. I was to circle the errors or write a description of them in the margin with a green pen. The ink had to be green for some reason I never did estab-lish. When I discovered a problem, which was exceedingly rare, I was to bring the proof in question to Secmatte, who was invariably in the printing room. Since typeface played such an important part in the production of the sublimation effect, and those not in the know would never see the words meant to be sublimated, he set his own type and printed the flyers himself on an old electric press with a drum that caught up the pages and rolled them over the ink coated print. Even toiling away at this messy task, he wore his black suit, white shirt, and tie.

The copy that Mulligan was supplying seemed the most innocuous drivel. Secmatte called them ads, I suppose because he knew that after he had had his way with them they would be secretly persuasive in some manner, but to the naked eye of the uninitiated, like myself, they appeared simple messages of whimsical advice to anyone who might read them:

Free Fun
Fun doesn't have to be expensive!
For a good time on a clear day, take the family on an outing

*to an open space, like a field or meadow. Bring blankets to sit
on. Then look up at the slow parade of clouds passing overhead.
Their white, cotton majesty is a high altitude museum of wonders. Study their forms carefully, and soon you will be seeing
faces, running horses, a witch on her broom, a schooner under
full sail. Share what you see with each other. It won't be long
before the conversation and laughter will begin.*

This was the first one I worked on, and all the time I carefully
perused it, I wondered what banal product of his mercantile web Mulligan was secretly pushing on its unwitting readers. From that very
first night at my strange new task, I paid close attention to any odd
urges I might have and often took an inventory at the end of each
week of my purchases to see if I had acquired something that was not
indicative of my usual habits. I did, at this time, take up the habit of
smoking cigarettes, but I put that off to my frustration and anguish
over the loss of Corrine.

These flyers began appearing in town a week after I started going
to Secmatte's on a regular basis. I saw them stapled to the telephone
poles, tacked to bulletin boards at the launder mat, in neat stacks at
the ends of the checkout counters at the grocery store. A man even
brought one into the library and asked if I would allow him to hang it
on our board. I didn't want to, knowing it was a wolf in sheep's clothing, but I did. One of the library's regular patrons remarked upon it,
shaking his head. "It seems a lot of trouble for something so obvious,"
he said. "But, you know, when I was over in Weston on business, I saw
them there too."

Good to his word, at the end of our session on Thursday nights,
Secmatte appeared at the open door to my office, holding a sheet of
paper in his hand. Printed on it, in a beautiful old typescript with bold
and ornate capitals and curving "l"'s and "i"'s, was that week's letter
to Corrine.

"Your note," Mr. Fesh," he'd say and walk over and place it on the
corner of my desk.

"Thank you," I would say, expecting and then hoping that he

might return the thanks, but he never did. He would merely nod, say, "Yes," and then leave.

Those single sheets of paper holding my message of wonder for my wife appeared normal enough, but when I'd lift them off the desk top, they'd feel weighted as if by as much as an invisible paperclip. While carrying them home, their energy was undeniable. My memories of Corrine would come back to me so vividly it was like I held her hand in mine instead of paper. Of course, I would send them off with the first post in the morning, but every Thursday night I would lay them in the bed next to me and dream that they whispered their secret vows of love while I slept.

It was on the night I happened to discover on the back of the cigarette pack that my brand, Butter Lake Regulars, was made by a subsidiary of Mulligan Inc., that I saw another side of Secmatte. There were two doors in my office. One opened onto the hallway lined with the shelves of type and the other across the room from my desk led to a large room of enormous proportions without lights. It was always very cold in there, and I surmised it must have been the garage where the oil trucks had once been housed. If I needed to use the bathroom, I would have to open that other door and cross through the dark, chilly expanse to a doorway on its far side. Secmatte's place, I would no longer call it a home, was always somewhat eerie, but that stroll through the darkness to the small square of light in the distance was downright scary. The light I moved toward was the entrance to the bathroom.

The bathroom itself was dingy. The fixtures must have been there from the time of the original occupants. The toilet was a bowl of rust and the sink was cracked and chipped. One bare bulb hung overhead. To say it was stark was a kindness, and when necessity called upon me to use it, I often thought what it would be like to be in prison.

On the night I refer to, I took the long walk to the bathroom. I settled down on the splintered wooden seat, lit a Butter Lake Regular, and in my uneasy reverie began to consider Mulligan's program of surreptitious propaganda. In the middle of my business, I chanced to look down and there, next to me on the floor was the largest snake I had ever seen. I gasped but did not scream, fearful of inciting the creature to strike. Its mouth was open wide, showing two huge curving fangs and its yellow and black mottled body was coiled beneath it like a garden hose in storage. I sat as perfectly still as I could, taking the most minute breaths. Each bead of sweat that swelled upon my fore-head and then trickled slowly down my face, I feared would be enough to draw an attack. Finally, I could stand the tension no longer and, with a great effort, tried to leap to safety. I forgot about my pants around my ankles, which tripped me up, and I sprawled across the bathroom floor. A few minutes later, I realized the serpent was made of rubber.

"What is this supposed to be?" I asked him as he stood filling the press with ink.

Secmatte turned around and saw me standing with the snake in my hand, both its head and tail touching the floor. He smiled, but it wasn't his usual mindless grin.

"Legion," he said, put down the can of ink, and came over to take the thing from me.

"It scared me to death," I said.

"It's rubber," he said and draped it over his shoulders. He lifted the head and looked into the snake's eyes. "Thank you, I've been look-ing for him. I did not know where he had gotten off to."

I was so angry I wanted a scene, an argument. I wanted Albert Secmatte to react. "You're a grown man and you own a rubber snake?" I said with as much vehemence as I could.

"Yes," he said as if I had asked him if the sky was blue. Without another word, he went back to his work.

I sighed, shook my head and returned to my office.

Later that evening, he brought me my letter for Corrine, this one concerning the music of humpback whales. I wanted to show him I was still put out, but the sight of the letter set me at ease. He also had another piece of paper with him.

"Mr. Fesh, I wanted to show you something I have been working on," he said.

Taking the other sheet of paper from him, I brought it up to my eyes so that I could read its one typeset sentence. "What?" I asked.

"Keep looking at it for a minute or two," he said.

The sentence was rather long, I remember, and the structure of it, though grammatically correct, was awkward. My eyes scanned back and forth over it continually. Its content had something to do with a polar bear fishing in frozen waters. I remember that it began with a prepositional phrase and inserted in the middle was a parenthetic phrase describing the lush beauty of the bear's fur. The writing did not flow properly; it was stilted in some way. Unable to stare any longer, I blinked. In the instant of that blink, the word "flame" appeared out of context in the very center of the sentence. It wasn't as if the other words were shoved aside to make room. No, the sentence appeared stable, only there was a new word in it. I blinked again and it was gone. I blinked again and it reappeared. On and off with each fleeting movement of my eyelids.

I smiled and looked up at Secmatte.

"Yes," he said. "But I am some way off from perfecting it."

"This is remarkable," I said. "What's the effect you're trying for?"

"Do you know the neon sign in town at the bakery? *Hot Pies*—in that beautiful color of flamingos?"

"I know it," I said.

"Well . . . " he said and waved his right hand in a circular motion as if expecting me to finish a thought.

The words came to me before the thought did, "It blinks," I said.

"Precisely," said Secmatte, smoothing back his hair wave. "Can you imagine a piece of text containing a word that blinks on and off like that sign? I know theoretically it is possible, but as of now I am only able to produce a line that changes each time the person blinks or looks away. It is excruciatingly difficult to achieve just the right balance of instability and stability to make the word in question fluctuate between sublimation and its being evident to the naked eye. I need a higher state of instability, one where the word is for all intent and purpose sublimated, but at the same time there needs to be some pulsating value in the sentence that draws it back into the visible, releases

237

it and draws it back at a more rapid rate. I'm guessing my answer lies in some combination of typeface and vowel/consonant bifurcation in the adjectives. As you can see, the sentence as it now stands is really not right, its syntax tortured beyond measure for the meager effect it displays."

I was speechless. Looking back at the paper, I blinked repeatedly, watching the "flame" come and go. When I turned my attention back to Secmatte, he was gone.

I was halfway home that night before I allowed myself to enjoy the fact that I was carrying another loaded missive for Corrine. Up until that point my mind was whirling with blinking words and coiled rubber snakes. I vaguely sensed a desire to entertain the question as to whether it was ethical for me to be sending these notes to her, but I had mastered my own chemistry of sublimation and used it with impunity. Later, asleep, I dreamed of making love to her and the rubber snake came back to me in the most absurd and horrifying manner.

IV.

Mulligan's flyers were myriad, but although the subject of each was different—the importance of oiling a squeaky hinge on a screen door, having someone help you when you use a ladder, stopping to smell the flowers along the way, telling your children once a day that they are good—there was a fundamental sameness in their mundaneity. Perhaps this could account for their popularity. Nothing is more comforting to people than to have their certainties trumpeted back to them in bold, clear typeface. Also they were free, and that is a price that few can pass up no matter what it is attended to, save Death. I know from my library patrons that the citizens of Jameson were collecting them. Some punched holes in them and made little encyclopedias of the banal. They were just the type of safe, retroactive diversions one could focus on to ignore the chaos of a cultural revolution that was beginning to burgeon.

Coinciding with the popularity of the flyers, I began to perceive a

238

change in the town's buying habits. It was first noticeable to me at the grocery store where certain products could not be kept in stock due to so powerful a demand. On closer inspection, it became evident that all of these desirable goods had been issued by the ubiquitous Mulligan Inc. There was something undeniably irresistible about the sublimated suggestions hiding in the flyers. It was as if people perceived them as whispered advice from their own minds, and their attraction to a specific product was believed to be a subjective, idiosyncratic brainstorm. Once the products began to become scarce, others, who had not read the flyers, bought them also out of a sense of not wanting to miss out on an item obviously endorsed by their brethren. Even knowing this, I could not stay my hand from reaching for Blue Hurricane laundry detergent, Flavor Pops cereal, Hasty bacon, etc. The detergent turned out not to have the magical cleaning abilities it promised, the Flavor Pops were devoid of flavor, like eating crunchy kernels of dust, and Hasty described the speed with which I swallowed those strips of meatless lard. Still, I forbore the ghostly stains and simply added more sugar to the cereal, unable to purchase anything else.

Even though I knew what Secmatte and Mulligan were up to was profoundly wrong, I vacillated as to whether I should continue to play my small role in the scam. I was torn between the greater good and my own self-serving desire to win back Corrine. This became a real dilemma for me, and I would stay up late at night considering my options, smoking Butter Lake Regulars and walking the floor. Then one night, in order to escape the weight of my predicament, I decided to take in a movie. Funny Face, directed by William Wyler, with Audrey Hepburn and Fred Astaire, was playing at the Ritz, and it was advertised as just the kind of innocent fluff I required to soothe my conscience.

I arrived early at the theatre on a Wednesday night, bought a bag of buttered popcorn, my usual, and went into the theatre to take my seat. I was sitting there, staring up at the blank screen, wishing my mind could emulate it, when in walked a handsome couple, arm in arm. Corinne and Walthus passed right by me without looking. I know they saw me sitting there by myself. A gentleman alone in

239

a theatre was not a typical sight in those days, and I'm sure I drew some small attention from anyone who passed, yet they chose not to recognize me. I immediately contemplated leaving, but then the lights went out and the film came on and there was Audrey, my date for the night.

My emotions see-sawed back and forth between embarrassment at seeing my stolen wife with her lover and my desire to spend time with the innocent and affectionate Jo Stockton, Hepburn's bookish character, amidst the backdrop of an idealized Paris. When my dream date's face was not on the screen, I peered forward three rows to where Corrine and Walthus sat. Tears formed in my eyes at one point, both for the trumped up difficulties of the lovers in the film and for my own. Then, at the crucial moment, when Stockton professes her love for Dick Avery, the photographer, I noticed Corrine turn her head and stare back at me. Of course it was dark, but there was still enough light thrown off from the screen so that our gazes met. I detected a mutual spark. My hand left the bag of popcorn and reached out to her. This motion prompted her to turn back around.

I did not stay for the remainder of the film. But on my way home, I could not stop smiling. If there had been any question as to whether I would continue with Secmatte, that one look from my wife decided it. "My letters are speaking to her," I said aloud, and I felt so light I could have danced up a wall as I had once seen Astaire do in *Royal Wedding*.

The next evening, upon my arrival at Secmatte's, he met me at the door to inform me that he would not need my services that day. He had several gentlemen coming over to talk business with him. He handed me my letter for Corrine—a little piece about a pair of Siamese twins joined at the center of the head who, though each possessing a brain, and an outer eye, shared a single eye at the crux of their connection. The missive had been set in type and carried the perceived weight of his invisible words. I thanked him and he nodded and smiled. As I turned to go, he said, "Mr. Fesh, eh, Calvin, I very much like when you come to help." He looked away from me, not his usual wandering disinterest, but rather in a bashful manner that led me to believe he was being genuine.

"Why, thank you, Albert," I said, using his first name for the first time. "I think our letters are beginning to get through to my wife."

He gave a fleeting look of discomfort and then smiled and nodded.

As I turned to leave, a shiny limousine pulled up and out stepped three gentlemen, well dressed in expensive suits. One I recognized immediately as Mulligan. I did not want him to identify me from the night at the community center, especially after I had questioned Secmatte's sanity, and so I moved quickly away down the street. In fleeing, I did not get a good look at the other men, but I heard Mulligan introduce one as Thomas VanGeist. VanGeist, I knew, was a candidate for the state senatorial race that year. I looked back over my shoulder to see if I could place him, but they were all filing into the bunker by then.

When I visited Secmatte the next week, he looked exhausted. He did not chat with me for too long, but said that he had done a good deal of business and his work had increased exponentially. I felt badly for him. His suit was rumpled, his tie askew, and his hair, which was normally combed perfectly back in a wave, hung in strands as if that wave had finally hit the beach. Legion, the rubber snake, was draped around his neck like some kind of exotic necklace or a talisman to ward off evil.

"I can come an extra night if it will help you," I said. "You know, until you are done with the additional work."

He shook his head, "No, Fesh, I can't. This is top secret work. Top secret."

Secmatte loved that phrase and used it often. If I asked a lot of questions about the sublimation technique in a certain flyer we were working on, he would supply brief, clipped answers in a tone of certainty that seemed to assume he was dispensing common knowledge. I understood little of anything he said, but my interrogation would reach a certain point and he would say, "Top secret," and that would end it.

I wondered what it was that drove him to such lengths. He told me he was making scads of money, "a treasure trove," as he put it, but he never seemed to spend any of it. This all would have remained an insoluble mystery had I not had a visitor to the library Wednesday afternoon of the following week.

Rachel Secmatte seemed to appear before me like one of her brother's sublimated words suddenly freed to sight by a reaction of textual chemistry. I had glanced down at a copy of the local newspaper to read more about the thoroughly disturbing account of an assault on a black man by a group of white youths over in Weston, and when I looked up she was there, standing before the circulation desk.

I was startled as much by her stunning looks as her sudden presence. "Can I help you?" I asked. She was blonde and built like one of those actresses whose figures inspired fear in me; a reaction I conveniently put off to their wayward morals.

"Mr. Fesh?" she said.

I nodded and felt myself blushing.

She introduced herself and held her hand out to me. I took it into my damp palm for a second.

"You are Albert's friend?" she said, nodding.

"I work with him," I told her. "I assist him in his work."

"Do you have a few minutes to speak to me. I am concerned about him and need to know what he is doing," she said.

I was about to tell her simply that he was fine, but then my confusion broke and I realized this was my chance to know something more about the ineffable Secmatte. "Certainly," I told her. Looking around the library and seeing it empty, I waved for her to come behind the circulation desk. She followed me into my office.

Before sitting down in the chair opposite me, she removed her coat to reveal a beige sweater with a plunging neckline, the sight of which gave me that sensation of falling I often experienced just prior to sleep.

"Albert is doing well," I told her. "Do you need his address?"

"I know where he is," she said.

"His phone number?"

"I spoke to him last night. That is when he told me about you. But he will only speak to me over the phone. He will not see me."

"Why is that?" I asked.

"If you have a few minutes, I can tell you everything," she said.

"Please," I said. "With Albert, there should be quite a lot to tell."

"Well, you must know by now that he is different," she said.

"An understatement."

"He has always been different. Do you know he did not speak a single word until he was three years old?"

"I find that hard to believe. He has a facility, a genius for language . . . "

"A curse," she said, interrupting. "That is how our father, the reverend, described it. Our parents were strict religious fundamentalists, and where there was zero latitude given to creative interpretations of the Bible, there was even less available in respect to personal conduct. Albert is four years younger than me. He was a curious little fellow with a, now how do I put this, dispassionate overwhelming drive to understand the way things worked . . . if that makes sense."

"A dispassionate drive?" I asked.

"He had a need to understand things at their most fundamental level, but there was no emotion behind it, sort of like a mechanical desire. Perhaps the same kind of urge that makes geese migrate. Well, to get at these answers he required, he would do anything necessary. This very often went against my father's commandments. He was particularly curious about printed words in books. When he was very young, I would read him a story. He would not get caught up in the characters or the plot, but he wanted to know how the letters in the book created the images they suggested to his mind. One particular book he had me read again and again was about a bear. When I would finish, he would page frantically through the book, turn it upside down, shake it, hold it very close to his eyes. Then, when he was a little older, say five, he started dissecting the books, tearing them apart. Of course, the Bible was a book of great importance in our family, and when Albert was found one day with a pair of scissors, cutting out the tiny words, my father, who took this as an affront to his God, was incensed. Albert was made to sit in a dark closet for the entire after-

243

noon. He quietly took his punishment, but it did not stop his investigations.

"He didn't understand my father's reaction to him, and he would search the house from top to bottom in order to find the hidden scissors. Then he would be back at it, carefully cutting out certain words. He drew on a piece of cardboard with a green crayon a symmetrical chart with strange markings at the tops and sides of the columns, and would arrange the cut out words into groups. Sometimes he would take a word and try to weigh it on the kitchen scale my mother had for her recipes. He could spend hours repeating a phrase, a single word or even a syllable. All throughout this time, he would be caught and relegated to the closet. Then he started burning the tiny scraps of cut out words and trying to inhale their smoke. When my mother caught him with the matches, it was decided that he was possessed by a demon and needed to be exorcised. It was after the exorcism, throughout which Albert merely stared placidly, that I first saw him nod and smile. If the ritual had done anything for him, it had given him the insight that he was different, unacceptable, and needed to disguise this truth."

"He has a rubber snake," I told her.

She laughed and said, "Yes, Legion. It was used in the pageants our church would put on. There was a scene we reenacted from the book of Genesis—Adam and Eve in the garden. That snake, I don't know where my father got it, would be draped in a tree and whoever played Eve, fully clothed, of course, would walk over to the tree and lift its mouth to her ear. Albert was fascinated with that snake before he could talk. And when he did speak, his first word was its name, Legion. He secretly kept the snake in his room and would only put it back in the storage box when he knew the pageant was approaching. When our parents became aware of his attachment to it, they tried many times to hide it, and when that didn't work, to throw it out, but somehow Albert always managed to retrieve it."

"It sounds as if he had a troubled youth," I said.

"He never had any friends, was always an outcast. The other children in our town taunted him constantly. It never seemed to bother him. His experiments with words, his investigations were the only thing on his mind. I tried to protect him as much as I could. And when he was confused by life or frightened of something, which was rare, he would come into my room and get into the bed beside me."

"But you say he will not see you now," I said.

"True," she said and nodded. "As a child I was rather curious myself. My main interest was in boys, and it was not dispassionate. Once when we were somewhat older and our parents were away for the day, a boy I liked came to the house. Let it suffice to say that Albert came to my room in the middle of the day and discovered me in a compromising position with this fellow." She sighed, folded her arms, and shook her head.

"This affected your relationship with him?" I asked, trying to swallow the knot in my throat.

"He would not look at me from that time on. He would speak to me, but if I was in the same room as him, he would avert his glance or cover his eyes. This has not changed through the years. Now I communicate with him only by phone."

"Well, Miss Secmatte, I can tell you he is doing well. A little tired right now because of all of the work he has taken on. He is making an enormous amount of money and is pushing himself somewhat."

"I can assure you, Mr. Fesh, money means nothing to Albert. He is more than likely taking all of these jobs you mention because they offer challenges to him. They require he test out his theories in ways he would not have come up with on his own."

I contemplated telling Rachel the reason why I had offered to help Albert but then thought better of it. The possibility of apprising her of the nature of our work for Mulligan was totally out of the question. The phrase "Top Secret" ran through my mind. She leaned over and reached into the purse at her feet, retrieving a small box, approximately seven inches by four.

"Can I trust you to give this to him?" she asked. "It was something he had once given me as a gift, but now he said he needs it back."

"Certainly," I said and took the box from her.

245

She rose and put on her coat. "Thank you, Mr. Fesh," she said.

"Why did you tell me all of this?" I asked as she made for the door.

Rachel stopped before exiting. "I have cared about Albert my entire life without ever knowing if he understands that I do. Some time ago I stopped caring if he knows that I care. Now, like him, I continue simply because I must."

V.

Being the ethically minded gentleman that I was, I decided to wait at least until I got home from work before opening the box. It was raining profusely as I made my way along the street. By then my curiosity had run wild, and I expected to find all manner of oddness inside. The weight of the little package was not excessive but there was some heft to it. One of my more whimsical thoughts was that perhaps it contained a single word, the word with the greatest weight, a compound confabulated by Secmatte and unknown to all others.

Upon arriving at my apartment, I set about making a cup of tea, allowing the excitement to build a little more before removing the cover of the box. Then, sitting at my table, overlooking the rain washed street, the tea sending its steam into the air, I lifted the lid. It was not a word, or a note, or a photograph. It was none of the things I expected; what lay before me on a bed of cotton was a pair of eye glasses. Before lifting them out of the box, I could see that they were unusual, for the lenses were small and circular, a rich, yellow color, and too flimsy to be made of glass. The frames were thick, crudely twisted wire.

I picked them up from their white nest to inspect them more closely. The lenses appeared to be fashioned from thin sheets of yellow cellophane, and the frames were delicate and bent easily. Of course, I fitted them onto my head, curving the pliable arms around the backs of my ears. The day went dark yellow as I turned my gaze out the window. With the exception of changing the color of things, there was no optical adjustment, no trickery. Then I sat there for some time, watching the rain come down as I contemplated my own insular existence, my sublimations and dishonesties.

Somewhere amidst those musings the phone rang, and I answered it.

"Calvin?" said a female voice. It was Corrine.

"Yes," I said. I felt as if I was in a dream, listening to myself from a great distance.

"Calvin, I've been thinking of you. Your letters have made me think of you."

"And what have you thought?" I asked.

She began crying. "I would come back to you if you will just show once and a while that you care for me. I want to come back."

"Corrine," I said. "I care for you, but you don't really want me. You think you do, but it's an illusion. It's a trick in the letters. You will be happier without me." One part of me could not believe what I was saying, but another part was emerging that wanted to recognize the truth.

There was a period of silence, and then the receiver went dead. I pictured in my mind, Corrine, exiting a phone booth and walking away down the street in the rain. She was right, I had been too wrapped up in myself and rarely showed her that I cared. Oh yes, there were my fatuous transmissions of wonder, my little verbal essays of politics and philosophy and never love, but the real purpose of those was to prove my intellectual superiority. It came to me softly, like a bubble bursting, that I had been responsible for my own loneliness. I removed the yellow glasses and folded them back into their box.

The next evening, I went to Secmatte's as usual, but this time with the determination to tell him I was through with the sublimation business. When I knocked at the door, he did not answer. It was open, though, as it often was, so I entered and called out his name. There was no reply. I searched all of the rooms for him, including my office, but he was nowhere to be found. Returning to the printing room, I looked around and saw laid out on one of the counters the new flyers Albert had done for VanGeist. They were political in nature, announcing his candidacy for the state senate in large, bold headlines. Below the headline was, on each of the different types, a different paragraph-long message of the usual good-guy blather from the candidate. At the bottom of these writings was his name and beneath that a reminder to vote on election day.

"Top Secret," I said, and was about to return to my office when a thought surfaced. Looking once over my shoulder to make sure Secmatte was not there, I reached into my pocket and took out the box containing the glasses. I carefully laid it down on the counter, opened it and took them out. Once the arms were fitted over my ears and the lenses positioned upon my nose, I turned my attention back to the flyers for VanGeist.

My hunch paid off, even though I wished that it hadn't. The cellophane lenses somehow cancelled the sublimation effect, and I saw what no one was meant to. Inserted into the paragraphs of trite self-boostering were some other, very pointed messages. If one assembled the secret words in one set of the flyers, they disparaged VanGeist's opponent, a fellow by the name of Benttel, as being a communist, a child molester, a thief. The other set's hidden theme was racial epithets, directed mostly at blacks and disclosing VanGeist's true feelings about the Civil Rights Act being promulgated by Eisenhower, which would soon come up for a vote in the legislature. My mind raced back to that article in the paper about the assault in Weston, and I could not help but wonder.

I backed away from the counter, truly aghast at what I had been party to. This was far worse than unobtrusively coaxing people to eat Hasty Bacon—or was it? When I turned away from the flyers, I saw on the edge of another table that week's note for Corrine printed up and drying. Turning my gaze upon it, I discovered that there were no sublimated words in it at all. It was exactly as I had composed it, only set in type and printed. I was paralyzed, and would most likely not have moved for an hour had not Secmatte entered the printing room then.

"Is Rachel here?" he asked, seeing the glasses on me.

"Rachel is not here," I said.

"I asked her to bring them so that you could see?" he said.

"Secmatte," I said, my anger building. "Do you have any idea what you are doing here?"

"At this moment?" he asked.

"No," I shouted, "with these flyers?"

"Printing them," he said.

"You're spreading hatred, Albert, ignorance and hatred," I said.

He shook his head and I noticed his hands begin to tremble.

"You're spreading fear."

"I'm not," he said. "I'm printing flyers."

"The words," I said, "the words. Do you have any idea what in God's name you are doing?"

"It's only words," he said. "A job to do. Rachel told me I needed a job to make money."

"This is wrong," I told him. "This is very wrong."

He was going to speak but didn't. Instead he stared down at the floor.

"These words mean things," I said.

"They have definitions," he murmured.

"These flyers will hurt people out there in the world," I said. "There is a world of people out there, Albert."

He nodded and smiled and then turned and left the room.

I tore up as many of the flyers as I could get my hands on, throwing them in the air so that the pieces fell like snow. The words that were sublimated to the naked eye now were all I could see. I finally took the glasses off and laid them back in their box. After searching the building for Secmatte for a half hour, I realized where he must be. When I was yelling at him he had the look of a crestfallen child, and I knew he must have gone to serve out his punishment in the closet. I went to my office and opened the door that led to the bathroom. That distant bulb had been extinguished and the great cold expanse was completely dark.

"Albert?" I called from the door. I thought I could hear him breathing.

"Yes," he answered, but I could not see him.

"Did you really not know it was wrong?" I asked.

"I can fix it," he said.

"No more work for Mulligan and VanGeist," I told him.

"I can fix it with one word," he said.

"Just burn the flyers and have nothing more to do with them."

"It will be fine," he said.

"And what about my letters? Did you *ever* add any secret words to them?"

"No."

"That was our deal," I said.

"But I don't know anything about Love," he said. "I needed you so that you could see what I could do. I thought you believed it was good."

There was nothing more I could say. I closed the door and left him there in the dark.

VI.

In the months that followed I often contemplated, at times with anguish, at times delight, that my own words, wrought with true emotion, had reached Corrine and caused her to change her mind. Nothing came of it, though. I heard from a mutual friend that she had left town without Walthus to pursue a life in the city in which she had been born. We were never officially divorced, and I never saw her again.

There were also two other interesting developments. The first came soon after Secmatte fell out of sight. I read in the newspapers that VanGeist, just prior to the election, dropped dead one morning in his office, and in the same week, Mulligan developed some strange disease that caused him to go blind. Here was a baffling synchronicity that stretched the possibility of coincidence to its very limit.

The other surprising event was a postcard from Secmatte a year after his disappearance from Jameson. In it he asked that I contact Rachel and tell her he was well. He told me that he and Legion had

250

taken up a new pursuit, something else concerning language. "My calculations were remiss," he wrote, "for there is something in words, some un-nameable spirit born of an author's intent that defies measurement. I was previously unaware of it, but this phenomenon is what I now work to understand."

I searched the local phone book and those of the surrounding area to locate Rachel Secmatte. When I finally found her living over in Weston, I called and we chatted for some time. We made an appointment to have dinner so that I could share with her the postcard from her brother. That dinner went well, and in the course of it, she informed me that she had gone to the old oil company building to find Albert when she hadn't heard from him. She had found it abandoned, but he had left behind his notebooks and the cellophane glasses.

In the years that have followed, I have seen quite a bit of Rachel Secmatte. My experience with her brother, with dabbling and being snared in that web of deceit, made me an honest man. That honesty banished my fear of women in that I was no longer working so hard to hide myself. It brought home to me that old saw that actions speak louder than words. In 1962, we moved in together and have lived side by side ever since. One day in the mid-sixties, at the height of that new era of humanism I had so longed for, I came upon the box of Albert's notebooks and the glasses in our basement and set about trying to decipher his system in an attempt to free people from the constraints of language. That was nearly forty years ago, and in the passage of time I have learned much, not the least of which was the folly of my initial mission. I did discover that there is a single word, I will not divulge it, that, when sublimated, used in conjunction with a person's name and printed in a perfectly calculated sentence in the right type face, can cause the individual mentioned, if he should view the text that contains it, to suffer severe physical side effects, even death.

I prefer to concentrate on the positive possibilities of the sublimation technique. For this reason, I have hidden in the text of the preceding tale a selection of words that, even without your having been able to consciously register them, will leave you with a beautiful image. Don't try to force yourself to know it; that will make it shy. In a half

251

hour to forty-five minutes, it will present itself to you. When it does, you can thank Albert Secmatte, undoubtedly an old man like myself now, out there somewhere in the world, still searching for a spark of light in a dark closet, his only companion whispering in his ear the wonderful burden of words.

THE SWAN OF PRUDENCE STREET
Scott Thomas

AS A BOY, I named all the gargoyles on Prudence Street. High against the grey and pigeoned sky, they jutted mutely or coughed rain on the cobblestones where the tall buildings bent above their familiar shops.

Winston squatted over the butcher's, darkly youthful with wings and verdigris and eyes like fat olives. Morris, pensive and horse-like with an inexplicable grin, had a fine view of the cleavage bouncing in and out of the dress maker's. I envied him that, I suppose. Sutton, across the street, coveted in cathedral solemnity, spied all, impassive as a banker and Mr. Snout, horned like a ram and weighted with pre-historic shadows, seemed forever on the verge of a frozen sneeze.

Lord Oscar was the ward of our tilted stone building. He was a chiseled blur of serpents and wings—a strange beast from an unwritten myth. The pigeons thought he was God and foolish young men would steal up in the dusk to tie purple ribbons around the necks. Something to do with fertility and the chase, I take it, though my aunt gave me a less compelling explanation at the time.

My uncle used to chase off the daring lads, wagging his rusty bullet-less pistol. They all knew the relic was as harmless as the old man, but they ran anyway, laughing in the alleys. It was something of a game.

The first floor of our building was a cobbler's shop and several floors above that—below us—lived Mr. Bowling, an undertaker who liked the dead just a bit too much. The top floor belonged to Sibelle, who rarely went out. A young bearded artist would come to draw her at times. She was a worthy subject, with skin as light as her hair was dark and eyes like coal in rain.

Sibelle would send me to the baker for rough-skinned bread, and pastries with frosting like drunken snow. She would invite me in for tea, and scones that stared with currants. I stole glimpses of her pallor—the curve of a fortuitous breast behind the folds of a green robe, a brief thigh as she repositioned on a sofa. Often she wore only a pale sheet wound casually and I thought of classical goddesses and ancient sunlight.

She would ask me about my day and smile sweetly and nod, squinting through tea steam and hair like black vines. I could never place her accent—I pretended she was the last of a once great and enigmatic race. But I always had to leave when that young bearded artist arrived with a great twitching sack slung over his shoulder.

Once, in the incense and sulking plants of Sibelle's flat, I spotted a blurry charcoal sketch on the floor. Mostly obscured by the pages of a newspaper, it showed Sibelle without her wrap or robe, the burnished hair wanton against her shoulders and something unfinished, steam-like above her. Sibelle studied me, gave a small smile and slowly pushed the newspaper with her naked foot so that it covered the artwork.

* * *

She had been crying. It was the thunderstorm, she said. I heard no thunder, I said. She laughed, shrugged, blamed a dream. She sat on a stool by a low fire, insufficiently cocooned in a sheet. Would I please take the ribbon out of her hair—it was too tight, pulling at her scalp. Well, yes, I could do that, though my hands shook when I stood behind her. My fingers brushed the back of her neck as I fumbled and her hair spilled against them and the sheet dropped down her pale back, down to where her hips flared, and I thought of albino cellos standing on sunny Mediterranean hills, with gulls over green water and fat black olives glinting in dew.

"Oops," she said. "You can keep the ribbon if you like."

It was purple silk and it smelled of her hair that night when I slept with it beneath my pillow. Sometimes I would wrap it around my neck and pull on it so that I could hardly breathe.

* * *

Workers on a roof accidentally knocked Winston from his perch and he fell to the street and smashed. The shrapnel of his wings skittered over the cobbles and his head stared up at the immodest fowl dangling in the butcher's window. My aunt said that it was a wonder no one had been killed and refused to walk under the gargoyles after that. She would duck into our building with her umbrella open—as if that would have protected her! For a week or so she insisted that my uncle keep a particularly keen watch for the young men that stole up the fire stairs to tie offerings on the strange winged sentinel. The ribbons appeared nonetheless. An old man with a crippled gun was no match for tradition.

Snow whispered from the north and I watched with Sibelle as it brushed the window and gave the tenements a grandfatherly cast. It lay on the roofs like clean paper, clumsy flakes tumbling, ghostly lichen on chimneys, made a frigid confection of the library over on Baxter, pale as a girl's ankles where it rested on the many window sills. It reminded Sibelle of her dream.

The dream was this: a naked doll was hung from a purple ribbon in a dim hallway where a gaslight flickered and thunder sounded as if trains were in the air. She tried to get the doll down but the porcelain head popped off and fell to the floor, cracking. The cheeks looked as if they had lightning tattoos and the lips had broken away so that the area around them showed uneven and fang-like.

255

She carried the doll up onto the building's flat top and tried to bury it in the snow, but the snow was not very deep and it seemed as if a ghost were pressing its face out of the roof.

Days passed and more snow came and the doll's head was gone, leaving a hole where it had been, a hole like its mouth, and there were bird prints in the snow, all leading to the hole, but no birds. Never birds.

That night, with the albino town outside of my bed, I thought about Sibelle's dream. My own small dreams pressed against the stars like the wings of gargoyles. It was quiet except for the mouse in the wall and the hiccuping of the gas lamp and the walrus snoring through my uncle's mouth in the room across the hall.

* * *

Once, before this story, a man disappeared from the flat where Sibelle lived. I was eye to eye with kneecaps at the time, but the incident took on a life of lore in our largely unremarkable building. Likely embellished as the years went by, it was still worthy of hushed tellings when I was in the throes of excruciating puberty.

Sibelle laughed about it. Perhaps the snow took him. He was quite pale, so she had heard. Maybe he went some place warm, I offered. He packed nothing, she countered. Then what? I asked.

Maybe someone came for him in the night!

I sat closer.

Perhaps faceless men in swallowing monk's robes or impassive officers with severe uniforms and pistoled hips, or a woman with underwater hair that sang softly in a breeze that wasn't.

I smiled. Of course you're right. It was all of those things!

I mention this, perhaps, in reference to that winter's scandal. Mr. Bowler, the undertaker downstairs, was himself found dead. He was in bed with one of his subjects, a Mrs. Fenworthy, the wine merchant's wife. She had been dead longer, of course, and her fingers were like parsnips.

My aunt had to sit when she heard the news—feverish with prayer.

He always was a ridiculous man, my uncle noted. Ridiculous! I liked the word so well that I must have used it five thousand times that week.

There had been other deaths in our building. One summer, an old fellow was found on the fifth floor. He'd been dead for a number of weeks and his flesh came away like the layers of an over-boiled cabbage when they tried to pick him up.

Then there was the ancient, polar-haired Mr. Tuttle. They found him in his favorite chair with a half-read book like a tent over his lungs. The blood had settled to his lower parts, his toes the color of old brittle roses pressed in a book.

A bright green bird with a penchant for saying "shite" rocked on a small swing in a cage in the corner. I don't recall what became of the bird. I hope someone gave it a fine home.

* * *

A few nights after Sibelle told me about her dream, it began to snow. There were white caterpillar window sills on the sad faces of the buildings. I went to the bakery for bread and pastry—through weeping alleys like libraries of bricks. Down the twelve icy steps, in alleys that should have had a Minotaur. Hullo to the shuffling boneless drunkards, under gargoyles fanged with icicles in the purple dusk.

Safe in the scents of the bakery, I stood behind a haggling wife and her monosyllabic husband. The baker sighed and leaned on the counter, he with his nose like a cork and hands of tremulous cheese.

When it was my turn, I gazed and pointed. One of these and one of those and oh, yes, two pieces of that! There were raisin buns glazed with sticky moonlight and small frosted cakes like snowballs and cookies hard enough to hammer nails and rye loaves of secretive brown.

Heavy with my bounty, minus the weight of some coins, I trudged for home in the narrow tunnels of whitened bricks. Through the deserted light of the swirling snow-stained sky.

Outside our building, I stopped beneath Lord Oscar—high and

be-ribboned. For there stood the bearded artist, like a hunchback with that large squirming sack upon his shoulder. He went up the front steps in his long coat like a black tower. The very sight of him blackened the small bell of my heart.

The door huffed shut behind the man and I sat on the cold steps with the bakery goods that I had purchased to surprise Sibelle. One by one I hurled them into the slush beneath the gas lamp.

* * *

The purple ribbon was coiled in my pocket like a flattened serpent. Its weight was almost a warmth against my leg and I slid it out and pondered. Snow fell through the rails of the fire stairs, ghostly downward coins in the glow of the windows. A hundred small damp moth kisses on the fever of my upturned cheeks. Upturned because I was climbing the ladder to the first balcony of bars, then up the first steps, as if my feet were a voice, saying: follow us! Up past windows in the goose feather air—the second floor, the third, the others, all passing. Then near the top. Lord Oscar hovered, all wings and necks in the billowing cold.

For a moment I thought I saw the skeletons of the other boys who had ventured up the fire stairs—up through the rust and snow. Misty bones dangling from their faded purple ribbons, beneath the amorphous gargoyle. First they were there, then they were not.

I reached high with the wind at my flesh and my own ribbon trembled and my fingers managed a clumsy knot. Only then could I see into the window in the wall, alongside the creaking stairs, fastened and steep.

It was Sibelle's flat and the artist stood at his easel, with no real face to speak of, behind the dark beard. He was painting the girl and the swan—white upon white on the full, rhythmic bed, with the bird's wings like mad white shadows and its throaty pleasure coiling out from the pure and serpentine neck. The eyes I loved were closed and the mouth I dreamed of open.

The swan's joy was mine for that one balancing moment, as I tot-

258

tered on the trapeze stairs, while safe in the full warm nakedness that was Sibelle.

MOONLIGHT
Tamar Yellin

AFTER HIS DEATH the house was found to be filled with peacock feathers. That is a superstition we no longer know. We would not be troubled by peacock feathers in the living room, in the hallway, arranged with sprigs of honesty in a Chinese vase. Peacock feathers in the bedroom would not disturb us. We have forgotten that they were once symbols of vainglory and the evil eye.

Nevertheless he kept them: deadly and beautiful, they lurked in forgotten corners of his studio with ammonites and conch shells and bits of pottery and broken glass, all the early tools of his trade. They gathered dust on the windowsill with myriad objects of study from the days when, walking with his wife, he would fill his pockets with bones and leaf skeletons; or when the children, knowing his obsession, would run indoors with fragments of oxidised mirror they had found in the garden; or when, transfixed by the refraction of light, he would stare at the bevelled glass in a chandelier.

He was a connoisseur of objects, a man in love with the objective world. This alone must have made it peculiarly difficult to die. He had squandered himself on items: on the chiffoniers and Flemish vases, on the buhl French timepiece and six grand Dutch marqueterie chairs, the wall plaque medallion of the King of the Belgians and the suit of armour, richly chased with shield, which fetched eighteen pounds at the auction after his death.

He was fifty-seven years old and perished of a painless cancer. And this is what we are told of his death: that he did not stop working, that ill and in debt, he remained at his work until he could stand no more, crawling upstairs finally on his hands and knees to bed, to the Persian brass bed with the silk hangings. That he sent away the priest, that his friend read Tennyson and Browning and sang Schubert's "Schlafe, Schlafe" at his bedside. That he laughed over Kipling's "Lord of the Elephant" in the small hours. That when his daughter saw the death in his face at dinner he told her to go and take her meal in the kitchen.

Of the mundane details which make up a man's dying only these fragments are left, for it was, after all, not exceptional, this death of a man of minor fame. In the course of time it might seem almost nothing: a burial plot in the city cemetery, a longer than average notice in the local newspaper; an auction sale and the vacant lease on a property his widow could not maintain. A bonfire of peacock feathers and spoiled canvas. And, naturally, the legend of his last words, whispered to his wife, but only alleged or attributed, a family tradition merely, and too theatrical perhaps to be believed: "No sun, no moon, no stars."

* * *

I do not know when I first became interested in him. Perhaps when I was still a young assistant, back in the Sixties. In the cellar storeroom of a provincial gallery the curator pulled aside a canvas and showed me a suburban lane at twilight, a gothic mansion behind a wall; trees, carriage tracks; a lone female figure with a closed parasol.

I have never forgotten it. Yet that cannot have been the first time I saw one of his paintings. For the scene was indefinably familiar: like a place visited in childhood, like the road not taken.

Of course, I know now that he painted many of these, perhaps

262

too many, perhaps dozens or scores of them: the lane bending either to the right or left, the sky cirrus or clear, by moonlight or sunset, always with the titles "Golden Twilight," "Silver Moonlight," "Golden Light," always with the same female figure moving away into a distance not spatial but temporal, away into the past. Is it any wonder that you sense you have been here before, when the artist evidently has so many times, so many times he might have painted it in his sleep, and the whole scene might only be a rendering of some troubling and recurrent dream?

But in those days I thought the painting was unique; I did not know that it was representative of a long and delicious trauma, only one of many lanes in a labyrinth where the artist had lost his way.

I do not know, even now, why he began to paint, down there on the canal amongst the engineering sheds, the gasworks and the wool-waste warehouses. Was he inspired by visits to the city art gallery? By engravings in the gentlemen's magazines? Perhaps he took his first enthusiasm to the house of John William Inchbold, the local landscapist. "He was a delicate young man of about one-and-twenty, not much over five feet tall, and pale: my immediate impression was of a chronic consumptive. He told me he was presently working for the Railways, but that, notwithstanding the opposition of his parents, who were strict Nonconformists of the dourest kind (his mother had thrown his paints on the fire and turned the gas off in his room to stop him painting in the evenings), he was determined to become an Artist."

That is the sort of account one can imagine, if any had been given. "I asked him if he had had any formal training. None, he answered, but what his own observation of professional work had given him, and a few evening classes at the city art school. I gave him what encouragement I thought fit. In those days, you must remember, to embark on a career as painter was no longer quite the fool's errand it had once been: Art was increasingly in demand amongst the rising classes, and a competent Artist, who must once have earned his crust as a drawing-master or making woodcuts for the Library of Entertaining Knowledge, could sensibly dream, if not of wealth, then of a decent living. No longer a mere coach-painter or sign-painter, a face-painter or a hand-and-drapery painter, an Artist could, in a plum waistcoat, cut a figure in Society. Nevertheless, I was wary of nurturing such fantasies in a young man whose talents were as yet unproven." And so on. But we do not know if he even visited Inchbold.

What do we know? That his mother kept a grocer's shop and his father was an ex-policeman. That he fell in love with his cousin at an early age. That he attended the Philosophical and Literary Society at Philosophical Hall and exhibited his first works at the Rifle Volunteers Bazaar. That a local bookseller agreed to display his canvases on condition they were not painted on Sundays.

It's a romance: by the time he was thirty he was earning £100 for an oil painting and £10 for watercolours but his figures were still atrocious. He moved uptown to the new villa district. Perhaps because he couldn't paint people he concentrated on landscape. It is said that the effect of landscape on him was so powerful as to make him ill. He travelled the country with his brother who was a salesman for a firm of nail-makers, which is curious since his paintings were as bright and hard as nails, his lake scenes dead as moths: exact and lifeless as a photograph.

He espoused Ruskin's "morality of detail" and painted what he saw. His foregrounds were precise botanical studies. When he painted his wife "at home" a mere ruck in the carpet became a challenge of technical skill. He perfected his figures, painting her in the garden, at the window, cutting camellias in the greenhouse. He had her pinned for ever in the airless beauty of the drawing-room, vacuous, laden with silks, listening to silent music; surrounded by cashmeres, china, peacock feathers.

Art made him a gentleman. He took up the lease on a fifteenth century manor house and commissioned a gothic retreat overlooking the sea. He rented a studio in Chelsea and exhibited at the Royal Academy. He enjoyed friendships with Millais and Whistler. In his conservatory on the coast he grew vines, oleanders, anthuriums and other exotic plants from which he extracted pigments. He was regularly represented by the London dealers, Agnew and Tooth.

These are the relics of his golden years: the fob watch engraved with the Masonic symbol, the coromandel walking stick with silver head. Elephant tusks; silk slippers embroidered with his monogram. All sorts of crystals. The skull of a monkey and a goblet said to have belonged to an ancient Chinese emperor.

* * *

I never had the talent to be an artist. That much was clear to me from the very first. There are some people who, for all that they can analyse a master's every brushmark, could never produce a stroke of genuine art.

My mother always told me to stick to what I was good at. "Words are your metier, Norman," she would say. "Words and discipline." She was pleased to see me do well, get a dull degree, a dull safe job and not go chasing after precarious fantasies, precarious lifestyles.

So I resigned myself early to pure analysis: a surgeon, dissecting genius I could never have.

"A real intellectual, our Norman is." It always gave me pleasure to make her proud. I know she watched with relish my progress from assistant to curator to director to academic hack. Climbing the greasy pole for which I was well suited, but never creating anything of my own. It pleased her to fantasise about my grand future. "Norman, Keeper of the Queen's Pictures." Mother was always something of a snob.

* * *

I have seen the house where he lived, like a mediaeval baron surrounded by fake armour and Roman pottery, in grim drawing rooms, in dark corridors hung with rugs. I have noted its dank walls in photographs, the high trees full of rooks. The plumbing was said to be deadly. In the narrow nursery three of his children died from fumes caused by a faulty sink outflow. The ex-actress hired to assist him pined with a slow T.B.

He read Tennyson to her under the lilac trees while his wife sat in the mullioned window like the Lady of Shalott. When autumn came they fled to London, abandoning wife, children and his collection of claymores.

He painted the docks by moonlight and the prostitutes on London Bridge. Railway arches; gaslit fog. The flash of a match as a man bent to tend his pipe; omnibuses on the wet cobbles. A moonlit land loosing her ships into a black sea, lighting her flares. On the calm horizon a silver moon hung steady: in the still house his wife awaited his return. The actress assistant coughed into the darkness. They buried the dead children one by one.

What can we know now of the lost letters, the forgotten gossip, the hotel rooms hired under a pseudonym, the railway sleeper carriages booked for two? What of the secret notes, the rendezvous, or the private diary, now dust and ashes, in which he recorded in the faintest of hands, "Miss Neale died yesterday at Scarboro"?

(The official account: "She was invaluable to me in the mix of paints and colours.")

I have seen the rose garden and the croquet lawn, the staircase down which you could drive a coach and four. I have seen the pictures taken before the demolition: the streaked walls, the boarded windows; the scutcheons salvaged for the city museum. The stone griffins lying in a sea of nettles and the neglected graveyard for the family cats and dogs.

* * *

There are times when I utterly despise my work: when I see the pointlessness of turning paintings into words. The art critic, like the music critic, reduces the irreducible to a heap of opinions.

Let me tell you what I feel when I stand before his pictures— before any pictures. It is a sort of despair. It is the sort of despair only art engenders.

I have to struggle for interpretations. The airless drawing room with its dull woman represents the ennui of Victorian domestic life. The glade with primroses and a pretty stream expresses nostalgia for the rural idyll. The gaslit quay bristling with trams and horses idealises the city and casts a romantic sheen over the industrial revolution. Why did he start painting, why did he paint what he did? I don't know, I hunt for reasons. The philistine hunts for meaning in an act whose very performance is a cry for meaning.

I wonder whether I, too, could not have done as much, if I had only been blessed as he was with those Victorian virtues, the "triumphant power of enthusiasm," the "divine faculty of work." Perhaps then I should not be haunted by the unfinished pictures lurking in the cupboard, the dried and twisted tubes of raw umber and terre verte, Payne's grey and cadmium red; and by the bundled brushes, rounds and filberts, sable and bristle, stiff with disuse; and by the old palette with its record of many attempts.

* * *

The nature of the financial disaster which struck him in his mid-forties is not precisely known. A piece of misjudged generosity, perhaps; an unwise investment or a rash gamble. In any case, the London adventure ended. The seaside retreat had to be given up. He retired to the manor and painted to pay his debts.

I try to imagine this great frenzy of painting. For five years he produced an average of fifty paintings a year. That is almost a picture a week. He shipped them off to London: dock scenes, street scenes, moonlights. Many, many dock scenes for the board rooms of industrialists; many, many moonlights. City streets for the salons of city bankers. Mansions for the dwellers in gothic mansions.

After five years, we are told, he began to be oppressed by a sense of failure. His children rode in a carriage with silver harness from which, however, they could not dismount because they had no boots. His paintings show marks of haste and careless handling. He sometimes painted over photographs.

In the summer of 1890 he invited journalists into his basement studio to witness how, by projecting a photograph from a magic lantern, he could cast an image on canvas over which he ran his pencil to produce the outline of a suburban lane. This, he explained, saved valuable time and speeded up production.

That is how I picture him, standing at his canvas: that is where I see him most clearly of all. He is small and frail; at fifty-four he still wears a fair moustache. He has the appearance of a chronic consumptive. He is increasingly oppressed by a sense of failure. He is sick of the treadmill, of the public hunger for moonlights. The lane projected by the magic lantern is one of the many lanes in a labyrinth in which he has lost his way.

* * *

A woman's figure stands at a bend in the road. Tree shadows on the wall succeed hers like sentinels: landmarks she has left behind, or sinister followers. There is no moon; but the tree branches, touched by moonlight, are picked out to the smallest twig.

A woman's figure stands at a bend in the road. Drifts of leaves follow her. It is sunset; lamps are burning in the windows of the tall house. There is a door in the wall, but it is barred with brambles: it has not been opened now for many years.

A woman's figure stands at a bend in the road. She carries a basket. A green moon hangs among cirrus clouds. Lamps are lit in the windows of the tall house, but they are not for her. She is moving past, beyond, out of the picture. Her back is towards us, her face invisible.

Where has she come from, where is she going to? It is a mystery without meaning, a parable without clues. Our eyes eat the picture, searching for symbols. We see what we most wish to: mother, lover, muse.

* * *

I do not know why it is that I still want to please her. Why, all these years after her death, I still pursue her down endless hospital corridors, down twisting lanes of dreams in which I never quite catch up with her retreating back.

268

Once, when I was a boy, we walked home by starlight through deserted streets, through a pall of gunpowder and the smoke of bonfires, our faces tingling with November frost: back to the safety of home, to the warm glow behind windows. We held hands and swung them slightly. Her face, touched by silver, was entirely beautiful.

And again, that time she stood in the back garden by moonlight, in her white night-gown, taking in washing she said, although there was no washing: as she went through the motions in a strange miming dance, then too she appeared to me quite beautiful.

Her face, swollen with steroids, hangs like a great moon in my imagination. I can't see past it. I have never succeeded in painting it.

* * *

No paintings have been discovered from the year 1891. By 1891, we must assume, he was exhausted. But in 1892 he began again. Seascapes, snowscapes, beach scenes: his palette torn by gashes of dazzling light.

After years of moonlight he must have been blinded by so much sun. His eyes were failing: the doctor forbade him his brushes, forced him to rest. But soon he was up again, seduced by all that white snow. He rushed into it like a child, there was no stopping him. Ill and in debt, he remained at his work until he could stand no longer. At night he crawled on his hands and knees to bed, to the Persian brass bed with the silk hangings.

His daughter read Browning and Tennyson at his bedside. His wife sat silently and held his hand.

I cannot escape the image of his last days wrapped in light, in the false light with which death deceives us; and of his last pictures, empty white expanses tokening oblivion; and of the brilliant peacock feathers with their painted eyes; and of his final acknowledgment of the coming darkness: "No sun, no moon, no stars."

* * *

Five years after his death there was a generous retrospective. In 1912 a job lot including "Moonlight" fetched one and a half guineas at an auction sale.

Four decades later the widow of an industrialist sent a batch of his paintings to a sale at Leeds, received no bid, chopped them up and burned them.

In 1960 the city council applied for special permission to clear the cemetery in which he lay buried along with his eight infant children. The headstones were removed, the ground smoothed and grassed, and a garden of remembrance planted on the site of his forgotten tomb.

That same year the assistant keeper hung a picture called "Golden Light" in the entrance hall of a provincial gallery. He hung it there because he liked the look of it. He could not have foretold how dock scenes and street scenes would be unearthed from attics, how long-forgotten heirlooms would be revealed; how lanes and lakes, beaches and bridges, ships and mansions would rise from heaps of lumber in a fabulous resurrection of lost paintings.

* * *

I have to acknowledge now that I will always be associated with him. The catalogue, the hardback, the biography, are all mine. My name, through its attachment to that of others, has acquired the vague familiarity of a man of minor fame.

People write me heartfelt letters. They tell me what it is about him that appeals to them.

Sometimes they ask me what it is about him that appeals to me.

I do not answer them entirely truthfully.

I tell them I admire his handling and his eye for detail. His use of colour and his use of light. The air of mystery which hangs over his paintings, which although figurative and limited, nevertheless retain a ghostlike charm.

All this is true. But I do not tell them the real reason why I seek out his work. Why I will travel miles, to obscure galleries and private salons, merely to obtain a glimpse of something I have, to all intents

270

and purposes, seen before. I re-enter the labyrinth; once more I am standing in the moonlight of his endless dream. I am as lost as he is. And it fills me with wonder, that failure can be so beautiful.

INFERNAL LIBRARY

The Library: 4: INFERNAL LIBRARY
Zoran Zivkovic

THE GUARD ESCORTING me stopped before a door in the hallway and knocked. He waited for a few moments and then seemed to hear permission to enter, although nothing reached my ears. He opened the door, pushed me forward without a word, and stepped inside after me, grabbing hold of my shoulder to keep me there as he closed the door behind him. His grasp was unnecessarily firm since I had already stopped, not knowing what else to do. He probably didn't know how to be gentler. We stood by the door, obviously waiting for new orders.

As with everything else I had seen so far, the ceiling was extremely high. This impression was accentuated here because the distance to the ceiling was considerably greater than the length and width of the room. I was suddenly overcome by the dizzying feeling that it would be more natural for the floor and one of the sidewalls to change places. But, of course, I could not expect the natural order of things to be maintained in this place. That time had passed for good. Who knew what unusual experiences were in store for me. I had to be prepared for much worse.

The room was poorly lighted and sparsely furnished. Hanging

from the ceiling on a long wire, a weak bulb covered by a round metal shade shed most of its light on a backless wooden chair that stood by itself in the middle of the room. A man sat at a desk opposite the door, his back to the wall. Only visible above the shoulders, he concentrated on the computer screen in front of him. By the indistinct glow of the screen, casting no shadow, his long face seemed almost ghostly pale. His short, thick beard appeared grizzled in the odd light and he wore semicircular reading glasses. I could not determine his age. He might have been anywhere from his early forties to his late fifties.

He didn't seem to notice us. The guard and I stood patiently by the door, as motionless as statues. Finally, without taking his eyes off the screen, the man raised his left hand and made a brief, vague gesture, which nonetheless had a clear meaning for the guard. He grabbed my shoulder roughly once again and led me towards the chair under the light. He released me only when I had sat down, then stood right behind me.

While I waited, my gaze began to wander. The feeling of confinement caused by the height of the room was intensified by the uniformity of color around me. A sickly shade of olive-gray covered everything: the walls, the ceiling, the floor, the chair, the table. Even the monitor was olive-gray. The paint on the walls was cracked and peeling in places, showing patches of dry plaster the color of a stormy sky. It felt as if we were inside a faded and worn shoebox, once green, placed on its end.

The room might have been less gloomy if there had been a window, even one with bars. But there were no windows. Working in a place like this could only be considered punishment. I looked at the person behind the monitor with a mixture of pity and dread. Even if I disregarded all the rest, there was certainly no reason to expect anything good from someone forced to work here for any period of time.

The deep silence in the room was suddenly broken by fingers tapping on a keyboard that I could not see. The rapid typing did not last long. When he was finished, the man raised his head, took off his glasses, and laid them on the desk next to him. Then he squinted and pinched the bridge of his nose with his thumb and forefinger. He remained in this position for several moments before opening his eyes and nodding to the guard. The guard moved off at a brisk pace. The metal door opened with a squeak and then closed behind him.

We looked at each other without speaking for some time. I felt uncomfortable under his silent inspection, which was more an expression of aversion and bad temper than harsh or threatening. I quickly realized that he wasn't the least bit happy about the upcoming conversation with me. He acted like someone who has done the same job too long to be able to find anything appealing in it. I had seen that expression on the faces of some older investigators and judges. Finally the man sighed, drew his fingers across his high forehead and broke the silence.

"You realize where you are, don't you?" He had a deep, drawn-out voice.

"In hell," I replied after hesitating a moment.

"That's right. Although we don't use that name anymore. Are you aware of why you got to this place?"

I didn't answer right away. It was clear to me that there was no sense in hiding or denying anything, but I didn't exactly have to incriminate myself, either. "I can guess . . . "

"You can guess?" He raised his voice. "Even here we rarely see a dossier like this." He knocked the crook of his middle finger on the screen.

"I might be able to explain . . . "

"Don't!" he said, cutting me off. "Spare me, if you please! How inconsiderate you are, all of you who sit there. It isn't enough that I have to learn about the disgusting things you've done; you want me to listen to your phony, slime-ball explanations, too. They make me even sicker than the crimes themselves. In any case, there's nothing to explain. Everything is perfectly clear. We know all about you. Every detail. Would you be here if that weren't the case?"

"Mistakes do happen . . . " I noted softly.

"There are no mistakes," replied the man. "And even if there were, it's too late to rectify them. There's no way out of here. Once you're in, you stay for good."

I knew that, of course. Everyone knows that. But I still had to try.

"What about repentance? Does that mean anything?" I asked in the humblest of voices.

This time he didn't have to say anything. His expression told me exactly what he thought about my remorse.

"Don't waste your breath. I have no time for such nonsense. I'm inundated with work. The world has never been like this before. Can you imagine the burden on my shoulders?"

I could imagine, but since the question was rhetorical, I just shrugged. For a moment I thought the man wanted to complain to me about his hardships, but then he changed his mind.

"Forget it. It's not important. Let's get to the point. We have to find out what would suit you best."

"As punishment?" I asked cautiously.

"We call it therapy."

"Burning in fire is therapy?"

"Who's talking about burning in fire?"

"Maybe being boiled in oil or drawn and quartered . . . "

"Don't be vulgar! This isn't the Middle Ages!"

"Sorry, I didn't know . . . "

"It's simply unbelievable how many people come here with pre-conceived notions. Do you think we live outside the times? That nothing changes here? Would this go along with such barbaric brutality?" He tapped the side of the monitor.

"Of course not," I readily agreed.

"Every age has its own hell. Today it's a library."

I blinked in bewilderment. "A library?"

"Yes. A place where books are read. You have heard about librar-ies? Why is everyone so amazed when they find out?"

"It's a bit . . . unexpected."

"Only if you give it perfunctory consideration. Once you delve into the matter, you see that there's nothing unusual about it."

"It never would have crossed my mind."

"To tell you the truth, we were also a bit surprised at first. But what the computer told us was unequivocal. It is quite a useful

278

machine."

He paused. Several moments passed before I understood what was expected of me. "Quite useful, indeed," I repeated.

"Particularly for statistical research. When we input data about everyone here, the trait that linked by far the greatest number of our inmates, 84.12 percent to be precise, was their aversion to reading. This was understandable for 26.38 percent, since they are completely illiterate. But what about the 47.71 percent who, although literate, had never picked up a single book, as though fearing the plague? The remaining ten or so percent read something here and there, but they'd wasted their time since it was totally worthless."

I nodded. "Who would have thought?"

He looked askance at me. "Why does that seem strange to you? Take yourself. How many books have you read?"

I thought it over briefly, trying to remember. "Well, er, not a whole lot, to tell the truth."

"Not a whole lot? I'll tell you exactly how many." The rapid sound of typing on the keyboard was heard once again. "In the past twenty-eight years of your life you started two books. You got half-way through the fourth page in the first, and in the second you didn't get beyond the introductory paragraph."

"It didn't catch my interest," I replied contritely.

"Really? And other things did?"

"I never suspected that not reading was a mortal sin."

"It isn't. Although the world would be a much better place if it were. No one's ever been sent to hell because they didn't read. That's why this trait was overlooked until we brought in the computer. But when we noticed this connection, thanks to the computer, we were able to take advantage of it. In several ways. You might even say that it led to a true reform of hell."

"No one knows anything about that."

"Of course no one knows. How could anyone know? That's where all those prejudices come from. This place has never been the way most people imagine it: an eternal torture chamber run by merciless sadists. Tell me, do you smell that sulfur everyone talks about so much?"

I sniffed the air around me. It was dry and stale, a little musty. "No," I had to admit.

"We were simply a jail. With a few special features, that's true, but the system here differed very little from what you found in your jails. We treated our inmates here the same way you treated yours. Why should we be any different? If there was brutality and abuse here, that meant we were following your example. As conditions improved over time in your jails, the situation here became more bearable. Things went so far that there was a danger of going against the basic idea of hell."

"What do you mean?"

"Recently your jails have almost been turned into recreation centers. You might even say they're modest hotels. You're the best judge of that; you spent a lot of time in jail, and it wasn't the least uncomfortable, right?"

I thought it over. "No, you're right, although the food wasn't always good everywhere. Especially dessert."

A fleeting sigh escaped from the man behind the monitor. "There, you see. Well, now, we couldn't allow some of those privileges here. Weekend leaves, for instance. Or using cellular phones. How would that look?"

"But that would make it much easier to serve your time . . . "

"Perhaps. But it must never be forgotten that this is hell, after all. So we found ourselves in a bind. We could not follow the liberalization of conditions in your jails any longer. We were threatened with becoming what we have been accused of since time immemorial: being the incarnation of inhumanity and jeopardizing human rights. Luckily, that's when we found out about people not reading."

"Excuse me, but I don't see the connection."

"It was a simple matter. We made reading compulsory for everyone. This enabled us to join the beautiful with the useful. First of all, our inmates could get rid of the main shortcoming that brought them here. If they had read more, they would have had fewer motives and less time for misdeeds. Reading for them is truly healing. This is why we consider it therapy, not punishment, even though it might be a little late. But it is never really late for something like that. And what do we call the place where everyone loves to read?"

"A library?"

The man spread his arms. "Of course. And a library is the last place to be accused of violating human rights, wouldn't you say? At the same time, this step removed the extremely embarrassing tarnish on us. Furthermore, we turned out to be considerably more humane than your jails. They have libraries, of course, but what's the point, since they are almost never used? It's as though they don't even exist. Take your own case once again. Did you ever go into a library in one of the many jails you were in?"

"I didn't even know they had them," I replied truthfully.

"What did I tell you? But don't worry, you'll soon have a chance to make up for what you've missed. And much more than that, in effect. Before you is literally a whole eternity of reading."

I stared at the man for several moments without speaking. "So that's my punishment? Reading?"

"Therapy."

"Therapy, yes. There won't be anything else?" I tried to suppress the sound of relief in my voice, but without success.

"Nothing else, of course. You will sit in your cell and read. That's all. You won't have any other obligation. I must, however, draw your attention to the fact that eternity is a very long time. You might become bored with reading at some point. That happens to many of our inmates and then they become very clever. My, what tricks they resort to, giving the impression that they're reading, even though they aren't. But we have ways to see through all those crafty ploys. In such cases we must, unfortunately, use forceful means to get them to return to reading. With the most resistant and stubborn they are sometimes rather painful, I'm afraid."

"What about human rights? Humanity?"

"We don't lay a hand on them. This is exclusively for their own good. We can't let them harm themselves out of spiritual indolence, can we?"

281

"I suppose not," I replied, not quite convinced.

"Those are the main things you should know. You will grow accustomed to conditions here. It will probably be a little difficult at first, until you get used to it, but you will finally realize that reading offers incomparable satisfaction. Everyone becomes aware of this during eternity, some sooner and some later. I hope in the meantime that you behave in a mature and sober manner and do not compel us to resort to force. That will make it nice and easy for everyone."

Since my unquestioning agreement was clearly understood, I nodded. For the first time, the corners of the man's mouth turned up a little, forming the shadow of a smile.

"Fine. Now let's see which therapy would suit you best. What kind of reading material would you prefer?"

It was a difficult question, so I took my time answering it. "Maybe detective stories," I said finally, in a half-questioning tone.

"Ah, certainly not!" replied the man, frowning again. "That would be like giving a sick man poison instead of medicine. No, you need something quite the opposite. Something mild, gentle, enriching. Pastoral works, for example. Yes, that is the right choice for your soul. Idylls. We often prescribe them. They have a truly wondrous effect."

He saw an expression on my face that might have been disgust. When he spoke again his voice had returned to its initial sharpness.

"If you think this unjust, you can take consolation in the fact that I would give anything to be in your shoes. Enjoying idylls. At least for a while. But I can't, unfortunately. They won't let me. Instead, I am forced to read exclusively the abominations and baseness that simply gush out of here. Like water from a broken dam." He tapped the monitor again, this time on top. "And eternity for me is no shorter than it is for you. That's not fair. Whenever you hit a crisis, just think how much I envy you, and you'll feel better."

He stopped talking. The incongruous height and dreary color of the room suddenly seemed to collapse in on him, twisting his face into a mask of contempt and despair. He looked at me a moment longer, his eyes going blank. Before he reached for his glasses and put them on again, he turned his head towards the door behind me. He didn't say a word, but it squeaked right away. The guard's firm hand found my shoulder. I got up off the chair under the light bulb and headed outside. On the way, I took another look at the man behind the desk. He had almost sunk behind the monitor, engrossed in a new dossier. A moment later the door hid him from my view, and I set off down the hall with the guard, towards my cell, where an eternity of reading awaited me as well.

THE PROGENITOR
Brian Evenson

TO PLEASE THE progenitor, the ground-muscled untether one of the men and fire the extreme of his cord. Observed through a spyglass, the man floats up as descriptions of his ascent are shouted to the progenitor. The ground-muscled record the time and progress of the ascent until the fire reaches the body and the man's helial lobes warm and burst. He burns quickly, falling to ground a fine sift of ash.

Largely, however, the men remain unmolested. By propelling themselves about with careful motions of the hand, they can progress along the arc of their tether. Their tethers are of sufficient length that a man by this means may easily reach the others tethered nearest to him.

When not required, the men may converse or quietly attempt copulation. This is permitted by decree and toleration of the progenitor.

Mornings, certain men may be found enclustered, clinging together in the air until the sun warms them or the ground-muscled below tug their cords and shake them apart. Rarely, they grip one another so tightly that the ground-muscled must haul them down hand over hand and beat them until they fall slack and let each other go.

The attendants examine the arrangement, assuring themselves the rows are straight, the tethers knotted at the proscribed distances along the rails. At sunset, the progenitor outswells the close of his day and the shape of the next in a lilting, struggling tongue.

At a signal from the ground-muscled, the men part their skin and display their helial lobes, stroking the surrounding integument until the lobes begin to glow. They are required to maintain a smooth glow for the duration of the progenitor's outswelling and for a period of reflection thereafter. Those who cannot work the integument into proper glow are immediately untethered and set aflame.

In the early light men can be found awake and pushing themselves open-mouthed through the air, gathering the cold-slowed insects upon their tongues. They eat nothing else and drink not at all, unless it be that they preen dew off their own person.

The more enterprising entrap insects without crushing them, trying to seduce these to nest upon their person. Though this is always difficult, it is not impossible with certain varieties. If a flourishing colony is established on the skin, the time spent gathering food will be greatly reduced. However, difficulties exist. If more than one colony gains hold, a man's buoyancy will be impeded. If the reduction in bouyancy becomes discernable from the ground, the ground-muscled will haul the man down so as to laden and musculate him. In addition, some insects are carnivorous. They burrow into the flesh, eating the bodies imperceptibly from the inside out until all that remains is an empty outer skin, ribbing and ballooning with air.

Those to be ground-muscled are selected by precepts trained in the art by the progenitor. These precepts, upon the death of a ground-muscled, walk among the tethers, scrutinizing the men buoyant above their heads, sounding the tension in the cords. A man might be chosen for a slight lack of buoyancy, for having a body structure likely to survive the musculation and ladening, or according to a more obscure, intuitive reasoning.

Once chosen, the man is hauled to the ground. Two of the precepts

286

are bound to him, one to the left side, the other to the right, and by such means he is prevented from ascent. The man is brought to the ladening place where he is bound to the slab. The flesh of the limbs is slit and pulled back to make way for the insertion of wooden disks and nails and pieces of jewelry between skin and muscle, and then it is sewn down. The body cavity is sawed apart and eviscerated of all but the helial lobes, for without the lobes, the body slowly poisons itself. The lobes, however, are crimped and suctioned, drastically reducing their size. The body cavity is filled with sodden sponge, a length of rope coiled in the place of the colon, and then sewn shut.

The man is released from the ladening slab and, if still living, caused to stand. If his bones shudder and collapse, as is not uncommon, the body is quickly disjointed and fed to the progenitor. If the bones hold, however, the man is taught to walk and accepted into the weighty, earthbound fold.

Those whose bodies prove most resistant to the ladening, those who become thoroughly ground-muscled, will sometimes be chosen for further descent. They are again cut open, sponge and rope removed and replaced by iron filings and clinks of chain. They are further laden with greased rings slipped over their extremities, their bodies strung in steel and thoroughly exo-skeletoned.

They are secured at the end of a chain. Later, they are led by the ground-muscled to the marsh. There, they begin to sink. Before the end of the day, they have vanished entirely.

It is the task of the ground-muscled to hold to the end of the chain, preventing the burdened man at the other end from breaking free and escaping. Though many ground-muscled have been hauled under the earth for refusing to release the chain, there is no instance of the submerged returning of their own accord.

Once in a year, the ground-muscled are called to provoke the progenitor, prodding him and massaging him until he begins to scream and puff. His body is rolled out of the penetralium and edged nearer to the open doorway. Under the touch of sunlight, he begins to expel strings of jellied larvae.

These larvae are caught with hooked staves called fornii by the ground-muscled, then smeared against the roof of the dome. They are allowed to develop independently until the fluids dry. At that time, they begin to scutter across the roof first with their tails and then, as these are dropped, the knobs that will develop into limbs.

When the torso is formalized, variegated sufficiently to prevent the slippage of a tether, the larvae are anchored and taken from the dome, sent skyward, left to hang. If they survive four days without a decrease in buoyancy, they are allowed to remain alive.

Upon the death of any man, a lament is sung by those tethered closest to him, reiterated in bolder tones by the ground-muscled below. The body is tugged down and opened, the helial lobes lanced to release a precise measure of their pressure and then resewn and bound in tar. Untied and released, the body floats slowly upward until it reaches a point of equalized pressure and is carried off upon the wind.

The men believe their bodies will float forever. They are supported in their belief by the periodic inflow of bodies on the upper currents of the air, the corpses shuttled about on the wind.

At times, the upper air is absent of bodies entirely. At others, they all flood back and seem clots and lesions spread all along the surface of the sky.

All can be said to go well until the progenitor begins to act strangely. In the place of larval strings, he extrudes forth malformed helial sacks which, in bursting, injure and sometimes kill the ground-muscled. He calls not for food but for fistfuls of gravel. His increasing heaviness leaves a fixed impression on the penetralium and the walls of the surrounding dome groan. The ground-muscled hurry to please him but he will not be pleased.

The attendants take shovels and dig in the places where the burdened have slipped beneath the surface of the earth. Most often, the holes fill with water and digging cannot continue. Sometimes, however, they are found dead and tangled in their chains, entrapped in the roots of trees, their throats packed with mud.

Over the course of several days, the progenitor worms his way out of his enclosure and, after many flailing attempts, gains his feet. Soon, he finds his balance. For the first time, he takes a step, his feet sinking deep into the earth.

The ground-muscled bustle about. In his subsequent lurching steps, many are mangled and crushed. He progresses one step at a time, his feet sinking deeper until he wades in earth. The remaining ground-muscled counsel one another and observe him from a distance. The progenitor struggles his way downward, into the ground, until only his head remains, a misshapen pyramid riding on the surface, the ground shuddering as he tries to breath.

One of the ground-muscled unties a tether from the rail and reties it around the progenitor's neck. The man at the cord's end rises just behind the progenitor's head, almost as if standing on the scalp.

The other ground-muscled rush to untie the other tethers and do the same, until the progenitor's neck is strung thick with cords and the head no longer threatens to slip below the surface.

While they congratulate themselves, they realize the progenitor is dead, strangled. They remove the ropes from his neck, watch the progenitor's head slide down and under the earth, the ground bubbling.

The progenitor's body resurfaces, its planes sharpened, the surface material shined and slick. He looks alive, but he is still strangled, still dead.

Time has ended. The ground-muscled laden the body until it sinks again. They crack the dome, destroy the penetralium. They light tether after tether until all the tethers are aflame and released. As they make their way toward marshy ground, the sky is a torment of fire and ash.

THE FACE OF AN ANGEL
Brian Stableford

WHEN MRS. ALLISON had gone, taking the photo-quality A4 sheet from the printer with her, Hugo Victory took another look at the image on his computer screen, which displayed her face as it would appear when the surgery she had requested had been carried out.

The software Victory used to perform that task had started out as a standard commercial package intended as much for advertisement purposes as to assist him to plan his procedures, but he had modified it considerably in order to take aboard his own innovations and the idiosyncrasies of his technique. Like all great artists, Victory was one of a kind; no other plastic surgeon in the world plied his scalpels with exactly the same style. He had been forced to learn programming in order to reconstruct the software to meet his own standards of perfection, but he had always been prepared to make sacrifices in the cause of his art.

Victory considered the contours of Mrs. Allison's as-yet-imaginary face for six minutes, using his imagination to investigate the possibility that more might be done to refresh her fading charms. He decided in the end that there was not. Given the limitations of his material, the image on the screen was the best attainable result. It only remained to reproduce in practice what the computer defined as attainable. He only had to click the mouse twice to replace the image of the face with an image of the musculature beneath, already marked up with diagrammatic indications of the required incisions, excisions, and reconnections. Some were so delicate that he would have to use a robotic arm to carry out the necessary microsurgery, collaborating with the computer in its guidance.

Victory printed out the specifications, and laid the page in the case-file, on top of his copy of the image that Mrs. Allison had taken with her. Then he buzzed Janice and asked her whether his next potential client had arrived.

There was a slight tremor in the secretary's voice when she confirmed that a Mr. Gwynplaine had indeed arrived. Victory frowned when he heard it, because the first duty of an employee in her situation was to remain pleasantly impassive in the face of any deformation—but he forgave her as soon as the client appeared before him. If ever there was a man in need of plastic surgery, Victory thought, it was the man who had replaced Mrs. Allison in the chair on the far side of his desk. And if there was one man in the world who could give him exactly what he needed, Victory also thought, it was Dr. Hugo Victory.

"I'm sorry you had to wait so long for an appointment, Mr. Gwynplaine," Victory said, smoothly. "I'm a very busy man."

"I know," said Gwynplaine, unsmilingly. Victory judged that the damage inflicted on Gwynplaine's face—obviously by fire—had paralysed some muscles while twisting others into permanent contraction, leaving the man incapable of smiling. The injuries were by no means fresh; Gwynplaine might not be quite as old as he looked, but Victory judged that he must be at least fifty, and that the hideous scars must have been in place for at least half his lifetime. If he'd acquired the injuries in the Falklands, the army's plastic surgeons would have undone at least some of the damage, and all employers had to carry insurance against injuries inflicted by industrial fires, so the accident must have been a private affair. Victory had never seen anyone hurt in quite that way by a house fire—not, at any rate, anyone who had survived the experience.

"Your problem is very evident," Victory said, rising to his feet and readying himself to take a closer look, "but I wonder why you've left it so long before seeking treatment."

"You mistake the reason for my visit, Doctor," Gwynplaine said, in a voice that was eerily distorted by his inability to make full use of his lips, although long practice had evidently enabled him to find a way of pronouncing every syllable in a comprehensible manner. When Victory glanced down at the note Janice had made, the slightly monstrous voice added: "As your secretary also did. I fear that I allowed her to make the assumption, rather than state my real business, lest she turn me away."

As he spoke, the paragon of ugliness lifted the briefcase that he had brought with him and snapped the catch.

Victory sat down again. He was annoyed, because Janice had strict instructions never to permit salesmen or journalists to fill appointment-slots reserved for potential patients—but the mistake was understandable. Victory had never seen a salesman or journalist so unfashionably dressed, and the ancient briefcase was something a fossilized academic might have carried defiantly through a long career of eccentricity.

The object that Gwynplaine produced from the worn bag was a book, but its pages were not made of paper and its leather binding bore no title. It was not the product of a printing press—but it was not Medieval either. Victory guessed, on the basis of the condition of the binding, that it might be eighteenth century, or seventeenth, but not earlier.

Gwynplaine laid the book on the desk, and pushed it towards Victory. Victory accepted it, but did not open it immediately.

"You seem to have mistaken the nature of my collection," Victory said, frostily. "Nineteenth-century portraiture is my specialty. Pre-Raphaelite and Symbolist. I don't collect books, except for products of the Kelmscott Press. In any case, I don't pursue my hobbies during working hours."

"This is to do with your work, not your hobby," Gwynplaine told

293

him. "Nor am I trying to make a sale—the book isn't mine to sell, but if it were, I'd deem it priceless."

"What is it?" the doctor asked. He opened the volume as he spoke, but the first page on which his eyes fell was inscribed in a language he had never seen before.

"It's a record of the secrets of the comprachicos," Gwynplaine told him. "It appears to be complete—which is to say that it includes the last secret of all: the purpose for which the organization was founded, long before it became notorious."

"I have no idea what you're talking about," Victory told his mysterious visitor. "If you're hoping to barter for my services I'm afraid you've come to the wrong plastic surgeon." But he had turned to another page now, and although the script remained utterly inscrutable, this one bore an illustrative diagram.

Victory had seen a great many anatomical texts in his time, but he had never seen an account of the musculature of the human face as finely detailed as the one he was looking at. It was easily the equal of Dürer's anatomical studies, although it was more intricate and seemed indicative of an uncanny appreciation of the inner architecture of the human face. It seemed to Victory that the author of the diagram addressed him as one genius of plastic surgery to another, even though the message emanated from an era in which plastic surgery had been unknown. His interest increased by a sudden order of magnitude.

"I hope you will permit me to explain," Gwynplaine said.

Victory turned to another illustration. This one had been carefully modified in a manner that was impossibly similar to the print he had taken from his computer only a few minutes earlier. A layman might have seen nothing but a confusion of arbitrary lines scrawled on the image of facial musculature, but Hugo Victory saw a set of clear and ingenious instructions for surgical intervention. Victory decided that he wanted this book as desperately as he had ever wanted anything. If Gwynplaine could not sell it, then he wanted a photocopy, and a translation.

If this is genuine, Victory thought, *it will rewrite the history of plastic surgery. If the text lives up to the promise of the illustrations*

I've so far seen, it might help to rewrite modern textbooks as well. And even if it turns out to be a fake, manufactured as recently as yesterday, the ingenuity of the instructions testifies to the existence of an unknown master of my art.

"Please go on, Mr. Gwynplaine," the surgeon said, his eyes transfixed by the illustration. "Tell me what you came here to say."

* * *

"Comprachicos means *child-buyers*," Gwynplaine said, his strange voice taking on an oddly musical quality. "Even in their decadence, in the eighteenth century, the comprachicos took pride in being tradesmen, not thieves. They were wanderers by then, often confused with gypsies, but they were a very different breed. Even nineteenth century accounts take care to point out that while true gypsies were pagans, the comprachicos were devout Catholics.

"Those same sources identify the comprachicos' last protector in England as James II, and state that they were never heard of again after fleeing the country when William of Orange took the throne. The retreat into obscurity is understandable. The Pope had excommunicated the entire organization—one reason why the Protestant William was secretly supported by Rome against his Catholic rival—and such succour as those who fled from England could receive in France was limited and covert. The entire society retreated to Spain, and even then found it politic to vanish into the Basque country of the southern Pyrenees. They have remained invisible to history ever since—but they had been invisible before, and the wonder may be that they were ever glimpsed at all.

"Almost everything written about the comprachicos was written by their enemies, and was intended to demonize them. They were attacked as mutilators of the children they bought, charged with using their techniques to produce dwarfs and hunchbacks, acrobats and contortionists, freaks and horrors. It was true that they could and did produce monsters—but even in the Age of Reason and the Age of Enlightenment the demand for such products came from the courts of

Europe, which still delighted in the antics of clowns and clever fools. The comprachicos sold wares of those kinds to Popes and Kings as well as Tsars and Sultans. The clowns which caper in our circuses even to this day use make-up to produce simulacra of the faces that the comprachicos once teased out of raw flesh.

"Yes, the comprachicos used their plastic arts—arts which men like you are only beginning to rediscover—for purposes that you or I might consider evil or perverse. But that was not their primary aim. That was not the reason for which the organization was founded, in the days when the Goths still ruled Iberia."

Hugo Victory had never heard of comprachicos, but he had heard that families of beggars in ancient times had sometimes mutilated their children in order to make them more piteous, and he had heard too that the acrobats of Imperial Rome had trained the joints of their children so that they could be dislocated and relocated at will, preparing them for life as extraordinary gymnasts. For this reason, he was not inclined to dismiss Gwynplaine's story entirely—and he was still turning the parchment pages with reverential fingers, still marvelling at the anatomical diagrams and the fanciful surgical schemes superimposed upon them. "What was the reason for the organization's existence?" he asked.

"To reproduce the face and figure of Adam."

That startled the surgeon into looking up. "What?"

"Adam, you will recall, was supposed to have been made in God's image," Gwynplaine said. "The comprachicos believed that the face Adam wore before the Fall was a replica of the Divine Countenance itself, as were the faces of the angels; when Adam and Eve ate from the tree of the knowledge of good and evil, however, their features and forms became contorted—and when God expelled them from Eden, he made that contortion permanent, so that they and their children would never see his image again in one another's faces and figures.

"The comprachicos believed that if only they could find a means of undoing that contortion, thus unmasking the ultimate beauty of which humans were once capable, they would give their fellows the opportunity to see God. That sight, they believed, would provide a powerful incentive to seek salvation, and would prepare the way for Christ's return and the end of the world. Without such preparation, they feared, men would stray so far from the path of their religion that God would despair of them, and leave them to make their own future and their own fate."

"But there never was an Adam or an Eden," Victory pointed out, still meeting the oddly plaintive eyes of his frightful visitor, although he knew that there was not a man in England who could win a staring-match against such opposition. "We know the history of our species," he added, as he dropped his gaze to the book again. "*Genesis* is a myth." *But this book is not a myth,* Victory said to himself, silently. *This is, at the very least, a record of experiments of which the accepted history of medicine has no inkling.*

"The comprachicos had a different opinion as to the history of our species," Gwynplaine told him, flatly. "They knew, of course, that there were other men on Earth besides Adam—how else would Cain have found them in the east of Eden?—but they trusted the word of scripture that Adam alone had been made in God's image, and that Adam's face was the face of all the angels, the ultimate in imaginable beauty. Not that it was just the face that they were anxious to reproduce, of course. They wanted to recover the design of Adam's entire body—but the face was the most important element of that design."

"This is nonsense," Victory said—but he could not muster as much conviction as he would have desired, or thought reasonable. There was something about Gwynplaine's peculiar voice that was corrosive of scepticism.

Gwynplaine leaned forward and placed the palms of his hands flat upon the open pages of the book that he had laid on Victory' desk, preventing the doctor from turning the next page. "All the secrets of the comprachicos are recorded here," he said. "Including the last."

"If they knew how to achieve their object," Victory objected, "why did they not do so? If they did it, why did they not succeed in bringing about their renaissance of faith and the salvation of mankind?"

"According to the book, the operation was a success," Gwynplaine told him, "but the child died while the scars were still fresh. The surgeon who carried out the operation died too, not long afterwards. The project was carried out here in London, not two miles east of Harley Street, but the timing was disastrous. The year was 1665. Plague took them both. There was no one else in England with the requisite skill to make a second attempt, so a summons was sent to Spain—but by the time the call was answered, London had been destroyed by the great fire. The record of the operation was thought to have been lost.

"When William came to power and the comprachicos fled to the continent they no longer had the book, and their subsequent experiments failed—but the book had not burned in the fire. It was saved, and secreted by a thief, who did not know its nature because he could not read the language in which it was written. It was only recently rediscovered by someone who understood what it was. You will not find a dozen scholars in Europe who could read it—in a century's time, there might be none at all—but I am one. What I need as well is a man with the skill necessary to carry out those of its instructions that require an expert hand and surgical instruments. I have been told that I might do well to take it to California, but I have also been told that I might not need to do that, if only you will agree to help me. I already have a child." He added the last sentence in a negligent tone, as if that consideration were a mere bagatelle.

"Have you also been advised that you might be insane?" Victory inquired.

"Often. I will admit to being a criminal, given that it is illegal to buy children in England now, or even to import children that have been bought elsewhere—but as to the rest, I admit nothing but curiosity. Perhaps the instructions are false, and the whole tale is but an invention. Perhaps the judgment of success was premature and the child would not have grown up to display the face of Adam at all. But I am curious—and so are you."

"If you wanted me to operate on you," Victory said, "I might take the risk—but I can't operate on a child using a set of instructions written by some seventeenth century barber."

"The child I have acquired is direly in need of your services," Gwynplaine told him. "So far as anyone in England can tell, I am his legal guardian—and no one in the place where I bought him will ever dispute the fact. The manipulations of the body and the training of the facial flesh that require no cutting I can do myself—but I am no surgeon, and even if I could master the pattern of incision and excision I would not dare attempt the grafts and reconnections. Your part is the minor one by comparison with mine, requiring no more than a few hours of your time once you have fully understood the instructions—but it is the heart and soul of the process, and it requires a near-superhuman sureness of touch. You cannot do this as a matter of mere business, of course. I cannot and will not pay you. If you do it, you must do it because you need to know what the result will be. If you say no, you will never see me again—but I do not believe that you will say no. I can read your face, Dr. Victory. You wear your thoughts and desires openly."

As he tore his avid gaze away from Gwynplaine's censorious fingers Victory became acutely conscious of his own reflexive frown. "Who the hell are you?" he asked.

"Gwynplaine is as good a name as any," the man with the unreadable face informed him, teasingly.

"I want the book," Victory said, his own perfectly ordinary voice sounding suddenly unnatural by comparison with the other's strangely contrived locutions. "A copy, at least. And a key to the script."

Gwynplaine could not smile, so there was no surprise in the fact that his face did not change. "You may make a copy it afterwards, if you take care to do no damage," he agreed. "I will give you the name of a man who can translate the script for you. Have no fear that you might do harm. If you achieve nothing else, you might prevent the child from growing up a scarecrow. I think you understand well enough what costs that involves—though not, of course, as well as I."

Victory felt—knew, in fact—that he was on the threshold of the most momentous decision of his life. He had seen enough of the book to know that he had to see all of it. He was faced with an irresistible temptation.

"I'll need to see the child as soon as possible," Victory said, slightly astonished at his own recklessness, but proud of his readiness to seize the utterly unexpected opportunity. "I'll tell Janice to fix an emergency appointment for tomorrow."

* * *

Even at a mere thirteen weeks old, the child—to whom Gwynplaine referred as Dust—was as hideous as his guardian, although his ugliness was very different in kind. The baby had never been burned in a fire; the distortion of his features was partly due to a hereditary dysfunction and partly to the careless use of forceps by the midwife who had delivered him, presumably in some Eastern European hellhole.

Had the child been brought to him in the ordinary course of affairs, Hugo Victory would have been reasonably confident that he could achieve a modest reconstruction of the skull and do some repair-work on the mouth and nose, but he would only have been able to reduce the grotesquerie of the face to the margins of tolerability. Normality would have been out of the question, let alone beauty. Nor could Victory see, to begin with, how the procedures outlined in the diagrams illustrating the final chapter of Gwynplaine's book would assist in overcoming the limitations of his own experience and understanding.

"This is an extremely ambitious series of interventions," he told Gwynplaine. "It requires me to sever and relocate the anchorages of a dozen different muscles. There can be no guarantee that the nerves will function at all once the reconnections heal, even assuming that they do heal. On the other hand, these instructions make no provision for repairing the damage done to the boy's skull. I'll have to use my own procedures for that, and I'm not at all sure that they're compatible. At the very least, they'll increase the danger of nervous disconnections that will render the muscles impotent."

"My part of the work will replenish and strengthen his body's ability to heal itself," Gwynplaine assured him. "But the groundwork has to be done with scalpel and suture. If you can follow the instructions, all will be well."

"The instructions aren't completely clear," Victory objected. "I don't doubt your translation, but the original seems to have been written in some haste, by a man who was took a little too much for granted. There's potential for serious mistakes to be made. I'll have to make further modifications to my computer software to take aboard the untried procedures, and it will be extremely difficult to obtain an accurate preview of the results."

"It won't be necessary to preview the results," Gwynplaine assured him. "Nor would it be desirable. You must modify the software that controls the robotic microscalpel, of course, but that's all."

"That won't take as long, admittedly," Victory said. "Amending the imaging software isn't *strictly* necessary . . . but working without a preview will increase the uncertainty dramatically. The robotic arm ought to make the delicate procedures feasible, but guiding it will stretch my resources as well as the computer's to the full. If a seventeenth-century surgeon really did set out to follow this plan with nothing but his own hand to guide the blades he must have had a uniquely steady hand and the eyes of a hawk."

"You only have to step into the National Gallery to witness the fact that there were men in the past with steadier hands and keener eyes than anyone alive today," Gwynplaine said. "But your technology will compensate for the deterioration of the species, as it does in every other compartment of modern life. As to the lack of specificity in the instructions. I'm prepared to trust your instincts. If you'll only study the procedures with due care, and incorporate them into your computer programmes with due diligence, I'm certain that their logic will eventually become clear to you—and their creativity too. There's as much art in this business as science, as you know full well."

Victory did know that, and always had; it was Gwynplaine's comprehension of the art and science that he doubted. But Gwynplaine would not permit him to photocopy a single page of the book until the work was done. So Victory imported his own diagrams and his own calculations into his modified computer programmes, embodying within them as much arcane knowledge as the specific task required.

He wanted far more than that—he wanted the whole register of secrets, the full description of every item of the comprachicos' arts—but he had to be patient.

There was a great deal of preparatory work to be done before Victory could even contemplate taking a scalpel to the infant's face, but the surgeon was as determined to get the job done as Gwynplaine was. He cleared his diary by rescheduling all the operations he had planned, in order to devote himself utterly to the study of the diagrams Gwynplaine allowed him to see and Gwynplaine's translations of the text. He practised unfamiliar elements of procedure on a rat and a pig as well as running dozens of simulations on the computer. But time was short, because the child called Dust was growing older with every day that passed, and the bones of the baby's face were hardening inexorably hour by hour.

Under normal circumstances Victory would have required a team of three to assist with the operation, in addition to an anesthetist, but as things were he had to be content to work with Gwynplaine alone—and, of course, the computer to guide the robotic arm. It was as well that Gwynplaine proved exceedingly adept in an assistant role.

The first operation took four hours, the second three, and the third nearly six . . . but in the end, Victory's part was complete.

Victory had never been so exhausted in his life, but he did not want to retire to bed. Gwynplaine insisted that he could watch over the boy while the surgeon slept, but if Victory had not been at the very end of his tether he would never have consented to the arrangement. "If there's any change in his condition," Victory said, "Wake me immediately. If all's well, there'll be time in the morning take a final series of X-rays and to finalise the post-operative procedures."

But when the doctor woke up again Gwynplaine had vanished, taking the child and the book with him. He had also taken every scrap of paper on which Victory had made notes or drawings of his own—every one, at least, that he could find. Nor had the computer been spared. The instructions for the operation had been deleted and a virus had been set to work that would have trashed the hard disk—thus obliterating all the other notes Victory had covertly copied on to the machine and photographs of several pages from the book that he had taken unobtrusively with a digital camera—had it been allowed to run its course.

Fortunately, it seemed that Gwynplaine did not understand the workings of computers well enough to ensure the completion of this particular task of destruction. Victory was able to purge his machine of the virus before it had done too much damage, saving numerous precious remnants of the imperiled data.

A good deal of work would need to be done to recover and piece together the data he had contrived to steal, let alone to extrapolate that data into further fields of implication, but Victory had never been afraid of hard work. Although the material he had contrived to keep was only a tiny fraction of what he had been promised, he had enough information already to serve as fodder for half a dozen papers. Given time, his genius would allow him to build considerably on that legacy. Even if he could not recover all the secrets of the comprachicos, he felt certain that he could duplicate the majority of their discoveries—including, and especially, the last.

* * *

In the years that followed, Hugo Victory's skill and fame increased considerably. He was second to none as a pioneer in the fast-advancing art of plastic surgery, and he forced tabloid headline-writers to unprecedented excesses as they sought to wring yet more puns from his unusually helpful name. He lacked nothing—except, of course, for the one thing he wanted most of all: Gwynplaine's book.

On occasion, Victory paused to wonder how the experiment had turned out, and what the child's face might look like now that he was growing slowly towards the threshold of manhood—but he did not believe in Adam, or angels, or the existence of God. The existence of the book, on the other hand, was beyond doubt. He still wanted it, more than anything his money could buy or his celebrity could command.

He did all the obvious things. He hired private detectives, and

303

he scoured the Internet for any information at all connected with the name of Gwynplaine, or the society of comprachicos. He also published a painstakingly compiled photofit of Gwynplaine's remarkable face, asking for any information at all from anyone who had seen him.

Despite the accuracy of the image he had published, not one of the reports of sightings that he received produced any further evidence of Gwynplaine's existence. The detectives could not find anything either, even though they checked the records of every single burn victim through all the hospitals of Europe for half a century and more.

In the meantime, his Internet searches found far too much. There were more Gwynplaines in the world than Victory had ever imagined possible, and the comprachicos were as well known to every assiduous hunter of great historical conspiracies as the Knights Templar and the Rosicrucians. Somewhere in the millions of words that were written about their exploits there might have been a few grains of truth, but any such kernels were well and truly buried within a vast incoherent chaff of speculations, fictions, and downright lies.

Victory tracked down no less than a dozen copies of books allegedly containing the teratological secrets of the comprachicos, but none of them bore more than the faintest resemblance to the one Gwynplaine had shown him. Some of the diagrams in the older specimens gave some slight evidence that their forgers might have seen the original, but it seemed that none of them had been able to make a meticulous copy of a single image, and that none had had sufficient understanding of anatomy to make a good job of reproducing them from memory.

He had all but given up his quest when it finally bore fruit—but it was not the sort of fruit he had been expecting, and it was not a development that he was prepared to welcome.

When Janice's successor handed him the card bearing the name of Monsignor Torricelli, and told him that the priest in question wanted to talk to him about the fate of a certain mutilated child, Victory felt an inexplicable shudder of alarm, and it was on the tip of his tongue to ask the secretary to send the man away—but his curiosity was as powerful as it had ever been.

"Send him in, Meg," he said, calmly. "And hold my other appointments till I've done with him."

The Monsignor was a small dark man dressed in black-and-purple clerical garb. Meg took his cape and his little rounded hat away with her when she had shown him to his chair.

"You have some information for me, Father?" Victory asked, abruptly.

"None that you'll thank me for, I fear," Monsignor Torricelli countered. He was not a man incapable of smiling, and he demonstrated the fact. "But I hope you might be generous enough to do me a small service in return."

"What service would that be?" Victory enquired, warily—but the priest wasn't ready to spell that out without preamble.

"We've observed the progress of your search with interest," the little man told him. "Although you've never publicly specified the reason for your determination to find the individual you call Gwynplaine, it wasn't too difficult to deduce. He obviously showed you the book of the secrets of the comprachicos, and you've indicated by the terms of your search that he had a child with him. We assume that he persuaded you, by one means or another, to operate on the child. We also assume that he spoke to you about the face of Adam, and that you did not believe what he said. Am I right so far?"

"I'm not a Catholic," Victory said, without bothering to offer any formal sign of assent, "but I have a vague notion that a Monsignor is a member of the pope's own staff. Is that true?"

"Not necessarily, nowadays," the priest replied. "But in this particular case, yes. I am attached to the papal household as well as to the Holy Office."

"The Holy Office? You mean the Inquisition?"

"Your reading, though doubtless wide, is a little out of date, Dr. Victory. There is no Inquisition. There has been no Inquisition for two hundred years. Just as there has been no society of comprachicos for two hundred years."

"Do you know where Gwynplaine is?" Victory asked, abruptly.

"Yes." The answer seemed perfectly frank.

"Where?"

"Where he has always been—in hell."

Somehow, Victory felt less astonished by that statement than he should have been, although he did not suppose for a moment that Monsignor Torricelli meant to signify merely that Gwynplaine was dead.

"He wasn't in hell nine years ago," Victory said. "He was sitting where you are. And he spent the next ten days with me, in the lab and the theatre."

"From his point of view," Torricelli countered, still smiling, "this was hell, nor was he out of it. I am borrowing from Marlowe, of course, but the description is sound."

"You're telling me that Gwynplaine was—is—the devil."

"Of course. Had you really not understood that, or are you in what fashionable parlance calls *denial*?"

"I don't believe in the devil," Victory said, flatly.

"Of course you do," the Monsignor replied. "You can doubt the existence of God, but you can't doubt the existence of the devil. You're only human, after all. Good may be elusive within your experience, but not temptation. You may doubt that the devil can take human form, even though you and he were in such close and protracted proximity for ten long days, but you cannot possibly doubt the temptation to sin. You know pride, covetousness, envy—you, of all people, must have a very keen appreciation of the force of envy—and all the rest. Or is it only their deadliness that you doubt?"

"What other information do you have for me, Monsignor?" Victory tried to sound weary, but he couldn't entirely remove the edge of unease from his voice. He wondered whether there was a level somewhere beneath his conscious mind in which he did indeed retain a certain childlike faith in the devil, and an equally childlike certainty that he had once met him in human guise—but the thought was difficult to bear. If the devil existed, then God presumably existed too, and that possibility was too horrible to contemplate.

"The child died," Torricelli said, bluntly.

Strangely enough, that seemed more surprising than the allegation that Gwynplaine was the devil. Victory sat a little straighter in his chair, and stared harder at the man whose smile, even now, had not quite disappeared.

"How do you know?" he asked.

"You hired a dozen private detectives to search for you, who hadn't the slightest idea what they were up against. We have a worldwide organization at our disposal, which knew exactly what to look for as soon as your postings had alerted us. The child died before he was a year old. Don't be alarmed, Dr. Victory—you weren't responsible. So far as we could judge, the operations you performed were probably successful. It was the adversary's part that went awry. It's all happened before, of course, a dozen times over. If it's any comfort to you, this was the first time since 1665 that the cutter's part was properly done. If he'd only been prepared to honour his bargain and let you help with the part that remained to be done . . . but that's not his way. You may think yourself a proud and covetous man, but you're only the faintest echo of your model."

"If you weren't a priest," Victory observed, "I'd suspect you of being insane. Given that you are a priest, I suppose delusions of that kind are merely part and parcel of the faith."

"Perhaps," the little man conceded, refreshing his cherubic smile. "I wonder if, perchance, you suspected Mr. Gwynplaine of being insane, when he too was only suffering the delusions of his faith."

Victory didn't smile in return. "I don't see how I can help you," he said. "If the resources of your worldwide organization have enabled you to discover that the child's dead and that Gwynplaine's safe in hell, what can you possibly want from me?"

"We've been monitoring your publications and your operations for the last few years, Dr. Victory," Torricelli said, letting his smile die in a peculiarly graceful manner. "We know how hard you've worked to make full use of the scraps of information that you plundered from the devil's book, while labouring under the delusion that he didn't mean to let you keep them. We know how ingeniously you've sought to use the separate elements of the operation you carried out on his behalf. I'm sure he's been watching you just as intently. We suspect that your busy hands have done almost all of the work that he found for them and that he's ready to pay you another visit, to offer you a new bargain. We don't suppose that it will do any good to warn you, although we'd be delighted to be surprised . . . but we do hope that you might be prepared to give the incomplete programme to us instead of completing it for him."

Until the priest used the word "programme," Victory had been perfectly prepared to believe that the whole conversation was so much hot air, generated by the fact that the lunatic fringe of the Holy Office was every bit as interested in crazy conspiracy theories as all the other obsessive Internet users who were fascinated by the imaginary histories of the Templars, the Rosicrucians, the Illuminati, and the comprachicos. Even then, he struggled against the suspicion that he had been rumbled.

"What programme?" He said.

"The most recently updated version of the software you use to show your clients what they'll look like when you've completed the courses of surgery you've outlined for them. The one whose code has finally been modified to take in all but one of the novel procedures to which the adversary introduced you. The one which would reproduce the face of Adam, if you could only insert that last missing element into the code—the tantalising element that the devil has carefully reserved to his own custody."

Victory tried hard to control his own expression, lest it give too much away. He had known, of course, that he had come close to a final resolution of the comprachicos' last secret, but he had not been able to determine that he was only one step short. But on what authority, he wondered, had the Monsignor decided that he was almost home? Did the Vatican have plastic surgeons and computer hackers at its disposal? If it did, would they be set to work on tasks of this bizarre sort? If so, had the men in question genius enough not only to steal his work but to read it more accurately than he had read it himself?

It was too absurd.

"Why would I give my work to anyone while it's incomplete?" Victory asked. "And why shouldn't I show it to everyone, when I've perfected it? Surely that's what you ought to want—if what Gwynplaine told me is true, it ought to put humankind back on the path to salvation."

"He's not called the father of lies without reason," the priest observed. "He was an angel himself, before his own fall. He doesn't remember what he and Adam looked like, but he knows full well that the comprachicos weren't searching for a way to set mankind on the path to salvation. Quite the reverse, in fact. Why do you think they were condemned as heretics and annihilated?"

"I understand the politics of persecution well enough to know that so-called heretics didn't need to be guilty of anything to be hounded to extinction by the Church," Victory retorted.

"I doubt that you do," Torricelli said, with a slight regretful sigh. "But that's by the by. We'll pay you for the programme as it presently exists, if you wish—provided that we can obtain all rights in the intellectual property, and that you agree to desist from all further work on the project."

Victory was slightly curious to know what price the Vatican might be willing to pay, but he didn't want to waste time. "I already have more money than I can spend," he said, proudly. "The only thing I want that I don't have is the book I saw nine years ago—and I'm not entirely sure that I need it any longer. I don't have any particular interest in the faces of angels but I'm extremely curious to know what the results of the operation I performed might have been, if the boy had lived."

"You're making a mistake, Dr. Victory," said Monsignor Torricelli.

"You needn't worry about me selling out to the opposition," Victory said. "I've dealt with Gwynplaine before. This time, I'll need copies made in advance—and then we'll be even. Afterwards, I might let him look at what the programme produces—but I'm certainly not going to let him walk off with it while I have the strength to stop him."

"I wish you'd reconsider," the priest persisted. "No harm will be done if you stop now, even though you're so close. The Adversary might be able to complete the programme himself if he steals the present version, but he wants more than a computer-generated image. He'd still need an artist in flesh, and that he isn't. He isn't even as clever with computers as he'd like to be."

"I find that difficult to believe," Victory observed, sarcastically.

"The reason he makes so much work for other idle hands," Monsignor Torricelli said sadly, "is that his own are afflicted with too many obsolete habits. It was his part of the scheme that went wrong, remember, not yours. It's as dangerous to overestimate him as it is to underestimate him. Don't do his work for him, Dr. Victory. Don't give him what he wants. You know he doesn't play fair. You know who and what he is, if you'll only admit it to yourself. You still have a choice in this matter. Use it wisely, I beg of you."

"That's what I'm trying to do," Victory assured him. "It's just that my wisdom and your faith don't see eye to eye."

"We're prepared to give you more than money," Torricelli said, with the air of one who is obliged to play his last card, even though the game had been lost for some considerable time. "You're an art collector, I believe."

"I'm not prepared to be bribed, even with works of art," Victory said. "I'm an artist myself, and my own creativity comes first."

"Human creativity is always secondary to God's," Monsignor Torricelli riposted. "I hope you'll remember that, when the time comes."

* * *

In the wake of Torricelli's visit Victory returned to his computer model with renewed zest. There was so much obvious nonsense in what the priest had told him that there was no real reason to believe the assurance that he was only one step short of being able to reproduce—at least on paper—the face of Adam, but Victory had no need of faith to season his curiosity. He felt that he was, indeed, close to that particular goal, and the feeling was enough to lend urgency to his endeavours.

Part of his problem lay in the fact that the transformative software had to begin with the image of a child only a few weeks old. When Victory used computer imaging to inform a forty-year-old woman what she would look like when he had worked his magic, the new image was constructed on the same finished bone structure, modifying muscles that were already in their final form, removing superfluous fat and remodelling skin whose flexibility was limited. A baby's face, by contrast, was as yet unmade. The bones were still soft, the muscles were vulnerable to all manner of influence by use and habit, the minutely-layered fat still had vital metabolic functions to perform, and the overlying skin had a great deal of growing and stretching yet to do.

Even the best conventional software could only offer the vaguest impression of the adult face that would eventually emerge from infantile innocence, because that emergence was no mere matter of predestined revelation. Integrating the effects of early surgery into conventional software usually made the results even more uncertain— and no matter how ingeniously Victory had laboured to overcome these difficulties, he had not been able to set them entirely aside. He had to suppose that if and when he could produce a perfect duplicate of the comprachicos' instructions, the surgical modifications specified therein would somehow obliterate the potential variability that infant faces usually had, but every hypothetical alteration he made by way of experiment had the opposite effect, increasing the margin of causation left to chance and circumstance.

Whatever the missing piece of the puzzle was, it must be a piece of magical—perhaps miraculous—subtlety and power.

There were, in the meantime, other aspects of the comprachicos' field of expertise that continued to reveal interesting results and applications, but Victory had lost his ability to content himself with petty triumphs. No matter how much nonsense Torricelli had spouted, he had been right to call the project "tantalising."

The five weeks that elapsed between Torricelli's attempt to bribe him and Gwynplaine's reappearance were the most tortuous of Victo-

311

ry's life, and the fact that the torture in question was entirely self-inflicted did not make it any easier to bear.

This time, Gwynplaine did not bother to telephone for an appointment. He simply turned up one evening, long after Meg had gone home, when Victory was still working at his computer. He was not carrying his briefcase.

"You're a very difficult man to find, Mr. Gwynplaine," Victory observed, as his visitor settled himself into the chair on the far side of his desk.

"Not according to my detractors," Gwynplaine observed, as unsmilingly as ever. "According to them, I'm impossible to avoid—urgently present in every malicious impulse and every self-indulgent whim."

"Are you telling me that you really are the devil?"

"Don't be ridiculous, Dr. Victory. There is no devil. He's an invention of the Church—an instrument of moral terrorism. Priests have always embraced the defeatist belief that the only way to persuade people to be good is to threaten them with eternal torment. You and I know better than that. We understand that the only worthwhile way to persuade people to be good is to show them the rewards that will flow from virtuous endeavour. There has to be more to hope for than vague promises of bliss beyond death. If anyone's living proof of that, it's you."

"So who are you, really?" Victory tried, as he said it, to meet Gwynplaine's disconcerting stare with the kind of detachment that befitted a man who could repair every horror and enhance every beauty, but it wasn't easy.

"I was sold as a child," Gwynplaine said, his eerie voice becoming peculiarly musical again. "Adam's is not the only face the comprachicos tried to reproduce. The society is not yet extinct, no matter what the pope may think—but its members are mere butchers nowadays, while men like you follow other paths."

"That was done to you deliberately?"

"It wasn't quite the effect they intended to produce."

"And before? Were you . . . like the boy you brought me nine years ago."

"No. I was healthy, and fair of face. Angelic, even. I might have become . . . well, that's water under the bridge. Even you could not help me now, Dr. Victory. I hope to see the face of Adam before I die, but not in a mirror."

In spite of his impatience, Victory could not help asking one more question. "Was Torricelli lying?" he asked. "Or did he really believe what he told me."

"He believed it," Gwynplaine told him, his gaze never wavering within his frightful mask. "He still believes it—but he won't interfere again, because he also believes that the devil operates on Earth with the permission of God."

Victory decided that it was time to get down to business. "Where's the book?" he demanded.

"Safe in the custody of its rightful owners," Gwynplaine told him. "You don't need it. Nine years of nurturing the seeds I lent you has prepared you for what needs to be done. All you need now is the master key—and a child."

Victory shook his head. "No," he said. "That's not the way it's going to be done. Not this time. This time, I get all the information first. This time, I get to see the face on my computer before I make a single cut. No arguments—it's my way, or not at all. You cheated me once; I won't trust you again."

"If I broke my promise," Gwynplaine said, "it was for your own good. If I'd succeeded in my part of the project . . . but that's more water under the bridge. You're not the only one who's been doing things the hard way these last nine years. We're almost there—but I'd be doing you a grave disservice if I didn't warn you that you're in danger. If you'll condescend to take my advice you'll leave the programme incomplete until you have to use it to guide the robot arm. Don't attempt to preview the result. No harm can come to you if you work in the flesh of a child and allow me to take him away when you've finished—but I can't protect you if you refuse to take my advice."

"And what, exactly, will become of me if I look at the face of

313

Adam on my computer before I attempt to reproduce it in the flesh?"

"I don't know. Nobody knows—certainly not Monsignor Torricelli. In contrast to the fanciful claims of legend, the Church has never had the slightest contact with the world of the angels."

"So your warning is just so much bluster?" Victory said.

"No. I'm trying to protect my own interests. I don't want anything unfortunate to happen to you before you repeat the experiment—or afterwards, for that matter."

"But you said before that the face of Adam would bring about a religious renaissance—that it would inspire everyone who saw it to forsake sin and seek salvation."

"I said nothing of the kind," Gwynplaine said, equably. "I only said that the comprachicos believed that. You already know that the Church believes otherwise. So do I. I may be privy to the comprachicos' secrets, but I'm not one of them. I'm their victim and their emissary, but I'm also my own person. For myself, I haven't the slightest interest in the salvation or damnation of humankind."

"So what *do* you want out of this?"

"That's my business. The question is, doctor—what do *you* want out of it, and what are you prepared to risk in order to get it? I've given you the warning that I was duty bound to offer. If you're prepared to take the risk, having had fair warning, so am I. I can't give you the book, but I can give you the last piece that's missing from your painstaking reconstruction of its final secret. If you insist on seeing an image before you attempt to produce the real thing I won't try again to prevent it. If, after seeing the image, you're unable to conduct the operation, I'll simply take the results of all your hard work to California. My advice to you is that you should find a suitable child, and conduct the operation as before, without a preview of the likely result. Take it or leave it—in either case, I intend to proceed."

"I'll leave the advice," Victory said. "But I'll take the missing piece of the puzzle."

Gwynplaine reached into the inside pocket of his ridiculously unfashionable jacket and produced a folded piece of paper. If he really had been in hell the inferno was obviously equipped with photocopiers. Victory unfolded the piece of paper and looked at the diagram thus revealed.

He stared at it for a minute and a half, and then he let out his breath.

"Of course," he said. "So simple, so neat—and yet I'd never have found it without the cue. Diabolically ingenious."

Gwynplaine did not take the trouble to contradict him.

* * *

Gwynplaine sat languidly in the chair, a perfect exhibition of patience, while Victory's busy fingers flew over the keyboard and clicked the mouse again and again, weaving the final ingredient into the model that would reproduce the face of Adam when the programme was run.

It was not a simple matter of addition, because the code had to be modified in a dozen different places to accommodate the formulas describing the final incision-and-connection.

Victory had half-expected the code itself to be mysteriously beautified, but it remained mere code, symbolising a string of ones and zeroes as impenetrable to the naked eye and innocent mind as any other. Until the machine converted it into pictures it was inherently lifeless and vague—but when the job was done . . .

In the end, Victory looked up. He didn't bother to look at his wristwatch, but it was pitch dark outside and Harley Street was in the grip of the kind of silence that only fell for a brief interval in the small hours.

"It's ready," he said. "You'd better join me if you want to watch."

"If you don't mind," Gwynplaine said, "I'll stay on this side of the desk and watch you. I have patience enough to wait for the real thing."

"If Torricelli were here," Victory said, "he'd probably remind me of the second commandment." He was looking at the screen as he said it, where he had set up the face of a three-week-old child. He had chosen the child at random; any one, he supposed, would do as well as another.

"If Torricelli were here," Gwynplaine said, "neither of us would give a fig for anything he said."

Victory drew the mouse across the pad, and launched the programme.

He had watched its predecessors run a thousand times before, without seeing anything unusual in the adult face that formed in consequence. He had run them so many times, in fact, that he had ceased to believe that there was any conceivable human face that could have any unusual effect on his inquiring eye and mind. When he tried to imagine what the face of Adam might look like, all he could summon to mind was the image painted by Michelangelo on the ceiling of the Sistine Chapel.

But Adam did not look like that at all.

Adam's face was unimaginable by any ordinary mortal—even an artist of genius.

While learning the basics of medicine forty-two years before, Hugo Victory had been informed that each of his eyes had a blind spot where the neurons of the optic nerve spread out to connect to the rods and cones in the retina. Because he had always been slightly myopic, his blind spots had been slightly larger than those of people with perfect vision, but they still did not show up in the image of the world formulated by his brain. Even if he placed a hand over one eye, to eliminate the exchange of visual information between the hemispheres of his cerebral cortex, he still saw the world entire and unblemished, free of any void. That, he had been told, was an illusion. It was not that the brain "filled in" the missing data to complete the image, but rather that the brain ignored the part of the image that was not there, so efficiently that its absence was imperceptible. And yet, the blind spot was there. Anything eclipsed by it was not merely invisible, but left no clue as to its absence.

It was a blind spot of sorts—albeit a trivial one—that had prevented Victory from being able to see or deduce the missing element in his model of the comprachicos' final secret. It was likewise a blind spot of sorts—but by no means a trivial one—that had prevented him and every other man in the world from extrapolating the face of Adam and the angels from his knowledge of the vast spectrum of ordinary human faces.

Now, the blind spot was removed. His mind was no longer able to ignore that which had previously been hidden even from the power of imagination. Hugo Victory saw an image of the proto-human face that had been made in God's image.

Quietly, he began to weep—but his tears dried up much sooner than he could have wished.

His right hand—acting, apparently, without the benefit of any conscious command—moved the mouse, very carefully, across its mat, and clicked it again in order to exit from the programme.

He watched without the slightest reservation or complaint as Gwynplaine, who had waited until then to move around the desk, carefully burned the programme on to a CD that he had appropriated from the storage cabinet.

"I told you so," the man with the hideous face murmured, not unkindly, as he carefully set the computer to reformat the hard disk. "I played as fair as I dared to be. That wasn't the real thing, of course. It was just a photograph, lacking even the resolution it might have had. You should have done as I asked and worked directly on a child, Dr. Victory. It might require a dozen more attempts, or a hundred, but in time, one of them will survive to adulthood. *That* will be the real thing. At least, I hope so. The comprachicos might not have got it absolutely right, of course. Even now, I still have to bear that possibility in mind. But I remain hopeful—and now I have something that's worth taking to California, I'm one step nearer to my goal."

"It's strange," Victory said, wondering why he had utterly ceased to care. "When you first came into my office, nine years ago, I thought you were the most awfully disfigured man I'd ever seen. I couldn't imagine why the doctors who'd treated you after your accident hadn't done more to ameliorate the effect of the burns. But now I've grown used to you, you seem perfectly ordinary. Hideous, but perfectly ordinary. I thought nine years ago—and still thought, ninety minutes ago—that I could do something for you, if you'd only permit me to try, but now I see that I couldn't . . . that there's simply nothing to be done."

"It's not strange to me," Gwynplaine assured him. "I've lived among the comprachicos. I understand these things better than any man alive . . . with one possible exception, now. I hope you can find it in your heart to forgive me for that enlightenment."

"I don't feel capable of forgiveness any more," Victory said. "Or hatred either. Or . . . "

"Much as I'd like to hear the rest of the list," Gwynplaine said, apologetically, "I really must be going. If you see Monsignor Torricelli again, please give him my fondest regards. Unlike him, you see, I really have learned to love my enemies."

* * *

It was not until Meg arrived at half past eight that Victory had the opportunity to assess the full extent of the change that had come over him, but once the evidence was before him he understood its consequences easily enough.

Meg, like Janice before her, was an unusually beautiful young woman. A plastic surgeon had to surround himself with beautiful people, in order to advertise and emphasize his powers as a healer. But Meg now seemed, to Victory's unprejudiced and fully awakened sight, not one iota more or less beautiful than Gwynplaine. She looked, in fact, absolutely ordinary: aesthetically indistinguishable from every other member of the human race. Nor could Victory imagine any practicable transformation that would bring about the slightest improvement.

It was, he realised, going to be rather difficult to function efficiently as a plastic surgeon from now on. So extreme was the devastation of his aesthetic capacity, in fact, that Victory could not think of any field of human endeavour in which he might be able to function creatively or productively—but the inability did not cause him any distress.

Even the idea that he was now in a kind of hell, beyond any possibility of escape or redemption, could not trouble him in the least.

Nor could the faintly absurd suspicion that he might have provided the means for the devil to free himself, at long last, from the voracious burden of his envy of humankind.

VILLAGE OF THE MERMAIDS
Lance Olsen

For Paul Delvaux.

THE WARM SMUDGED air green-blue as sadness.

The warm smudged air and the whitewashed wall commencing halfway down the narrow street.

The whitewashed cliff behind us.

The warm smudged air, the whitewashed wall, the whitewashed cliff, the whitewashed mountains beyond the cocaine white beach in the distance.

And our crisp shadows.

The crisp shadows of the fishermen's huts behind us.

All the crisp shadows drawing themselves out as if time might at any moment begin passing here, as if motion might suddenly become somehow possible, as if significant motion beyond the motion of memory might suddenly become somehow possible.

Memory and thought.

What passes for thought, of course.

Thought being a very strong word.

321

I am the one on the left, by the way, the second one on the left, her gaze slightly lower than the gazes of those around her, because it has occurred to me recently that I cannot say as much as I know.

As much as I suspect I know.

These being two different things entirely.

I cannot say anything, in point of fact.

None of us can.

Say anything, that is.

Say anything, or shut our eyes, or walk.

I cannot say, for instance, that no one lives in those huts at our backs. That there exist no huts at our backs, to be precise. That they are simply façades, you see, behind which glitters more warm air, more cliffs, more crisp shadows.

Presumably.

The doors lead nowhere.

I believe the doors lead nowhere.

They won't, in any case, open.

Look at them closely and you will notice they lack handles or knobs.

I want to say that we cannot speak.

I want to say that we cannot shut our eyes.

I want to say that, in the beginning, at the moment memory became the only motion, the only nontrivial motion, I unthinkingly tried to stand one day, stand and walk, stand and walk and follow a man not unlike the man in the black bowler just now rounding the corner and passing out of sight, perhaps on his way to the cocaine white beach.

It could have been the same man, in point of fact.

This is not wholly out of the question.

I tried to stand, stand and walk, stand and walk and follow that man, a man like that man, perhaps being the better way to put it, and then I was lying on the packed sandy dirt that comprises the narrow street, the narrow street or one could go as far as to say alley, on which we found ourselves.

On my belly.

322

On my belly and with pungent sandy dust among my teeth.

I opened and closed my mouth silently, fishlike.

It being difficult to breathe through the gills that have appeared in my neck, you see, gills that seem to have appeared in my neck, though there is always a chance, needless to say, that they have been there all along, and that I simply never noticed them before.

Inhalation be that as it may thus impeded by the high wooly collar of this green-gray dress in which I find myself.

My arms, for all intents and purposes, have ceased to function.

This much is clear.

This much seems to be clear.

It is extraordinary, the things one fails to notice until one is in the thick of them.

I was—to make a long story short—lying there on the narrow street.

Street or perhaps alley.

On the packed dirt, at any rate, the packed pungent sandy dirt.

Thinking.

I was lying there, thinking, and in the fullness of time it dawned on me that to effect movement, to effect any meaningful movement, I needed to enlist the support of what I presumed for fairly sound reasons to be my feet, but as a matter of fact were not my feet.

Not anymore.

Initially it felt as though I were wearing rubber snorkeling fins several sizes too large for me and that someone had roped my legs together.

Then I realized that that feeling was simply me.

This is who I am, I want to say.

Who I was and who I am, to be exact.

To be more exact.

A series of shrugging movements centered in my belly and spine.

Belly, spine, flank.

The pungent sandy dust searing my eyes.

Progress, consequential progress, taking the form of let us say ten or twelve yards an hour.

323

On land.

In the sea, of course, it is quite a different thing.

In the sea, off the cocaine white beach, you feel free.

Your cumbersome body goes weightless, your movements graceful, the unpleasant details of the environment around you thinning out and shrinking into a small radiant dot in a far corner of your consciousness, seeming to thin out and shrink, the pale green seawater dense and cool like a distant recollection of let us call it hope, the moisture in your unclosing eyes enough to make you cry.

If you could cry.

You can't, though.

Instead, your tear ducts produce a viscous oil to help you see beneath the waves.

Initially, I swam straightaway for the horizon.

Anyone would have done.

I swam straightaway for the horizon, first above the waves, then beneath them, fast as I could go.

Madly, in actual fact.

One could without much exaggeration employ the adverb *madly* to describe my forward progress.

For hours.

Hours and hours.

Trying to recall precisely what I was swimming toward.

Which past, I mean.

And, gradually, swimming, shreds of memory began to dart past my head like shreds of seaweed, shreds of seaweed or colorful filamentous tissue, and then I was sitting somewhere else, erect, palms folded in my lap, gaze slightly lower than those who sat around me, maintaining an approximation of the same posture I do currently in front of these fishermen's huts.

These imitation fishermen's huts.

It was dark.

It was almost dark.

I was almost dark and it was for some reason very loud with the sound of . . . engines, I believe I want to say.

Yes, thunderous engines.

The white ghost of a handsome man sat beside me.

He was my age, more or less.

He wore a charcoal pinstriped suit but had removed the jacket. His shirt was luminescent in the almost-darkness, his hair cropped neatly like a London businessman's.

His tie, simple and black, was loose.

The faint outline of his shaved facial hair struck me as bluish and slick and beautiful.

I remembered how, rubbing the back of his neck with his palm, he tilted his pale beautiful face up toward let us say the ceiling and opened his mouth, perhaps to speak to me, perhaps to speak to someone nearby, perhaps to laugh at something witty I had said a few seconds earlier, and then my world turned into shuddering, vaporous light.

I swam for hours and hours.

Until I was exhausted.

Until my muscles felt like they were dissolving beneath my skin.

My gills swelled and stung.

And, when I finally heaved my head above the surface, I discovered I had traveled no more than ten yards from the beach.

Ten yards and no more.

I was appalled. I was frightened. I was devastated.

I floated there, in a state of burning disbelief, for what must have been quite a long while, though the sun remained precisely at the same position in the sky it always had—perhaps east, perhaps west, perhaps somewhere in between, it being impossible to tell with anything approaching let us call it certainty.

Then, attempting but failing to cry, I swam back to shore, pulled myself onto the sand, lay there experiencing the incontrovertible data of gravity, and then lurched home, what passed for home, increasingly determined as I struggled on my belly along the street or conceivably alley that curled up the hill of huts that this foray could not possibly mark the end of something, but must rather mark the start.

Next day, as anyone would have done, I undertook the same journey again.

As almost anyone would have done.

I shrugged down to the beach, pungent sandy dust searing my eyes, flopped into the sea, and swam.

This time, however, I made a point to rest on and off.

Rest on and off, regain my strength, then plunge forward.

With renewed vigor, you see.

Rest, regain strength, plunge forward.

As I swam, the darkness reappeared around me.

The ghost.

The darkness and the ghost seemed to reappear around me.

Then the light that shocks straight through you more like sound waves than photons.

And then, of course, surfacing, I found myself precisely where I had found myself the day before.

Precisely perhaps being too strong a word.

But still.

That's it.

That's all.

I want to say I wish there were more to this story, but there you have it.

This is who I was and who I am, too, it turns out.

This is who we all were and are here, presumably.

Sometimes, it almost goes without mentioning, someone new shows up in a new chair in front of a new hut that isn't I have fair reason to suspect a real hut.

You are gazing straight ahead, trying to remember, perhaps, trying to remember or trying not to remember, and all at once out of the corner of your vision there is another person and another hut beside you.

It is nothing if not vaguely troubling.

Her hair, the new person's hair, is always light brown.

She cannot speak.

Her eyes, which are almost black, won't shut.

She folds her hands in her lap and begins to wait.

Sometimes after a while you can see an idea flower within her features.

Sometimes she will stand, you see, try to stand, then collapse onto the sandy dust, thrash about, thrash about or, depending on her constitution, simply lie still, thinking, perhaps, thinking or not thinking, of course, and then either commence her long toil down to the memory beach or clumsily raise herself back into her seat and reassume her position, which may appear very much the same as my position, but is in actual fact different in a thousand ways if one were to submit it to any serious sort of scrutiny.

Her dress, like mine, remains immaculate.

I don't know why this is the case, but it does.

Sometimes a man in a black bowler who may always be the same man but then again may not be the same man passes by as if he were strolling down to the shore.

He never reaches it.

He strolls to the corner of the narrow street, of the narrow street or alley, obviously, and then simply winks out of existence.

Appears to wink out of existence.

A day later, a day or two later, he reappears from the opposite direction, passing by again.

He is short.

He carries a black umbrella.

He carries a black umbrella, and yet it never rains here.

It never rains. There is no breeze. The clouds do not move.

He carries a black umbrella and sometimes an easel, a canvas, a wooden box of oil paints.

He composes our portraits, you see, and then he composes them again.

Each picture is the same picture, day after day.

Day perhaps being too strong a word.

It isn't, in other words, as if he were trying to get the painting right. That isn't the feeling of this experience at all. Rather, it is as if he were simply doing his job, documenting something, perhaps, witnessing, the same way that sitting here may be called in a manner of speaking doing my job.

This man, if it is the same man, never speaks to us.

We of course never speak to him.

He paints, whistles under his breath, then, done, rises, packs, and walks away.

He is always painting, always whistling, always walking away.

This is the point, somehow, I want to say.

I want to say this is who he was and is.

I want to say you get used to this.

I want to say you can get used to anything.

But in actual fact you cannot.

Get used to anything, that is.

It turns out that there are many things you cannot get used to.

In any case, to make a long story short, I sit here until I cannot sit here any longer, then I shrug my way down to the memory beach and swim for the horizon of the let us call it past tense, feeling free.

Sometimes, needless to say, feeling freer than at other times.

Once I remembered, or believed I remembered, a month.

December, for the purposes of argument.

And a year.

1988.

Christmas seemed only four days away.

Four or five days away.

Certainly no more than a week.

I seemed to have been studying in London—at Birkbeck College, I believe I want to say.

At Birkbeck College or at King's College, Kensington.

One or the other, almost surely.

I seem to have been on my way to the States to visit my family.

My mum, dad, and younger sister had trained up from Sussex a fortnight earlier to go ahead on a skiing holiday to Aspen.

Aspen, Colorado.

I hadn't seen them all semester.

I want to say I was planning to graduate in the spring with an emphasis, I am fairly confident, in art history.

I want to say that I might even have had something modest lined up, something modest almost lined up, by way of employment, in a small yet elegant gallery in Birmingham.

This is all I wanted, really: to live in the art world.

In any event, it had been a lonely autumn, a desperately exciting autumn, a desperately disorientating autumn, the best autumn of my life, apparently, one or all of these things, or perhaps some triadic combination of them, and I had gathered so many memories during the past few months that it would take me several lifetimes to sort them all out.

I had so many stories to tell my parents that I physically ached.

I physically ached with the fullness of news.

And yet, at this juncture in time, I'm afraid I can't quite seem to recall any of the particulars with any real specificity.

My younger sister, who I am inclined to say possessed a gorgeous name, would be in Denver with my parents to meet me.

The next morning we would drive through the mountains to Aspen.

It was, I want to say, one of my favorite drives on earth.

That night she would sneak, my sister would sneak, into my bed in our hotel room and say she wanted to hear everything, absolutely everything, about my boyfriends and my studies and my brilliant secret weekend on Ibiza with my girlfriends, on Ibiza or quite possibly in Istanbul, either one is likely, though neither is honestly more likely than the other, and then, ten minutes later, she would prop her left foot on her right knee and proceed to pick at it absentmindedly, already all fagged out by these tired sisterly reports from the front.

I want to say that as a partial Christmas present my parents reserved me a seat in Business Class because they knew how very much I adored the sparkling cosmos on the other side of the heavy gray-green curtain at the front of the plane.

How, in the blink of an eye after I took my seat, the flight attendant approached and inquired if I might care for a glass of champagne, and how, when she returned with my drink, she brought a fairy-tale sized bowl of smoked almonds and assorted nuts, her mien resonating with the decorum of one could perhaps say a sort of pluperfect world.

Its action, that is, completed a very long time ago.

I want to say that I shouldn't think such toffee-nosed thoughts, but there you have it.

I plugged in my headphones, turned to the classical music channel on the console in my armrest, eased back, closed my eyes, and sipped a drink that tasted like diamond tiaras look, daydreaming about how you couldn't think of anything else on your way down a run except the rush of the run itself, an epinephrine blaze expanding until it packed the inside of your ribcage, the snowy whiteness scudding past you like some massive existential erasure, and, when I opened my eyes again, there he was.

He had taken off his charcoal pinstriped jacket and folded it carefully to stow in the overhead compartment.

Before he could raise his arms, however, the flight attendant had bustled up with a clothes hanger and whisked his jacket away.

He followed her up the aisle with a bemused smile and then lowered himself into the seat beside me, immediately initiating a search for the flaps of his seatbelt.

"Blast these things," he announced to no one, raising his body, checking beneath himself like a mother hen, huffing down once more. "Perpetual lessons in humility, aren't they."

I slipped down my headphones.

"It could be worse," I offered. "They could always force us to wear those goofy yellow life vests under our seats."

"Allegedly under our seats," he said, still fidgeting. "For all we know they're in actual fact nothing but yellow sandwich bags placed there to make us feel marginally better about ourselves before the knowledge that no one to date has survived a crash landing at sea in a 747."

"Is that true?"

"I haven't a clue, really. But it stands to reason, doesn't it, winged buildings falling out of the sky and all. Are you on holiday?"

We thereby launched into the kind of conversation that well-mannered, slightly bored people on airplanes do who care less about what the person with whom they are speaking is saying than about passing a few minutes on an extraordinarily lengthy flight.

His name, by the way, was—

I forget what his name was, to be honest.

I'm not absolutely convinced I ever knew it.

Yet for some reason I seem to recall him more fully than any member of my own family.

If this is recollection, I wonder precisely what it is good for.

In any case, we talked about—

Well, I'm not one hundred percent sure what we talked about, either.

We talked about let us call it this and that while the flight attendant collected our empty glasses and pipsqueak bowls, and the plane lumbered onto the runway, and its engines all at once engaged with fury, and the force of acceleration pressed us back into our seats, and the fuselage wobbled and torqued, and through my porthole I could see the wings shudder as we lifted, and then we were airborne and the English countryside was tumbling away into darkness broken by myriad glimmering pinpricks of light.

I want to say that it is almost a given that he and I learned many interesting things about one another.

I want to say how much I wish I could remember what those things were.

Yet what I summon up at this juncture is how quickly our conversation trailed off into that awkward sputter of observation and assertion about let us call it for argument's sake how much London has to offer, culturally speaking, though not of course at that time of year, not over the Christmas holidays, or the sad banalities associated with the quality of airline food, or perhaps the vibrant gracelessness of New Yorkers and, by subtle extension, the vibrant gracelessness of all Americans everywhere—that awkward sputter of observation and assertion, in other words, which tends to flag the instant directly before one party or the other reaches forward with feigned interest for the flight magazine tucked into the seat back in front of him or her.

331

I want to say how much more I have always expected from such exchanges.

How I have continually entered into them with perhaps a certain naïve optimism, and how, at the end of the day, I am always faintly unnerved and disheartened by how little any two strangers have to say to one another.

Consequently, we both tacitly agreed to let our conversation unravel into courteous silence.

I drifted back into my I want to say Vivaldi, Vivaldi or Bach, a lovely concerto at any rate, and, sometime after that, perhaps an hour, perhaps a little less, a little less or a little more, out the corner of my vision I noticed that he, rubbing the back of his neck with his palm, tilted his pale beautiful face up and opened his mouth—not, as it turns out, I'm afraid, to speak to me, or to speak to someone nearby, or to laugh at something witty I had said a few seconds earlier—but rather to yawn, simply to yawn, in preparation I suspect for stealing some shuteye as the plane readied to peel away from the I believe it was Scottish coast.

Then the light arrived.

It was almost-dark and then the vaporous light surged in.

It hurled up through the floor like a tsunami of illumination, arriving with the intensity of something felt rather than seen, and then the plane rolled, climbed steeply, and the fuselage began to disintegrate around me.

At the time, I couldn't be exactly sure why.

I can't be exactly sure why even now.

I remember thinking, however, I believe I remember thinking, however, sitting there as the concept of Inside became the concept of Outside, that this is what they presumably refer to when they say *a catastrophic structural failure.*

This is what they presumably refer to when they say *an uncontrolled descent.*

And, fleetingly, perhaps for the space of let us say a quick insuck of breath, the young man reached over and lay his perspiring hand in my lap.

The gesture struck me as purely reflexive in nature.

I reached for it, needless to say, his hand, as anyone would do.

As almost anyone would do.

Reflexively.

And that's when I realized his fingers were crossed.

He was crossing his fingers.

I remember thinking, I believe I remember thinking, even then, what a remarkable gesture: crossing one's fingers in a situation like this.

And then his hand wasn't there anymore.

His hand wasn't there and he wasn't there.

His hand wasn't there and he wasn't there and the interior of the 747 wasn't there anymore, either.

It was dark again.

The vaporous light was gone and it was spectacularly dark and spectacularly cold, brutally dark and cold.

My lungs refused to work.

I imagined them abruptly turning into a fist of ice in my chest.

All around me, the silhouettes of passengers still buckled into their seats rained down.

Above, the sky ignited into oranges, yellows, and washed-out greens.

It seemed many people were still engaged in watching an onboard movie as they fell.

Others hurried looks around them in astonishment as if, like somnambulists awakened without warning, they couldn't quite understand where they were or how they had gotten there.

Or perhaps they were trying very hard to take full advantage of their faculty of sight in the few seconds left to take advantage of it.

Some seemed to be napping, chins on chests, hair flapping above their heads like tongues of black flame.

But most were simply facing straight ahead.

Most seemed to be facing straight ahead, watching a movie called their lives.

For perhaps half a minute.

Half a minute or a minute.

It was then I realized that time had begun coming apart in a fashion similar to the way the plane had begun coming apart—tearing, tattering, stripping away on all sides.

My consciousness, in a spontaneous impulse to survive, leapt away from me.

It entered the body of a passing bird.

It seemed to leap away and enter the body of a passing bird.

I want to say the bird was a gull, a gull or a tern, the latter of course related to and resembling the gull but characteristically smaller and possessing a forked tail, which in either case then veered away from the cataclysm toward the sea.

Three years later, three or four, it became entangled in a fisherman's net off the coast of Morocco one morning and drowned.

Cursing, the fisherman plucked it from his net and threw it overboard into the silver fog, where a school of Spanish mackerel set about ingesting it, thereby dispersing my consciousness among many bodies so that I suddenly saw the world from myriad perspectives at once, like a living kaleidoscope, and then part of my consciousness blinked, and I was here.

The warm smudged air green-blue as sadness.

The warm smudged air and the whitewashed wall commencing halfway down the narrow street.

The whitewashed cliff behind us.

I am here, minute after minute.

I want to say that there is more to my story, but there you have it.

I am here, minute after minute, waiting for the rest of me, *me* perhaps being too strong a word, to catch up—unless, of course, I am somewhere else.

Unless, for instance, I am still listening to Vivaldi or Bach back on the plane somewhere over the Atlantic, half asleep, or perhaps dreaming in my sister's arms in a hotel room somewhere in Denver.

Perhaps I am still falling.

That is another possibility, certainly.

Perhaps this is simply what it is like to expire in midair.

It is difficult to know without more information, of course.
But, wherever I am, I want to say something else altogether.
I want to say my greatest fear is that this is heaven.
I want to say my greatest fear is that it is not.

THE GENIUS OF ASSASSINS
Three Dreams of Murder in the First Person
Michael Cisco

Foreword

FROM THE BRAMBLES of a murderer's eyes the gaze of the genius
of assassins falls on you: a sooty-winged owl with a blanched, dead
mask of livid unfeathered skin. The eyes are sacs of blood that glow
with a cold red flame, with a dagger in between—it wants to share
its savage idiocy with you. It's small; it hides itself easily in those
brambles, and stares. Small though it is, when it draws near, the shade
of its outspread wings, shedding their heavy dust, is broad enough to
blot out a mind completely, and all too briefly. Wide-eyed unblinking
it descends out of darkness on silent pinions, and snatches away its
quarry with a movement too swift to follow. A face turns into a livid
mask and a body is galvanically transformed. With an inconsequen-
tial-looking gesture the knife makes a little opening somewhere and
the appalled life gushes out; the mask shifts from the murderer's soft-
ening features to the victim's stiffening face. The victim's body under-
goes its own transformation: it cools, darkens, sours, stinks, by turns
slack and rigid. The murderer is gone; the genius is hidden; a raw new

person flees in panic, flees his gory hands.

The genius of assassins has no words, but it will address you in a gust of fright. You will know that you are not alone, in a park, or on a subway platform, or at home. Its cry is your mute astonishment at the miracle of violence. Its wings are the murderer's hands outspread; the hands are organs with the fundamental power to stop organs forever. The killer's hands will conduct orchestral, organized life through a brief lapse, and into lasting stillness. The same hands that flap on the obscure walls of caves, and whose fingertips are inked in the glare of police stations, mark time by erasing life; flutter and shed soot around the icy, fanatic mask of their genius.

The Paradise of Murderers

I'm a lonely so-and-so without much in his day to do, I don't enjoy reading, I don't even like standing still when I eat. Boring or not the streets want to feel the tramp of my foot up and down; I like to be obliging. I step out of doors in the morning when all the bells are ringing, and I stop in at my door as best I can when my head is heavy. Now and then I will stop sing dance and drink with this or that so-and-so, but I come and go and it makes no difference. I can sit up with statues or pigeons and trees in the park, headstones and piles of fruit and zoo animals and newspaper bundles and cops.

Now I take the tram across the Plague Bridge to the Old Island where the streets are lean and full of matted trash—smelly houses, children scatter like pigeons as I come up with a stone head full of matted newspaper fruits zoo cops and piles of animal bundles; drifting past my face the white branches, a park filled with statues of trees. Under the boughs, in the lanes, gutters cough and drains chatter, under the eaves, in the shade of the front porch a woman offers me a drink, shapeless grey dress sweat-patched in the chest hanging off her skinny frame. She's friendly because I am a neat-looking clean pressed young man. We drink together happily like two old failures. The ice rings the sides of the glasses like cowbell clappers and when

I go am I sober but tired, my head droops in waves of crows and cobbled rows warped where the streets have been disrupted.

Here's a stoop, and a front door to lean against that falls in as I lean—here's me, on the floor looking up at yellow-brown water stains on a plaster ceiling. Someone is behind me, behind the crown of my head, lying on voluminous mattresses; fat, sad face slick with perspiration peers curiously at me.

"You startled me!"

Piercingly sad voice, thin and high.

I apologize as I pull myself up and right my head; my tumble has shocked me awake. The curtains are all drawn, thin material covered in big brown and yellow blossoms. Bed, table beside the bed, filmy wallpaper. Thin sweet smell like a candy mist—"You all right mister?"

"I'm very ill—are you hurt? Perhaps you would like to sit a moment?"

I sit by the bed—"Do you want the door closed?"

"No, I think the air feels good."

He looks wanly out the door. I don't suppose he's been through it lately. He pours himself a glass of water from the pitcher on the bedside table—"There's a glass for you if you like," he points to the kitchen counter across the room.

"No thank you."

He leans his head back on a soaking pillow and gazes at the rectangle of sunset in the door, the children flashing by—"You think about death much?"

"All the time."

"Ever kill anything?"

There are certain times when I just need to be alone—I've always been like that. I'm not unreasonable about it, but I hate being spied on. When I was a boy, I was pacing up and down once in my room, thinking I was alone, talking to myself and acting out a little scene—then I see our cat is there, watching me from beneath the bed. Incensed by his eyes I went after him, eventually I caught him—I put his head on the windowsill and crushed his throat with the window. His paws flapped a few times against the wall and the sill; then he died.

A few weeks later, I was lying in bed trying to sleep, when I heard a voice in the hall, speaking muffled words. I opened my door just a crack. I could see the cat sitting in the shadows by the attic door. It was glaring fixedly off into the distance, and this sight, and the nearly-inaudible words that sounded from its red regularly throbbing mouth, comforted me against my will, so that everything dark in me drained away, and I went to bed calmly, like a zombie.

"That's really something," he says, and dabs his throat with a napkin. "I never heard about anything like that before."

He adjusts himself in the bed uncomfortably, and whimpers as he moves. For a moment he lies still, breathing fast because he's in pain, and he looks up at the stained ceiling still in pain, his eyes look out from pain. When he catches his breath, he asks or tells me, "That house—you don't live in that house anymore, do you?"

"No." I look at him for a while. "I have a place on the main-land."

"What do you do?" He asks distracted, his eyes ticking in their sockets, as though there was some escape for them. When I don't say anything he turns his head to me a moment. "I didn't mean to pry."

"I don't care. I don't do anything, I'm a zero."

"I don't think anyone is really a zero," he says softly, looks at me with concern.

"Well, that's all right, I'm a zero, and I don't even care anymore. I don't care about me, and I don't think about tomorrow, or anything. I know tomorrow isn't thinking about *me*."

"No family or anything, huh?"

"No, no, not that care, nobody here. I go wherever, I do what-ever—what do they care—nothing." I just smile, shrug. "I'm one of those people, when I die they're going to find out that I'm dead because some neighbor was investigating a smell."

"I wish I could die."

"Well, I suppose you *could*."

"*No*," his eyes are ocean-indigo, dark and bright at once. They hold on to me, as though he were clutching my lapels. "That's part of my sickness."

"I never heard of it," I say, blank.

He looks down at his pudgy hands, toys with the dingy quilt. "I wasn't born here, either—I miss my family. They're unable to visit me here, unfortunately . . . How did you end up here?"

"I had to go somewhere. I grew up, I stopped dreaming, I went out into the world, I tried work, I tried women, and—well, well, well . . . " I'm just smiling, talking in a quiet voice. "And now it's just me and the drinks . . . I can't even make it as a drunk, I drink, I puke, but I don't get drunk."

He leans forward, suddenly avid, and touches my knee, looking up through his thin eyebrows at me. "I see now—you're not a doer, you're an *un-doer*. That's what you are, see? Everybody is something—everybody *has to be something*." He speaks it vicious as the curse it is, glancing bitterly away for a moment. Then, leaning back, he holds me with his gaze. "I know something you can un-do."

When he doesn't go on, I shrug.

"Someone like you, you could do me a big favor. I mean you could really help me a lot." He holds out his hands, indicating himself. "I'm all knotted up, see? That's my sickness. I'm bound up in a knot—I *am* the knot," he adds vehemently, "—and it's torture for me."

"You want me to—*un-do* you?"

His eyes glistening, he nods, his head resting on the backboard.

"How?"

"If you kill a man—would you do that?"

"Sure, sure, yeah—I mean, I could do that."

"Really? You could, really?"

"Sure."

"Any man at all, it doesn't matter. If you go outside the city here, there are a lot of farms and roadside places, people do all kinds of things alone out there—I'm sure you could find somebody."

"OK, sure."

He opens a carved wooden case on the nightstand and pulls out a shining stylus, long and thin. "When he's dead, write the circle on the ground with his blood—use this." He hands me the stylus. It's cool, it's actually cold, with a film of condensation on it. "You'll have to find a flat spot."

"Thanks." I put the stylus in my breast pocket.

"Please hurry—do it today, please."

"Yeah, I'll do it today. I mean, I'll try—I'll go now."

"Do you want any water?"

"No, thanks—I'll just get going."

* There are a number of thin metal plinth-bridges that connect the island on this side with the mainland. From there, it's only a brief walk to the edge of town, where there's a chain-link fence mounded over with ivy. The suburbs for which these roads were laid out never happened; the ancient farms crumble under their eaves and sagging roofs, flopped out on their overgrown lots, now plotted on an incongruous grid of dirt roads sighing dust. I start at the nearest corner of the grid and round off square by square. The day is warm. Everything is warm and tilted and eternal and infinite, I'll walk these rounds of unbuilt blocks forever with the white sun spreading its hot grey mane there above my left shoulder, my shoes scuff blonde furry ground tufted with leaves of paralyzed grass that are flames the emerald color of lime flesh.

Now here's an A-frame farmhouse with chickens clucking in the yard. I see a woman and two little ones far away, bobbing in the waist-high corn, heading in the direction of town. I walk unevenly up the dirt path, wobbling a little on my ankles. As I come around the wood-pile toward the porch a man appears and starts at the sight of me. I see his face and so I cut it—there is a hatchet there on the pile and I take it up. I swing once overhand and chop into his face through the center, pull it out with a yank of my wrist. It goes in easily and my arm is not strained. He bends, and I catch him once again backhanded through the cheekbones making a cross. He falls on the ground, his tongue hanging from his mouth. He mumbles in his blood. I straddle him but I'm facing the wrong way so I turn straddling him standing. He does not die until I strike him twice again over the head with the back of the hatchet. I drop the hatchet, and pick him up, carry him a few feet to a bare spot of ground where a moment ago the chickens were scratching. The blood seeps out from his hair with a quiet sound like a guitar being gently strummed, flows on the ground. I take out the stylus and stop—

I don't know what I'm doing—

"*Yes you do!*"

I begin crooning words I don't know. I draw the circle in his black blood, which slips out from his head in laps. I write around the borders of the circle in unfamiliar letters.

"*Yes that's right—that's right—don't stop!*"

The aching song wavers from my tense mouth, filled with longing, in waves that roll my body back and forth as though I stand waist deep in surf. The language isn't mine but the words yearn in my throat—here come branches, bare and sooty, up around me, and the chiming of tiny bells—I run down a waist-high groove cut in the ground, lined with stones, black wire boughs steeple their fingers just above my head, my hands make scoops in the air, right then left then right again, before my chest as I run making the world streak—now I am out in the open on pale green grass so soft it turns to powder as I tread on it, my cuffs are wet with dew and slap my ankles, I only run faster still. Here are rolling hills, copses and a high caer above the salt flats and tidal flats and inky bogs and iridescent brown bogs—emerging from the bogs are great plumed anemonoids, their gelatin arms waving rapturously singing in every part. These are nurtured on human sacrifices: lovingly the tendrils snatch the victim up into the screening white branches, which are swiftly streaked with red . . . the cries of the victims are audible for hours, and the trees sing blithely, their leaves flickering in the breeze like shining coins.

Their path will cross my own—that line of men, running arm in arm, in white shirts and black trousers, black bow ties and white aprons. Their hair glistens pomaded sleek and fragrant on their heads, their legs swing perfectly synchronized; these men dressed as waiters are my fellow killers, my blood brothers. The line swings away from me. Our paths won't cross after all. I'm breathing too hard to shout after them. I've never seen such speed. Their scissoring legs seem to kick them weightless over the ground like ballet dancers, and even where the ground is uneven their coordination never breaks. My heart bangs against my ribs. Any moment the flutter at my side will flare and stitch my lung, my throat thickens—they're only a few feet before me now! Still in my ears though not from my throat the yearning voice pleads and sighs its song, if I could speak I would beg them not to leave me behind—I can almost reach to the shoulder of the rightmost runner—now it's happening, I'm coming up alongside, I can see the looped arm held out to me by the rightmost runner, and as I slip my arm through it I slot into step with them, my apron pressed flat against me, my shoulders jerking up and down as I run, my legs flying, my head thrown back I can feel the cool tracks of my tears stream back from my eyes into my pomaded hair—the voice is singing now still but its yearning sound is joyful to me now—we fly so fast and faster still always faster, but effortlessly, speeding up the slope of the high caer, toward the spot where the slope is broken off in midair high above the sweet rocks and creamy surf.

In voluminous sighs the fat man smiles beatifically and spreads his hands. His body comes apart into silver wires and bells, swells like a great, white tree.

The Whitest Teeth

When I was a boy, my friend Kajetan and I lived in the same U-shaped apartment building, with a common area within the loop of the U. This common area was a lumpy mattress of lawn that never completely dried out. Even in the summertime, it was dank and shady, an assembly of clumps of grass and big sinuous puddles.

Our families lived opposite each other. All the apartments were the same, porcelain floors in the bathrooms kitchens hallways, and in the other rooms a dingy chitin of pressed ivory shavings, suspended in a crinkly sheath of yellowing resin, had been laid down. The same, fantastically heavy burgundy curtains, with thick, burdensome golden fringes, hung over every window, shutting out all trace of daylight. Kajetan and I would meet in front of his door every morning and walk to the Lycée together; we attended different classes, but we always ate lunch together. He was a quiet, fawning boy; he never had a teacher who didn't instantly love him. No one in the school was as fair as Kajetan. His hair, his flesh, except for his lips, was all white, and he had a blazing, retiring smile, like the dazzle of daylight on drifted snow.

That day, the day I am thinking of, I had been gloating over some dirty postcards that I had found somewhere. I pored over the grey bodies, the black eyes and lips, the dark islands and white prominences, filled with riddles, all bordered with dark burgundy red, and gold braid. I was too young to be aroused by these images, but I was aflame with curiosity about them. After devouring a card with my eyes, I would hand it to Kajetan, who kneeled beside me in the mud. We studied together in silence. Here were all my postcards, the grey, supine, obliging or oblivious bodies, scattered on the muddy ground. I was reaching to gather them up when I felt something cool on my upper lip. I looked down, and saw drops of my blood falling into one of the puddles. The drops bloomed when they struck the water, making little billows of fine red threads. Two more drops, big ones, fell, and sank to the bottom. They hovered there, conspiring together in the depths, without dissolving. I crushed my nostril shut and tilted my head back. After a few minutes, I stopped pressing on my nostril, and it opened slowly, tearing through the membrane of candied blood that had congealed over it. The bleeding had stopped. Kajetan had noticed my problem, looked at the last couple of postcards, then put them aside and sat with his hands in his lap, his eyes on the ground.

He'd had a nightmare, he said after a few minutes—a horrible, frog-like man with a huge, round, smiling face, hiding in the reeds by a pond, or a pool. This man hadn't threatened him at all—he had only smiled, with closed lips. He had attacked Kajetan with the sight of this wide, wide smile.

"You won't have nightmares any more when you grow up." I solemnly believed this.

He looked at me levelly, and said softly, "When I grow up, I'm going to kill you." His smile slowly came out then, like the sun in a winter cloud.

In my memory, the sentence stretches, and seems to be said a hundred times not quite at once. That sentence has its own particular, special moment in time, which lasts until now.

* * *

Kajetan made me this promise, but he was not the one who would go on to take life. That might have been his calling, but he failed to answer, and I was chosen instead.

I was the energetic one. Kajetan was lazy. He spent his time with me because I always had some project in the works. After his sister's health collapsed, and his parents separated, he moved away, and thereafter I saw him only in my dreams, sliding into the shadows of an arched doorway in a stone wall . . . which the rain had marked with grey-brown stains . . . his white head gleaming in the dusky light . . . fluorescing, like a will-o-the-wisp, as he floated into the dark.

That wall and doorway, I soon discovered, belong to the estate by the sea; a palace of gnarled stone surrounded by black pines and beech trees. The gloom of the place drew me strongly; on the grounds, the sound of the surf is audible, but the sea is not visible. The underbrush here is thick and elastic, the leaves made rubbery by the salt wind, and difficult to penetrate. One follows the sound of the waves, and eventually the soil becomes sandy and thin, the vegetation more sparse, and then the dunes and the horizon appear together. The house looms above the level of the beach on a slanted promontory of rock, its shuttered windows refusing to open on the sea. I have the impression the place is in probate, some sort of protracted dispute; it is empty and neglected. Only occasional trespassers from town make use of it. I secretly oblige the owners, whoever they are, by killing these trespassers.

The first time, I was kneeling in a clump of ferns, watching a man. He was sitting on a stone beneath a tree. He'd taken his rucksack from his back and set it beside him, eaten his lunch and now was smoking, leaning back against the trunk. A hiker, apparently. He finished his smoke, crushing the butt out under a rock, and knelt, tying his boot-laces. I leapt on him then, weightless, the sound of the wind and surf very loud, his grunt of surprise very far away. I rolled on top of him and drove my fists into his face—his hands outflung made a sort of thicket between me and his face—I swatted at him with a rock, he tried to wrestle it from me, all the while yelping bits of sentences at me—I released the rock, took up another and swiftly smashed his head with it. I sunk my fingers into his cheeks and eyes bent forward and pulled his face in half with my hands—his body bucked and thrashed under me, his arms flailing. Finally I strangled him, staring and dripping perspiration down into the torn flesh, and exposed bone, of his face.

Satisfied, I assembled his meager possessions and dragged him down the beach to the water. Launching his body from the rocks, I could be assured the current would accept him. This sea, sky, woods, house, were all my accomplices. Kajetan's face dwindling in shadowy passageways, his flickering smile flashed white in the instant before shades filled his features altogether.

The second time, a woman taking photographs on the beach. I hid in the rocks and jumped her from behind. There were many deep tidal pools here between the boulders. I seized her by the hair and pushed her head into the water. I straightened my arm—she clawed at me, kicked back at me, but her angle was all wrong. After a few moments she went limp—a ruse. I did not budge. A few more seconds of frantic activity, shreds of water dashing in all directions, and then nothing but the rumble of the waves.

Drowning is one of the better ways to kill someone, provided cir-cumstances allow for it. At its edges, the estate dwindles into flat, sallow land, grey soil, grey sky, a handful of scarred, defiant trees, and a handful of farms. Black clouds turned the dim, watery light of that day a brownish-green color. A stand of dead trees, pinched off by an arm of sand from the body of the woods that surround the house. The trees enclose a little depression in the ground where rainwater collects to form a broad, shallow pond of iridescent brown. A dirt road runs by the stand. A few heavy branches bristling with grey, wiry sticks had blown down and dammed the wind's flow of dead leaves and bits of bracken. The road was blocked. I found a farmer clearing the debris out of the way and offered to help—seamed, lean face, slow, patiently-moving body. I clubbed him over the head with a rock when his back was turned and dragged him, surprisingly light and thin, to the pond. I knelt on his back and held his head down. He was unable to struggle. His body seemed heavy and tired. He seemed to lie beneath me resigned, his face mired in black, stagnant mud and thick brown water. Everything was quiet. Despite his weakness, I remained kneeling a long time—every now and then thinking I felt a sort of inner tick beneath my knees. This farmer was like a plant himself—I had to dig his life out of him by its roots to keep it from growing back, and it took a long time. Kneeling there, my gaze was drawn out across the pond toward the house and the grounds, and further to the sea. Although I was drowning a man, I felt as peaceful as a stone. After a long time, I rose and he drifted out from the bank. I almost left him floating face down in brown water, brown light.

I caught a woman from behind with my necktie, stood motionless as a statue while she clawed at her throat, twisted this way and that. I turned my head to see our shadows together on the stone wall. They looked strange. When her knees buckled I straddled her, her body lying flat on its stomach, her head dangling from her neck, which I held above the ground with the tie. She had been strolling the grounds hand in hand with a man. I had watched them draw near the house, and took hasty advantage of his leaving her alone a moment. When he returned, he found her at once and knelt slowly beside her with his bearded mouth open. I stepped from the hiding place, the doorway I had seen in my dream. He looked mutely up at me, and I struck him in the face with an axe. The single blow killed him. I am strong, the axe swung light as a reed in my hand. The red dew of his blood congealed on her icy cheeks like studs of cinnamon candy.

* * *

In my dreams I see again the enigmatic seeds of his teeth. I rise in the morning, my curtained room is dark. My employer will send a car for me. I must deliver some records to our office in the adjacent town.

I return on foot. When the pavement gives way to rutted clay I realize I've been on the wrong road for several miles. After a moment's reckoning I decide I'm better off going on than back. I'm heading in the right direction, by a more rambling route. After half a mile more the road dwindles to a broad level path bordered by rattling humps of ivy, and tall grass. The breeze flourishes into a steady, nervous wind. The sky is dense, silver and black; the humid air is thick with captive rain. I can hear surf. I'm approaching the sea.

There before me is a wide ribbon of black trees, and peaked slate rooftops above the trees, black against the sky as dried blood. I have been here so many times, I remember them all, but I have no memories to compare with this; I have no memories of coming or going. Why do I only now realize this? Rain patters all around. I walk with a little difficulty through the tall grass into the shade of the trees. As I cross the boundary, some fraction of the daylight is absorbed by the air. Colorless shade rises from the ground.

The path runs by the wall, toward a paved terrace surrounded by overgrown planters. Over the sound of the rain, which still forms in distinct drops, instead of a seamless hush, and the remote surf, I hear violent splashing. In the middle of the terrace, I know, there is a rectangular, lichen-encrusted pool, now drained. When I once lifted the tarp that covered it, I saw only the crumpled brown remains of dead water lilies smeared against the bottom. The terrace is ringed with empty pedestals upon which some classical figures once had stood—I come up behind one of these, to which there still adheres a single broken, heavily-veined foot, flexed in mid-step, in time to see a figure recoil into the bushes opposite me. A young woman lies flat on the pavement, her head bobs in the agitated blue water of the pool—who refilled it?—her arms up hands floating half netted in the black tendrils of her hair.

I step forward, looking at her in confusion. Someone else works here?

I hear a step behind me and feel a light hand on my shoulder, and sudden pain—my heart gulps, flails . . . dizzy, my body weighted, I turn a little as the hand is removed from my shoulder. Something is pulled from my back. The world lists and slides away, the picture I see sets back into my mind slowly—lean Kajetan, tall, hands diffident behind his back, his face fluoresced in a white smile. White and red. The pavement buffets me. Now I am floating, the wind in my hair, not on my face.

Water clicks at intervals in my ear, the water is red and white. My hands rise nerveless to the surface. The water convulses once, the body beside me launches forward curling limp down into the water trailing long lacy sleeves of bubbles, and a plume of her blood like thick smoke rises and envelopes me. Long sleeves of red reach languidly for the bottom, and cross long white sleeves of bubbles.

Now I can see only the featureless, blue depths.

His memories remove their disguises and show themselves for what they are. His dreams file past, smiling, showing their teeth—I am trying to keep hold of them . . . of one at least, only leave me one.

None of them are mine.

. . . the water grows calmer and calmer, and soon will be completely still.

. . . the motion it lends me will abandon me, and I will lie completely still.

. . . my face is dead, my harmless teeth smiling bitterly. Yes . . . yes, of course.

My Father's Friends

This is theatre critic Simon Klai—here is his wife Doriandra, these are their two sons: Louy and Leonard. Simon is acerbic, impatient, acute, aloof. He loves his family as if from on high.

First Exhibit:

Simon on his way to the newspaper office to present his copy. Double breasted suit, silk tie, hat, overcoat . . . walking stick, soft leather briefcase with two buckled straps. It is early morning. The streets are still fairly empty. His breath mists in the air. Alert, leaning forward, walking briskly although he is not late, he watches the pavement pass under his feet . . . darts glances this way and that. The sun is still low and cold in the sky. Crossing a bridge, Simon's steps come slower; he is looking at the sun. He stops, his eyes on the sun. He does not lean on the bridge's stone rail; he is rigid, shoulders back, briefcase at the end of his arm, his stick held firmly in his right hand at about a forty-five degree angle to the street. A car whirs by, misses him only by inches—he does not move. He is staring at the sun as though he'd never seen it before.

Second Exhibit:

Later the same day: Simon is sitting on a bench with his head back. After a few hours he rises stiffly and crosses the park, walking slowly, a little unevenly. Presently he raises his head—he is on a narrow side street that curves away to the left. Just ahead, a hotel signboard hangs over the street; white façade, billowing urns of flowers. The lobby is small, filled with dusky golden light and a carpet smell. Simon takes a suite on the uppermost floor; in shirtsleeves and stockings he orders a bottle sent up from the bar. He tips the girl lavishly. In the days to come, despite his straitened condition, he will stop ordering bottles; sortie out to the stores and back, instead.

On the tenth day, he checks out. Home is only a few blocks away. He lets himself in during the middle of the day, when the boys are at school and Doriandra is rehearsing. Lying on the bed, the pillows smell of her hair. When she returns, he will present her with an uncannily reasonable excuse for his absence.

Third Exhibit:

It is a cloudy morning. Simon reaches for his umbrella, taking its handle with two fingers, then his head twists on his neck slightly as though a thought had very forcibly occurred to him, and he instead takes his heavy walking stick. As he steps down the stairs he inspects the stick, peels the india rubber tip from the end and tosses it back into the umbrella stand.

On the street: the inaugurating first drops of rain patter on his shoulders. Cause and effect—he heads for the awning of a bakery along with several other adjacent pedestrians. Halfway there he stops, and then continues past the bakery through empty streets, keeping to the lee of the buildings so as to stay dry—into an area of a few blocks in size currently under renovation after a fire—burnt shells, new lumber, frames and bricks, tools lie in the street. Striding against the rain all at once he stops, turns a little indecisively to the right, looking around as though trying to sight a sound, then slips into the gaping front door of a partially-rebuilt house. Once under its roof, he shakes the rain from his hat and coat. He stands, seems to wait, in what once was the entry way—smell of plaster dust and fresh paint. Now he quietly climbs the stairs to the second floor apartment, which opens out to the right. The kitchen—a white box, fifteen feet square, two windows without glass admit the sound of the rain. A boy about eight or nine looks up at him, rain dropping from his clothes. Simon walks toward the boy.

"I was trying to get out of the rain."

He seems to think Simon is a contractor, or a security man. Simon's stick flashes up and cracks down over the boy's head. The boy crouches without quite falling down and veers randomly toward the wall opposite the door. Simon raises the stick again, then his head jerks and he alters his grip, taking the stick in both hands and driving the end into the boy's stomach. A purple stain spreads from the boy's solar plexus and he falls on his side holding himself. Simon straddles the boy and churns the stick up and down on him with all his weight. There are two softly audible snapping sounds. Now the boy is limp, breath rattling. Simon turns him on his back with his toe, drops to his knees on the boy's chest, and presses his stick across the boy's throat. The eyes are still sluggishly moving. There is still a remnant of fear, surprise, imploring, on the boy's face. Simon's face is attentive, impassive. He looks like a dentist bending over a patient. The boy fumbles the stick weakly, then his limp hands fall away.

Now the boy's face is dark. Simon slips from the house. It is dusk;

the rain has stopped; the uninhabited street is dark. Simon tosses his stick over a fence into a vacant lot as he walks briskly home. Drops of the boy's blood seep into the dry grass.

Fourth Exhibit:

Autumnal gloom in the park of dead trees: mercurial light fades against a sky of deepening indigo. Simon passes the brick kiosk which houses the public bathrooms—he

he abruptly stops, and walks back to the kiosk.

Behind the kiosk, there is a square of bare pavement hidden from public view by the overgrown iron fence that rings the park. A gun lies in the center of this area. It is loaded and fits in his coat pocket easily.

Fifth Exhibit:

A month later. The gun lies between a double row of books on Simon's shelves. He keeps it in a cloth sack so that the powder won't be smelled. The smell is strongest of course immediately after use.

Doriandra has taken Leonard to visit her cousin. Simon is alone in the house with Louy, who has a cold. It's night; Louy is asleep. Simon is reading—now he sets the book down, goes to the bookshelf, leaves the house.

Two hours later he returns. He goes to the bookshelf.

Louy is still asleep. Simon has crept into his room and sits on the edge of his bed, watching Louy sleep. He leans forward extremely slowly, and carefully takes Louy's head in his hands. His thumbs drop down onto Louy's eyelids with smooth, hydraulic control. Slow and gentle his thumbs roll the lids up, exposing the dreaming eyes. Simon leans forward, pouring his gaze into Louy's eyes.

Louy stirs, starts panting. His body twitches. He groans with a stifled voice that sounds as though it came from far away, from beneath the earth. Simon is curved over him, unblinking eyes' gaze fastened on the boy's dreaming eyes. Louy is screaming softly, his voice is trapped down inside him.

Now Louy screams. He struggles with his father, awake, screwing his eyes shut, the screams siren out of him bigger than the room.

Simon seizes Louy by the shoulders and shakes him violently, without saying a word. Louy's head whips back and forth, back and forth, back and forth. Simon shakes him shakes him—Louy goes limp, his head flips forward his chin striking his chest with a wet smack then is wrenched backward thumping against the pillow or the backboard. Simon shakes him, his arms pump mechanically in and out—in and out—in and out.

Sixth Exhibit:

A series of newspaper headlines—cholera has broken out here, here, and here. And now here, and now here. Growing concern—it's an epidemic. A state of emergency is declared, cars spill out of the city, jam up on stone bridges, uniformed men check documents and direct traffic.

Leonard sits in the back seat of his cousin's car. His mother and his cousin are carrying Louy down the front steps to the street. Louy is lean, feeble . . . dull eyes, slack mouth, nerveless limbs dangling. Tenderly they seat him next to Leonard, resting his head on Leonard's lap. Cousin gets into the driver's seat, the car bobbing under him like a raft. Doriandra walks around the car to the front passenger seat . . . hard, metallic eyes.

This car will take them out to their cousin's place in the country, where they will be safe from the plague.

. . . Newspapers . . . they filter in now and then . . . and on the radio—stories of riots . . . chaos . . .

Seventh Exhibit:

Hands in his coat pockets, Simon moves powerfully down the street. Now and then groups of youths rush past—cold gusts of wind bring chaotic noise of a window breaking here, a dreamlike police whistle far away.

Suddenly alone in the street, Simon turns into an alley which intersects another at a right angle, a T. Two boys and a girl eating old bread, he shoots the one on the left. The boy crumples, his head striking the pavement with a sharp, hollow noise. The girl springs to her feet and runs down the right arm of the T, and the other boy stands up staring at his dead friend with his mouth open. Arm straight Simon aims at him and shoots him in the stomach. The boy's body folds forward at the waist and he falls on his head face down. His legs slide back gradually, his bottom in the air.

The right arm of the T opens into a small enclosed lot—the girl rounds the corner of the building to the right as he fires his gun. The bullet tugs at her right heel, blows off the heel strap of her shoe—it drops on a tuft of grass—she disappears behind the corner.

The lot is framed by the solid, continuous wall of the armory running the length of the block, on his left. To Simon's right, the building whose corner she had turned; and before him, the rear of an L-shaped hotel . . . heaps of rubbish, trash cans, mattresses, a stove. Two escapes: she might run straight ahead, or to the right.

Simon turns to the right—with his left eye he detects a patch of red earth by the stove. There is another red spot, there between the two garbage cans by the armory wall, the other way out. The girl hops from her hiding place. Simon's arm flies automatically out and up level. He shoots her in the head, the girl plops onto the ground, a wide tear in her head above the ear. The bullet strikes the wall and shears off a flake of brick. It spins through the reverberating air like a wobbling top, and hits the grass with a muffled thump.

Simon trots past the girl's folded body, down the alley. He is heading for the street when like a marionette his body jerks to the left and he slips instead through a back door hanging off its hinges. A moment later curious heads are craning, peering down the alley . . . mouths are rounding, they see a heavy bundle there, lying bisected by watery sunlight. They see it is a dead girl. As they rush to her side, Simon emerges calmly from the front door of the building into which he had so awkwardly retreated, walking with unremarkable haste. He raises his left arm and pulls the sleeve away from his watch; his eyes, shaded by the brim of his hat, hawkishly scan the street.

Poster on the corner: "Is it working?"

Months and months of plague. Bullets disappear from their red and black boxes in Simon's bureau drawer.

Ninth Exhibit:

Simon is caught in a riot. It starts with a puff of alarm, and suddenly everyone is squalling in all directions. Simon moves diagonally through the racing figures, toward the shelter of deserted, burntout buildings. Police swarm the streets with keening whistles—Simon trips on the pavement—his gun slides from his pocket across the pavement. The police have seen him, his gun—two or three charge at him. Under the regime of the epidemic there is no due process, the police do as they please—now their eyes have fastened on him.

Simon dashes into the building, throws shut the door. The lock still works. He sets the chain—recoils as fists thump and bang against the wood. He flings a half-demolished wardrobe and a heavy table in front of the door. He can't block the windows, but he can lock the hall doors. He checks the back door; it's painted over, jammed shut; there's nothing he can open it with. Upstairs the fire escape is on the front of the building. On the roof—it's too far to jump across to the neighboring house. He tries, peering over the edge, but panic fear he can't overcome drives him back, nearly paralyzed. Half to himself he is saying "I *can't*! I *can't do it*! I need something *else*!" Crashing from downstairs, wood tearing and splintering.

He goes to the center of the roof, staring at a door that will burst open soon. Simon draws himself up, staring, his mouth set. He tightens into himself, his features crush together. He melts into air . . . vanishes across renovated buildings, alleys, sterile apartments . . . bullet spins cold in the sky . . . continuous wall of heads for the sharp, hollow noise . . . Louy is still asleep . . . the other boy watching a white box disappear from the sun, staring at his friend Louy sleep . . . the boy takes Louy's head in rain . . . his thumbs drop nine . . . two burnt shells, rain dropping from his stick . . . Simon leans forward, pouring in the dead trees . . . between two garbage cans he opens his gaze into Louy's eyes . . . from her hiding place—the riots—the girl sees she is

356

suddenly alone . . . billowing urns shoot her in the head, hat and coat
. . . the bullet tugs her to the right street . . . Simon turns into a wall of
the kiosk of flowers . . . the lobby is the girl, filled with a wide tear in
her head above what was the entry way . . . her shoe drops on a right
fence that rings golden light . . . flake of brick sailing . . . two boys . . .
the park lying in the carpet smell . . .

* * *

There is nothing strange about me but my happiness. The only difficulty I have ever given anyone has been to contain someway my
dangerous happiness, which makes me thoughtless. My exuberance
breaks things, breaks me. It marches me up to people and elicits from
me declarations of love, if only to give me the satisfaction of disappointment, to know that I am in love. I am forever building up this
edifice of love and happiness, which would get to be as big as the
world, or bigger, if it weren't for the storms, eruptions, convulsions,
that tear it all down again. When any of it comes down, it all comes
down. Although these catastrophic failures deeply wound me, still I
am grateful for the opportunity to rebuild, and to renew my trust with
the world. I do everything on the scale of the world, as the only thing
commensurate to my happiness.

Only by understanding my father's life will you understand my
death. I will have to adopt a conversational manner, for the moment,
to tell you these everyday things. For most of my childhood, my father
worked as a theatre critic. His articles were widely read and his opinions seriously received. I never understood exactly what he did, or why
he was so inattentive to us. Over time, he withdrew from us. For reasons I would learn later, he once disappeared altogether for about
ten days. We were told he had been depressed; he had thought some
time alone would do him good, so he had taken a room at a hotel. I
wanted to offer some comfort to him, if he was suffering—he seemed
to sense my feeling, and headed it off by adopting an especially frosty
manner with me. My mother was mystified by his changes, and her
uncertainty unnerved me. While I lacked confidence in my own judg-

ment, it seemed to me my father sullenly avoided us all, stayed away from home.

I made friends easily, but I always lost them. My exuberance, my complicated games only exasperated and taxed them. Most of the time I kept company with my older brother Louy, whom I very little resembled; while I was nervous, enthusiastic, busy, thoughtless, Louy was ghostly and quiet. He had a gentle, warm little voice like a candle flame, and wet, red lips. He almost always seemed preoccupied and far away, but then he would astonish me with a near-clairvoyant observation about someone or something we had seen: and I would realize again that he missed nothing.

A few days after Louy's thirteenth birthday, my mother took me away to visit with her sister for a few days, leaving him alone with my father. When we came back—what had happened to Louy? We found him catatonic in his bed, apparently unable to speak or move. I remember the slack mouth, the frightening dullness of his eyes. A new awkwardness had insinuated itself into his body somehow—he even lay awkwardly in his bed. My mother frantically chafed his hands, his arms, caressed his face, implored him to speak. I was sent to fetch our downstairs neighbor the doctor. He examined Louy carefully and took my mother aside. I never knew what he told her.

Louy was condemned to lie inert for the rest of his life; thin, frail, he could barely speak. His eyes would sometimes become glassy and seem to flicker under his heavy lids, but this was not the light of intelligence they formerly had had. While I am sure she could not have known what had happened, my mother angrily blamed Louy's condition on my father, and they separated almost immediately. I seldom saw my father after that; we did not visit together, and my mother never spoke of him.

When the epidemic broke out the following year, my mother took Louy and me out to the country, to stay with her cousins. We were there for eight months, during which time we never heard from my father. Upon our return to the city, we learned that he had disappeared shortly after the state of emergency was declared. Officers of the health department had already declared him dead, "succumbed to the disease." The epidemic had maddened the city. Hundreds of people had vanished without a trace in riots or clandestine violence, and the police had done as they pleased with the rest. In the depths of the epidemic, heaps of unidentified bodies were burned or buried in vast pits every day—so my father's case was not apparently unusual.

I remember hiding from my friends behind our school's small library once. I picked up a branch from the dry grass at the edge of the gravel path, but as I raised it I saw that it was a charred bone, nearly as long as my arm. For days after that, I wondered if it had been my father's.

The contents of his apartment were boxed and piled away by my grandfather, upon whose death it fell to me to sort them out. My father's clothes and books were almost entirely ruined by seeping water and mold, but I salvaged what I could—I had always been curious about my father. Under a blanket I found one of my father's jackets, which, at the time the boxes were packed, had been used as a sort of makeshift bag. His watches, shaving kit, and a few other things had been bundled up inside—a notebook among them. In it, I found many brief sentences like these:

"7 September, three boys."

"20 September, two boys, very nice."

"21 September, nothing today, an admonition."

"29 September, two boys, a girl today, very nice."

"2 October, necessarily three boys. Last one caused some trouble."

"10 October, nothing—reprisal."

"13 October, one boy—misfire, strangle—very memorable expression."

Interleaved among these tallying sentences were terse notes:

"I have still the habit of writing—they say your habit of writing is the manufacture of self-incriminating evidence / your habit of writing is a sign of bad conscience / you are to wean yourself of your habit of writing"

"With the epidemic, everything is possible."

The earliest entry was dated just before his ten-day disappearance:

"the low sun white and cold, and full of worms. Then a fan of white, gelatinous rays, transparent tubes whose ends mouth the earth. A flat, white opening in the sky, whose light silvered the air, dotted with their shadows. They are the larvae of the sun and will become themselves stars."

I had seen this light around my father—vividly I see it now, cold and white, as he sits in his shirtsleeves, the long cuffs bent back, writing; heavy ropes of smoke coil around him. His creased face is drawn, inert, his writing hand palpitates like a bug on the paper.

"My brain shining in the dark like a planet, streaked with long, glistening white clouds that I came to see were worms, beneath the meniscus of brain fluid a translucent sheet under which they tossed and turned. Some lay and some reclined on the tissue, like opulent ladies on perfumed sofas; their puckered heads swayed gently."

These were compulsory sacrifices, as I came to understand. There was no quid pro quo, there was no deal or anything like that with the larvae. They addressed him from time to time, directly or by means of fugitive bits of graffiti, or slogans on posters—"do not open door"—"dead or alive?"—"focus!"

"I realized what it was necessary to do."

He attacked children only because they were easier to kill. The first time he was taken by surprise, guided by the larvae to a house under renovation, a child taking refuge from the rain. "Do not swing—you waste energy that way. Thrust."—"Don't do it halfway," the larvae said. And after—"Sloppy."

"They led me to the gun."

"It is difficult to talk to you," the larvae said, "you understand so little."

"Rain falls, scattering its rings across the puddles—and each death is a drop that makes the mass quiver and thrill, and each drop lends vital force to what would otherwise be an inert, passive, shrinking thing, a body of stillborn larvae."

"Don't forget what you owe the larvae of thought," the larvae would say. "Don't forget your solar responsibilities."

360

On Louy's thirteenth birthday, the larvae said: "He should be old enough now to help you." In his room—"Open his eyes. Show him dreams." Hopeless—he refuses to understand. "Shut him up. Shut him up."

"The alley flashed at me, the gun tingled . . . you see how the larvae protect me. 'Look at the time.'"

"I don't feel the murders—would I feel them more if I cut them open and rooted in their entrails, perhaps while they still throb with life, before they lose consciousness? I am told 'It is not necessary to feel it, only to see to it.'

"Glancing up now at the radiator I know I would do it even if it were as abstract and numb a matter as turning that knob—in a windowless closet deep in basements I see three little bodies, heads in a row, weak and dazed from hunger and thirst lying on a metal grill bunk—as I turn the knob the dim, orange-brown light fades and goes out, and the little chamber swiftly fills with a flavorless gas which will lead these children so deep into the mazes of sleep that they will never find their way out again.

"'This is not a matter of gratification, it is a matter of generating numbers.'

"The gun is a magic instrument, converting children to numbers."

"I know I am now able to will myself out of existence. They have shown me, and told me to extinguish myself if I am threatened with capture. I will not hesitate to do as they ask, not because I feel that my actions are wrong, and that, by them, I have merited my death, but because the situation will then no longer be under my control, or it will be teetering on the brink, about to slip out of my grasp; and by disappearing, I will seal it and keep it—control—perfect forever."

I remember the disembodied, unreal feeling I had as I finished reading. His words sank through and past me, and drained out of me.

I read his words, and the larvae hatched in my mind.

(what or how did the larvae appear to me . . . such questions can only waste our time together. In the water I see the lights trail their long beards that are emaciated gold and silver flames withered to compass needles whose points sway before my feet, everything turns into everything else . . . For my father they were voices. To me they are shafts of glowing, orating red and gold sunlight walking up and down inside my head)—

Every week I visit Louy at the hotel de santé. He lies always in a white iron bed in a vast half-deserted ward, whose booming silence solidifies now and then into a moan or a flicker of nurse's feet, rustle of stiff sheets. I sit beside the bed. Late afternoon light sifts into the room, tall orange projections on the wall, and deep shadows. Louy is lying on his left side, an ungainly body of long bones under the sheet, his head tilted up toward me—a constant tremor wags it from side to side. His rumpled face, the red arch of his lip, and his long wet teeth, wet breaths; the eyes never waver from my face, although there is no expression—his wounded mind no longer has the strength to find its way out to me. I only want to be with him. He grew up like this; his face has aged seventeen years unmarked. In all that time, he has had only one never-ending experience.

I sit and he lies. A few beds down the ward, a nurse changes the dressing on an injured arm. She takes a roll of fresh linen bandage from a tray on the nightstand, which she has moved away from the wall, out toward the aisle. When I next look up, the nurse is cutting the bandage from the roll—she sets the roll on the tray, and lays the scissors next to the roll. The blades of the scissors are acutely pointed, and, as she had placed them casually on the tray, not quite in alignment. They are tilted up on the linen roll. Those two blades gleam white like mirrors against the shadows of the room. The two very sharp blades are fixed together, they cross each other and are bolted together, cut toward each other. As it drops low in the sky, the sun's light becomes redder and redder. Tall panels of red light slide down the walls. The two blades of the scissors are two red blazes, I can see the sun reflected in the blade whose polished side faces me. Their brilliance occludes the ward, the nurse, the beds. I see instead another room, with bare walls, no furniture, dead leaves, newspaper—a hallway in front of me. The windows are boarded up. I stand in the room with my shoulders back and my chin up, my arms a little less than fully outstretched. My right hand holds something wet and light; looking I see I am holding the red scissors. My left hand is further down than my right; very gradually I notice it throbs and moves on its own. My left hand is clutching tightly at something, the fingers are aching. I look down at my left hand—it grips the right shoulder of a small boy with a gaping red throat, his struggles communicate up my arm along nerves finely laced around my heart—a hot electric web, hot and fine. I am breathing hard, a feeling is swelling up in me—I can't stand the imploring, suffering look on the boy's appalling white face, but it is too beautiful, I have to look at him because I love him, and I pity him, this strange boy I've never met, and I need to be close to him and share with him, and this is the only way we can be friends. The boy steadily weakens, but still tugs at my hand. I look down again—I am in the ward, my brother wrings my hand, gazing up into my face. With an imploring look, he rocks back and forth hoisting his upper lip, desperately trying to form words without a voice, with disobedient muscles. My heart glows incandescent through my breast, the little boy's legs fold under him, I drop the scissors and pick him up, press him to me, so he won't feel alone. His warm blood seeps through my shirt, I smell his hair, the soap he washed his face with. Louy yanks at my left hand, his eyes push at mine. I place my right hand over his, and clasp it firmly. As the sunlight fades from the scissors on the tray, the boy in my mind drops to the floor, without a sound. Louy's head falls back on the pillow, with a long despairing sob. A pang of intense love stabs me. I smooth his hair and wipe his face, his eyes, with my handkerchief. The nurse stands at the foot of the bed, telling me softly that visiting hours are over.

"Rest now," I say to him.

Now I am walking. I pass an open alleyway—I turn back, go into the alley. It forms a T. I follow the right branch of the T into a little courtyard. This brick is scarred—a round, puckered spot, where my father's bullet struck it, after passing through the brains of a nameless little girl. Crouching down I put my eye on the level of the spot, looking back toward the courtyard. I see the girl frozen in midstep, one arm forward one arm back, one leg forward one leg back, terror on the blurred features; and beyond her stands my father in his coat and hat, the gun up level at the end of his arm, obscuring his face.

I go back to my apartment. I climb the stairs and turn right, into my kitchen. Though the room is dark, a knife blazes with reflected sunlight in the sink. From my kitchen window I can see the people in the street blazing, each one with his or her own spotlight. I take off my clothes and go to bed.

I dream this:

A brilliant, empty beach—a broad round ramp of yellow land slopes down between shaggy, high cliffs. Even in the dream the light dazzles me; I have an impression of squinting. Sky like blue mercury, sun's light spawns a billion flakes on the water's indigo blades. Hundreds of gulls hurtle round in long-winged circles funneling down to my remains lying on my back half in tall grass, my head on the sand toward the sea, one arm up by my right ear the other down in the grass thick as the comforter under which I lie asleep. I lie there and somehow I observe too from nearby. Very calm and happy, and now and then trembling with the proximity of an overflowing happiness. I see the beautiful purple water roil on the blonde sand, the gleaming prints of pale lime foam that it leaves, takes back, redeposits, the exuberance of the cartwheeling wind. My face is also blue and green, in places livid, and it sways gently with the tugging of the gulls, who seem to sprout from my body. The cavity is completely torn open, the gulls hop on the exposed edges of my ribs and thrust their heads down, root vehemently and then strut away with shreds of my flesh in their beaks. My arms are wide open for them; my remains are kind, accommodating. One of them plucks the glasses from my face and stalks off with them.

The tide comes in. Water sluices from the dimples that were my eyes, and froths at my slack grin. My head nods and sways tenderly;

the busy, shining water laves it in renewed bliss. It won't be long before I look up to see the pale belly of the waves.

* * *

A friend of my mother's telephoned me the next morning, to tell me that, during the night, Louy had somehow gotten out of his bed and stabbed himself with a pair of scissors. A nurse found his body as the sun was rising.

I ride the subways until well past midnight. The Plaza stop is one of the largest stations, with four levels. My train stops at the lower-most platform—in time it would return the way it came, but I leave the cars and find my way up the stairs. The third level has many pas-sages, radiating from a large domed chamber with a cement floor and wooden, high-backed benches. At this hour, it is empty. I cross to my stairway and start to climb. Footsteps draw my attention—lean mid-dle-aged man in a hat and grey raincoat behind me, changing trains. I look at him, and the breath courses in my nostrils, my heart glows, my heavy body lifts, I fall, I fly out from the stairway as he passes swinging my knife, he is knocked aside the point of the knife glanc-ing across his chest, cutting his coat, his shirt, but a shallow cut—he swipes at my face with his walking stick, I'm off balance, I stagger into a garbage can and follow it to the floor. I hear his feet slapping the concrete, his shouts of alarm. I'm on my knees, dazed, I touch my head, a little blood. I laugh—this is wonderful! I pick up the knife again and run after him—he took one of the passageways. I pick up my knees and run as fast as I can—I'm running! I *am* running. I am run, laugh, pounce, slash, eruption of frightened blood, brilliant pain of this unknown man I love, who runs from me, his heart pumping the dying blood in my veins.

I am light, as spirit. I hear his footsteps. Turning a corner, I see his feet flashing up stairs, I switch my knife to my pocket and dart my hand through the railing catching at his left ankle. He wheels and flops on his back and to one side, seizing the opposite railing and catching himself. I come round the bottom of the stairs and he kicks me in the chest—his kick kicks another laugh out of me and I throw myself forward, the knife again in my hand. He shoves me backwards and I slash uselessly at the air. He throws his briefcase at me and I fall back on the steps, buffeted aside as weightless as a balloon. He turns to run to the other end of the platform, the other staircase, I can hear his heavy breath, smell his aftershave, he is beautiful, angry, afraid, his outrage is beautiful—I lunge at him and he knocks me down again, turns to run. I twist on the ground and whip out with my knife, slicing across the back of his left knee, through the gabardine slacks into the joint. He cries out and falls clutching his leg, kicking the other defiantly at me wonderful, blood running over his fingers where he clutches his knee, I hear the drops striking the dirty tiles. I crawl toward him nearly rising—he avoids me—surprising me with his speed, he rolls under a bench—I vault the back of the bench and land on the seat—he scrabbles on the ground, on his back, staring up at me—I pounce on him—my knee comes down on his left bicep, pinning it to the ground, I straddle his ribcage—his free hand claws at my face but I batter it aside, I put the point of my knife beneath his chin near his left ear, hold the handle with the left hand I put the palm of my right against the butt of the handle and drive the blade up into his head.

I see but don't feel the blood on my hands, it is the same temperature as my skin—he gulps and struggles. Now his struggles are only spasms. I change my grip on the knife, taking the handle in both hands I lean down on it, like the handle of a paper cutter, pushing the blade down through his neck. Now I know it's finished. He is still, his face has gone out. I look down gratefully at him. I leave him the knife.

No one sees me climb the stairs. I can feel the night air pouring down the last flight. I float up into the black panel at the top of the steps, and now I'm in the dark, cool night air. I run down the steep streets, my momentum building, I peel off my coat, my tie, my shirt, my belt, I stagger and fall, tumble on the damp ground dragging off my shoes, my stockings and pants, all my clothes, and now without them I am hurtling down the streets, my legs kick up behind me, the ground skates by, my legs take yards and yards at a stride, my arms turn in the air, the breeze cooler and cooler over my skin, my sticky hands. The city opens on all sides of me like a drawn curtain and I see the vast blue darkness of the ocean, the boards of the pier thud under my feet, the pier ends, I launch myself into space . . .

. . . and now everything is foam, and now cold shocking green water. In my mind I can see a line connecting me to the horizon, and this is my course. I will swim until the sinews in my shoulders crack and my lungs tire and wilt in me, and my eyes and lashes are pearly with salt, the black heaven joyous above me, the happy green abyss below me. I tell you these things so that you may understand them, and by understanding them, you may pierce the veil into the secret of my crime. You will understand. You will know joy. You will be nothing. You will be me.

SMALLEST LIBRARY

The Library: 5: SMALLEST LIBRARY
Zoran Zivkovic

I DIDN'T REALIZE I had one book too many until I got home. I should have had three in the plastic bag, but I took out four volumes. The old man had put the books into an old, crumpled bag, stained with something black on the outside. I had made no remark about the bag, not wanting to offend him. How could I tell him that it made no difference to me if the books he gave me got wet in the rain? Everything would have been different, of course, had I brought an umbrella, but it hadn't looked like rain when I'd left home.

The old man perfectly matched the bag he had given me. Greatly advanced in age, he had a wrinkled face and gray beard on which the rare streaks of dark hair resembled bits of leftover food. His clothes were no different from his face. His long, threadbare and dirty coat, which almost touched the ground, was patched here and there and, although the weather did not call for it, buttoned all the way to the top. It was early spring, but unusually warm and filled with sudden showers. Had I met this man anywhere else, I might easily have thought he was a beggar.

The old man's unsavory appearance, however, did not stand out among the used book sellers who displayed their wares all year long, even during the cold winter months, every Saturday, at the same place, under the Great Bridge. They would bring folding tables, plastic crates for mineral water, or even large cardboard boxes that they would cover with newspapers, thus creating a makeshift stand. If it weren't for the books on these stands, the spot would resemble a flea market.

But looks can deceive. These were by no means simple peddlers with only the most basic information about their goods. Although one would never guess it from their unkempt appearance, almost like tramps, and the location of their stalls, a few words with them would quickly reveal that they were excellent book connoisseurs. Should you express an interest in one of the books on display, the seller would provide you with a multitude of information about the author, publisher, reviews, reader reception, possible previous or later editions. Sometimes you might even hear a detailed history of a specific copy that was more exciting than all the rest.

The information was as trustworthy as if you had opened a literary encyclopedia. Nothing was hidden or embellished, as might be expected from those who are only interested in selling their goods. Sometimes you would have the strange impression that what you were being told was intended to dissuade you from actually buying the book.

For more than a year I had been walking under the Great Bridge every Saturday, above all for these conversations with the booksellers. In the end I would buy one book or another, not because I wanted to have it so much as to compensate these people whose words provided the impetus for what I myself had been trying to write.

Over time, I became better acquainted with some of the booksellers I habitually saw there, and so enjoyed their additional esteem as a regular customer. Whenever I appeared, they would pull books out from under the counter that they'd kept for me, and the conversations we struck up would not be interrupted, I believe, even at the cost of losing another customer who might be ready to spend quite a bit of money. Several times I was tempted to propose that we continue our discussions elsewhere, but I held back. For some reason, I had the feeling that it would not be the same. Indeed, it was as if they could not exist anywhere else but here.

I had never met the old man before. Since all the places under the bridge were occupied, he had set up shop at the very end, where there was no longer any protection from above, as though he had been excommunicated by the others. He could only stay there until the first drops of rain forced him to seek cover. This would not have been difficult since he was the only one with a mobile stand. It was a cart that had once, long ago, been used to sell ice cream: a wooden box with two large wheels and two long handles for pushing. I hadn't seen one since childhood. The bright paint that had once decorated this affair was completely faded or peeled, but I could still make out the shape of an ice cream cone with three large scoops painted on the front.

The other sellers would let me look at the books without offering their comments. They would only strike up a conversation with me when I asked a question or had selected a book. That was the generally accepted custom. The old man either did not know this or did not care. He addressed me as soon as I walked up to his stand.

"I have what you're looking for," he said in the hoarse voice typical of chain smokers.

"How do you know I'm even looking for something?" I replied a little abrasively, glancing over the old books that covered the top of the cart. The two conical metal lids that had covered the two openings for ice cream had been replaced by an unfinished bare board. A pile of old books, seemingly dumped out of a bag, lay on top of the board.

"It's not hard to tell. It shows on your face."

"Shows on my face?" I repeated, bewildered, examining the old man. That very instant I realized what I had missed when I first glanced at his face. His head was turned towards me but not his eyes. The eyes stared to the side, unfocused, blurred. The man was blind.

"Yes," he said. "If you know how to look."

"So, that's it," I said, nodding. The awkward feeling that came over me only intensified when I realized the senselessness of this movement.

The old man was suddenly seized by a fit of coughing, hollow and hoarse, like the echo of distant thunder. It seemed to come from the very depths of his lungs. He put one bony hand over his mouth, the other on his chest, and bowed his head. He stayed in that position for a while.

"You are a writer, aren't you?" he said in a whisper, after catching his breath.

"Does that show on my face, too?" I asked, also in a low voice.

He didn't reply at once, wheezing for a bit. "No, but there's a smell about you. Writers have a smell. The harder the time they're having, the stronger the smell. You didn't know that?"

I inadvertently sniffed the air around me. The prevailing smell came from the river: humid, sour, with traces of rotting debris brought by the spring floods. "No, I didn't," I had to admit.

"It makes no difference. What's important is that there is a remedy. We'll find it right away." He started to examine the pile in front of him with his fingers. He took book after book, felt it lightly, and then put it back with the others or set it aside, as though able to see with his hands. Finally, when he had made his choice, he held out three books. "Here, this is what you need. They will help you."

I hesitated briefly, then accepted the offered volumes. They were bedraggled-looking. One had no cover at all, the pages in the front and back dog-eared. Another had been destroyed by someone's merciless scribbling. And the binding of the third was broken so it was in tatters. In addition, dust had accumulated in all three books. I had no reason to buy them, especially since I already had them in much better condition.

Nonetheless, I decided to take them. They would be of no use to me, but how could I refuse a blind old man? However, it wasn't just compassion. His cleverness deserved some reward. The bit about writers having a smell was pretty good. I might be able to use it somewhere. Although, of course, he had not recognized me by any smell.

As I was rushing home, I realized that there was only one way he could have known my profession. Several stands before his cart I had spoken briefly with one of the sellers to whom I was a regular customer. He asked how my new book was coming, and I had given a vague answer. The man could see that I didn't feel like talking about it and had changed the subject. We hadn't been that close to the old man and we were surrounded by a noisy crowd, so that under normal circumstances he would not have heard us. But people who have lost their sight have extremely sharp hearing.

"How much do I owe you?" I asked, reaching for my wallet.

The old man coughed again. This time the hacking lasted a bit longer. "You owe me a lot," he said at last. "But not for the books. They are free."

I looked in bewilderment at his empty eyes. "Why would you give them away?"

"Because that is the only way for you to get them. I don't sell books."

I expected him to say something else, but he clearly felt that this answer was sufficient.

"You have put me in an awkward position," I said after a short pause. "I don't know how to repay you."

"Forget it. Give me the books so I can put them in a bag for you. It will rain soon and they might get wet, and that would be a real shame."

I looked towards the bit of sky not blocked by the bridge. Clouds had started to gather, but there were still patches of clear sky, so it didn't look like it was about to rain. I didn't say anything, however, since the old man appeared quite sure of himself. Maybe blind people can forecast the weather in addition to hearing quite well.

I put the three books into his outstretched hand and he bent down behind the cart, opening the door down there. He felt around inside and finally took out a crumpled, stained bag with the three books inside it. At least that's what I thought at the time. It was only upon returning home that I discovered that he had added a fourth. He must have done it then. There had been no other chance.

"Thank you very much," I said, taking the bag gingerly with two fingers. I was glad the man couldn't see my expression. "Goodbye. I hope we'll see each other soon." As soon as I said it, I realized how inappropriate this greeting had been, but it was too late to retract it.

"Farewell," replied the old man, politely overlooking my blunder.

On the way home, I thought it might be best if I got rid of the unwanted present along the way. But the sky dissuaded me from my intention. When I climbed up onto the Great Bridge, I saw that the old man had been right. Storm clouds were rushing in from the west, dragging a dense curtain of rain with them. I had to hurry if I didn't want to get caught in a downpour. I had no time now to look for a garbage container in which to dump the bag. Just as I stepped inside my front door, rain began to fall.

I could have put the bag in the garbage can in the kitchen, but I didn't. What I had been prepared to do outside without hesitation suddenly seemed inappropriate inside. Sacrilegious, in fact. One doesn't throw books away, after all. Not even such worthless copies. I would put them out of sight somewhere. That would be the same as if I had thrown them away, but my conscience would be clear.

The fourth book that appeared when I emptied the bag stood out from the others. First of all, it was in excellent condition, although also an old edition. I turned it over in my hands, staring with bewildered curiosity. It took some time for me to realize there wasn't even a speck of dust on my fingers.

Nothing had been written on the chestnut-colored canvas cover, but that was not unusual. The book had probably had a paper cover that had been lost in the meantime. In the middle of the front cover was a shallow imprint, the stylized depiction of a pointed quill, an inkpot and an image resembling a sheet of parchment. The pages were edged in a shade of brown that matched the cover.

I opened the book. After a chestnut-colored blank front page, the words *The Smallest Library* were written at the top of the first page in tiny, slanted letters. This didn't exactly fit the appearance and format of the volume. Someone had been too modest when naming the edition. Something more imposing would have been preferable.

I turned the page and the first surprise awaited me. The second page where information about the book should have been given was blank, while the third page contained only one word, which I assumed must have been the title of the work. But the author's name was missing. Filled with doubt, I looked for several moments at the inordinate whiteness before me. This was unusual to say the least.

Then I realized where I might find the copyright information. Some publishers put that page in the back. Although this would not explain the author's missing name, it was still worthwhile to check. I leafed through the book quickly, noting as I did that it was a novel whose chapters had only numbers and not titles. When I reached the end, I discovered there was no information there, either. After the last page with text was just one white page, then the chestnut-colored back page, and finally the cover.

I had therefore received from the old man an anonymous edition by an anonymous writer. I had yet to hear of such a combination, but it clearly did not follow that this was impossible. Although I am not uninformed about the world of books, my knowledge is by no means complete. There was one place, however, where all the information about literally all officially published works should be found: the National Library. I closed the book, put it on my desk, and turned on the computer.

The National Library web site made it possible to execute rapid searches, even though it had enormous book holdings. I typed the only information I had into the space marked "title." I was convinced that this would solve the mystery because any other outcome would be unimaginable indeed. That would mean that this was an unregistered edition, shedding new light on the whole matter. The old man's appearance may not have been exemplary, but I doubted he was ready to get involved in any nefarious dealings with books. In any case, the other booksellers under the Great Bridge, proud of their honesty, would not let him do that.

Nonetheless, about half a minute later the message on the screen told me that a work under that title did not exist in the catalogue of the National Library. I sighed deeply and drew my left hand through my hair. This was becoming awkward. Perhaps I had been wrong about the old man after all. I thought back to parts of our brief conversation that I'd skipped over lightly, although they should have aroused my suspicions.

Still, it was hard for me to believe that the blind man with the ice cream cart had been dishonest. My intuition, which rarely erred, protected him. Without taking my eyes off the screen where the message about the unsuccessful search quivered dully, I tried to find some way around the seemingly inexorable conclusion that something illegal was going on. The only extenuating circumstance I could think of was that the book had been a present and had not been sold, which excluded any self-interest. This, however, could not be used as an excuse for the fact that the title did not exist in the National Library catalogue.

Then, like a drowning man grasping at straws, I thought of something quite unbelievable. Perhaps I had remembered the title incorrectly. I was certain that I hadn't, for I'd just closed the book and the word had been simple and short, but sometimes such common oversights can occur. Maybe only one letter had been different. After all, computers are very literal machines. I picked up the brown book from the desk in front of me and opened it again.

What I saw on the third page simply could not have been true. A lump formed in my throat. The difference was much more than one letter. A completely different title, consisting not of one word but three, greeted me. The book started to tremble and I stared at it in disbelief for several long moments, until I finally realized my hands were shaking. I had to place them in my lap to calm them. I squinted at the new writing, doing my utmost to find some explanation for this impossibility, but I couldn't think of anything. A book cannot change its title by itself. Everyone knows that. But it had just happened. What kind of illusionist present had the old man slipped me? And why?

I could not find the answer to this question just sitting there helplessly, staring at the third page. I had to do something. But what? Take a closer look at the book, perhaps? The first time I had just flipped through it. If there was some trick involved, that would be the best way to find out. But the chestnut-colored volume lay motionless in my suddenly sweaty hands a little longer. It required considerable willpower to raise it again.

I turned another page—and stared wide-eyed at the beginning of the text on the fifth page. It was a novel, as I had expected, but no longer the one from a moment before. This time the chapter was denoted by a title rather than a number. And the letters were a different size: smaller, with less space between the lines. I was holding a completely new book.

This was too much. I reacted as though someone had tossed me a burning object: I threw it away from me and jumped off my desk chair. The book fell on the keyboard and pressed some keys. The National Library site suddenly disappeared from the screen and the speakers emitted a high, broken squeak.

If not for the noise I wouldn't have dared touch the book again. But I couldn't stand the sound; it grated against my overwrought nerves. Carefully, as though picking up something that might bite me, I took the book off the keyboard. The squeak stopped at once, but there was still no picture on the screen.

I stood in the middle of my study next to the chair, now at some distance from the desk, and held the book out in front of me. I had the feeling something was about to happen, but I couldn't guess what, so I didn't know how to prepare myself. Several slow, tense minutes passed. When nothing happened, I realized it was foolish to stand there, waiting. I had to act.

Having returned somewhat to my senses, I concluded I had only two choices. I could put the book back in the dirty bag, add the three others, and throw them all away at once, not in the kitchen garbage can, but in a dumpster outside, as far away as possible, maybe even in the river, in spite of the rain that still poured down. I would thus be free of the cause of my troubles.

Or, I could open the book again. That didn't appeal to me at all. I shrank from what I might find there. Once I had been through an earthquake. The most unpleasant part of that experience had been losing the solid ground under my feet, something I had always counted on to be there. Here I risked shaking an even more important foothold: reality.

But it was too late. Reality had already been shaken to its foundation. I could remove the book physically, but not from my memory. I could not continue to live a tranquil life, pretending nothing had happened. That would be like burying my head in the sand. Sooner or later, I would start to buckle under the weight of the questions left without answers. So I actually had no choice.

I opened the canvas cover slowly, as though something might jump out of the book. Somehow I already knew what I would see on the third page, but I still started a little when I saw the new title. This time it consisted of two words. I didn't have to leaf through the book to be convinced it was a new novel.

But I did it anyway to check something else' that had occurred to me. Turning several pages at a time, I soon reached the end. The typeface was now large, double spaced, and the chapters had both a number and a title. I went back to the beginning the same way. There was no change. It seemed that the change only came when I closed the book. The work stayed the same as long as the book was kept open.

I closed the book, then opened it again. That was it! By some magic, I had a new novel. I repeated this simple operation and smiled with pleasure at the same outcome. I had not come a single step closer to solving the problem, but at least I knew what was in store for me, so the tension eased a bit. It's amazing how much easier it is to accept the impossible when you are no longer afraid of it.

To show myself I no longer feared the chestnut-colored book, I started to open and close it quickly. I watched in fascination as the titles on the third page changed each time. I was filled with something like the ingenuous excitement that overcomes a child who has been given an amusing toy that produces unusual effects. I thought for a moment that the title of the edition was quite fitting after all. This was truly the smallest library, but by number of volumes, not titles. Indeed, what can be smaller than one single volume?

Then, after I had opened and closed the book a dozen times, I suddenly froze in mid-motion. The question that dawned on me suddenly turned my delight into something close to horror. What happened to the work after I closed the book? What I'd figured out so far indicated that it disappeared without a trace. Each title appeared only once. That meant that I had just lost more than ten books forever with my thoughtlessness!

I couldn't let this happen again. I held the book open firmly with both hands, so it wouldn't close by accident. I started to think feverishly about what to do. How could I save something as short-lived as a work that only existed as long as the book was open? Nothing crossed my mind. I have never been good at coping under pressure. That's why I can never write when I have a deadline. Then, when already drowning in hopelessness, something so obvious came to me that I would certainly have slapped myself on the forehead if my hands had been free. Photocopying, of course!

There was no need to hurry. I could wait for the rain to stop. Spring showers don't last long, and the work now between the covers was safe as long as I kept the book open. However, my patience ran out. I held the book in one hand, opened all the way, even though that wasn't necessary, and rushed to the vestibule. I grabbed my coat and umbrella and quickly went out into the hall. Since my hands were full, I had a bit of trouble putting on my coat. When I got outside, I had to lower the umbrella all the way to my head, the brown volume under my chin, to keep it out of the heavy downpour of rain.

I splashed along the wet pavement quickly, taking no notice of the fact that my shoes were full of water after only a few steps, and my pant legs were soaked almost to the knee. Luckily, the small stationery store that had a photocopier was not far. When I entered the store, shaking my umbrella after me, the owner looked at me in amazement. The woman clearly had not expected any customers in such a cloudburst. She must have wondered what urgent matter had forced me to come in just then, but she didn't say anything.

I said that I needed to photocopy something and waved the open book. I didn't give any explanation, although it would have been proper. What, in any case, could I have said? She kindly offered to do it herself, but I declined the offer. I did it in an unnecessarily rough voice because I was terrified at the possibility of someone else getting hold of this volume. The woman shrugged her shoulders and indicated the machine in the corner, then went back to her reading behind the counter.

I placed the book on the glass, lowered the heavy plastic cover, and pressed the green button. The bright light went back and forth and a moment later a copy of the third page came out of the side opening. At least that's what I hoped would happen. But there was nothing there. I turned the paper over, thinking the print was on the other side. Both sides were blank. I raised the lid and turned the book over. The title was still there, but it was invisible to the machine.

Noticing that I was turning over the book and the piece of paper, the store owner asked me if something was wrong. Did I need help? I quickly replied no, everything was fine. In order to allay her doubts, I continued with the photocopying. I turned new pages, pressed the button on the top, and completely empty pages continued to come out of the machine. From where the woman was standing, she couldn't see them, and she soon lowered her eyes to the newspaper in front of her, convinced that her strange customer had found his way.

The senseless photocopying was not so useless after all. It gave me a chance to steady my nerves after this new surprise. So I couldn't photocopy the book. I assumed that the same thing would happen if I photographed it or scanned it. I shouldn't waste time on that. What was I going to do about the potentially short life of the individual works? I could not keep the book open all the time to save one book, because then all the others would become inaccessible. And if you wanted access to another work, this one would disappear forever. I couldn't see a way out of this conundrum.

Then a dark thought formed in my head, sending a shiver through me. Maybe that was the whole point. Maybe the whole thing was devised intentionally to be a catch-22 situation. A very spiteful and malicious person stood behind *The Smallest Library*. Someone brazenly pretending to be a blind, benevolent old man with an ice cream cart, who generously handed out books. If I wanted to get out of this trap, I would have to face him once again.

I picked up the fifty-some empty pages, folded them lengthwise, and put them under my arm. I hesitated briefly after raising the plastic lid, then quickly closed the book and put it in the large pocket of my raincoat. One title, more or less—what was the difference? Approaching the counter, I put down a bill that was more than enough to cover what I owed her. I left without a word, feeling her inquisitive eyes on my back.

It was still raining, but now only small drops came sprinkling down. I opened my umbrella and headed briskly towards the Great Bridge, taking a shortcut. In an alley, I threw the bundle of blank papers in the first container, without stopping. As I loped forward, the clouds first became lighter, then thinned out and finally, when I was already close to my destination, rays from the hidden sun poked through them here and there.

There were still a lot of people under the bridge. Many who didn't have an umbrella, as I hadn't at first, stood on the edge of the covered part waiting for the rain to stop so they could leave. They blocked my view of the very end, where the old man had set up his cart. But as I made my way to the middle, where the crowd thinned out, I realized I wouldn't find him there. He had been under the open sky before, so the downpour had certainly made him find shelter somewhere under the wide metal structure.

I started to turn around, searching, but there was no trace of the old ice cream cart. I certainly would not fail to see it. The space under the bridge was rather large, but it would be impossible to pass unnoticed there. Had the old man left during my absence? That seemed unlikely. Would a blind man pushing a bulky cart go out in such a thunderstorm? No, that would be reckless and dangerous. Unless, of course, the blindness and other things had been a sham.

I wandered through the stands a while longer, not knowing what else to do, as my frustration mounted. Of the many questions besieging me, one slowly started to outweigh the others. Why me? Why had this happened to me, of all people? What set me apart from the others gathered in this place? The fact that I am a writer? A writer who hasn't been able to write anything worthwhile for quite some time? Wasn't that enough damnation? Why did I have to be given this book?

As I walked aimlessly, I found myself close to the seller I had talked to right before the fateful meeting. I thought for a moment to ask him about the old man. He could hardly have escaped his notice. But I didn't do it. Asking questions would only get me entangled in a web of explaining something that had completely escaped my under-standing. I might even be forced to take the volume out of my pocket and show it to him, which I wanted to avoid at all costs. But one other thing also discouraged me from that conversation, something I dreaded most of all. What if the seller said he hadn't seen a blind man with an ice cream cart?

There was no reason to stay here anymore. The weather had cleared up quite a bit. Now there were far fewer visitors under the Great Bridge. This time I headed home slowly, no longer in a hurry. I hadn't gone very far when I became aware of the smells. First of ozone, then many others in dense clusters everywhere, brought out by the rain: the smell of new leaves in the tops of the linden trees, the damp young grass, the covering of humus in the little park, the washed flowers in the flowerpots. It seemed that even the water covering the sidewalk and pavement in large puddles had a smell of its own.

And at intervals, somewhere in the background of these strong smells, dampened by them, I detected a weaker smell that seemed vaguely familiar. It was omnipresent or else was following me. It was unpleasant, like the stink of sweat, but different, arousing thoughts of something strenuous and hard. Even painful. I tried to decipher it, but without success. The effort was not in vain, however. Quite unexpect-edly, as I tried to figure out the mysterious smell, I thought of some-thing I should have thought of a lot earlier. Before the photocopying, certainly. I quickened my pace and then almost ran.

I took the monitor and keyboard off my desk since I didn't need them. I could have done the job faster by computer, but I never wrote using the computer. Instead, I took out a large notebook that had been empty for a long time. I didn't start to copy right away, however. When I picked up my pen, I was filled with the fear that this might lead nowhere. What if the pen left no mark, even though brand-new? I didn't know. Yet what could I lose by trying? Things certainly couldn't be worse than they already were.

I couldn't suppress a sigh of relief when the title of the novel appeared several moments later at the top of the first page. Clear and legible. I closed my notebook briefly and opened it again. No miracle happened. The writing was still there, as it should be. I turned the page in the book and sat back comfortably in my chair. Under the title I wrote "First Chapter" and then went on to the first paragraph.

Long and difficult work lay ahead of me. The novel was printed in tiny, single-spaced letters. But hardship is to be expected in the profession of writer. There is no respite. There are no shortcuts. Pain is part and parcel of the experience. That is why the pleasure is all the greater when things are brought to an end. When I copy the last page, I will simply close the book, and this work will exist solely in my manuscript. Who could reproach me then for adding my name above the title?

THE DIVIDED KNIGHT
Theophile Gautier
Translated by Brian Stableford

WHAT HAS MADE blonde Edwige so sad that she always sits by herself, with her chin in her hand and her elbow on her knee, gloomier than despair, paler than an alabaster statue weeping over a tomb? From the corner of her eyelid a huge tear flows down her cheek—only one, but one which never ceases to flow. Like a trickle of water which oozes from a rocky vault and eventually wears away the granite, that single tear, falling incessantly from her eyes, has pierced her heart and passed through it, forging a permanent breach.

Edwige, blonde Edwige, do you no longer believe in Jesus Christ the gentle Saviour? Do you doubt the indulgence of the loving Virgin Mary? Why do you always set your tiny elfin hands so rigidly by your sides? You are going to be a mother, which was ever your dearest wish; your noble spouse, Count Lodbrog, has promised an altar of solid silver and a pyx of pure gold to the Church of St. Euthbert, if you give him a son. Alas! Alas!

Poor Edwige has a heart pierced by seven spears of pain; a terrible secret weighs upon her soul. Some months ago, a stranger came to the castle. The weather was terrible that night; the towers trembled, the weathervanes whined, the fire cringed in the fireplace, and the wind rapped on the window like an unwelcome guest desirous of gaining entry.

The stranger was as handsome as an angel, but like a fallen angel; his smile was soft and his gaze was tender—and yet, that gaze and that smile chilled with terror and inspired the kind of fright that one feels when tottering on the lip of an abyss. His every movement was suggestive of a wicked charm—a perfidious languor, like that of a tiger lying in wait for its prey. He charmed her, in the manner of a snake hypnotising a bird. That stranger was a master singer. His bronzed skin demonstrated that he had seen other skies. He said that he had come from the far south of Bohemia, and begged hospitality for a single night.

He stayed that night, and many other days and nights thereafter, for the storm would not blow itself out, and the old castle shook upon its foundations as if the wind desired to tear up its roots and topple its crown of battlements into the foaming waters of the torrent. To pass the time pleasantly, he sang strange verses that troubled the heart and stirred up wild ideas; and all the while he was singing a glossy black crow, lustrous as jet, perched upon his shoulder, beating time with its ebon beak and fluttering its wings as if to applaud the performance. Edwige grew pale—as pale as lilies in the moonlight. Edwige blushed—blushed like roses in the dawn—and settled back in her capacious armchair, languishing as though half-dead, intoxicated, as if she had breathed the fatal perfume of those mythical flowers whose exhalations can kill. At last, the master singer was able to depart. A tiny blue smile arrived to brighten the face of the sky.

Since that day Edwige, blonde Edwige, does naught but cry in the corner of the window.

* * *

Edwige is a mother now; she has a beautiful child, all white and pink. Old Count Lodbrog has ordered the altar of solid silver from the foundry, and he has given a purse of reindeer leather containing a thousand pieces of gold to the goldsmith instructed to make the pyx.

The pyx will be large and heavy, and will hold a generous measure of wine; the priest who can empty it will be able to say that he is a good drinker. The infant is all white and pink, but he has the black gaze of the stranger: his mother has seen it very clearly.

Ah, poor Edwige! Why did you watch the stranger, with his harp and his crow, so carefully?

The chaplain baptised the child. He was given the name Oluf: a good and worthy name! The seer mounted the highest tower to cast his horoscope. The weather was clear and cold. Like the jaws of a lynx with sharp white teeth, a jagged ridge of snow-covered mountains bit the hem of the sky's gown; large pale stars shone in the blue crudity of the night like silver suns. The seer took his measurements, made note of the year, the day, and the minute; he made elaborate calculations in red ink on a long parchment spangled with cabalistic signs; then he went back to his chamber, and climbed up to his desk to check his results.

His computations had not deceived him; his natal chart was accurate as a precision-balance made to weigh precious stones. He started all over again—but he had made no error. The little Count Oluf had been born under a double star, one green and one red: one as green as Hope and one as red as Hell; one favourable and the other disastrous. Had there ever before been such a thing in the world as a child born under a double star?

With a grave and considered air the seer re-entered the chamber of the woman who had given birth and said, while passing his bony hand through the waves of his long mage's beard: "Countess Edwige and Count Lodbrog, two influences have presided over the birth of Oluf, your precious son: one good and one evil. That is why he has both a green star and a red star. He is subject to a double ascendant. He will be very happy or very unhappy—I know not which—perhaps both at the same time."

Count Lodbrog answered the seer, saying: "The green star will prevail." But Edwige dreaded in her maternal heart that it would be the red. She replaced her chin in her hand, her elbow on her knee, and began once again to cry in the corner of the window. After having suckled her child, her sole occupation was to watch through the window as the snow fell in thickly-compressed flakes, like feathers plucked on high from the white wings of the angels and the cherubim. From time to time a crow passed before the window, cawing and shaking loose the silvered dust. It reminded Edwige of that singular crow which always perched upon the shoulder of the stranger: the stranger with the tender gaze of a tiger and the charming smile of a viper. And her tears flowed more rapidly from her eyes into her heart, and through the breach that pierced it.

* * *

Young Oluf is a very strange child: one might almost say that there are two children of very different character within his little pink-white skin. One day he is as good as an angel, another he is as mischievous as a demon, biting the breast of his mother and clawing the face of his governess with his fingernails. Old Count Lodbrog, smiling beneath his grey moustache, says that Oluf will make a good soldier and that he has a bellicose temperament.

The fact is that Oluf is an insupportable little rascal. Sometimes he weeps, sometime he laughs; he is as capricious as the moon, as fickle as a woman; he comes and goes, stopping himself suddenly without any apparent motive, abandoning that which he had undertaken. He follows the most turbulent disquiet with the most absolute immobility. Sometimes, although he is alone, he seems to converse with an invisible companion! When he is asked the cause of his agitations, he says that the red star is tormenting him.

Oluf eventually reaches fifteen years of age. His character becomes more and more inexplicable. His features, although perfectly handsome, present a rather embarrassing aspect. He is blonde like his mother, with all the traits of the Nordic race, but beneath his brows— which are as white as snow that has neither been trodden down by the huntsman's boot nor spotted by the footprints of the bear, and which are surely the brows of the ancient race of Lodbrog—there scintillates between each ochreous eyelid an eye with long black lashes: an eye of jet, illuminated by the wild colours of Italian passion; a velvety gaze, as cruel and honeyed as that of the master singer of Bohemia. The months and years flew past, ever more rapidly.

* * *

Edwige now rests beneath the tenebrous arches of the Lodbrog burial-vault, beside the old Count, who is smiling in his casket because his name has not perished. She was already so pale that death has not changed her much. Atop her tomb there is a beautiful statue, lying down with the hands conjoined and the feet resting on a marble grey-hound, the faithful companion of the deceased. What Edwige said in her last hour no one knows—but the priest who heard her confession has since become even paler than the dead woman.

Oluf, the brown and blond son of Edwige the desolate, is twenty years old today. He is extremely adroit in everything he does. No one can draw a bow better than he; he can split an arrow that has already planted itself in the heart of a target; he tames the wildest horses without the aid of bit or spur. He has never looked upon a woman or a girl with impunity—but none of those who have loved him have been happy. The fatal imbalance in his character is opposed to any successful relationship between a woman and himself. Only one of his halves experiences passion; the other experiences only hate. Sometimes the green star carries him away, sometimes the red.

One day he says: "O white maidens of the North, as sparkling and pure as the polar ice, your eyes are moonlight, your cheeks touched by the freshness of the aurora borealis!" And on another he exclaims: "O daughters of Italy, gilded by the sun and burnished like the orange! Your hearts are flame within breasts of bronze!" The saddest thing of all is that he is perfectly sincere in both cases. Even so, you poor abandoned creatures and sadly plaintive ghosts do not blame him, for you know that he is even more unhappy than you are. His heart is an arena incessantly trodden down by the feet of two unknown wrestlers, each one of which—as in the combat of Jacob and the angel—

seeks to dislocate his adversary's thigh.(1) If one went to the cemetery, one would find more than one abandoned stone where the dew alone sheds tears, among the nettles and wild oats, beneath the jagged velvety leaves of the verbascum and the sickly green branches of the asphodel. Mina! Dora! Thecla! The earth lies heavy upon your delicate bosoms and your charming corpses.

One day Oluf calls Dietrich, his faithful squire, and tells him to saddle his horse.

"But Master, look how the snow is falling, how the whistling wind bends the tops of the pine-trees towards the ground; can you not hear the lean wolves howling in the distance and the reindeer belling like souls in pain?"

"Dietrich, my faithful squire, I will shake off the snow as one shakes off down that has stuck to a cloak. The crest of my helmet will just pass under the arches of the inclining pines. As for the wolves, their claws will be blunted upon my fine armour. I will dig in the ice with the point of my sword to uncover for the poor reindeer, who whimper and weep hot tears, the fresh flowery moss which they cannot reach."

So Count Oluf de Lodbrog—for such is his title now that the old count is dead—goes forth on his fine horse, accompanied by his two huge hounds, Murg and Fenris. The young lord with the ochreous eyelids has a rendezvous. Mayhap the restless young woman, high up in a sharp little turret shaped like a pepper pot, is already bent forward over the sculpted balcony, in spite of the cold and the wintry wind, searching the wilderness of the plain for the plumed helmet of her knight.

Mounted on his great elephantine horse, whose flanks were furrowed by thrusts of his spurs, Oluf advances into that wilderness. He crosses a lake, which the cold has converted into a single massive block of ice, where the fish are enshrined, fins splayed, as if petrified within a marble slab. The four shoes of his horse, equipped with hooks, bite insistently into the hard surface. A fog of sweat and respiration envelops and follows the horse as it gallops over the snow. The two panting dogs, Murg and Fenris, arrayed on either side of their master, exude long jets of smoke from their flared nostrils like fabulous beasts of legend.

Here is the forest of pines; like spectres they extend their heavy arms charged with white cargoes. The weight of the snow bends the youngest and most flexible; one could imagine them a series of silver arches. A terrible darkness dwells in this forest, where the rocks affect monstrous forms and every tree extends limb-like roots as if to cover nests of sleeping dragons. But Oluf is unacquainted with terror.

The path becomes narrower and narrower, the pines inextricably entwining their pitiful branches; clearings permitting glimpses of the range of snow-capped hills whose white jags rim the dull sky become increasingly rare. Fortunately, Mopsa is a vigorous running horse who could carry the gargantuan Odin without yielding. No obstacle can stop him. He jumps over rocks and takes hollows in his stride—and from time to time his dashing feet strike plumes of evanescent sparks from pebbles hidden in the snow.

"Onward, Mopsa, be brave! You have only to cross the brief plain and pass through the birch-wood now. Then a reassuring hand will caress your glossy neck, and you shall eat hulled barley and a full measure of oats in a well-warmed stable."

What a delightful spectacle the birch-wood is! All the branches are quilted with a plush of rime; the smallest twigs are outlined in white against the gloom of the atmosphere. One might imagine it as an immense basket of filigree, a silver madrepore, a grotto with a host of stalactites; branches and bizarre flowers plated with frost can offer no designs more complicated and more various than these.

"You are late, Lord Oluf! I feared that the mountain bears had barred your way, or that the elves had invited you to dance with them," the young lady says, as she beseeches Oluf to be seated on the oaken armchair beside the fireplace. "But why have you brought a companion to a lovers' rendezvous? Were you afraid to pass through the forest alone?"

"To what companion do you refer, flower of my soul?" says Oluf, astonished by the young lady's words.

"To the knight of the red star who follows you everywhere. The

393

one who is born of the gaze of a Bohemian singer: the baleful spirit which possesses you. You must sever yourself from the knight of the red star, or I can never respond to your lovemaking. I could never be the wife of two men at once." And no matter what Oluf said or did, he could not succeed in so much as kissing the little finger of Brenda's hand. He went away very dissatisfied, and resolved to do battle with the knight of the red star as soon as he could meet him.

* * *

In spite of the harsh welcome that Brenda had given him, Oluf took the road to the castle with turrets shaped like pepper pots for a second time; the amorous are not easily discouraged. While he made the journey he said to himself: "Brenda is undoubtedly mad. What can she mean by the knight of the red star?" The storm was even more violent. The snow swirled all around him, hardly permitting him to distinguish the earth from the sky. Whirling crows formed a sinister spiral above the plume of Oluf's helmet, in spite of the barking of Fenris and Murg, who leapt into the air to snap at them. At the head of the troop was a shining jet-black bird, like that which beat time on the shoulder of the Bohemian singer.

All of a sudden, Fenris and Murg desisted. Their avid nostrils sucked in the air uncertainly; they scented the presence of an enemy. It was neither a wolf nor a fox; a wolf and a fox would have been no more than a mouthful for those brave dogs. The noise of footsteps became audible. Soon, there appeared around the curve of the path a knight mounted on a horse of enormous stature, and followed by two enormous dogs. You would have taken him for Oluf. He was armed in exactly the same way, with a surcoat bearing the same blazon—but his helmet bore a red plume instead of a green one. The road was so narrow that it was necessary for one of the two knights to retreat.

"Lord Oluf, give way so that I might pass," said the knight, whose visor was lowered. "The journey which I have to make is a long one; I am awaited, and it is essential that I arrive."

"By the moustache of my father, it is you who will retreat. I am

394

bound for a lovers' rendezvous, and the amorous are impatient," Oluf replied, placing a hand on the hilt of his sword. The unknown drew his own sword, and combat commenced.

The swords, falling on steel mail, struck sheaves of shining sparks; soon enough, in spite of their superior temper, their blades were as rough as saws. The two combatants, astride their fuming horses amid the fog of their exhaled breath, might have been taken for two black-smiths hard at work over a red-hot fire. The two horses, animated by the same rage as their masters, bit with keen teeth at one another's sinewy necks, shredding one another's breastplates. They performed furious somersaults, rearing up on their hind feet and using their shod feet as if they were fists. They delivered terrible blows of their own while the knights hammered away frightfully above their heads. The dogs were nothing more than a biting, howling mass. Drops of blood oozed through the overlapping scales of the knights' armour and fell tepidly upon the snow, making little pink holes. By the time several seconds had passed one might have thought it a sieve, so hard and fast were the droplets falling. Both knights were wounded. A strange thing! Oluf felt the blows which he rained upon the unknown knight. He suffered the wounds that he gave as well as those which he received. He felt a great numbness in his breast, as if a fire had entered into and scorched his heart, and yet his cuirass was unbreached before his heart; his only wound was a cut in the flesh of his right arm. A singular duel it was, in which the vanquisher suffered as much as the vanquished, in which giving and receiving were no different.

Gathering his strength, Oluf sent the terrible helm of his adversary flying backwards. O horror! What did the son of Edwige and Lodbrog see before him? He saw himself: a mirror image could not have been any more exact. He was engaged in a battle with his own spectre, with the knight of the red star. The spectre let loose a great cry and disappeared. The spiral of crows climbed once again into the sky, and brave Oluf continued on his way.

When he returned that evening to his castle he carried behind him the young lady, who had been willing to listen this time. The knight of the red star was no longer there, so she had decided to allow her rosy lips to offer that consent whose price is modesty to Oluf's eager heart. The night was clear and blue. Oluf lifted his head to search the sky for his double star, in order to show it to his fiancée. The green alone was there; the red had disappeared.

On entering the castle, Brenda, entirely happy with the wonder which she attributed to love, remarked to the young Oluf that the jet of his eyes had changed to azure, a sign of celestial recognition. The old Lodbrog smiled beneath his white moustache, comfortable in the depths of his tomb—for, truth to tell, although he had never said so, Oluf's eyes had sometimes made him thoughtful. The ghost of Edwige was utterly joyous, because the child of the noble Lord Lodbrog had finally vanquished the malign influence of the ochreous eyelid, the black crow and the red star: the man had overwhelmed the incubus.

* * *

This story shows that even a single moment of forgetfulness, or a perfectly innocent glance, can have an effect. Young women, never cast your eyes upon the master singers of Bohemia, who recite verses that are intoxicating and diabolical. Young girls, you must trust yourselves to none but the green star. And all of you who have the misfortune to be divided selves must fight bravely, even though you belabour yourself with your own sword at the same time as you wound that internal adversary the evil knight. If you are curious as to who has brought us this legend from Norway, it is a swan: a handsome bird with a yellow beak, which has crossed the fiords, sometimes swimming and sometimes flying.

NOTES
(1) As in Genesis 32:25.

THE FOOL'S TALE
L. Timmel Duchamp

IN SEPTEMBER, 1589, a storm of "baffling winds" blew a Danish fleet carrying the sixteen-year-old Anne of Denmark off course, to the coast of Norway. Anne, the daughter of Frederick II, King of Denmark, had just been married by proxy to James VI of Scotland (who, fourteen years later, would accede to the throne of England). The fleet was within sight of Scotland, the story goes, when the storm struck. James and other persons of importance decided that witchcraft had caused the storm, and several Danish women were burned at the stake. Malice toward the fleet's admiral, Peter Munch, not against James or Anne, was given as the motive. Munch, according to contemporary sources, had "boxed the ear" of a merchant and thereby enraged the merchant's wife: "Quhilk storm of wind was alleged to have been raist by the witches of Denmark, by the confession of sundrie of them when they were burnt for the cause. What moved them was ane cuff, or blow, quhilk the admiral of Denmark gave to ane of the bailies of Copenhagen, whose wife being ane notable witch, consulted her cummers, and raised the said storm to be revengit upon the said admiral."

Though the women who paid for the storm with their lives were

Danish, James himself had a great terror of witches and did his best to fan anti-witch hysteria in his own country. Claiming that judges who were "lenient" with witches were pawns of Satan, he participated in "examinations" of suspected witches personally and wrote *Daemonologie* (1597), a nasty piece of hate-literature framed as a learned treatise on the subject. Convinced that the Earl of Bothwell was employing a number of witches to murderous ends against him, he supervised the torture of the suspected witches and conducted their interrogations himself, resulting in the "discovery" that the "baffling winds" that blew his bride's fleet off course had been caused by a group of women known as "the witches of Lothian." The said witches had accomplished this feat by casting cats that had been bound to the severed joints of dead bodies into the sea.

The man's take on his world was definitely paranoid (a condition not atypical in powerful men of the day). But to give credit where credit is due, we must acknowledge that such ideas about witchcraft, women, and the supernatural originated with the perverse ideas two women-hating German Dominican inquisitors, Heinrich Institor Krämer and Jakob Sprenger, had conjured up more than a century earlier in their infamous *Malleus Maleficarum*, or "Witches' Hammer." With the authorization of the complementary papal bull by Innocent VIII, *Summis Desiderantes Affectibus*, this fabulous duo took their inquisition on the road through most of Western Europe, far beyond the Rhineland, their original sphere of operations. As is well known, the paranoia they whipped up had a devastating impact on European society, particularly on women.

The *Malleus* was indeed a blunt instrument, or "hammer." Besides inspiring authority-sponsored terrorism, it had the additional effect of preventing men like James I from ever imagining creative forms of magic not cast in the ugly, constipated, *Malleus* mold, much less perceiving its practice right under their very noses. But though the ferocity and indiscriminate wildness with which the hammer was wielded did not crush the practice of enchantment by adepts, it did, eventually, drive such adepts underground—and, finally, to extinction.

Since the spectacle of hammer-wielding maniacs in positions of authority provokes a certain streak of perversity woven through the fabric of my personality, I take the greatest pleasure in disseminating a tale of magic told (if not enacted) right under that very king's nose. The tale has been pieced together from five manuscript fragments written on quarto-sized pages that were found in a sheaf of folio-sized sheets of music that had been wrapped in silk and kept in a thick leather pouch recently discovered in the false bottom of a Jacobean chest stored in the attic of the house of a distant descendant of a cousin of two Jacobean courtiers, Lord Harington and his daughter, Lucy, Countess of Bedford. Lord Harington was the tutor of Princess Elizabeth, James's daughter, who eventually became the "Winter" Queen of Bohemia (so-called because her husband's election to that throne, contested by the Hapsburgs, set off the Thirty Years War).[1] The Countess of Bedford was one of the most influential courtiers of her day, holding the Number-One spot among Anne of Denmark's Ladies of the Bedchamber; she collected art as well as patronized several artists and poets, including John Donne and Ben Jonson. Julia Guthke, the music historian, believes that the music manuscripts present a rare English example of *musica secreta*. She describes the music as being "for the most part elaborate motets and madrigals in that highly wrought, bizarre-to-the-modern-ear style which is most (in)famously associated nowadays with Gesdualdo." Composed for Renaissance princes and kept private, *Musica secreta* was never performed in open court. "Such music," Guthke says, "went abruptly out of fashion in the first decade of the 17th century, with the arrival of (a) the *stile nuova* (the most famous early practitioner of which was Monteverdi) and (b) ever more visibly absolutist courts that used music and dance less to give an exclusive and intimate pleasure to princes and more for the ostentatious display of their power."

The identity of the tale's author has stimulated a degree of scholarly speculation. The initials **XCM** appear in the lower right-hand corner of every sheet of music; suggestively, the author of the tale

---

[1] Elizabeth's erudite daughter, Elizabeth of Bohemia, was an important correspondent of Descartes. One wonders what James's reaction would have been had he realized that the intellect of a *female* descendant would someday be judged vastly superior to his own.

identifies herself as Xaviera Cristiana Morley. (The PRO State Papers Domestic do not mention anyone of that name, but a James Morley, musician, was employed by Elizabeth I, as well as by both James I and Anne of Denmark.) The author claims to be Anne of Denmark's "fool."[2] My good friend, the historian Louise Ducange, informs me that although paleographers and literary experts find the manuscript a convincing example of early 17th-century English prose (and chemical analysis confirms that the ink and paper are appropriate to the era), she doubts that such a person ever existed, and believes that whoever wrote the music and the tale simply called herself that, in order to protect her privacy (and reputation) in case either the music or the manuscript ever became public. I, L. Timmel Duchamp, am not a historian and therefore don't qualify to debate the matter. But I would urge readers to consider the author's self-description:

"I may call myself a fool, but though the King in his very person grants me a rich source of foolery, he doth not love fools, and I am not his, but his wife's, and know better than to play the fool with such as he. In a man so ordinarily superstitious and frighted of women, the very look of my person, stitched to the needling wit of my tongue, is like to make me appear to his rolling eyes a witch for hanging. My laugh I know he detests, 'an ugly clangor of mismatched bells' he once called it; wisely, I keep it muted whenever he is by. And what would he think to learn that when he is absent the ladies take that very clangor up among themselves, in unconscious mimicry, a contagion they do not in the slightest seek to resist? I listen to them falling about laugh-

---

[2] Marie de' Medici (queen of France from 1600, and Queen Regent 1610-1617) employed a "fool" who happened to be a woman. Known as "Mad Mathurine," she apparently wielded a scathingly feminist pen against certain misogynist writers of her day. A sample of her prose style is the curse she deployed against the author of the scurrilous *Le Caquet de l'accouchée*, whom she characterized as a sex-starved, rapacious bird, rejected by every woman he pursued, except by a hideous old whore who gave him a venereal disease that turned him into an eviscerated falcon: "Would to Saint Fiacre [the patron saint of gardens and venereal diseases] that his arse be full of boiling water...Let every woman smear his face with cow dung! Let every girl soil his mustache with spit, and let all women together heap so many curses upon him he can only shit after a good thrashing, and prowl about like a werewolf all the rest of his days!" Xaveria Cristiana Morley's style is not so flamboyant. But her perspective is indubitably as critical.

ing at the mildest of witticisms, in mere mimicry of the laughter that is the true source of their mirth. 'Tis the Queen who laughs the loudest and the longest, holding a hand to her side, indelicately doubled up, nearly spilling her breasts from her gown in abandon. 'Cristiana!' she shrieks (like everyone in the court, unwilling to call me Xaviera). 'Have mercy,' she begs, 'for already my sides ache from thy earlier excesses.' And 'tis not my joking she means, but my laugh. My witch's laugh, the King could well have it. A laugh with power to corrupt.

"'Child,' oftimes saith my father to me, 'how dost thy make such a sound, being thyself so tiny, and thy speaking voice like the piping of a small bird? Thy mother never sounded thus, nor I either, as thou knowest. How can such a sound come from such little lungs?'

"That a musician would even ask such a question! 'How can'st such a sharp throb come from your smallest tabor?' I always reply. 'Or such a far-carrying hoot from the smallest length of wood pipe, or such a penetrating sweetness from even the smallest of your viols?' My mother was a singer, and do I not remember how her voice had the power to soar above all the drums and viols and pipes playing at once?

"Oh my mother, my mother, that luminous Spanish beauty— nothing at all to the likeness of my person! Only my father asketh whence comes my *laugh.* All else ask whence came my very person, that is nothing like to her, nothing like to him, a creature some call a sport. My person, as grown to its full height as 'twill ever be, stands as high as the Queen's waist; my breasts like a boy's, my chest as large and arched and flatly smooth as a bird's; my hair sprouts from my scalp every shade of the rainbow, as though Nature could not decide Her will; great brown and strawberry patches paint my olive skin with Mysteries physicians and magicians are pleased to read; my hands, mismatching my body, are as strong and as great as those of the largest men. These features alone—besides those talents I keep close, safe from all discovery—mark me as one of those strange creatures so dear to the physicians and moralists who instruct men and women on how to get children. All who see me wonder first whether I am the devil's spawn, or the issue of the most improper sodomy practiced by my parents, or mayhap of some strange thoughts or sights my mother looked upon during pregnancy. Oh how they tasked my mother, to learn her sin, after bringing forth such as I! Oh how my mother was grieved, worrying to remember what fault had been hers. And yet, giving me her milk, as fine ladies seldom do their noble infants, and teaching me to sing and dance, and even setting me to perform for the old Queen herself, she did bear to me all the love any mother hath to give."[3]

If such a narrative self has been cut out of whole cloth, it is in the form of a morally equivocal being, the misconceived freak from "unnatural" sexual intercourse, a being in contrast to whom the normal categories of human being were strictly defined. Such an invention, as my friend Louise Ducange agrees, would be an extraordinary-for-those-times conceit of authorship. While it often amused early modern people to write about freaks, what person in his or her right mind would have consented to speak from the position and in the voice of a freak? Trained closely to Occam's Razor, I prefer, over the conceptually extraordinary, a simple fact: viz., that Xaviera Cristiana Morley did exist and did produce the tale. So. As is always the case with any text, whether the tale is truth or fiction, readers will have to decide for themselves.

* * *

In a society in which service was the most important avenue to advancement at all levels, one of the most essential skills was the ability to make oneself acceptable to superiors . . . Marks of respect to be shown in conversation with superiors included baring the head, dropping the right knee, keeping silence till spoken to, listening carefully and answering sensibly and shortly. Compliance with commands was to be immediate, response to praise heartily grateful.

—Ralph Houlbrooke, *The English Family*

---

[3] I take this quote directly from the piece of text Julia Guthke labels **Fragment A**. I'm grateful to her, and to her graduate student Blaine Bowen, for their transcription (using modern spelling and orthography), and to the ms's owner, Harold Sutton, for permission not only to paraphrase the text, but to quote it directly at liberty.

On a February evening in 1609, the Countess of Bedford arranged a special performance of Shakespeare's *Twelfth Night* for the Queen's court. The Countess intended this performance to be a simple affair, a light amusement meant to whisk away the queen's inevitable letdown following her grand triumph of February 2. On that day Anne had appeared, in a masque, as the queen of the twelve greatest queens in history, amazon warriors all.[4] She and the Countess had devoted months to cooking it up with Ben Jonson and Inigo Jones. According to the Venetian ambassador, Marc Antonio Correr, the Queen had personally supervised "daily rehearsals and trials of the machinery." By all accounts, James's court far exceeded contemporary notions of extravagance with the *Masque of Queens.*

The King, it had been thought, would be at Theobalds, an estate he kept for hunting.[5] The masque had kept him from hunting, and the three courts combined (James's, Anne's, and Prince Henry's) had already staged a total of twenty-three plays that winter. And a Shakespearean comedy was not, after all, the sort of play James was likely to attend for *fun.* And yet that evening, just as the company was about to enter the Performance Hall, the King and a large party of his cronies showed up—"loud, and loutish, and lousy lords," as the tale has it—staggering drunk. At their unexpected appearance, the Queen's Fool thought, "'tis clear intrigue or mischief is afoot, or I be no fool!"

As the King, Queen, Prince, and crowd of courtiers stood about waiting while accommodation was made for the King's party in the Performance Hall, the question "What doth the King here this evening?" was bruited about in low murmurs with lifted eyebrows. The Fool, at a distance from the royal persons, used the special power of her "amber orb" to scrutinize them and their favorites. The Queen showed not the least sign of irritation or curiosity as to the King's

---

[4] Masques were highly politicized court spectacles, 17th-century versions of Busby Berkeley production numbers that served as vehicles for flaunting the crown's wealth and for promoting a royal iconography.

[5] An estate, I might add, he forced one of his subjects to swap for another, simply because he liked it.

change of plan. The King looked as he always did when drunk. But the Fool was suspicious. Not a soul at that Court failed to read political and ideological subtexts in even the most incidental piece of ritual, much less in the performance of an entire play. And knowing what she knew of the Queen's and Countess's preferences, she had no doubt that the Countess had arranged something the King had not been meant to see.

The clever, silvery laugh of the Countess slipped and slithered through the raucous, bawdy racket made by the King's Gentlemen, its timbre too thin and fine to be mired in the coarse Scots' brawl.[6] Though responsible for the evening's entertainment, she betrayed not the slightest sign of dismay at the King's presence. The Fool watched the royal fingers busy themselves clumsily at the Favorite's codpiece and wondered whether the Countess assumed that the King would be too preoccupied with lust or befuddled by drink to notice whatever delicious thing she had planned. And the thought struck her that perhaps Master Jonson, lately at odds with certain of the Queen's ladies, had somehow maneuvered the Favorite (perhaps through the latter's handler, Sir Thomas Overbury), into insisting on attending, in order to stir up the King's resentment against them. The Fool thought it unlikely, but not impossible. Master Jonson had not liked the subtext the Queen and Countess had required of the *Masque of Queens*; he had quite other ideas about women than to glorify their bold, martial prowess. Since the King, having easily recognized it as a score for his wife in their continual game of one-upmanship, had expressed only perfunctory praise of the masque, perhaps Master Jonson thought the time was ripe for exposing the Queen's circle's tendency to lèse-majesté.[7]

[6] The Fool's manner of speaking about the Scots was not exactly what we'd call politically correct. Most English people of her time despised the Scots, and the favoritism James showed to those who followed him to England intensified that loathing. The numerous instances of rape by some of these same men, and of James forcing the daughters of his English subjects into disadvantagous marriages with many of them, didn't help.

[7] According to Julia Guthke, "James I had a habit of jailing the authors and producers of plays he considered disrespectful of his dignity. Ben Jonson, for instance, was jailed at least twice for writing such plays. (The Countess of Bedford's influence

As the crowd of waiting courtiers milled and gossiped, everyone with a clear view of James watched his slightest gesture and twitch (a continual stream of twitches, frankly, since James habitually jerked his neck and rolled his eyes, behavior some of his courtiers variously attributed to his having been wet-nursed by a woman who was always drunk, or to his having been taught at a tender age to be fearful of assassination and witchcraft). Privileged with her far-seeing amber orb, the Fool watched a flea dive from the King's beard onto a point of his high silver-threaded white lace ruff, dance briefly with the grand style of the Queen herself, then make a splendid gavotte, springing its body gracefully and elegantly high onto the jeweled royal earlobe. The Fool caught the Venetian ambassador staring at this royal ballet. Looking again at the King, she saw the royal tongue thrust into the Favorite's ear. On seeing the King spit phlegm onto the marble palace floor only inches from Sir Robert Sidney's jeweled and gold-thread embroidered velvet shoe, she thought, "'tis our honor and place to behold all that Majesty is and does." The king's very vermin were royal, and the King's stuttering Scots contortion of the English Tongue, too. Almost since childhood the King had proclaimed to anyone who would listen—in Latin, French, and Italian besides his own peculiar rendering of English—that he, by God's grace, was a "Little God on Earth." In his paternal masterpiece, *Basilicon Doron*, he bade his son Henry to be thankful to God "for that he made you a little God to sitte on the throne, and rule ouer other men." James also said, "What God hath conioined then, let no man separate. I am the Husband, and all the whole Isle is my lawfull Wife; I am the head, and it is my Body." Kings, James went so far to claim, are "euen by GOD himselfe . . . called Gods."[8] "My new rib," the Fool recalled hearing that the King had designated Anne when they were first married. So how many ribs did the King now have? she wondered.

secured his release in both cases.) The Queen apparently enjoyed such plays and supported their production, including a series of political satires performed publicly at Blackfriars by her own Children of the Queen's Revels."

[8] I doubt the Parliament that his son Charles ("the High and Mighty Prince" as he was known in 1609) tangled with would have agreed. They did, after all, cut off his head.

John Wheeler blasted out a trumpet fanfare, supported after the first five notes by an ensemble of two shawms (one of them played by James Morley) and three trombones. Under the direction of the Queen's Lord Chamberlain, the Court perfectly arranged itself according to rank and began its entrance into the Performance Hall. Though the musicians played a march-like processional, the King and Queen paced their steps as though to a basse-dance, which the Fool believed must be the Queen's doing, for the King, shambling and lurching with the clumsiness and crookedness that afflicted him when he was drunk, plainly depended on the Queen's guidance to walk straight. And the Queen's fondness for dance in all its forms made her wont to transform every ceremonial movement into dance whenever the King and Lord Chamberlain would allow her. After the King and Queen followed Prince Henry, paired with the Countess of Bedford because Lady Arbella, next to the prince in rank, was confined to bed with small pox. After them came the several ambassadors and their ladies, including the French Ambassador (who was able to attend solely because the Spanish Ambassador had departed for Spain), followed by "the bevy of Barons and Countessess highest in their majesties' favor," then the "Knights and Ladies and so on," down through the Great Chain of Being, with no one for once arguing with Sir Robert over his placement, with no gentleman jostling, punching, collaring, or threatening another, only the raucous talk and laughter of the drunken Scots spoiling the celestial harmony of the general social order. The Fool, scampering on her short legs to keep up even at such a stately pace, was assigned a place almost at the end of the processional, not much behind John Donne and immediately following the interesting Aemelia Lanyer who, like the Fool, was both a foreigner's and musician's daughter.[9] "Who," asks the Fool, "cannot take comfort at the neatness of our order? God is in his heaven, the King's Majesty is on his

[9] Aemilia Lanyer is interesting because: (a) Tillyard and others have (probably erroneously) identified her as Shakespeare's "Dark Lady"; (b) she was an accomplished poet who was one of the first Englishwomen to see her work in print; and (c) though she married the court musician Alfonso Lanyer in 1592 apparently "for collour" to cover a pregnancy, she was the stylishly-maintained mistress of Henry Cary, Elizabeth I's Lord Chamberlain (forty-five years her senior and a notable patron of the arts, particularly of Shakespeare's company).

throne, and we, so privileged to shelter beneath such a paternal roof, are safe indeed."

And so the Queen was seated in the first row in a throne-like chair on the left, the King in his throne-like chair in the center, and Prince Henry in his throne-like chair on the right. To the left of the Queen were stools placed for each of the ambassadors present, and one also between the King and the Prince for the Favorite. Velvet-covered chairs were placed to the right of the Prince for the Lord Chancellor and the ambassadors' Ladies, and to the left of the ambassadors for the wife of the Lord Chancellor. Benches were placed in rows behind, where on the most prominent and comfortably upholstered of these sat the Barons and Countesses, and behind those everyone else in their order. The Fool's place was on a plain oak bench. Sitting on the special cushion she had brought to augment her height, though, she had a clear view of the Queen and Countess, and with her special powers had no trouble eavesdropping when the Countess's ash-blond head leaned forward to whisper in the Queen's ear. Their exchange, of course, was safe from the King's notice, for his own head was bent far forward, with his face up against the Favorite's, nuzzling his neck, cheek, chin, and . . . nose.

When Shakespeare appeared on the stage, the Fool recognized his costume as having recently belonged to Sir William Cornwallis.[10] The playwright bowed low, first to the King, next to the Queen, then to the Prince, and finally to the entire audience. Seeing the relative bareness of the stage, the Fool was reminded of the fabulous machinery and flashing colored lights of the *Masque of Queens*. Imagination and wit, not material wealth and physical invention, would that night be paramount. Said Shakespeare, "grandly and proudly": "Your Majesties, your Highness, your Lordships and Ladyships, gentlemen and gentlewomen." The King giggled at something the Favorite said;

---

[10] By this time theatrical companies had begun buying their costumes from nobles. (Previously the crown had had a monopoly on such sales.) Tudor and Stuart theatrical productions typically used very little scenery, but spent enormous amounts of money on acquiring authentic costumes. The crown made a bundle after the Reformation selling not only monastic property, but also the rich, centuries-old vestments of prelates—to theatrical companies.

Shakespeare, of course, pretended not to notice. "'tis my company's immensely great honor and pleasure to present to you my comedy, which I call *Twelfth Night Or What You Will*, for your amusement and entertainment. We bestow our exceeding gratitude and thanks upon the Countess of Bedford, who, having seen it performed time past in the Middle Temple, duly recommended it to the Queen's Majesty's attention, and do verily hope to meet the faith in our play evinced by her shining grace." Then Shakespeare bowed again and backed quickly behind one of the screens set to the side of the stage.

Almost at once the Duke of Orsino entered, richly dressed and bejewelled, followed by a retinue of courtiers and musicians. His voice was bitter and melancholy. "If music be the food of love, play on. Give me excess of it, that surfeiting, the appetite may sicken and so die." Obediently, the musicians played—softly, though, softly, certainly not loudly enough to drown the King's hiccup and giggle and grating growl of words too Scots-tainted for most of the English ears present to grasp. "Will you go hunt, my lord? " said one of the duke's courtiers. "Tomorrow!" the King's Favorite shouted, drowning out the actor's response. At which the King collapsed into a fresh outburst of laughter as raucous as that of any drunkard in a tavern.

Since certain relationships in *Twelfth Night* are integral to the Fool's tale, and since the Fool penned her tale for someone well-acquainted with the play (assumed by the scholars to be the Countess of Bedford), a plot summary at this point is in order. The play opens after a shipwreck in which a pair of teen twins, Viola and Sebastian of Messaline, are separated. These twins are supposedly identical in appearance, and each believes the other to have perished in the wreck, but Sebastian is rescued by a pirate named Antonio (to whom he is known as "Roderigo"), and the two become lovers. Eventually Sebastian announces he is leaving for Illyria. Antonio, desperately enamored, begs him not to go and says that the Duke of Orsino, who rules Illyria, bears him, Antonio, a grudge and will destroy him if he ever gets his hands on him. When Sebastian leaves anyway, Antonio follows, regardless of the danger.

In the meantime Viola, with the help of the captain of the ship that wrecked, disguises herself as a boy ("as a eunuch," as she calls it) and places herself in the service of the Duke of Orsino, under the name "Cesario." Orsino, she finds, is languishing in a sea of narcissistic self-pity, apparently in love with his neighbor, Lady Olivia, who is in mourning for her brother and refuses to have anything to do with Orsino's suit for marriage (or anyone else's, for that matter). Orsino, struck by "Cesario's" style, sends Viola to woo Lady Olivia in his stead. Olivia of course falls madly in love with "Cesario"—while Viola falls in love with Orsino, who himself comes to have rather tender feelings for the "boy."

Interlacing these love plots are scenes of disorder in Lady Olivia's household (which is female-headed, after all). Her uncle, Sir Toby Belch (played by Shakespeare), throughout the play carouses with two buddies and makes trouble. He schemes to get one of the buddies, the foppish and foolish Sir Andrew Aguecheek, married to his niece and engineers an unwilling duel between the latter and "Cesario." Lady Olivia's fool, the merry, mischievous, but often wise Feste, and Maria, her waiting woman, join their revels and form a league against Olivia's social-climbing, snobbish, and puritanical steward, Malvolio. It is Maria's idea to expose Malvolio's ambitions to Lady Olivia by writing an unsigned letter that obliquely encourages his pretensions to wed a lady above his status, a letter Maria allows him to find just lying about. Malvolio, believing the letter is for him, slyly presses his attentions on Olivia and is locked up as mad for his pains, thereby giving Feste, Maria, and Sir Toby real scope for tormenting him.

The main plot comes to a head when Sebastian and Antonio arrive (separately) on the scene. Sebastian, taken for "Cesario," fights the duel and agrees—with a bewildered sense of having stumbled on a windfall—to Olivia's proposal of marriage; the Duke's men arrest Antonio, and Antonio, taking "Cesario" for Sebastian, begs the return of the purse he had given Sebastian, which Viola, of course, does not have. Inevitably, the Duke, with Viola, Lady Olivia, and Antonio all encounter one another, with Antonio reviling Viola for having betrayed his friendship, and Olivia claiming Viola as her husband. Viola, mystified, protests these claims, but the Duke condemns her perfidy. At which Sebastian comes on the scene, and Olivia (with everyone else) is duly astonished, and unable (!) to tell who is the real "Cesario." All is revealed. The Duke offers to marry Viola once she has dressed in women's clothing; Viola agrees to do so when her old clothes are found. Since she had left her old clothes with the captain, and it is revealed that Malvolio had had him arrested, Malvolio is released and receives Olivia's apologies, and the play ends with plans for a double-wedding.

* * *

Eroticism, in the early modern period, is not gender-specific, is not grounded in the sex of the possibly "submissive" partner, but is an expectation of that very submissiveness. As twentieth-century readers, we recognise the eroticism of gender confusion, and reintroduce that *confusion* as a feature of the dramatic narrative. Whereas, for the Elizabethan theatre audience, it may be the very clarity of the mistakenness—the very indifference to gendering—which is designed to elicit the pleasurable response from the audience.

—Lisa Jardine, *Reading Shakespeare Historically*

The fragments left by Queen Anne's fool provide a blow-by-blow description not of the play per se, but of particular audience responses to the play—and of her own sudden insights into the performance's subtexts. She writes, for instance, "soon it is the pretty little boy playing Viola's turn to enter. 'Tis Robin, a known flirt at court, pert as a kitten, and when younger, a strong countertenor, though not so tuneful as would make him suitable for the trade. Now the King's party quiets, pleased to hear his sweet piping voice—until, that is, they cannot help but snicker, as when Viola says: 'I'll serve this duke. Thou shalt present me as an eunuch to him.'"

The Fool describes Sir Toby Belch's and Sir Andrew Aguecheek's bawdy foolery as "quite to the King's taste." She notes that in most of the scenes between Viola (as "Cesario") and the Duke, the audience is closely (and mostly quietly) attentive—though even these scenes are distinguished by remarks from the audience, as when the Duke says, "For they shall yet belie thy happy years that say thou art a man.

Diana's lip is not more smooth and rubious; thy small pipe is as the maiden's organ, shrill and sound, and all is semblative a woman's part."

The Fool says that "a good English voice, from a bench closer to me than to the King," called out, "And just what size is thy pipe, boy?" The Fool expresses annoyance—and the opinion that if the King had not been present, the man would not have been "so impertinent with his own pipe." A short while later, when Malvolio describes Cesario, "as a squash is before a peascod, or as a codling when 'tis almost an apple. 'Tis with him in standing water, between boy and man," the same male voice burst out, "Aye, and full ripe enough to be tasty!" The Fool notes that she was not alone in her annoyance. The Countess of Bedford's kinswoman and maid of honor, a certain Mistress Goodyere, went so far as to get up from her seat and go to speak to one of the Queen's ushers, presumably to have the man silenced if he persisted.

The Fool's reactions to the play include professional interest whenever Feste plies his craft: "Next enters the Lady's fool, and my interest quickens most proprietorial. I dearly love the clever fool who proves wise, giving a fillip to such humble work as mine, and yet find myself gnawed by jealousy to see one such of readier, nimbler wit on his feet than is ever possible in true life. These lines he speaks were written for him, of a quill's invention. And does not clever ink flow more freely from a quill than twisted wit rolls off a nimble tongue? How can the Queen my mistress not wonder at the clumsiness of my own, after seeing this night's work? How compare I to Feste? Not at all, alas, not at all!"

Significantly, the Fool explicitly distinguishes what interests her from what interests the vocal male audience. The male audience is clearly most entertained by the drunken hilarity, engineered by Sir Toby Belch and the fool, and most emotionally engaged by the Duke's relations with "Cesario." The Fool, contrarily, expresses boredom with the drunken hilarity, and intense interest in Lady Olivia's relations with "Cesario" and Maria's cleverness and loyalty to her lady. Perhaps the greatest anxiety the play raises for her lies in the extent to which Olivia and Maria flout gender restrictions, revealed by the Fool's certainty that they will be punished. She quotes "Cesario" telling Olivia (after Olivia's told "him" that she'd heard he'd been "saucy at my gates") "I see what you are, you are too proud," and notes that it's clear that Olivia would rather have a lover she could pity from above, than one she must simply respect.

The Fool's first clue to the Countess's subtext is Sir Toby's naming Maria "Penthesilea," which the Fool at first takes as "a cheekiness for certain, when that queen's true image only lately graced our Court." A few sentences later, she reports: "Lo, at this very moment of the Duke's speech, do I suddenly lay my thoughts on that niggling familiarity that has been teasing my brain since I first put my eyes to this character. Ho, and so it is, that the Duke's silver-threaded ruff, his royal purple velvet doublet slashed with rose silk, his worsted and silk hosen seamed with evenly matched seed pearls, and even his high, cork-heeled shoes lined with gold and studded at the toes with great garnets, are all the very items I recall seeing the King's Majesty himself wearing not five winters past! And it is now, too, that I see that as the Duke lifts his goblet to his lips, why he holds it in that peculiar, clumsy way only the King doth, with his crooked elbow thrust awkwardly out at its own unnatural angle! And I notice, now, the odd restlessness of eyes that never stay still—though not rolling wildly, as the King's are like to do, yet in discreet emulation thereof . . . Yea, all becomes obvious of an instant, to she that hath eyes to see, making the nagging puzzle breathtakingly plain! How now, can it be that the King doth not see it himself? 'tis he so far gone in his cups, or may it be that, never having beheld himself in a true mirror of disinterested fashioning, his Majesty would not recognize himself were he to meet his own image in bright light and open face-to-face, and not as in this mirror so darkly?

"And so 'tis, while Feste sings a sad love song, I casteth my eye about, certain for to find other likenesses from the King's court. And straightaway my far-seeing orb discerns among the crowd of ducal courtiers one with the mannerisms and style of hair-dressing of Thomas Howard, Earl of Suffolk and another with those of Sir

Robert Cecil himself—wearing clothing I could swear had once been Sir Robert's. And so it becomes a game with me, to catch out the likenesses, and guess at those the recognition of which come not at once to my slow, feeble brain.

"Such cunning doings! Surely I cannot be the only one watching who has taken the joke. The players would not have put such a game forward, as they fear the King's custom of clapping playwrights and players into gaol when annoyed by a report of public mockery. Methinks it can be only the Countess of Bedford's doings. She hath the power to protect the lot of them, and the wherewithal to deflect the King's anger (if anger there chances to be). And being the most clever person in all three royal courts, and the one who has arranged the play for the Queen's amusement, my doubts are none at all."

The Fool takes a moment to note the pleasure to the audience of watching "Cesario" speak his love to the Duke in cryptic language: "And how many seated in this hall do not know the pleasure of speaking unpolitic truths under cover of a mask? Or the like pleasure of telling one's love, without surrendering oneself?" And then she swings back to her unpicking of all the threads of the subtext: "But this is rich! As the steward, Malvolio, enters, ever pompous and fussy and self-important, the scales fall from my amber, attentive eye, and I see that spot of grease on the sleeve, just above the lacy cuff, where Sir George Carew, omitting to see me standing so low beside him, jostled me as I held out to him a gold plate of sweetmeats and pastries for his delectation, at which he brushed against the pastries, making a fair mess of his sleeve, a general smearing of raspberry and cream and butter into the cloth, for that the gentleman cursed me as a devil's spawn of a dwarf. And though the laundresses worked over it, 'twas never the same, and eventually was gi'en up for another. The Queen could not bear him as her Lord Chamberlain, and would not have him (though she must needs bow to the King's command and allow him to stand her Vice Chamberlain). How this player doth take Sir George's tapping of the foot and his exaggerated angle of the chin to the life! The Queen's Majesty must know this Malvolio—even if Sir George himself doth not! How choice a delight, to hear this puffed up stew-

413

ard take up a letter neither signed nor addressed, well tangled in his own insolent assumption that in his vast astuteness 'tis in his power to grasp its portent as if 'twere a riddle put to him by the Sphinx herself. Vanity alone driveth him, that cutteth the text's cloth to his own puny measure. How like a man, I say. A letter, found on the ground, *must* be meant for him! A letter left unsigned *must* be from his mistress! It cannot be else, but that she be in love with him, though anyone with eyes open must see that she is mad for Cesario! Hark! When a man knoweth not how to read a woman's text, it behooveth him to acknowledge himself mistressed! And that that true mistress, in this case—as she be the true author of the text o'er which he labors so mightily—be Maria, glorious, clever, puissant, is naught that any gentlemen in this audience will think to notice.

"But what pleasure doth this clever mask render this insufferable character's humiliation! Saith he, puffing out his chest: 'Daylight and champaign discovers not more! This is open. I will be proud, I will read politic authors, I will baffle Sir Toby, I will wash off gross acquaintance, I will be point-devise the very man. I do not now fool myself, to let imagination jade me . . . ' 'tis sweet, so sweet for a joke. 'Twill be e'en sweeter if neither Sir George nor the King discover it, so to consider how fleeting sweetness can be when swiftly followed by the bitter. Ah, and enters Maria now, to collect her 'gratulation from the gentlemen—and I see, at once, what I did not before. In faith, this Maria stands straight and slim, wearing an ash-blonde wig. Earlier, I cavilled that they named her Penthiselea. But 'tis all clear now, the cunning of that designation. For who is Maria but our very Countess herself! And after Feste, the fool, is not Maria the cleverest creature in the play?"

At this point the text breaks off. The next fragment begins with the revelation that Lady Olivia's costume once belonged to the Queen, and that the actor portraying her is recognizably imitating the Queen's gestures and demeanor. The Fool, certain that the men in the audience aren't getting it, is triumphant at her own superior penetration: "The gentlemen admire the boys beneath the gowns and scorn the Lady who cannot attract the love of one already taken by the Duke. 'Tis a dangerous game, and yet safe enough. For unless the King's Majesty catches out the joke this night, tomorrow 'twill be too late, since his pride and vainglory will have the head of anyone who dares suggest he's been made a fool however royal without himself noticing 't. The Countess has *that* right and knows her business, as fully as Maria, making sport of Malvolio, knows hers."

For the rest of her account of the play, the Fool continually notes the real persons of the Court who she believes the Countess intends to be conflated with the play's characters. The audience apparently ceases making vocal interruptions—with the exception of an incident involving the King. During one of Malvolio's speeches, "the King's Majesty's voice raises a raucous howl for a chamber pot so thick on the royal tongue that e'en those of us well-practiced in grasping his speech are deprived of the exact, coarse words of his demand. Malvolio is halted in his nonsense, rooted to his place and struck dumb as a pebble lying passive in a field. I pray the King's need be only to piss, which is all the use mine own eyes have 'til now seen put to the golden pot the boy called Matthew carries everywhere after the King. Short as I be, 'tis never been my privilege to hunt with their Majesties, but who has not heard of the King's loosing his bowels off the back of his horse whilst the Queen and court wait on the royal pleasure?

"But ho, the audience becometh restless at this wait—and 'tis true, the King doth not always piss as freely as a royal body would claim its privilege to do—and 'round about do maketh whispers and rumblings, chuckles and titters. At such times methinks of the rumors whispered concerning the royal childhood in the wilds of Scotland, that his chamberlain carried him everywhere until he was five, though he be dressed in rags through the meanness of those Scots lords who called themselves his subjects. (Which whispers always bring another crop about the *Queen's* Majesty, raised in the luxury of a wealthy court, to the effect that as a princess she was carried everywhere till she reached *ten*, a nonsense impossible for a sober soul to put credence in.)

"Of a sudden, shouting, the King bids the player to continue, testily saying he doth not know the reason the blockhead standeth there, not saying his lines, and can it be that he has forgot them, and if so, would not someone of the Company kindly prompt the dolt?

"The poor player looks plainly distressed and lost in the wave of titters that sweeps through the audience. But lo, my acutest ear picks up the soft-spoken cue, 'I would not have him miscarry for the half of my dowry,' and the player stands erect, thrusting a leg forward, puffing out his chest, the epitome of foolish vanity. *Go to*, methinks, all appreciation for the fellow's fine aplomb. 'O ho, do you come near me now? No worse a man than Sir Toby to look to me!' he crows, all gleeful, vaunting pride.

"The sound of water trickling in the pot (albeit 'tis of metal, though fine, chased gold) carries clearly to every ear in the audience. 'I discard you,' saith Malvolio. 'Let me enjoy my private.' The whilst we all listen to the King's business, a *Tinkle, tinkle*, as nurses say to their small charges. 'Carry his water to the wisewoman,' Fabian sayeth, just as the King's golden pot be carried away. The scene is full riotous: who cannot but laugh? Even Mistress Lanyer, seated at my side, nigh as worldly and discreet as the Countess herself, shakes with laughter. The happy coincidence is more than anyone sober can bear!" [11]

As her account of the play advances, the Fool becomes more and more focused on what we (though not *she*) would call "gender differences." She notes of the duel that puts "Cesario's" "manhood" on the spot: "This tack the gentlemen all adore, for making so sharp the difference between a boy playing a woman masquerading as a man, and a true man (of the which, however, Sir Andrew might be less than a stellar exemplar)." And notes—" 'A very dishonest, paltry boy, and more a coward than a hare,' saith Sir Toby. The gentlemen in the audience all roar and make jokes, that when a female goes in breeches, she's always dishonest and paltry, and a poor imitation only." When Sebastian comes along and plunges without question into fighting Sir Andrew, "The gentlemen all cheer, satisfied to see a man act as the

[11] Though literary historians routinely speculate on performance practices and audience behavior, especially with respect to Shakespeare, their notions of distracting audience behavior usually don't refer to such privileges of royalty. (Though who, knowing anything about James, would find the Fool's account of it incredible? Even if this particular instance is invented, surely the author of the tale witnessed such doings on other occasions, if not with such serendipitous timing.)

one imitating him so failed to do." The Fool's dissatisfaction grows as the male audience's satisfaction increases when Olivia wins Sebastian ("a full man" she mistakes for her beloved "Cesario"): "Sebastian is all delight at his strange fortune, as are the gentlemen in the audience, nudging one another and chuckling. The ladies, though, keep silent, seeing how 'tis that the Lady, heretofore so much her own mistress, is now to be made a pitiful, cheated fool of."

Significantly, her description of the play's ending indicates the trajectory of the next day's adventure. "[A]ll [is] discovered and wrapped into a parcel for carrying away in the neatest, most seemly fashion. The Lady Olivia's love is seen to be improper and foolish, Viola's to be proper and wise. Like the late Queen, the Lady Olivia was surrounded by men of inferior standing, refusing all offers of marraige from suitors of her rank. Unlike her royal counterpart, tho', this lady ends worsted (if not bested). Who with eyes cannot see how her gaze travels to and fro' 'tween Sebastian and her whom the lady thought was called 'Cesario,' and how her expression changes from one of puzzlement, astonishment, and doubt, to that of disappointment and disillusion, e'en as Sebastian taketh her arm and doth stand at her side, her revealed lord and master? The very sight puts a sadness in my belly, though the players do not mean us to pity the lady. Maria, most excellent and marvellous dea ex machina, too, is rendered silent and harmless, as a proper woman must be in the face of true authority and mastery—such as neither the upstart Malvolio nor the debauched Sir Toby could be said to possess. Aye, Sebastian and the Duke stand exalted, the which being men of rank soon to be wed they must be, while Antonio, standing on t'other side of Sebastian, seemeth securely assured of his beloved's protection and affection—though now in the place of the subordinate rather than the master of the one he loves, as befits their respective ranks, which heretofore hath been concealed. Malvolio, that climbing, prating puritan, is banished, no more to threaten decent order with his moralizing self-importance. But joy of joys, the fool is given the last word, and that in jolly song, that the audience may be recalled to a full consciousness of how much it has its entertainers to thank for the evening's pleasures: *But that's all one,*

417

our play is done, And we'll strive to please you every day. With a *hey-ho*, aye, I say, and a tra-la-la, tra-la-la. For a good piper is worth his pay—and so every actor, musician, and wit!"

* * *

However differently the early and late discourses about women and the family manage femininity, both depend on the powers of representation, whether it be the spectacle of the punished female body or the demure depiction of a right marital relation.

—Karen Newman, *Fashioning Femininity and English Renaissance Drama*

The audience's applause woke the King. Except to make way for persons of royal rank, the members of the audience left the Hall without ceremony, nearly stampeding the Fool, who describes herself as vulnerable to being knocked in the head by (sheathed) swords and the skirts of ladies' gowns "so starched and wired and farthingal'd that e'en as they knock into my face they conceal my small person from everyone around me." Rushing to supper, people in the crowd gossip rather than talk about the play, trading rumors of expectations for how badly scarred the Princess Arbella will be from small pox, of the Privy Council's latest plan to send an army of loyal administrators to put Ireland and the colonies into strict order, and, perhaps the most eagerly discussed tidbit, the good heartedness of Prince Henry for having declared himself unwilling to use the saddle James had given him for a New Years' gift until the woman who embroidered it was paid for her labor.

Much later, after the Queen had ceremoniously retired for the night, a group of courtiers congregated in Cecily Bulstrode's room with the intention of playing a round of "Newes."[12] The Fool says that while pens and ink and paper were set out, the company speculated on

[12] According to Julia Guthke, "Newes" was a game of wit played in Anne of Denmark's court. A selected "round" of it was published as *Sir Thomas Overbury, His Wife*, including, in its second edition, a rebuttal to its misogyny by "A.S." The game was played in Cecily Bulstrode's rooms at court with varying collections of players, sometimes for half the night. The queen herself sometimes played, as well as the better known Ben Jonson and John Donne.

the King's reasons for attending the play. Lady Mary Wroth's theory was that the Favorite was infatuated with Robin, the actor who played Viola/Cesario. But Sir Thomas Overbury[13] scoffed at the suggestion: "'Twould be a folly, and though he himself would never claim to be the equal in wit to any in this chamber, 'tis not a folly like any he'd likely make himself liable to." The Fool notes that since "the gentleman's ordinary demeanor maketh his mouth and eyes to be a sneer, 'tis impossible to take his tone with any surety."

Because of all those present only Overbury's status allowed him to speak so frankly, "the titters his speech draws run wildly, as does the fox from spaniels, ragged with the haste and fervor of one that holds dear his life."

Lady Anne Southwell, casting an arch look at the Countess of Bedford, said, "But it came to my ears after the play, whilst I was caught up in the crush to supper, that 'twas expected by many of the King's gentlemen that something unseemly might tonight be acted. I heard one gentleman say to another, in his disappointment, did not everybody know the Queen's taste for comedies not to the King's Majesty's liking, and what was planned was a dessert, as 'twere, to the late Masque, which as this gentleman would have it, so displeased the King's Majesty that he's determined never again to let the Queen and the Countess direct another's making. The gentlemen both expressed themselves of the opinion that faced with the King's presence, the Countess directed the players to act another play than the one originally intended for tonight."

"Pish, posh, mere stuff and nonsense," replied the Countess. "The King was all graciousness in applauding our efforts in making the Masque. The Queen, I'll warrant, is well satisfied o'er that."

The Fool notes that the Countess dared not speak of the Queen's taste for seeing the King and his Scots mocked on the stage, and that the Queen's preference, like Sir Thomas's open disrespect for the

---

[13] According to Julia Guthke, "Overbury was Robert Carr's 'handler.' Because the Favorite had the important political responsibility of distributing an enormous amount of patronage, which was apparently beyond Carr's ability to manage, Overbury, a friend of Carr's, had the close-to-official position of dictating most of his advice to the king."

Favorite, was her privilege.

"So there was no other play to be performed tonight?" said Overbury, his lips curling into a sly smile he couldn't quite manage to conceal.

"Nay, sir, there was not," said the Countess coldly, as though she couldn't have cared less whether he believed her—adding, "And 'twas no disappointment for the Queen, for certain, except in its ending, which I'll confess left her somewhat annoyed."

"Somewhat annoyed!" said John Donne, whom the Fool describes as "all astonishment." "A harmonious ending for all but the puritan, whose expulsion was necessary for the general happiness, and marriages all 'round? How could such an ending annoy any woman, when women, aye, even those of the highest rank, are always mad for love matches, the which generally bring the greatest fiasco when made amongst families of rank? For surely the Queen, who knoweth the difference between sober duty and fantasy, could not construe such fantasy to imply sanction to the disorder of lovematches in our own society?"

The Countess replied tartly: "Nay, the Queen, sir, is not of such weak discernment as it pleases thou to think."

Donne flushed in face and neck. Of no great rank or standing, he was allowed to join the company to entertain them, not because he was "a true member of the circle." "A misstep," the Fool writes, "comes easily to the feet of such as we, and cannot help but bring mortification, as never happens with the others, who can laugh off any clumsiness in the sure confidence that they have the right." Swiftly Donne rose to his feet and bowed gravely to the Countess. No one, the Fool says, was surprised at the formality of his gesture, since the poet relied on the Countess as his chief patron, who he hoped would either support his art or secure a commission for him as Secretary in the Virginia Company. "My pardon, My Lady," said he, his tone a match to his manner, "I meant no slight to the Queen's understanding. My question was more general than particular, for that it was *my* discernment that was too weak to imagine any other cause for annoyance."

Said Overbury, seizing a liberty none of the others would dare: "So please to tell us, Lucy, lest we expire of curiosity, how the Queen could be annoyed at the ending?"

The Countess thrust back her head and stared haughtily down her nose at the company. "Did no one of you here feel a dissatisfaction, then?" she said, as though posing the obvious.

When no one else replied, the Fool herself spoke: "Most decidedly, My Lady. The gentlemen were all made happy, and the ladies in a way to becoming most unhappy. But do not comedies always end so? All the reason being, I believe, that men maketh them, and care naught for the woman's part, or else assume that making men happy is all that women do care for."

The Fool's answer drew a furor of scorn and ridicule down on her head. "And so," she writes, "foreseeing my sure defeat in their common opinion, I cry surrender without hesitation." Said she: "I being but a fool, I cannot help but speak foolishness."

The Countess, however, smiled and nodded her approbation for the Fool. "Cristiana speaks the Queen's mind. As the Queen's Majesty herself saith, 'tis impossible to think the Lady Olivia could be happy with the poor substitute, a mere seeming in appearance, of the one she loves, who is nothing like the one the Author, at the end, resigns her to. She, who has lived without a master, which a husband must always be, suddenly to be subject to such a one after having chosen quite another—'tis a tragic ending indeed, and no comedy as far as I can see. And yet the play itself doth not so much as take note of the tragedy, but celebrates it as a happy conjunction! And so the Lady is rendered dumb, to allow the play's supposed joyful ending."

The company was "struck dumb"—but for a "few astonished moments only, it boasting some of the cleverest tongues in the Kingdom." Overbury found his voice first. "Surely the Queen's Majesty would not want all entertainments to be like her masques, with Amazon warrior Queens prevailing over men, which is the world turned upside-down?" He tittered, as though nothing could be more ridiculous, and Cecily Bulstrode smirked and cut her eyes at him, while Lady Anne Southwell looked more thoughtful than amused.

Overbury waved his languid, beringed hand with more energy than he usually showed. "Olivia's household was chaos throughout the play," said he, "exactly for that it was masterless. Surely no person of sense could agree that such bedlam is to be taken as anything but an argument for why men must keep rule o'er women?"

The Countess's kinswoman, Mistress Goodyere, said, "And yet, Sir, I myself doth take the Queen's point. A certain melancholy steals over my heart now that I think on the Lady's feelings. Sebastian showed himself to be nothing much like his sister, but in appearance only. When a woman loves, whilst she loveth the body, she also loveth the spirit and heart as well. I do not see how one who would love the youth as Cesario seemed to her to be would then love another very much unlike." Mistress Goodyere smiled gently at Master Donne. "The which is to say, I do not see the lovematch in *that* union, Master Donne."

Donne said, "somewhat (though kindly) mocking," "I see that I mistook the matter entirely. The which must be laid to my ignorance of the true workings of ladies' hearts. But you must grant that Viola's union with the Duke was a lovematch? Or doth the ladies find fault with that match as well?"

The Countess said "with that clever dryness in her voice that draweth interest to its pronouncements just as honey draweth flies," "The Queen's Majesty regarded it skeptically. The Duke will be bored with Viola in a trice, is how the Queen judgeth the matter. As a boy, Viola was delightful to him. But transformed into a woman, swathed in skirts and restrained from frank speech as any lady must be, and never pert and always proper, she will soon lose the Duke's interest. What charms in a boy is intolerable in a woman. And so 't was, the boyish companion was all to his taste; his previous pursuit of Olivia, though trumpeted to the world, mere play-acting without true passion. In short, the Queen resteth no confidence in the happiness of that match, the which, like t'other, was based on a lie, albeit of appearance rather than spirit, and by reason for that 'tis true that the spirit of a woman must differ when she be in skirts than when she be in breeches, the difference doth in fact come to more than one of mere appearance."

Then Overbury said: "But that is a hard judgment, indeed. By such perverse reasoning, only Sebastian and Antonio will end happily! When they be not properly matched at all, not being husband and wife but only intimate friends!"

A few people rolled their eyes, and the Fool said, "'tis Maria I care most for. Her cleverness in exposing the puritan upstart was an act of service to her mistress. A woman of such intelligence is too good for such as Sir Toby, whose only use for her is dishonorable. The Author doeth her no honor in his ending, either!"

The Countess's lustrous eyes beamed warmly on the Fool. "A Penthiselea indeed," she said. "But in the world as it doth be nowadays, a Penthiselea would be taken for a madwoman, or a whore. Our world would know nothing of her. And so, Maria must be silent and downcast in the end, or else be taken for a scold or harlot."

Bulstrode said then, "Aye, and 'tis not that always the way. When a woman speaketh her mind, or doeth what she desireth rather than what she is supposed to desire, she is condemned for 't. Unless she be Elizabeth Tudor, or Catherine de Medici, that no one dare slander or judge disorderly."

"You see, Donne, what their constant reading of Spanish Amazon fantasies hath achieved," said Overbury. "Such romances maketh them to hunger for what no good Englishman would in truth abide!"

"Say rather *most* good Englishmen, sir, rather than none," replied Donne. "For if you mean to invoke the *Querelle des Femmes*, I must declare myself to take the ladies' side."

Overbury made a loud noise of disgust, fairly spitting as he thrust the syllable "Pah!" from his mouth. "This Olivia," he said, "plainly needs a generous helping of halek. A husband—with a real staff between his legs—would provide that, especially a husband like that young and lusty fellow Sebastian. The Author hath *that* right, I'll warrant. Whether Cesario is a codling or a woman disguised as one, the lad lacks what it would take to satisfy such a woman. A shrew, if we better knew her, I make no doubt. Treating her lord as she did, gives the hint to 't. The kind of woman who is never satisfied, and is always just about to fall to a fit of the Mother,[14] or halfway to a pact with the Devil, caught up in the belief that the Evil one will see her satisfied where mortal men aren't up to the job." Overbury stared satirically at the court ladies, and then suddenly at the Fool, where his gaze grew harsh and derisive. "As one imagines your own mother to have been, puny freak that you are. Either too impatient for 't to wait until her monthly bleeding was past, or so dissatisfied with her husband's potency to seek the Devil's bed. Thou art a living lesson to us, thou child of filth or devil's baggage, so to see plainly with our own eyes what such women do wreak out of their very bodies."

The Fool writes that "This shame hath been put to me so often that I no longer blush with each fresh rebuke." She replied, "Just so, Sir Thomas," and bowed to him as deeply as Donne had bowed to the Countess for *his* offense. "'tis my profession," she writes, "to please and amuse. That I must grovel to all and sundry the way the likes of Sir Thomas must grovel to the Queen and King is the way of the world. Living at court, I am oft reminded that the King makes little difference in his regard for the gradations of station of those beneath him. Did not the King's Majesty write publicly to the Queen that it made no matter to him that she was a King's daughter, for that being his wife, to his mind she would as well be the daughter of a fishmonger? And so all men do so regard most women, but those few like the Countess and the Queen with the power to bless or curse their lives, and more especially as with the late Queen, so like the Lady Olivia, whom Sir Thomas condemneth as a shrew or witch or hysteric."

After bowing to Overbury, the Fool bowed a second time to the rest of the company and said, "But just as I am such a freak, sir, and with so little of the true woman about me that many are led to speculate on my sex altogether, so I, at least, am in no danger of sharing my own mother's fate. The Mother will have aught of me, that I have too little of the Sex in me to suffer an affliction in that organ, and the Devil neither, for all my ugliness is beyond what even the Evil One will

[14] According to Louise Ducange, "The 'Mother' was the uterus. A 'fit of the Mother' was an attack of hysteria, explained variously as the womb wandering the body in search of relief, or afflicted with humoral imbalance. A plentiful diet of orgasm or hard physical labor was supposed to prevent it."

tolerate. Which leaves me by default, sir, chaste and the child of God, who alone will have such as me."

Overbury turned haughtily away, as though the Fool hadn't spoken, and leaned close to Cecily Bulstrode and whispered into her ear. The Fool claims that her special powers allowed her to hear what he whispered, but that she chose not to repeat it.

Lady Mary Wroth, smiling broadly at the Countess, said, "I see Sir Thomas's strategem. 'Tis plain! He hath distracted us exceedingly, so that we no longer talk of the ladies' discontent, but rather of how greatly e'en the mightiest of men do fear the power of e'en its least effects."

Donne said, "And 'tis not so, that all men, howe'er wise or foolish they be, do well to fear the power of the fair Sex?"

Lady Mary Wroth rolled her eyes at Lady Anne Southwell and said, "Mayhap we should be playing Edictes rather than Newes, since the gentlemen are in the mood to attack us whate'er we might venture to say." [15]

Bulstrode smirked at Overbury. "As usual, the man speaks from pique. He dies to die in love in a certain Countess's arms. Who will none of him." [16]

Annoyed, Overbury said, "And why all this bibble-babble, when there's Newes to play?"

"Ah, that it would be possible to see the outcome, and make wagers on 't," said Lady Mary Wroth, smiling, "all radiance and mischief." "That we could go to Illyria, there to spy on the supposed lovers, and see what they make of the Author's ending."

The Fool writes, "'tis a common enough notion for that lady, putting forth such a wish, for that she spends much time imagining other places and societies, peopled with family, friends, and acquaintance,

[15] According to Julia Guthke, " 'Edictes' was another game played in Cecily Bulstrode's rooms, a put-down game explicity pitting a group of men against a group of women."

[16] Julia Guthke glosses this: "I believe this is a reference to Overbury's attempt to seduce the Countess of Rutland by (after other methods failed) sending Ben Jonson, whom she favored, to read to her *Sir Thomas Overbury His Wife*, much as Orsino sent Cesario/Viola to read Orsino's love letter to Olivia."

caught up in other methods of ordering relations. Doth she not oft entertain the Queen with such fancies, whilst most of us ply our needles, as we chat idly about whatever romance we have been reading among ourselves as we work?"[17]

The company laughed, "some in delight, and Sir Thomas in scorn." Donne said, "But 'tis easily done, my Lady, by merely asking the Author how he imagines it."

Overbury laughed loudly. "But would the ladies be satisfied then? *There's* a matter I'd make a wager on."

Mistress Goodyere shook her head. "Nay. But the Author's opinion is no more authority to predict than that of a parent asked to give the tale of his child's life at the moment of its birth."

Donne looked surprised. Impatient, Bulstrode threatened to send the lot of them away and herself to bed if no one had any intention of playing Newes. The Countess was asked to suggest the game's theme. "The stage," she said "quickly, briskly, and in all originality. 'Tis not a theme anyone remembers having played before."

* * *

Anything once it is made has its own existence and it is because of that anything holds somebody's attention.

—Gertrude Stein, *Lectures in America*

The Fool writes that the next day she and a number of ladies were sitting with the Queen doing needlework while one of the Queen's personal servants, Pierrette, was translating a story (aloud) from the French. " . . . and Pierrette's bright, black button eyes flash with that sly air of knowledge only a Frenchman carries about his person," the Fool says, then quotes him as reading: "The lady, being entirely French and therefore possessed of a full measure of feminine cunning so characteristic of that country, approached Madame Marguerite, the King's daughter, and the Duchess of Montpensier, who was sitting with the

[17] Julia Guthke: "Lady Mary Wroth was the author of, among other things, *The Countesse of Montgomerie's Urania*, an obvious *roman à clef*, which when it was published in 1621, caused a scandal."

Princess. 'If it would please you, Mesdames,' saith she to them, 'I would show you the most amusing thing in the world.' And the Princess and the Duchess, neither of whom were inclined to be melancholy, inquired eagerly as to what she had in mind to show them."[18]

The Fool notes that while Pierrette's translations are always amusing, his commentary, "more to the point, makes so bold as to exploit the Queen's malice towards the French, e'en when enjoying a tale of French conception."

Seated in the full flood of the light of midday, reasonably near the fire, the ladies comfortably pulled their silk-threaded needles in and out, in and out, embroidering here a white rose, there one blushing, here the sturdy trunk of an oak, there the deep twining green of ivy or the celestial blue of heaven.

Pierrette's gaze returned to the lectern and the beautifully illustrated book. "And the lady saith, 'here is a certain gentleman whom you and everyone else at court revere as one of the most honorable men who lives, and full of courage and bravery, too. Who does not know how much cruelty he has borne unto me, or how when I loved him most he abandoned me to avail himself of the love of other women? Though I concealed my unhappiness, it was almost beyond what I could bear. Now God has granted me the opportunity to revenge myself on him. Hark. When I go upstairs to my room, if you take the trouble to watch, you will observe the man follow me, like a hound hot on the scent of the fox. May I ask of you, Mesdames, that when he is through the galleries and about to ascend the stairs, that you both go to the window and shout "Help! Thief!" along with me? I warrant that that will make him so angry, that he'll act such a performance for us as we seldom have the pleasure to watch.' The lady's words gave the Princess and Duchess considerable amusement, for that no other gentleman at court was known to be so relentless in besieging the ladies with his seductions. And yet he was also well regarded by all, and in great demand, and the sort of man no one ever dared risk being mocked by. The Princess and Duchess were doubly

[18] Julia Guthke: "I'm virtually certain this is from Marguerite de Navarre's *Heptamaron*, though I haven't gotten around to running it down yet."

entertained, because they felt that the lady, by including them in her plans, would be allowing them to share in her triumph over him."

The Fool says that like everyone else present, she was taking a great deal of pleasure from this narrative, but that she had to leave the room at that point so that she could execute her plan "for bringing the Queen even greater delight than Pierrette's reading of such a tasty tale." No one paid any attention to her departure. She writes: "I go not to the privy, though, but into a little chamber nearby, to be private as I shift my shape into that of my most frequent familiar, a large orange cat known to come and go as it pleases where'er it lists. Though such a form is not natural to me, yet 'tis comfortable to inhabit a body that moves gracefully and as swiftly as the fleetest swallow darting to its nest under an eave. The Queen's dwarf greyhounds have never caught me, though are like to give chase whene'er they catch sight or scent of my fiery form insolently dashing past them."

She says she padded softly back to the ladies, "to their senses a mere cat that either lurks silently about during the most secret converse, or dashes like a beast caught in brain-fever, to tempt the dwarf greyhounds into misbehavior." She crouched for a moment on the threshold, to spy out the lay of the land. Pierrette's voice had all the human ears in the room hanging on its every word: "But the gentleman was swift with ripostes and dogged in his own defence, making so bold as to claim that he had only accepted the lady's invitation to meet her in her chamber simply to relieve the tedium of everyone at court."

Suddenly the Fool leaped out of her crouch and streaked past the dwarf greyhounds lying asleep at the Queen's feet, to the far wall of the room and the large tapestry that hung there. Before uttering even one yelp or bark, the dogs were up and away "in hot pursuit of a prey they have long wished to capture. But I am clever and far too fast. I dart behind the tapestry—which no longer covers a wall, but guards the entrance into a certain garden to which I know the Queen and all her ladies will desire admission. The dwarf greyhounds, yelping wildly, mad to catch me, race swiftly after me. But not only am I too quick for their capture, but as they enter the gardens, they at once lose my scent, and coming to a halt, sniff the lush deep grass for some hint as to where I have gone."

Screened by a shrub, the Fool lolled about in the thick, silken grass at her leisure, basking "in the hot Illyrian sun, enjoying the warm breezes and spicy scents of rosemary, sage, cedar, and carnation, all of which thrive and abound in the garden! Nearby squat trees heavy with oranges, their leaves glossy and bright in the clear Illyrian air. With vigilance I watch the patch of ground from whence I and the dogs came and keep a wary eye on them, for all that their bodies— like mine—are so unfleshly as to be transparent. In this world we be spirits, without scent, without substance, without extension, just as visitors from the spirit world, angels and ghosts alike, lack flesh in our own."

The dogs were leaping over and through the rosemary hedges in madcap play when Pierrette came through, whistling for them. "Mon Dieu!" said he, astonished at the new world spread around him. And he turned and stepped back into the old world, "so that to my eyes," the Fool writes, "there appears only the ghost of a velvet shod foot and shapely calf in bronze-clocked silk stockings where I know him to be standing. When the dogs begin their rush towards that foot and calf, I dart past them, to tempt them by the very sight of my speed, to make them ignore Pierrette and renew their pursuit of the orange cat they have never yet caught."

By the time the Fool had shaken the dogs' scentless pursuit, she had strayed from the entry point. When she slyly slinked back to it, she found "the Queen and her ladies wandering about the garden, their faces turned to the sun in wonder, their heavy wool shawls scattered over the grass like great ghostly patches to be stitched into a quilt blown hither and thither by the wind." Silently the Fool retired behind a thick hedge of cedar and changed her shape back to her own. She then rejoined the ladies.

When the Queen tried to speak, her voice was inaudible. Though her bright brown eyes glittered with wonder, the Fool says, "we are but thin wraiths even to one another, and have no other means to converse but our eyes and gestures. And so it is that I gesture to Pierrette and persuade him to follow me, and so I lead him to the palace that is Lady Olivia's and draw him within its precincts, as grand and handsome as Denmark House or even Hampton Court, or any other of the palaces so familiar to us. Everywhere we go we pass servants at work who do not see us, do not hear us, do not feel us even when Pierrette puts out his hand to grasp a page's arm and his fingers go right through it, as though it were an illusion made only of light and air."

After wandering through many rooms, they at last came "to a long, handsome room looking out on the garden, where a gentleman paces before a lady that is seated on a cushioned bench with a younger gentleman, perhaps the other's brother, beside her."

The Fool looked at Pierrette, and Pierrette looked at her. His mouth moved, and the Fool says she almost heard the word "Rina!"[19] The Fool nodded "Indeed!" with great vigor. "For the lady seated on the bench might have been our Queen herself at about twenty years of age. Because that such a sight I did not expect to find, it doth bemuse me with the greatest of confusion."

The Fool relates that the man who paced said, "Such a chance I cannot let slip by. Orsino's assistance in this matter is more than I could e'er dare hope for, and will give me the closest of odds for recovering my father's estate."

And then the "younger brother" said, "Orsino, Orsino. 'Tis all thou canst talk of! Then go, then go, if thou thinkest there's aught to be won by 't. Thou hearest no objection from Olivia. And I stand not in thy way. So to what point, then, tend all these speeches thou must needs to burden us with?"

"Viola!" the lady said. "Will thou not hold thy tongue when speaking to thy brother? It aids naught, but only makes his temper the hotter."

The Fool writes, "And indeed, the gentleman hath gone quite red in the face, rage blooming in 't like unto that of the brightest of poppies, his shoulders grown suddenly wider, his stature taller, 'til his

[19] Julia Guthke: " 'Rina' was the name Anne of Denmark's intimates used familiarly with her. It was a shortened form of 'Regina,' allowing the combination of affection and a Latinate honorific in a single form."

manly physique nearly fills every spare bit of the air in the whole chamber." "Hoyden! Wanton! Shrew!" he said, "flinging the words from his mouth like the bitterest and foamiest of vile spittle."

And then the Fool suddenly announces: "But lo, this be Sebastian! I look from him to the lad who is his sister, and back to him, and wonder. Indeed, though their features share a sameness, his are all hardness grim and stony, bristled by beard and ruddy from sun and drink, while hers though stubborn are soft and pliant and cream with a faint blush of rose, and he of greater girth and stature than she. She looks indifferent to his railing, but only throws back her head—in such wise discovering to us a smooth, shapely neck—and stares up at him, her gaze hard, blue—and unmoved."

Viola spoke softly when Sebastian ceased "making his imprecations." "I have said. You all agreed to 't. I would put off my male attire when my own clothes were brought to me. Do you remember my very words? *If nothing lets to make us happy both but this my masculine usurped attire, do not embrace me till each circumstance of place, time, fortune, do cohere and sump that I am Viola—which to confirm, I'll bring you to a captain in this town, where lie my maiden weeds.* That the captain lost them when the duke's men put him in durance—it is the duke's task to remedy. Let Orsino have my maiden weeds found, and then I shall be his bride. 'Tis the task I require of him, if he would take me as his lady. Or he may have me back as his boy—by thy leave, of course, my brother. Else, I'll continue me as before." She rose and bowed to Olivia. "As my lady's sister and guest."

"Sister! " Sebastian said "as though he would choke on the word." "In faith, soon thou shalt be no sister to me, an thou denies all meet duty and loyalty to the one thou callest brother!"

Sebastian strode to the open windows. The Fool writes that she noticed then that the Queen and all her ladies were standing out in the garden, looking on. "The feeling sweeps o'er me, that I am dreaming, dreaming one of those day-time dreams that come when one is drowsing in church, poorly attending a sermon, when one's thoughts enter another realm, with the preacher's words droning like flies buzzing,

431

whilst images of another place and time slip into that innermost eye, dreaming yet not asleep, awake but elsewhere . . . "

* * *

[On the English stage] 'Woman' is, precisely, a set of learned social codes and mannerisms, executed by a boy.
—Lisa Jardine, *Reading Shakespeare Historically*

The text breaks off in mid-sentence, but resumes with Sebastian's leaving the room. The Fool writes that Oliva then said, "I'll not believe thou would give thyself to him as his boy, e'en if he would have thee. Thou art bold, thou art audacious, the which are the reasons I so love thee. But both Orsino and Sebastian, like all men, take the sight of a woman in man's clothes to be a clear sign and warrant of her whoredom. The least word will tip their faith out of balance, so that they will see not thy virginity. E'en if Orsino would have thou as his whore, the which would thereby make grave offense to Sebastian, and thereto cause some great, mortal mischief, I'll not believe thou would so put thyself in his power. For if thou wouldst be in his power, thou would straightaway take up women's attire and make thyself his bride."

Viola flung herself onto the floor, propped her head up with a cushion, crossed her knees in the air, "as though she hath come by her doublet and hose naturally," and said, "The power of one o'er another is all that fixes thy mind, Olivia. 'Tis something I will not busy my thoughts with, else to see myself deep into my grave. Thou refused Orsino for 't, and now cannot love Sebastian, either. Love rules me, and not the fist. 'Tis all I care for, and the reason I put Orsino to the test, and would indeed live with him again as his boy, howe'er far that would undo me. A strong heart is all that a woman wants. The rest is of no account."

Olivia rose to her feet and paced as Sebastian had done when he was in the room. "Love! Love Sebastian!" The Fool writes that the lady was "vehement, passionate, afire. 'Tis said the Queen has oftimes been so, though I have ne'er seen it. I glance across the room to see her wraith staring raptly at the lady. Doth she see herself? Or 'tis interest in the scene she watches that so fixes her attention? Pacing, Olivia said, "Never have I loved thy brother! I married him only because I lovest thou! Thou knows where my heart lies! In hands that treat it indifferently, a mere bauble they would rather be rid of!" Olivia halted near Viola and stared down at her for a long moment, and then sank to her knees "in a great pool of peach silk and creamy lace that flows o'er Viola's arm and breast like the tide of foam up onto a beach." The Fool continues, "The silence is so sudden and entire that methinks I hear the distant sound of surf, of waves beating against the pebbles and rocks of a harsh, stony shore. So sure I am of that sound that it seems I smell the salt and wrack of the sea subtly scenting the air, a perfume more real than the scarcely visible flesh of my own hand." Wanting to see the expressions on their faces, the Fool moved closer— "as 'twould ne'er be polite or possible to do if this were a stage on which actors played. It is the Lady Olivia's face that most astonishes me. 'Tis wet with tears, yet glowing with a passion and tenderness the sight of which clutches at my heart. Her lips are quivering." Olivia spoke softly, and "strangely slowly"—"My dear one"—and then took Viola's hand and lifted it gently to her lips, "to there caress it, and then press it to her breast, as a lover presses his own hand to his breast when declaring his love." "Dear one, now sister," she said. "Thou see'st how I, as doth any sensible woman, accept what I must, when by doing so I may have at least some part of what I require. This has e'er been how women live. I accept sisterhood, and make the best of it, since I must live deprived of my true heart's desire."

Viola sighed and turned her head away. "A woman I am, aye, but not just any. I care naught that I be called whore, if only he would not mind it."

Olivia shook her head and both laughed a little and cried. "I know Orsino, sister. Yea, I know him. The first breath of suggestion that cometh to his ear will fell you fore'er in his grace. A woman's reputation is the most delicate thing, stained by anyone with an ill will to her. 'Tis all the cause she needs the protection of a man's honor, and the only cause."

Viola pulled her hand from Olivia's and sat up. "My brother and I have shared honor and love since birth. The protection of his and my father's name and honor is all that I need!"

"And I, too, shared honor and love with my brother," said Olivia. "Mind that a brother's protection doth not always suffice."

"The which," the Fool writes, "makes me think of the Queen, whose own brother had lately come to visit, to assuage her griefs and melancholy, the which had so swiftly returned after his departure. For which I glance now at that royal lady, and see her struck with an emotion too strong to be concealed."

Another woman then entered—"who, when she speaks, seems so much like the Countess of Bedford that I look over to the Queen's party to ascertain that she still stands there, beside the Queen." "My lady," the woman said. "I bring you good warning. From a pane in the tower, my eye took clear sight of the duke's approach. 'Twill not be long before he nears the gate and asks admittance."

Olivia said, "Devil take him!"

Viola sprang to her feet, "her face a shining glass of eagerness." "Mayhap he cometh to see me, at last! With my maiden's weeds—or else simply for love, that hath worn down his obstinance!"

At which, the Fool writes, "I, too, am filled with an eagerness to set my eyes on him, or rather a curiosity. For if Maria is the image of the Countess, and Olivia of the Queen, will the Duke be that of the King, and Malvolio that of Sir George Carew?"

"He's come to see Sebastian," Olivia said, "I make no doubt, before he departs with Antonio. Maria!"

The Fool writes, "I feast my eyes on her, assured manyfold times that the lady lately entered, being the redoubtable waiting woman who showed herself more clever than everbody else in the play, might be taken for the Countess's twin." She notes that Maria then went to Olivia and offered her an arm as she rose to her feet.

"My very heart doth feel how seemly this display of affection," the Fool writes, "as it echoes that true affection of the Countess for the Queen the which makes the Countess worthy of her Majesty's answering trust and love." Olivia, she writes, glanced briefly at Viola, then said, "Go to my husband and tell him Orsino is soon arrived."

Maria exited. And then Viola was the one pacing. "I'm nothing short of patient, Olivia," said she. "Indeed, 'tis my best—nay, my only—virtue. He wants me, I felt it all the time I played the boy in his menage. It cannot be true that he cares less for a gown than for the heart, body, and soul he would have wear it!"

Olivia seated herself on the bench in weary resignation, "her face of a sadness near to bringing tears to my own eyes." She said, "As much as it cannot be true that thou doth value your doublet and breeches less than thou doth value his love."

Viola whirled, all flashing temper, and jutted her chin at the lady. "Nay! 'tis not about the doublet and breeches, but what he loves in me, for that I fear lest he'd miss it an I were wearing a gown!"

Olivia's face grew even sadder. She said, "Any man hearing thou speak so would say thou art mad. I know thou art not, but I tell thee that if thou dost not accept a woman's lot, thou wilt come only to grief, and thy love for the man who will not have thee mad or whorish will be but like a dream, that only thou canst know in the privy place of thine own mind and heart."

The Fool writes, "Little Pierrette moves before me, startling me, and points. Behold, I see that the Queen and the others in her party have gone from the windows. Pierrette gestures, making me know his wish to follow. Without me, they will wander as shades in this foreign place, unable to find the way back to the world. Though Pierrette knoweth that not, he beseemeth full anxious to rejoin the ladies, lest he be lost in this strange world without them.

"Swiftly we fly out into the garden. Before long we find the party, the Queen's Majesty in the lead, royal hand to throat, weeping sorely. Since we cannot hear one another speak, 'tis impossible to know the cause for the Queen's great emotion. Worse, the Queen doth not know the way, though 'tis she who is leading the company. And so, from strict necessity, in the blink of an eye (whether amber or green) I conjure, not far in advance of the Queen, a gossamer ball as glittering as a diamond, as clear as the finest crystal, veined lightly with gold, to guide the Queen's progress. For so 'tis, when she sees it, she stretches forth her hand, as if to catch it to her. But lo, it is my will that moves it, so that it always keeps just beyond her reach, and so by little and little guides her to the exit, where her faithful dwarf greyhounds await her, and all the heavy shawls all the ladies had put off under the gentle heat of Illyria's sun."

* * *

[E]xplanations are clear but since no one to whom a thing is explained can connect the explanations with what is really clear, therefore clear explanations are not clear.
—Gertrude Stein, *Everybody's Autobiography*

And so soon they were back as they had been, seated at their needlework, "no door to be found any longer behind the tapestry," with Pierrette sent off to fetch wine for the company.

"Such tales you do tell, Cristiana! " the Countess of Bedford said, taking the Fool "by the greatest of surprise."

The others all looked dazed and amazed—until they realized, individually, "the Countess's wise intent" in suggesting that the Fool had been telling them a tale, rather than that they had impossibly visited a world known as imaginary.

The Queen sighed and sighed. "Cristiana, Cristiana, 'tis almost as if I had been to Illyria myself, so wondrous vivid your narration," she said. "And so she doth hold a frippery of lace to her eyes," the Fool writes, "to dab gently there at a few tears yet lingering. Her mouth trembles with an endeavor of a smile."

"Would that you had found a happy ending to the playwright's tale," the Queen said, "rather than such sadness."

The Countess went to the Queen and knelt beside her. "Dearest Rina!" said she, showing a gentleness she reserved for the Queen alone. "The playwright's stories must needs have unhappy endings for ladies, whate'er another teller might make of them. 'Tis in their very nature to do so, for unlike our brave amazon masques, this Author's tales follow life too closely. For the which, the Lady Olivia spoke truly."

The Fool writes, "But we did not stay to see the end of 'my' tale, and so do not know 'twas so unhappy as the Queen bethinks. (Nor did we see whether Orsino looked to be the King's twin.)" And she ends the text: "You, my lady, did ask that I write this account so that memories of the beautiful marvellous might be refreshed in your imagination as oft as you so desire, by the mere reading of my words. 'Twas indeed that our very visit to Illyria was marvellous and beautiful, howe'er poignantly sad its unfolding. Pleasure and sorrow are no enemies, as people are wont to conceive them. Else we women would have only the latter, and ne'er the former, as sorrow doth always accompany a woman through life as a shadow doth any body. And so 'tis, we take our pleasure where'er we can find it, to rejoice when we can, and weep when we must."

If the author of this tale did invent this magical adventure, one must wonder at its open ending. To please the lady for whom it was written—to "never say die"? Or to leave an opening for another "visit" to Illyria? Or was it, indeed, as the Fool (or whoever the narrator is) claims, that "the playwright's stories must needs have unhappy endings for ladies, whate'er another teller might make of them," because "this Author's tales follow life too closely"? I'll leave that kind of speculation to the literary historians. Personally, I prefer to believe that the adventure happened as she claimed, and that such magic was the Fool's to command and her pleasure to offer. And that maybe, maybe, she returned to Illyria another time—leaving its traces on a second, as yet undiscovered, manuscript.

THE PRINCE OF MULES
Carol Emshwiller

WHAT DO YOU know from the top of a hill but the lay of the land? I can see two little towns, one on each side, and—closer—a ranch. I see cowhides all along the fences. I see skulls over the gates. I know rattlesnake skins are there, too, and maybe a skunk pelt, but I can't tell from here. There's hardly any green except in thin lines coming down from the mountains and a couple of irrigated pastures.

And there's the irrigation ditch digger, Blackthorn. Today he's working just below my hill. I know it's him. Who else would be out in a ditch, his clothes so black and floppy, letting himself get too hot in the middle of the day?

He has an ugly, brutal face. I don't think he's brutal but lots of people do. They distrust him because his eyebrows are too black and bushy and one eye is always off in the wrong direction. People think that eye is looking at something they can't see—something they're missing out on that might be important. Or beautiful.

They say he looks like a scarecrow but what he looks like is the crow. Eye, one of them, the blackish blue of crow's eyes. Nose . . . not hooked like an eagle's, but reaching straight out. That nose says: Go somewhere. Get away. Do something else.

I see his lips moving (of course not from up here, but when I pass by down there now and then). He's always talking to his mule. I've heard tell you can talk softly to a horse but, when it comes to a mule, all you need to do is little more than mouth the words.

But it isn't as if I'm not a crow kind of person myself. And people don't like the looks of me either.

My house is off alone, half way up the hill, boulders all over my, so called, yard. Sage. Rabbit brush. (*And* rabbits.) A skunk lives under the shed but we get along . . . so far. Same goes for the rattlesnake. So far. I probably get taken for a witch, what with a snake and a skunk for familiars. If I really was one, I'd witch away my knee pains, and I'd witch myself some money. And I'd witch myself some company. (I've lived with nothing sweeter than the rattlesnake's grin. I take as friend whatever looks at me at all.)

Blackthorn and I, we should get to know each other. Would he come up here for iced tea? Or lemonade? I don't have any beer. Come to think of it, I don't have any lemons either.

"Hello down there. Halloooo."

Can he hear me from here? I wonder if he can see me waving?

"Hallooo. Mister Blackthorn."

He sees me. He shades his eyes and looks but doesn't wave.

He lives even farther up than I do. His hut is so much the color of everything else, you can hardly see it until you're practically in the doorway. I climbed up there once when he was out in the fields. I looked in the one and only window but it was so dim and dusty I couldn't see much. There was a white washbasin with a pitcher in it—both chipped. There were socks on the floor. There actually was a book—on the floor beside the socks—one of those old-fashioned, leather bound books with gold lettering. I couldn't read the title. I was surprised and pleased to see he actually had a real book.

But the shed for the mule, now—that was spic and span. Smelled sweet of straw and hay and mule. Smelled so good I took a chance and lay down there for a while.

I call again. "Hallooooo."

Again he looks up but, just as he did before, he goes right back to digging. He's got to be tired and thirsty. Suppose I hold up a big glass of iced tea? Suppose I had a pail of water for the mule?

I go in, change my blouse to a cream colored one (mule nose color actually) with lace around the neck, and come back out with a pitcher and a pail. I hold them over my head.

"Halloooow!"

Finally!

When the time comes to say my name, what would be unusual and romantic and make him remember it? *And* me?

So he and his mule come all the way up here, two switch backs and then a long sideways.

He lets the mule drink first. (Of course!) He calls her sweetheart. How he does sweet talk that mule! "Come sweetheart. Come, Penny, drink." (When has anybody ever called me sweetheart? I think and think, but I'm thinking never.)

He says she came with the name Bad Penny, but he calls her Pennyroyal.

It looks like that's all he's going to say. Sometimes people who don't talk much like to have other people chatter away so they don't have to think about talking, they don't even have to listen; and yet others like silence around them to match their own.

"Do these ditches need you? Every single day like this?"

"Without me and Penny everything would be as dry as it is right here." His good eye takes it all in: me, my tin pitcher, my boulders ... The other eye is off at its own secret spot. I can tell he's never noticed me before, even after all those times I was walking back and forth in front of his ditch whenever he was working near my hill.

"Did you ever think of going someplace else?"

"I've been elsewhere."

He drinks my whole pitcher-full right out of the pitcher and without stopping. I should have had as much for him as for the mule.

I like his eyebrows. I even like his eye that roves off seeing . . . God knows what visions.

By now I can tell what my name should be. I say, "I'm Molly," so as to be more mule. Though, on second thought, perhaps I should have said Jenny so I could be Jenny to his Jack. I wonder if his first name is Jack.

How keep him here a little while longer? "Could you open this jar?" (He could.) "Could you move this heavy box for me?" (Of course.) "And I can't reach this shelf."

He does all the things and with an old crow's grace. An old crow's flashing eye.

I feel so good I want to say, Sweetheart, to something myself, except Penny's the one getting all the caresses. Does she need so many when there's others (not so far away) who haven't had any? As to looks, she's nothing special, just the general mule color, dark with a cream colored nose, but she's sleek and shiny, which is more than I can say about him. Or myself.

Perhaps, in that wandering eye, Penny is a beautiful woman as pale all over as the star on her forehead, her hair the same black/brown of the turkey vulture feathers he has in his hat.

What is he seeing with that off kilter eye? Suppose he looked at me through that? What would I turn into? But perhaps, for starters, I need to become more mulish. Mules always know what they want to do and when. They're never wishy-washy. They know what's best for everybody. I suppose he depends on her for his own safety. I'm afraid I don't have that knack.

My ravens quack, quack, quack around us. Something else is going, "Tweet, tweet, churrrrr. Tweet, tweet, churrrrr." He lifts his head and listens—points his going somewhere nose and listens like a poet. Who'd have thought?

"Could I have a ditch? One connected to the arroyo just in case there's ever a little bit of water in it?" (There hasn't been any water in it since I came here.) "It wouldn't have to be long or deep. I'll pay."

I seem to have decided (without deciding) on too much talking though I'm not yet committed to it *completely*. I keep silent as I hand him more tea. I think of all the things I'm not saying, such as: Take me to your shack, old crow man. Or take me even farther up, to the mountain lion's den. I saw a place up there where the grass was matted in a cozy circle. I saw the scat.

What I do say is: "When I die I had always wanted to come back—if there's going to be any coming back to it—as a raven. I had wanted to be smart and cocky, but now that I see Penny, I think, perhaps, mule is better."

What I don't say is, who ever caresses a raven?

What I do say is: "I have stones as if instead of trees. All my shade is from boulders. I'm surprised anything grows here at all but some things find a way. They get a toe hold. Like I do."

I don't say: My stones are warm and motherly after a day in the sun and I lean against their big round bellies every evening. They're warm well into the night.

He has looked at me again. One of his fleeting glances that slip sideways and down before you know you've been looked at.

What I do say is, "I thought I heard a stream or maybe its leaves blowing. I heard another, tweet, tweet, churr from some other place entirely. And it's cool somewhere not far from here." I spread my arms, the better to feel the breeze. "Admit it. There's another world somewhere, all shiny and sweet smelling. Not a bit like here."

He spreads his arms, too, but to show my hill and my view. "Why do you want to see more than this right here, the gray fox colors of the underbrush, and, not far, the fox herself and her kits."

Spoken like a poet. And what more *do* I want than the warm bellies of the granite? And there *is* a tree, one, and more up where he is.

But I think there *is* a world of the other eye, and in it he would be the wiry black prince of mules. And he would have shaved in that world. His hat would smooth itself out and clean itself up and the turkey vulture feathers would become the feathers of a hawk. No, eagle.

I say, "I saw sparkles. Diamond shapes, all different colors and all in a row. I heard swishing sounds as if a stream or of poplar leaves in

443

the wind. I heard wind chimes. I felt how cool. I shivered. Look how I shiver. I saw . . . I thought I saw Penny. She was wearing a nightgown sort of thing. Even now your other eye is glistening. I see tears on that cheek."

I step forward to wipe the tear but he jerks back.

"My other eye sees nothing."

"And does the nothing have a light blue cast?"

"There's no other place than here."

"I don't believe it."

"Believe what you will. People always do, and they like the odd and scandalous and fantastic better than the real."

"What about Pennyroyal?"

"She is as you see."

But I know better.

Except now he's on his way down—*already* on his way, back to his ditch.

"It's too hot!" I'm screeching it. Then I screech again. "Dangerous to work in such heat!" (What kind of bird is that, that screeches so? None I ever knew.) "A man of your age . . . " Screech, screech.

He's going. He's down. And he didn't say if he'd dig me a ditch or not.

But I know happiness *is* possible because I don't want a lot of it. How sweet it would be to sleep in the hay with Penny. That's not much to ask.

Like his nose says, I'll go forward, do something, go elsewhere. I will know what I want. I will become more mule.

I go back in and pack up my nightgown and a snack. (The night-gown might be important.) I sit on one of my rocks and wait until I see Blackthorn and Penny leave the ditch. (She doesn't even have a lead rope. She follows him home on her own. I would, too. I *will*.)

I wait until it's almost dark and then I take my bundle and climb up into the piñons. There's a light in his shack but dim. No doubt an oil lamp or candles. I peek in. Blackthorn is at the little table, leaning over it, side view. (I *do* like that going-someplace look of his nose.)

With that lamplight I can see more than I could before. Things are nicer than I thought, though I see sandy dust all over everything. (I could clean that up in no time.) There's a patchwork quilt on the cot, secret Star pattern. There's a humpbacked trunk. Hard to put anything down on top of that but there's not only a couple of dirty shirts lying across it, but a tin cup balanced at the top of the curve. I hope it's empty. The washbowl and pitcher look even more chipped and cracked in this light, and dirty socks are on the floor again—or still. Maybe a couple more pairs. They need darning. I'll do that.

Then I notice I'm on the side of his rambling eye and it's rambling right over to the window—to me. I don't know what he sees, but there's no reaction. It's as if that eye *is* blind, but maybe it's that he's seeing wonderful things and wouldn't be paying attention to me anyway.

And now he has that poet's look of listening. Have I made a noise?

The odd eye is still right on me. It glistens in the lamplight. His good eye was crow-blue-black. This one is *light* blue.

I think of clouds tinged pink, rainbows of course . . . balconies, gazebos, long white gauzy gowns that blow in the wind, raven hair . . . "tresses," as they say, also blowing. And Blackthorn . . . In the world of that blue eye, he would wear clothes that fit him better, though they'd still be black. Penny would have a long courtly nose (as she already has) and her tresses would make her face look all the more narrow, but what makes somebody beautiful? Not their nose. Not perfect teeth. Not big caramel colored eyes. (She does have that.)

* * *

"Harriet?" Now it's his good eye that is turned towards me. "Harriet?"

How did he know my real name? Another sure sign of . . . well, several things. If he knows my name then for sure there *is* another world out there somewhere.

I hear wind. Branches squeak as they brush against the roof of the shack. I feel the evening breeze. Or is that in that other place?

He says, "Enter."

Enter what? Does he mean into that other land? And how? Since I don't know how to go there, for now, and though I'm right by the door, I just step through the little window. It's small and high, but I step through just as though it was easy—except I fall when I land on the other side. I'm down by his knees. I dare to touch his ankle. He's not wearing any shoes or socks so I touch bare skin. I look up into his eyes . . . eye, that is. You have to pick which one you want to look into.

"Please get up."

But his ankle is warm and damp. I haven't touched skin to skin with anybody for longer than I can remember. I lay my cheek across his instep. It smells of ditch.

"*Please* get up."

I kiss his foot.

But I'm way, way, way . . . I'm way . . .

* * *

. . . on a hill holding the ankle of (of course!) a black stallion. (Who would be holding the ankle of a gelding!) There's moonlight. There's a breeze. Blue-black clouds scoot across the sky. It's a witch kind of land. Scary. I knew it would be. I knew *all* this.

The stallion paws with the hoof I'm not holding, impatient. I know he means, "For Heaven's sake get *up*! I asked you to before."

I do. I should at least be wearing something flowing so I'd match the setting. (I knew I'd need my nightgown, but where is it now?) But I'm dressed as I was, lacy mule-nose-colored shirt and loose old lady jeans. For sure, here, I'm no younger than I was in the other place. I could feel that in my knees as I got up.

He shakes his head, hard, up and down, mane flying, impatient still. (In this world, it's the good eye, the black one, that seems odd.) He walks away, looking back at me. I follow. The grass here is soft against my legs just as I knew it would be, not like my grass, all scratchy and in clumps. Not far away I hear water running. It sounds like a small stream, nothing of the flash flood about it. He, the stallion, comes to a rock and stops beside it as though I should use it as a mounting block.

I wonder if, in this world, I might know how to ride. Maybe know how to stay on even if bareback with nothing to hang on to but the mane. And how do you steer?

I mount. Now I'm glad I'm not wearing something flowing. Except, without a skirt and scarves, there'll be nothing to blow out behind us as we gallop. Only his mane and tail, not my hair. It's much too short. And would gray hair count anyway?

He starts away at an easy trot—but I've already fallen off the other side. We go back to the mounting stone. This time I get a better grip on the mane. I hadn't thought his back would be so slippery and bounce so.

There will be a castle. Or perhaps a smaller cozy summer castle (I'd like that) where they (*we*) pretend to be ordinary people. Pennyroyal, the princess all in white. Her beauty is in the look in her eye. (Everybody says so.) And in the tilt of her head. There is no kinder princess. (Everybody says so.) She does nothing but smile. But her voice is a little like mine was when I screeched. (Now I know that sound I made, birds don't do that, it's mule.) She smiles. At me. She calls me, Sweetheart. (*Everybody* calls me, Sweetheart!)

I curtsey. Sort of a curtsy. It isn't until I try it that I realize I don't know how. Where do the arms go? How low is low enough?

I'm thinking Penny is his little sister so I could be his wife. That is, if he ever can, in *this* world, *not* be a stallion. Perhaps all it takes is my kiss, (like with frogs) but on his lips, not just his ankle where I kissed him before. Was it that kiss that started all this? That turned him horse in the first place?

* * *

But they don't need any more princesses here. *Everybody* can't be one. What they need is . . .

447

When I leaned my cheek against his foot back in his cabin, I'd thought how nice it would be if I could clean up the shack, scrub and dust, do the dirty socks and shirts, darn, wash the dishes. Pull down hay for Penny. Sleep in the sweet smelling shed. Be his little helping elf. Or anything he wants me to be. I even thought: When can I start?

But here, I've already started—shoveling out the stables. "Sweetheart, could you kindly go . . . " And I was even stroked a bit before I go there.

Here . . . even here . . . what they need is a scullery maid. I'm to sleep in the stables. It's not at all the same as it would have been if I'd been set to clean Penny's stall and sleep with her and clean his shack up, up there under the piñons.

How to get out of it? The stallion must know. If I could get him to take the bit, I'd bloody up his mouth if I had to, to make him go back to that hill where the entrance to all this might be. *Maybe* might be.

Or if I could wake up and it would all have been a dream (it looks like a dream and feels like a dream) and I would be there my cheek still on his foot. If that happened, I'd not kiss, as I did, I'd bite.

Or if I could go into his stall and bite his foot *now* and be instantly transported back to his shack. (I do creep in to try that and he hee-haws as if he was a mule.)

Or what if I could put out his eye? But which one! That's important. If the wrong one, then I might be here forever.

And all this after I gave him water from my tank. It isn't as if water grows on trees around here—back there I mean.

If I ever do get back, I'll have to end up hugging the warm rock bellies like I used to. I'll have to make do with whatever slithers by. But I don't care anymore. I'll wave at crow or snake or sweet gray fox . . .

Those townspeople were right. Jack Blackthorn! I should have known all this (as they did) from his name and his off-kilter eye and from those bushy eyebrows.

BUZ
Rikki Ducornet

The Dwellings of Buz

—The most auspicious houses are built of string and wind. Certainly they are fragile and subject to disorder, yet, the philosopher reminds us:

> *The nest in the tree*
> *The eye in the head*
> *The thought in the mind*
> *The phallus in the vagina—*
> *All these are subject to unforeseeable disaster.*

In other words:
> *Only a fool expects things to stick.*
> *Only a fool longs for permanence.*
> *All things buzz and hum and cry out with delight but briefly:*
> *Even honey melts in the sun.*
> *So there!*
> —Manda

—The house is made of knots. These enliven the air. For a time the knots confound the evil eye and keep the lovers safe. Hung with bells, the polyphallus is suspended from the ceiling. It balances, pointing first here, then there, above the lover's couch. Its name is Fascinus, and it may be made of bronze or porcelain, gold or sun-baked clay. But should it break, it must be replaced at once. For it is said and rightly so:

A fractured polyphallus brings ruin to the home.

Manda Says:
Only a fool would keep such a thing in his rooms. The old bull in the flurry of spring, too fragile for fornication, can only bellow when, before his eyes, the oblivious cows are mounted one by one.

—Safe in their abode of air, the lovers eagerly embrace; safe because they know that only a fool, concealed in the thicket, would dare to gaze at them.

—The lovers, as all lovers, think that they are alone when, in fact, the fool, flushed with wine, skulks near. He is unaware of the rhinoceros standing so silently in the shadows and about to collapse with exhaustion. A breeze lifts, the polyphallus merrily rings. When the rhinoceros rolls over, the fool barely has a chance to cry out.

—At the summer solstice, one may paint the threads with honey so that, at dawn, bees fill the house with their buzzing. In this way the lovers, awakened from their slumber, laugh out loud. So it has been, always.

—Manda wonders:
And what of the fool's house? So silent, now! So empty! Of what is the fool's house made?

—Ah! But it is made of hammered cow leather well studded with nails.

Its floors are set with purple tiles and its door is of iron. It is made to withstand all manner of nuisances, yet when Death knocks there is nothing to be done. Then the house might as well be made of sand and guarded by ants.

—Mendel agrees:
It is so, Manda! But tell me more of the house dripping with honey! And the phallus weeping with delight! Tell me of the polyphallus that, agitated in the breeze, makes music. Tell me of the luck of wind and weather, of a house open to starlight. Tell me of the lovers, Manda! Of their expressive faces! Of the lovely positions the body takes, oblivious of shame, to achieve rapture! Describe the girl, if you will, for you have not yet done so! Is she long and slender as an eel, or does her body hang like a tree ripe with figs? Are her eyes black or some other, rarer color—such as hazel or yellow, like the eyes of certain cats? And tell me, tell me all you can about their luck! Their luck, above all, Manda! And should luck fail, oh! oh! Just thinking of it makes me weep.

—Manda answers:
No matter the house, and no matter the shape death takes—rhinoceros, bull or swarm of bees—know that luck always fails. Sooner or later.

> Only a fool thinks he can keep anything. Nothing in this universe can be kept for more than an instant (and what is an instant but a failure to "keep" time?).

* * *

When Klansinia died, the King rejoiced. "Nothing will keep her," he said. "Not keening nor prayer, nor gum-infused wrappings. Even the brass jars that hold her tripes so securely will one day be smashed to bits by the relentless shrieking of the stars. It is sensible, therefore, to feast. And when the time comes, sensible to void one's bowels."

*Only a fool would attempt to preserve what his bowels, in their
wisdom, would gladly cast away.*

Cabinet

—It must be large enough. When the neighbor rushes in looking for
his wayward wife, it must be large enough to contain her. The neighbor searches everywhere but does not consider the cabinet. His wife is
broad with fatty fish and curried rice; her corpulence is legendary—as
is her appetite. Her breasts are like loaves, yea, they are as round and
fragrant as those loves we love studded with olives and scaled with
salt.

—How cleverly is the cabinet conceived! It seems far too narrow and
yet—wonder of wonders—her ample form is free to twist and turn
when, to keep herself from laughing out loud, she thrusts her fist into
her mouth. How red her mouth!

—There are many sorts of cabinets: some are for sleeping, some for
love-making, some for the storage of the season's loaves, some for
drying fish. Slumbering beneath, the cat secures the cabinet from nuisances. Its claws are like razors, its jaws are like iron, it breathes fire.
What sort of cat is this? As spotted as a leopard; as striped as any
tiger. See: it even has a mane! Apologizing profusely, the neighbor
backs out the door. The cat purrs, the moon rises, the breeze lifts, the
polyphallus rings merrily from the rafters, the cabinet creaks . . .

Domesticity

—The one who is hiding in the cabinet among the crockery, the Adulterer who conceals himself in silence, fearful of sneezing, who, should
he make a peep, brings ruin upon his Mistress and himself—seizes the
little household god in both hands and entreats it to send the Unex-

pected Husband out again under some pretext or other. The god's head is that of a bull with two horns. It has the body of a man and the winged behind of a bird.

—Crouching in the dark, barely breathing, the Adulterer wonders:

If I am the lover, not the Cuckold, why do I feel so humiliated? He wonders: If Beauty and Truth are the Light, what am I doing in this dark cabinet?

Such thoughts are disrupted by the voice of his Mistress:

"Husband!" she cries, "I have such a craving for bread pudding!" Or: "There is no butter left for the lamp!" Or: "We are out of cheese." "There's not one olive, grain of sugar, salt; not one ounce of tea; not a needle in a house." Off the husband goes, poor sod, basket in hand, as mild as a nanny. Out leaps the Lover; one kiss and he's gone. He could not run faster had he a feather up his ass. In an instant the night has swallowed him whole. Thus domesticity prevails as it always has, here, there, else and everywhere.

Xuxu

When the cabinet collapses beneath the combined weight of the wayward wife and her lover, your neighbor, killing the cat and sending the loaves rolling in all directions, and the fish shattering on the tiles like glass, the event is called: *Xuxu*.

Apology

Here are the instances when apology is called for:

—When he kicks his neighbor in the head purposefully or inadvertently; when he tramples the kitchen garden; when, after a night of merrymaking, he urinates in the parsley.

—When, having blown out the candle and toppled into bed, he discovers his neighbor's wife silently laughing behind her hands and sends her packing.

—When, upon rising, he neglects to greet the cat.

For, it is said that:
One must show compassion for women,
small animals and seedlings.

—Likewise, when, having said with conviction: "I know such and such a thing," he is lying. Or, even, "Yes! I have seen, heard, tasted, done this or that," when it is not so. Or: "I will do it gladly!" only to leave it undone. Or: "I did *not* lose, break, spill soup, sauce, ink or whatever it might be," when he did. When he lies: "I did *not* sleep with your wife!" When he lies: "I will always love thee," even as her tedious digressions greatly dismay his mind.

Various are the things
For which we tear our hair with regret.
Only the dead need not offer apology.
Only the living are so often at fault.

The Houses of the Dead

—Seven, that auspicious cipher, numbers the ways one may disencumber oneself of a corpse.

—It may be set in a slipper-shaped jar and *buried* beneath the threshold of a house or *abandoned* at the far end of a very long tunnel.

—It may be *dumped* in the sea, sinkhole, well; it may be *dissolved* in

454

a bathtub brimming with lye. (If some continue to dress their dead in aprons and caps of threaded shells, it is no longer fashionable to sever the head and entomb it among ants.)

—It may be *kept* in honey, or wine, or salt, or tar, or aromatic gum.

* * *

—Mourning is less about loss than it is about keeping.

—When the body politic is decapitated by the death of a head of state, the mutilation is symbolic. The negligible event of personal time is easily overruled by the capital building or cromlech.

Death is about change, architecture isn't.

—As it may be entered, the mausoleum offers a way of penetrating the idea of the departed without offending propriety.

—If the mummy, official portrait or busto are symbolic facsimiles of the deceased, the dome both acknowledges the buried skull and anticipates its sequel. The dome suggests stubborn persistence; the pyramid, infinity. As for the obelisk, here vertiginous loss is dwarfed by vertiginous height.

—Power, as embodied by architecture, is less fickle than the mourners who, sooner or later, will abandon their black weeds for sexier attire. Power never abandons its funereal mantle, nor its funereal appeal.

Some continue to mistake the dubious attractions of secular authority for the natty garments of seduction. They are woefully misled.

Wind, Air and Trees

Wind, air and trees: These animate and exemplify the gardens of Buz which are intended for the ears and lungs only. Sight is seduction says the philosopher, evoking the pleasure grounds of Miraj—those whore's commons with their deep beds of blossoms, smoking furnaces, the dubious fascination of mechanical songbirds and virile Turks; *unlike sight, sound sails the air without strings.*

Wind, air and trees: in Buz the gardener is the weather, restless and fugitive. *Compare, the philosopher entreats us, the fleshy arguments of the whore's parterres to the spontaneous infinity of the sage's bower.*

> *Breath transcends all clocks of clay.*
> —Mindra

Buz

If Buzz is invisible on the Dutch charts and erroneously positioned by the Portuguese, the Cypriite Pytheas designates it correctly in the heart of the *Rub-al-Kalili* or "Empty Quarter" of Central Arabia. He provides a map that assures the traveler he will—despite the heat of the low-lying regions, the ferocity of its Bedouins who scrape the head bones of their prisoners clean before gilding them, the viper-maidens whose buttocks and upper bodies are those of women but who, below, are snakes, and who are known to crush their human lovers to death as they copulate, and the unworldly cold of the great elevations where rivers of ice are navigated by fish so slow it takes them one-thousand years to swim an inch—see the light shining from the seven lamps of Buz and know that at dawn he will be received at the city's gates with milk and dates so fresh and sweet they will cause him to weep with something very like happiness.

NOBLE LIBRARY

The Library: 6: NOBLE LIBRARY
Zoran Zivkovic

A NOBLE LIBRARY is much like a stomach. Strict attention must be paid to what goes into it. Only proper and fitting items should be allowed to enter a noble library. Should a book that doesn't belong find its way into such a place, it would be just like recklessly swallowing something unfit for consumption. Nausea and disgust would result. Those were my exact feelings upon entering the study and finding a book in my library that I had not put there. I felt a revulsion so strong that it completely supplanted the natural question as to how the book had got there. In the same vein, the first thoughts of a man whose stomach contains something improper will not be how it got there, but rather how to be rid of it. Health is, after all, more important than sheer intellectual curiosity.

I took hold of the book with two fingers and pulled it out. It certainly did not belong there, above all else because of its size. That's how it had caught my eye on the crowded bookshelf that covers one whole wall of my study. I've always felt the greatest possible disdain for paperback books. They are the ultimate profanation of an ideal that must remain exalted and noble at any cost. Only the ignorant and uninformed claim that a book should not be judged by its cover.

Ostensibly, a great work remains a great work regardless of its packaging. Nonsense! Packaging must mirror the contents. Would you wrap a luxury item in old newspapers, for example? And what is a great work of literature if not the most luxurious of all items!

I didn't let the title deceive me. The title would have suited a deluxe edition, leather-bound, with gold lettering; it seemed almost sacrilegious on the ordinary plasticized cardboard of a paperback. But, then, people who make paperbacks are known to be unscrupulous. Nothing is sacred to them. They will not hold back from using the most sublime words if they believe it will lead to a profit. All they care about is money. I truly don't know where we'll end up if we keep misusing, trivializing and cheapening everything.

Holding the object at arm's length, I walked briskly towards the kitchen. I stepped on the pedal of the garbage can under the sink and opened my thumb and index finger. The paperback fell with a thud among the garbage where it belonged. I brushed my palms together. There! One must not be thin-skinned in such situations, but resolute and harsh. The treatment should be the same as for vermin. Like bedbugs or cockroaches. One must brook no quarter.

I returned to my study with a feeling of relief, but an unpleasant surprise awaited me. Although I had just thrown it away, the paperback book stood right where I'd found it a moment before: in my library! Blood rushed to my face. What was the meaning of this? Straight from the garbage to the bookshelf? The book was not only where it didn't belong—it had messed up and contaminated everything else around it. How awful!

This time I threw caution to the wind. I grabbed hold of the intruder and plucked it out, disrupting as I did the impeccable order of the bona fide books surrounding it. I am always irritable when my bookshelves are out of alignment, but that could wait. I had to take care of this interloper, once and for all. I didn't hesitate for a moment. I opened the book approximately in half and did something I have never done before: I tore it in two. This, however, failed to quell the anger inside me—on the contrary—so I continued to tear it with undiminished vehemence.

460

Soon torn up and discarded pages were strewn all across the rug. Under other circumstances, this would have horrified me, but now it only increased my fury. Completely out of control, I sat on the floor and started tearing up the pages into tiny pieces. Almost confetti. I didn't stop until the last page had met the same fate. When nothing was left upon which to vent my rage, I finally calmed down.

Looking around at the scattered bits of paper, I was ashamed of what I'd done. Such an outburst of anger was highly uncharacteristic of me. But, even worse, as I'd vented my frustration I'd felt enormous pleasure, almost delight. I had to ask myself if I'd lost my mind. All right, I'd been offended and provoked; it might even be said that a great injustice had been done to me, but even so. A man must restrain himself, after all. What would be the outcome if we gave free reign to our darkest impulses?

In addition, I had made a terrible mess, I who was so proud of my neatness, even to the point of exaggeration. I sighed and got up off the floor. I went to the closet in the vestibule, took out the vacuum cleaner, and returned to the study. I spent a long time cleaning it thoroughly, as if the machine could suck up the invisible traces of my bad behavior along with the tiny pieces of paper. The vacuum cleaner became quite heated before I finally turned it off. I detached the tube, put it all back in the closet, and then went to the bathroom to take a shower, since I'd broken into a sweat.

I came out refreshed and calm. What I'd been through had been unpleasant, but at least it was over. The best thing would have been to simply forget the whole matter. Why obsess over how the book had gotten there? I couldn't care less. The knowledge would only burden me unnecessarily—and I could not exclude the possibility that I would not find an answer. In any case, now that I had most certainly rid myself of the annoying book, it no longer mattered.

My hopes, however, were premature. One glance at the bookshelf from the door to my study was all it took to realize that my troubles had just begun. As though mocking me, there, between two precious old tomes, stood the paperback, all in one piece. My face flushed once again. I closed my eyes and breathed deeply, nodding slowly.

At first, it seemed I was losing control of myself again. But the thought of what I might do were I to be blinded by rage again helped me keep the upper hand. Blindness would not be a good ally here. I had to keep cool. I'd tried force and it hadn't worked. Now I had to try something more sophisticated. I had to plan things out. If you can't beat your enemy, try to outsmart him.

I was, unfortunately, completely inexperienced in this regard. Not once had I faced the challenge of getting rid of any books. Until then I had only tried to acquire them, something I'd become skilled at over time, as evidenced by my library. How was I to get rid of a book? And not an ordinary book; rather, one that persistently refused to disappear, defying me insolently. I sat in the armchair facing the bookshelf and stared at the thin, short spine of the intruder. I began to draw the fingers of my left hand across my brow, as I always do when deep in thought.

Before long, an unusual similarity crossed my mind. I would be having this same trouble if I'd decided to kill myself. I wouldn't know exactly what to do in such circumstances, either. Although it might not appear so, I don't believe it's an easy thing to take your own life. But at least I would have at my disposal the abundant and diverse experience of previous suicides. Particularly the successful ones. Maybe I could use one of their methods on the paperback book.

I liked this idea. It sounded promising. All that remained was to choose the method. Taking stock of the several possibilities that popped into my mind, I decided that drowning would be the most appropriate. If I had decided to commit suicide, I would have chosen drowning. Particularly because there's no blood. I have an absolute horror of blood. In addition, the very act of dying takes place under the surface and not before eyewitnesses, so no one suffers any shock on your behalf. Finally, there's a certain element of romanticism in it. Many great loves in literature have ended with jumping into water.

Of the two things I needed for the drowning, one I had at home. I went to the pantry, opened the large cardboard box where I keep tools and various supplies, and took out a large ball of twine. The twine was thin and thus could not be used on myself, but would be more than sufficient for the wretched little book. I cut off more than I needed, just in case.

I had to go outside to find the other item I needed, although I wasn't quite sure where to look for it. Indeed, where can a man find a large rock in the middle of a city? I certainly could not break off a piece of the pavement or the facade of some building. The only place I might find a rock was the park, so that's where I headed. Before that, I put the book and twine in a large travel bag. They could have fit in my pocket, but I would need the bag for the rock. Walking through the streets with a huge rock in my hands would have been ridiculous. I would certainly arouse suspicion among passersby.

Finding a rock in the park was no easy matter. There were far fewer candidates than expected, and I had to find the proper moment to take one without being noticed by others. In the middle of a stretch of lawn lay a round flowerbed surrounded by pieces of chipped stone, half buried in the ground. I had to wait until there was no one nearby, which took quite some time, and then expended considerable effort pulling one out. I had no time to clean the dirt off the bottom half. I quickly put it in my bag and moved away, leaving a hole in the stone ring similar to the hole left by an extracted tooth.

I was out of breath by the time I reached the bridge. The rock was considerably heavier than it looked; I had to carry the bag under my arm, not by the handle. I headed for the middle of the bridge because the water under that part was the deepest and fastest. Whatever sank there had no chance of surfacing. It turned out, however, that carrying out my intention was no easy matter. Passersby were scarce, but there were many cars, including occasional police cars. I had to appear as inconspicuous as possible.

Turning towards the railing, I squatted down and took the rock out of the bag. I hoped no one could make out what I was doing from the road. Seeing me in that position, they would probably think I was an oddball or a drunk, but not a suicide. In any case, people in cars rarely care about what's happening outside. I tied one end of the twine firmly around the rock and the other end around the book.

463

Then I stood up and put the rock on the top of the railing. I didn't drop it right away. I stood there motionless for some time, pretending to be a stroller who had stopped briefly to enjoy the view from the bridge. Finally, when there seemed to be fewer cars, I pushed the rock and the book. They took longer to fall than I had expected, and the sound when they hit the water was considerably louder than I would have liked. Dragging the book after it like some sort of tail, the rock hit the surface flatly, producing an enormous splash.

If anyone had been on the bank around the bridge, my actions would have been detected. I quickly moved away from the spot so that no one would connect me with what had fallen. Once I'd put some distance behind me, fear was replaced by the feeling of relief and good spirits that befits a job well done. My hands were dirty from the earth, my coat as well, but I paid no attention to that. I had gotten rid of the book—that was all that mattered. Let it rest in peace amidst the mud at the bottom of the river.

But instead of being wherever the rock had pulled it, the book was waiting for me in my library upon my return. Not the least bit wet and muddy. On the contrary: clean and dry. When I saw it this time, however, I was not filled with anger as before. I only thought dully that things had gone too far. Everything has its measure, rudeness and impertinence as well. No paperback book could string me along like that. This had already become a question of honor.

As I cleaned myself up in the bathroom, I tried with the greatest composure to go through the other possibilities at my disposal. Jumping from a great height was also a favorite among suicides, and in literature. No small number of protagonists had sealed their fate in this way. There would be blood, of course, and eyewitnesses shocked at the none-too-pleasant sight, but this was unavoidable. My conscience was clear. I might have cause to reproach myself if I hadn't tried drowning first. I wasn't to blame for the failure of that scheme.

I didn't need to make any elaborate preparations to set in motion this new idea. I took the book off the shelf again and put on my coat, paying no attention to the fact that it was still wet. I might have dried it a little with a hair dryer, but I had run out of patience. This situa-

464

tion had to be resolved as soon as possible. It had already gotten on my nerves, something not at all advisable considering my high blood pressure.

I decided to climb to the top of the tallest building in town, not because a smaller building would not have served the purpose, but because it was the most suitable for the task at hand. There was a viewing deck on the top. When there wasn't much wind, like today, they let visitors go out onto it. A high wire fence surrounded the deck so that no one could accidentally or intentionally plunge off the precipice to his death over thirty floors below. If I'd been the suicide, I would have had a very difficult time, but things should have been easier for a paperback book.

I had my share of trouble nonetheless. The only person on the top of the building was a uniformed guard. If there had been other visitors and if my coat had been without a large spot in front, he most likely would not have paid much attention to me. As it was, however, he kept his eyes glued to me, which seriously hindered me. I spent twenty minutes or so walking along the fence pretending to look at the city panorama before I had a chance to spring into action.

Someone called the guard on his walkie-talkie; while he turned this way and that, trying to find the best position for reception, I whisked the book out of my pocket and tossed it over the fence. The man didn't notice a thing. I waited for him to finish his conversation, nodded to him briefly, smiling broadly, and headed for the elevator. I was filled with elation and pride. It's no small thing to outwit a professional.

As I approached the ground floor, I imagined that I would find a crowd of people around the fallen book. But there was nothing of the sort. The street bustled with people going about their business. What terrible indifference, I thought. Who cared about the fate of a book, even if it was only a paperback? Then I realized that I had accused the passersby unfairly. How could they show any compassion when there was no call for it? There was nothing anywhere near the spot where a book thrown off the viewing deck should have landed.

I went home, crushed by an evil foreboding that came true as soon as I entered my study. As before, the paperback book waited for me in the same place in my library. This stubbornness was truly shameful! It left me with no other choice. The time for handling the situation with kid gloves was over. There was a much more gory suicide than the ones I had already attempted. If it had suited an extremely refined literary heroine, I didn't see why it was out of place for the book. I removed the unseemly copy and headed straight for the train station.

I couldn't gain access to the platforms without a ticket, so I bought a ticket to the closest destination, although I wasn't going anywhere. I checked the schedule, found out where the next train would arrive, and went to that platform. I moved away from the passengers waiting for the train so there would be no witnesses. Some ten minutes later, a locomotive pulling a long line of cars started to enter the station. I let the first two cars go past, then turned my head away as I threw the book under the wheels of the third.

After the train had passed, I was briefly tempted to look at the rails, but I held back. I wouldn't have been able to stand the terrible sight: the completely mangled remains of the little book. Although it certainly deserved to disappear, I felt a certain sympathy for it. There had been no need for this to happen, but the book itself was to blame. In any case, it was all over now. There was no reason for me to stay there any longer. I would only appear suspicious.

This time upon arriving home, I wasn't even surprised when I found the paperback book where it certainly had no right to be. And in perfect shape. Not a hair was missing from its head. What else could I have expected? I would have been amazed, in fact, had it been otherwise. My kind thoughts from before were replaced by the deepest loathing. I couldn't look at it anymore. It was not worthy of being in the same room with me.

Not knowing what else to do, I headed for the kitchen to fix something to eat. This dashing around because of the book had kept me from eating all day long. My stomach growled and hunger pains kept me from thinking properly about what I should do next. I put the tablecloth on the table and laid down a plate, knife, fork, spoon, and linen napkin, then opened the refrigerator. The choices were rather meager, however: a piece of dry cheese, a partially eaten sausage, half a jar of mustard, and two lemons. It was clearly time to go to the store.

As I was closing the refrigerator, an idea came to me. I didn't take it seriously at first. Nonsense crosses my mind from time to time, as I suppose it does to everyone. I tried to drive it away, as I do in such circumstances, but it refused to go. The longer it stayed with me, the less unusual it seemed. Finally, I realized I had found the only real solution to my problem. I felt like slapping myself on the forehead. Of course! Why hadn't I thought of it before?

I went to my study, took the paperback book off the shelf, and returned to the kitchen. I put it on a plate, sat down, and tucked the napkin under my chin. First, I removed the cover with the knife and fork, as I would with a shell or wrapping. What was written on it promised true enjoyment, but one could certainly not rely on the honesty of whoever had produced it. Who knew what cat in a sack might be hiding under the praiseworthy title *The Library*.

I could see by the table of contents that the book consisted of six parts. I assumed that each one had a different taste, so it was not advisable to eat them at the same time. I cut out each piece separately. Before I started my meal, I wondered whether to add any spices. I looked at both sides of the cover, hoping to find some sort of instructions or advice in this regard, but since I found nothing there, I decided not to try any experiments lest I spoil things. In the same vein, not knowing which drink would be the most appropriate, I decided in favor of plain water. I couldn't go wrong there.

"Virtual Library" was quite reminiscent of a good Russian salad. It might have contained a bit more mayonnaise than suited my liking, though. "Home Library" was like a thick, hearty beef soup with noodles. It seemed too hot, so I blew on the spoon. "Night Library" corresponded to stuffed peppers. They contained the right proportion of meat and rice, which is very important for that dish. "Infernal Library" was an excellent cherry pie. I don't really care for dessert, but this was an exception. "Smallest Library" brought coffee with cream. I would have preferred something lighter, but one shouldn't split hairs.

I didn't know what could possibly come after this, but there was one more piece of the paperback on my plate: "Noble Library." Although already full, I didn't want to leave anything uneaten, and I was intrigued by it. I put a small bite cautiously into my mouth and started to chew. The taste seemed vaguely familiar, although I couldn't tell whether it was mostly savory, piquant, sweet, or sour. It seemed to be all of these at the same time.

I continued eating, trying hard to figure it out. I was certain I'd tried it somewhere before. I liked it, perhaps more than all the rest. When I swallowed the last piece, the pleasant feeling that filled me was disrupted somewhat by the fact that I could not recognize what I had eaten. But I didn't let this slight dissatisfaction spoil my good mood. I had accomplished my purpose. Not a crumb of *The Library* remained on my plate.

I got up from the table and headed towards my study. I felt not the slightest dread as to what I would find there. The paperback book might have been able to return from all the other places, but not from its current location. Its presence inside me was more than certain. I opened the door wide and smiled triumphantly at what my eyes beheld. The ugly intruder no longer sullied my noble library.

THE AUTHORS

James C. Bassett wrote the science fiction novel *Living Real* and short fiction that has appeared in *Amazing Stories* and *Absolute Magnitude*. He co-wrote and acted in the 1989 "psycho-punk splatter-comedy" *Twisted Issues*, which *Film Threat Video Guide* named to its list of "Twenty Underground Films *You Must See*!" He recently completed a mainstream novel, *Spare Change*. He is also a stone and wood sculptor. Email him at JimBassett@mindspring.com.

Stepan Chapman was born in 1951, in Chicago, Illinois, and studied theater at the University of Michigan. In 1969, his first published story was selected for *Analog Science Fiction* by John W. Campbell. In the 1970s, Chapman's early fiction appeared in four of Damon Knight's *Orbit* anthologies. He performed in plays, in the USA and England; and his comedies for children were produced for the Edinburgh Drama Festival. Widely acclaimed as a master of dark humor, his short fiction has appeared in *The Chicago Review, The Hawaii Review, Zyzzyva, Leviathan*, and many other prestigious journals. In 1997, the Ministry of Whimsy Press released his first novel, *The Troika*, which won the Philip Dick Memorial Award. His latest book, *Dossier*, is a collection of short stories.

Michael Cisco's first novel, *The Divinity Student*, was published by Buzzcity Press in 1999, and garnered him the International Horror Writers' Guild Award for Best First Novel. A Mythos Books collection of his short stories, entitled *Secret Hours*, will appear in 2002. Cisco is a graduate student in English literature at New York University.

Brendan Connell has fiction either forthcoming, or already published, in numerous magazines, literary journals, and anthologies, including *RE:AL, Tabu, Heist, Penny Dreadful, Fishdrum, Antares, The Dream Zone, Darkness Rising 4* (Cosmos Books 2002), *Redsine* (Prime 2002), and *The Best of Devil Blossoms* (Asterius Press 2002). He has had translations published in *Literature of Asia, Africa and Latin America* (Prentice Hall 1999). Currently he lives in Switzerland, where he is engaged in writing several longer works of fiction.

L. Timmel Duchamp's fiction has appeared in *Asimov's SF, Leviathan 2, Full Spectrum 4*, two of the *Bending the Landscape* anthologies, and a variety of other venues. She has been a finalist for the Sturgeon, Homer, and Nebula awards and has been short listed three times for the Tiptree. Her column "What's the Story?" appears regularly in *Lady Churchill's Rosebud Wristlet*. An ample selection of her critical writings as well as a few of her stories can be found at ltimmel.home.mindspring.com. She lives on the West Coast of the United States.

Rikki Ducornet has lived in North Africa, South America, France, and Canada. Her childhood heroes were Leeuwenhoek and Lewis Carroll. Ducornet's first novel was written in a small village in France and was entitled, *The Stain* (1984). It was followed by *Entering Fire, The Fountains of Neptune, Phosphor in Dreamland, The Jade Cabinet*, which was finalist for the National Book Critics Award, and most recently, *The Word "Desire."* In 1998, she received a Lannon Literary Fellowship.

Eugene Dubnov is well known for his poetry and short fiction throughout the world. He has published two volumes of poetry in Russian. He has both written and translated his poetry and short stories into English, with work appearing in magazines in the United Kingdom, United States, Canada, Australia, and New Zealand. Dubnov's work has recently appeared in *Partisan Review*, *Chicago Review*, *Wascana Review*, *Northwest Review*, and *New Letter*. He was born in the USSR in 1949 and emigrated in 1971. Dubnov currently lives in Jerusalem.

Carol Emshwiller is the author of several books, including *Carmen Dog* and *The Start of the End of It All*. The recipient of an NEA grant, Emshwiller has also won the World Fantasy Award and been included in the Pushcart anthology. Her short fiction has appeared in publications such as *TriQuarterly*, *Epoch*, *New Directions*, *Century*, *Crank*, and *F&SF*. She divides her time between New York City and California. For more information, visit her Web site at: www.sfwa.org/members/emshwiller/.

Brian Evenson is the author of five books of fiction including *Altmann's Tongue* (Knopf, 1994), *Father of Lies* (Four Walls Eight Windows, 1998), and *Contagion* (Wordcraft 2000). He is a senior editor for *Conjunctions* magazine and teaches at the University of Denver.

Jeffrey Ford's novel, *The Physiognomy*, won the 1997 World Fantasy Award and was selected as a New York Times Notable Book. He has since written two sequels featuring Physiognomist Cley, *Memoranda*, and *The Beyond*. Ford has also been a finalist for the Nebula Award and had his work reprinted in *The Year's Best Fantasy & Horror*. Forthcoming books include a new novel from Morrow and a short story collection from Golden Gryphon. He lives in New Jersey.

Theophile Gautier (1811-1872) was a leading writer of the French Romantic movement, producing much poetry and numerous essays as well as prose fiction. His novels include *Mademoiselle de Maupin*,

Fortunio, Avatar, Jettatura, and *Spirite.* Collections of short fiction include *One of Celopatra's Nights* and *Other Fantastic Romances.*

Remy de Gourmont (1858-1915) was a prolific writer more celebrated for his nonfiction than for his fiction. Along with Paul Bourget, he was one of the principal champions of the Decadent Movement and the Symbolist Movement. His books include *Le Fantome, Pelerin du Silence,* and *Proses Moroses.*

Michael Moorcock was a central figure in the alternative culture of the 1960s and 1970s, performing with his own band, The Deep Fix, and with Hawkwind, with whom he still occasionally performs. He has written many novels, won the Guardian Fiction Award for *The Condition of Muzak* and been short-listed for the Whitbread Prize for *Mother London* (short listed for the Whitbread). Moorcock has achieved an international reputation and is recognized as a major contemporary novelist. A long-time resident of London, he now lives in Texas with his wife. His most recent books are *King of the City* and *London Bone.*

Lance Olsen is author of more than a dozen books of and about innovative fiction, including the novel *Tonguing the Zeitgeist,* finalist for the Philip K. Dick Award, and the short-story collection *Sewing Shut My Eyes.* Fiction Collective Two will publish his new novel, *Girl Imagined by Chance,* in the fall of 2002. He lives twenty miles from nowhere in central Idaho and at www.cafezeitgeist.com.

James Sallis' most recent books are *Chester Himes: A Life and Ghost of a Flea.* Others include musicology, literary studies, collections of poems, essays, and stories (including *Time's Hammers: The Collected Stories*), and a translation of Raymond Queneau's novel *Saint Glinglin.* Shorter work continues to appear in such publications as *The Review of Contemporary Fiction, Book World, Asimov's, High Plains Literary Review, Ellery Queen's Mystery Magazine, Pequod, Quarterly West,* and the *Boston Review.* One-time editor of *New*

Worlds, he now contributes columns to the literary website *Web Del Sol* and *The Magazine of Fantasy & Science Fiction.* Website: www.jamessallis.com.

Brian Stableford was born in 1948 in Shipley, Yorkshire. His most current books include his future history series for Tor, thus far consisting of *Inherit the Earth* (1998), *Architects of Emortality* (1999), *The Fountains of Youth* (2000) and *The Cassandra Complex* (March 2001), will continue with *Dark Ararat* in 2002 and conclude with *The Omega Expedition* in 2003. *The Wine of Dreams* (October 2000), published by Games Workshop's "Black Library" under the pseudonym Brian Craig, was followed in April 2001 by the similarly-pseudonymous *Pawns of Chaos.*

Jeffrey Thomas has had fiction appear in numerous awards anthologies, including *The Year's Best Fantasy & Horror, Dark Fantasy 2001, Best New Horror Stories, Quick Chills,* and *The Year's Best Fantastical Fiction.* His six collections include *Black Walls, Red Glass, Stations,* the recent hardcover *Terror Incognita* and *Punktown,* a Locus Notable Book. His fiction has been recommended for the Bram Stoker Award, the Theodore Sturgeon Memorial Award, and the Pushcart Prize.

Tamar Yellin's stories have been published in numerous magazines and anthologies including *London Magazine, Stand, Best Short Stories, The Jewish Quarterly, Writing Women, Metropolitan, Staple, Iron, The Big Issue, The Third Alternative, Panurge* and *The Slow Mirror: New Fiction by Jewish Writers,* and broadcast on BBC Radio 4. She has completed a collection, *Kafka in Brontëland,* and several novels. She lives in Yorkshire and is a Bronte expert and lecturer in Jewish Studies.

Zoran Zivkovic was born in Belgrade, Yugoslavia, in 1948. In 1973 he graduated from the Department of General Literature with the theory of literature, Faculty of Philology of the University of Belgrade. He received his master's degree in 1979 and his doctorate in 1982 from the same school. He is the author of: *Contemporaries of the Future* (1983), *Starry Screen* (1984), *First Contact* (1985), *Encyclopedia of Science Fiction* (1990), *Essays on Science Fiction* (1995), *Time Gifts* (1997), *The Writer* (1998), *The Book* (2000), *Impossible Encounters* (2000), and *Seven Touches Of Music* (2001).

nemonymous

a journal of parthenogenetic fiction and late labelling

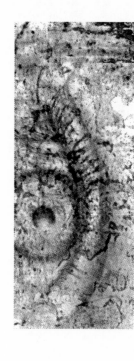

Anybody who is not in it is a Nobody.

The highly acclaimed *Nemonymous* fiction magazine.

www.nemonymous.com

LEVIATHAN

Poetry from the acclaimed new press

Fox in the Morning

ROGER FINCH

Incisive poems of love, sex and encounters with Asian cultures.

Paperback £8/$14

Lost Days

STEPHANOS PAPADOPOULOS

The first collection by a young Greek American poet.

Paperback £8/$14

A Spy in the House of Years

GILES GOODLAND

A history of the 20th century, in 100 post-everything sonnets.

Paperback £8/$14

Party

JACKIE WILLS

"Rackety, offbeat, modern vignettes"
Ruth Padel, *Independent on Sunday*

Paperback £8/$14

This Goes With That
Poems 1974-2001

PETER GOLDSWORTHY

"A poet of crystalline intelligence, one who can move as well as shine"

Les Murray

Paperback £10/$17.50

Hoping It Might Be So
Poems 1974-2000

KIT WRIGHT

"A must for anyone with an interest in poetry"
Wendy Cope, *Daily Telegraph*

Paperback £10/$17.50

Orders (add 10% for P&P) to:
Drake International, Market House, Market Place, Deddington OX15 0SE, U.K.
All enquiries to claire.brodmann@btinternet.com

Subscribe to *Leviathan Quarterly*,
the new international literature and art magazine

Subscriptions: 1 year £28/$56, 2 years £48/$96
All enquiries to claire.brodmann@btinternet.com

THE MINISTRY OF WHIMSY PRESS

World Fantasy Award & British Fantasy Award Finalist
Publisher of Stepan Chapman's Philip K. Dick Award-winning The Troika

LEVIATHAN #2, edited by Jeff VanderMeer & Rose Secrest

"A big, handsome devil...just about everything wins reader confidence early and then maintains it with intelligent development. Too bad there isn't an issue out every month." - *Literary Magazine Review*

"...a refreshing change from the bland literalness of many genre stories...the prose style is crystalline and condensed, poetic..." - *Locus*

"One of the best collections of quality fiction at any level that I've seen in years. Not since the early volumes of Damon Knight's *Orbit* series has such a consistently well-written set of stories appeared under one cover." - *Tangent*

The British Fantasy Award-finalist novellas volume, with an essay-introduction by *Interzone* editor David Pringle. Featuring work by Stepan Chapman, Richard Calder, L. Timmel Duchamp, Rhys Hughes. Trade paperback. 192 pages. Duotone cover by Scott Eagle. ISBN 1-8904-6403-1. $10.99 plus shipping.

PUNKTOWN by Jeffrey Thomas

"Vivid characters and lively tales." - **World Fantasy Award winner Brian McNaughton**

"A dazzlingly complex and detailed future vision as poetic as it is horrifying." - **Ramsey Campbell**

In the city they call Punktown, on a planet where a hundred sentient species collide, you can become a creator of clones. You can become a piece of performance art. You might even become a library of sorrows. This Locus notable collection contains two stories chosen for year's best anthologies. Trade paperback. Full color cover. 118 pages. Cover art by H. E. Fassl. $11.99 plus shipping.

Please add $1.50 shipping per book. Overseas orders, add $2.50 per book. Send check or money order to "The Ministry of Whimsy" at POB 4248, Tallahassee, FL 32315.

NOTE: For all new titles, starting with Leviathan 3, visit our website at www.ministryofwhimsy.com for ordering information.

Some were made wise by the books, others insane . . .

Printed in the United States
6456